EVERYONE IS RAVING ABOUT JAMES BRADY'S **FURTHER LANE**!

"Everybody in the Hamptons is reading FURTHER LANE . . . The hunt for the killer is fast-paced and unpredictable. Readers will also delight in the author's take on the ceaseless class wars in the Hamptons—a subject Brady, a resident, has long been watching with evident amusement."
—*Town and Country*

"As witty, erudite, and on the cutting edge as its author, James Brady's FURTHER LANE is a lot of fun and 'must' reading for everybody in the Hamptons set—and all those who aspire to be." —Michael Korda, Senior Vice-President and Editor-in-Chief of Simon & Schuster

"James Brady moves easily between fact and fiction, building composite personas in FURTHER LANE. Finding the celebrities as well as solving the crime is part of the fun of this who's whodunit." —Rochelle Udell, Editor-in-Chief of *Self*

"Brady combines his novelistic talents with his status as a bio-coastal insider to deliver the goods in this entertaining, fast-moving yarn." —*Publishers Weekly*

"Dry humor, literate tone, acid observation, and lots of name-dropping help characterize the village and its people."
—*Library Journal*

"Readers get taken on a Liz-Smith-meets-Agatha-Christie murderous romp through the celeb-studded hedges of East Hampton." —*Hamptons* Magazine

"An always-stylish romp through the playgrounds of the very pampered and vaguely famous." —*The Purloined Letter*

Further Lane

A NOVEL OF THE HAMPTONS

JAMES BRADY

St. Martin's Paperbacks

FURTHER LANE

Copyright © 1997 by James Brady.

Excerpt from *Gin Lane* copyright © 1998 by James Brady.

Cover photograph by Ken Miller.

Library of Congress Catalog Card Number: 96-53927

ISBN: 0-312-96598-2

Printed in the United States of America

St. Martin's Press hardcover edition published 1997
St. Martin's Paperbacks edition / June 1998

St. Martin's Paperbacks are published by St. Martin's Press, 175 Fifth Avenue, New York, NY 10010.

10 9 8 7 6 5 4 3 2 1

This book is for Sarah Kelly Konig.

Further Lane

ONE

Here, if anywhere in America,
you could still find the sweet life . . .

I'd been away from East Hampton, working in Europe and North Africa as a correspondent, and now I was back in a wonderful place where I'd grown up and found it even more desirable than I remembered, lovelier, more lush and sensual, richer if that was possible. More glitz as well, you had to admit, and that discomfitted the local gentry, who saw celebrity and its attendant publicity as a cross that decent Protestants were expected to bear. No matter. Here, if anywhere in America, it seemed you could still find the sweet life. A little money was required, of course. If only you had a little money, New Money or Old; in East Hampton anything was possible . . .

A pretty nice place.

Just east of our house, where Further Lane meets Spaeth Lane, there used to be an actual landing strip that Mr. Roberts put in, so that the small planes of that era belonging to the rich, to men with flair and imagination, could land and deposit their passengers within, quite literally, a few hundred yards' stroll of their own homes. You would have had to offer sedan chairs to provide greater ease and consideration. From my own bedroom at night when birdsong and the whir of insects and most things had stilled, you could hear the ocean, the surf slamming down, in a metronomic *bang! bang! bang!* over and over. If that didn't help you sleep, what would? And toward dawn, you might hear the far-off wailing whistle of the night freight at the grade crossings. That was nice, too, suggesting the lonely sounds Americans used to hear in lonely places. And as many houses had gone up here, how much development, the vast monies spent, early mornings along Further Lane you might still see, through the kitchen window, a deer browsing on the lower boughs of our fruit trees or a young red fox trotting purposefully along the road or a covey of pheasants scuttling to safety in the hedge or a rabbit rousing itself for a new day's frolic. Pretty nice as well to be back amid such memories in a familiar and congenial place, where generations of my family lived and where I had spent pleasant chunks of my own youth.

On my return, even the women seemed more gorgeous than I remembered.

You could see them, too, from the house, passing on Further Lane, the long-legged flat-bellied young women and girls who belonged to the rich men. Or who, arguably more erotic and exciting, were themselves rich. You couldn't really tell whose the wealth was; no Dun & Bradstreet reports being issued on the matter. Now that I was back and writing, I took occasional breaks from the laptop to stand lazily smoking in the sunshine of my father's lawn, and felt the familiar tug when they ran and biked and Rollerbladed by, or sped past in cars specifically designed to show off the exquisite aerodynamics of freshly washed hair, riding the slipstream in a summer's sun. Even their cars were right: old Bentleys and new Ferraris, classic Jags and the odd Aston-Martin, Land Rovers and Lamborghinis, tiny Porsches and histrionically stretched limos.

It was hard to tell along Further Lane which were more beautiful, which sleeker and more expensive: the cars or the women.

Further Lane is only two miles long but offers bonus

glimpses of the Atlantic as it ambles parallel to the ocean, across rich men's lawns and working cornfields and slim groves. Green farms, blue waters, and crashing surf; you might well be in Mayo or elsewhere on the west coast of Ireland. These were the pastures of what geologists call the "Eastern Plain" of the village. A local historian described Further Lane as "large estates . . . grand country houses with extensive gardens on parcels of five to ten acres and more," and concluded, glumly I thought, "The era of prosperity in America which made these estates possible ended in the 1930s."

Oh, but they were splendid, those estates, those gardens, those country houses, every bit as splendid as the hard-bodied women and girls who pranced last summer on Further Lane before the eyes of a young man who was roughly handled by the mullahs in far-off Algiers and, even more painful, bruised by a distant, careless London beauty. How could I resist being drawn to such women, smoothly cool yet erotically beckoning, all the while (and realistically) suspecting they were unattainable.

TWO

If you follow Liz Smith and *People* magazine or watch
Entertainment Tonight on the tube and have a subscription
to *Vanity Fair,* you may get the impression East Hampton
is a Hollywood production, founded quite recently by
Steven Spielberg, Demi Moore, and the Baldwin brothers.
Those of us who live here know it wasn't motion picture
people who first settled East Hampton but dry, cranky old
Puritans out of Maidstone, England, wandering down via
Massachusetts Bay Colony in 1640; the first movie stars
not to arrive until slightly afterwards.

In 1921 Rudolph Valentino made *The Sheik* along the
beach between East Hampton and Montauk at Napeague,
our local dunes impersonating the Sahara, the tents and
horses imported on the Long Island Railroad. Wally Reid,
the silent film actor so admired by Scott Fitzgerald for his
Arrow shirt-advertisement good looks, owned that big
ivied house with its mullioned windows on Further Lane
adjacent to the golf course, just west of Lasata, which was
"Black Jack" Bouvier's place where Jackie and Lee grew
up. Mary Pickford, briefly, had a place. So did Ring Lard-
ner and one of the Barrymores. In the postwar summer of
1946, Clark Gable visited East Hampton, played a couple
of rounds of golf at the Maidstone Club, and lunched there
on the clubhouse patio, thrilling female members. Frederic

March came out and so did Kate Hepburn and Spence-ah. She played ferocious tennis while his tastes ran sedately to croquet and old-fashioneds. Arthur Miller and Marilyn Monroe consummated their marriage here, one supposed passionately, honeymooning in a borrowed Amagansett cottage. More recently, Faye Dunaway took a place on Egypt Lane but sold it back when the Village wouldn't let her put in a pool that close to the wetlands. Until they split Dina Merrill and Cliff Robertson lived in a beach house set atop the dunes just off Highway Behind the Pond. She's still there. Designer John Weitz and his wife, Susan (she starred with Monty Clift in *Freud*), own a hilltop red barn of a place. Roy Scheider's here. Alan Alda. Alan Pakula who made *To Kill A Mockingbird* and *Klute* lives on Georgica Pond. Woody Allen was supposed to be building or buying a place. Never did, I don't believe. Randy Quaid. Kathleen Turner. Anna and Rupert Murdoch, before he purchased 20th Century-Fox, rented a beachfront place on Mrs. Tyson's Further Lane compound, and made an offer to buy but the old lady wasn't selling. Or else we would have had another Hollywood tycoon out here. When we already had Spielberg and Geffen and, of course, Mickey and Mikey: Mickey being Mr. Schulhof, who had been head of Sony USA and therefore the boss of Michael Jackson, among others; and Mikey being Mr. Fuchs, who headed HBO and did other clever things for Time Warner.

Diana Ross almost lived here; but you knew that. Nearly became a member of the Maidstone Club as well, which for some time now had Catholics and Jews, but not yet an African-American. There was considerable stir when Ms. Ross married her Norwegian shipbuilding magnate, who'd long been a member of the Maidstone, though rarely dropping by. And now, as his wife, Diana Ross would also be a member in good standing. Except that, for reasons of his own that may have had to do more with sailing than with snobbery, the Norwegian decided to drop his membership and concentrate his loyalties instead on a yacht club in Greenwich, Connecticut.

The Maidstone would have gathered Diana Ross to its bosom and been the better for it, I believe. But it was not to be. And off she went to Connecticut and an entirely different cast of snobs.

But hers was a somewhat unique situation. What it came down to was that film people liked the place and took to the Hamptons almost from the start. Trouble was, until the jetliner, planes from the coast were too slow and lacked range. By now, of course, all that's been fixed. Not only has the jet come along but the fast chopper, landing at small local airports and on spacious private lawns, and seaplanes, some of them quite old and classic, others new wave and high tech, that splash down on our myriad bays and coves and even the larger ponds. So that, to an extent that amuses or perplexes or infuriates local people, East Hampton is referred to as "Malibu East." Or rather more elegantly by the newly arrived essayist Peter Mayle, as "Hollywood *sur mer.*"

Old Money East Hampton chose to pretend the cinema had not yet caught on and that nothing at all had changed. Old Money out here is like that. But even in East Hampton things had changed and it was foolish to deny it. Take last summer.

With the great Barbra Streisand, Demi and her fashionable pal Donna Karan, Patricia Duff Perelman (was she about to drop the Perelman?), New Money Hannah Cutting and her decidedly Old Money rival Pam Phythian, Kim Basinger, and one-woman conglomerate Martha Stewart all in residence simultaneously for the summer, it seemed only a matter of time before, having achieved critical mass, East Hampton went up in some sort of spontaneous combustion.

The only surprise, with so many dazzling and impossibly high-powered egos enjoying "the season" in the same little old resort village, was that until the very end, nothing happened.

Well, almost nothing.

In mid-August a great white whale came ashore dead, gashed and bloody, a very rare thing here, leading those who believed in omens and portents to ponder and cluck about what it meant, if anything. The whale floated in after a collision at sea with the whirling steel screws of a big ship and already dead, but still bleeding, drew vast schools of feeding sharks that tracked its reeking course all the way in, until it grounded foully ashore on our famous Old Beach, where the sharks, large and small, slid wriggling on their bellies literally up onto the wet sand to hit again at the huge whale and tear away another chunk of flesh, before wriggling back again into the bloody water. That was something to see, eight-foot sharks up and feeding, on the same sand where pretty girls sunned and your kids built castles. A bloody whale in the shallows, with hungry sharks to boot, pulled crowds of the curious from all along the East Hampton shore, especially delighting little boys who darted excitedly this way and that, much too near the sharks for their nervous, scolding mothers. But as the novelty of a beached whale wore off, its stench became more powerful in the heat, and the whale eventually drove us all away, even the camera crews and small boys, until, at last, the Coast Guard threw a cable on the carcass and towed it out to sea. That, finally, emptied the beach.

Except for gloomy people with long, Old Testament faces who stood to windward of the bloody, stinking sand, and prophesied unprecedented and awful things.

Some of which would come about. Though not quite yet.

Instead, we had a season of relative peace and tranquility. The annual running of the au pair girls on the fairways of the Maidstone Club produced the usual number of adulterous liaisons between married members and the summer's crop of nymphets; but only a handful of broken marriages. Doc Whitmore the tree surgeon got back onto his rickety old bike following a hip replacement. Half-a-dozen chic new boutiques opened on Memorial Day, went bust, and were shuttered by September. A resurgence of the "brown tide" suggested the October scalloping wouldn't be much. Dunemere Real Estate huffily denied they were the agents for grunge singer Courtney Love, rumored to be buying a place. Two neighbors on Huntting Lane, one Old Money, his woman neighbor indisputably New, feuded over her dogs and he was suspected of shooting at them with a BB gun. Although, with the privet hedge masking his line of fire, little damage was done; another recommendation for growing a good privet. Deer ticks swarmed once more. Which was why, they said, Billy Joel bred and raised guinea hens at his spread on Further Lane, to keep down the ticks. Guinea hens like a nice tick. There were few unexpected personal bankruptcies and not a single front-page suicide. A wealthy husband, known locally and disparagingly by various epithets, suspicious his celebrity third wife was gathering evidence of abuse, verbal or otherwise, met her private jet with bodyguards and had her "patted down" to determine whether she might be wearing "a wire."

She was.

Decent people tut-tutted such yarns as tabloid inventions and piously hoped the couple might work out their differences. Even the season's resident charlatan, a New Age guru, who described himself, with deadpan solemnity, as "The Swami," maintained a discreetly low profile. Although he, at least, had amusement value.

Imported, lavishly housed, fed, and watered at the considerable expense of rich, foolish women who got their

names in the columns simply for going to lunch, the
Swami affected caftans, working his magic largely in private, levitating and chanting, going into trances, prescrib-
ing enemas and a diet of wheat germ, all the while smelling
up a lovely, old, borrowed house with incense. Thoughtfully, he promoted his scams, if that was what they were,
behind thick and sheltering privet hedges rather than on
village streets, where he might frighten leashed dogs or
roller-skating children.

"Conspicuous privacy is a big deal in the Hamptons."
Or so wrote someone terribly decorative and designery in
a summer's issue of the *New York Times*. And he was right.
We're as subject to the usual seasonal crazes as the next
place. An obsessive toting of bottles of Evian water, for
one. To stroll the three hundred yards from Hither Lane to
Middle Lane, people feel it essential to stock up on designer water as if they were setting out to cross Arabia's
Empty Quarter with T. E. Lawrence. But otherwise, we're
pretty sensible folk, sheltered and insulated from such
foolishness by all that boxwood and privet hedge out here,
why we seem so happily screened-off as well from the
cruel, more substantive realities that plague less fortunate
places.

But even in East Hampton, the harsh world occasionally
intrudes.

In mid-August, the whale washed up. A few days later,
Leo Brass, a brawny local Bayman who'd somehow gotten himself educated (Penn State and then grad school at
MIT!), was arrested for igniting a minor riot over wetlands protection (Leo personally bulldozed a police barri-
cade erected to keep Baymen from blowing up a dock
constructed in Accabonac Harbor by Krantz, the wine
baron). East Hampton was unaccustomed to such loud
posturing and some locals were offended, literally, by
Leo's "brass." Nor had MIT been an enormous success

for Leo. At Penn State he'd been welcomed, nurtured, li-
onized as a track and field star who narrowly missed making our Olympic team in the decathlon (the javelin his best
event). While at MIT, lost amid the Cambridge crowd, he
drank too much and in a Harvard Square bar one night
punched out a Ph.D. candidate over an arcane point of
ecology, and ended by being first busted and, eventually,
sent down by the institute.

No one, except possibly the unhappy Ph.D. candidate,
questioned Leo's instinctive feel for country, for earth and
water, the fragility of wetlands. There was no denying his
expertise no matter how erratic and surly he could turn.
Leo didn't like me very much but what did that matter?
When in the mood, Leo was fun but there was a nervy
edge to him and he could go mean in an instant; despite his
schooling, he enjoyed playing the crude rustic. Never-
theless, he was on the side of the Gods ecologically and
claimed to know more, and perhaps did, than anyone else
out here about the vulnerable nature of our sprawling,
boggy wetlands. Contemptuous of critics, whom he dis-
missed as effete "tree huggers," and hostile to the New
Money men putting his precious wetlands at risk, Leo was
not at all bashful when it came to taking contributions of
their "conscience money" and bedding their women; both
activities he characterized smugly as "screwing the rich."
To his adherents, Leo just might be, in many ways, "the
new man" people were waiting for.

People who understood such things stroked their chins
and predicted the demagogue Brass might have quite a future out here, Huey Long on a Caterpillar tractor.

And finally, as if Brass and his militant Baymen had
mischievously whistled it up, a mostly tranquil summer
would end, melodramatically, with a storm right out of
Lear, a great hurricane that came at us, deadly, destructive,
unforgiving, boiling, raging and writhing out of Africa,

through the Antilles and then the Caribbean, bouncing off Florida and bounding up the coast past Hatteras to target East Hampton, tearing at our barrier sandbars, lashing our dunes, ripping into our shores, splintering our great elms, swamping our roads.

That was the threat. But would the tempest actually get here or veer off out to sea? No one yet knew.

By mid-September in a village whose Main Street had been labeled by the *National Geographic* as the "most beautiful in America," with its miles of gorgeous ocean beach and scores of bays and ponds and inlets and snug harbors, its pine barrens and green fairways and golden sand, no longer did things seem quite so comfortable and predictable. Instead, everything . . . and even East Hampton itself . . . seemed as vulnerable as anyplace else to change, and not always for the better.

As, in a macabre sort of entr'acte, on the beach just east of the Maidstone Club, there washed up one dawn a famous woman's naked, skewered body.

THREE

A battered upright where Billy Joel
might play a few tunes . . .

My name is Beecher Stowe.

There are plenty of richer people here but our family's been in East Hampton since the time of the Rev. Lyman Beecher and his children, Harriet Stowe, who wrote *Uncle Tom's Cabin,* and her "amorous" brother Henry Ward Beecher. We don't go as far back as the Phythians or Buells or Hunttings or Gardiners, some of whom can count back eleven or twelve generations, but long enough. And like Ms. Streisand and Martha Stewart and the others, I spent last summer in East Hampton, at my old man's place on Further Lane, recuperating from that nasty business with the Muslim Fundamentalists in Algiers, and working on a book about terrorism based mostly on my dispatches to *Newsweek.* And since I'd been a guest at that final cocktail party and knew the victim, it wasn't entirely unexpected that when her body was found, the cops came to seek me out. Not only might I know something, but with my father having been for so long the chief of naval intelligence, a sort of super spy, a bright cop could be excused for imagining I might possess some potential for information.

I'm a working newspaperman. Have been since Harvard when I got a cub's job at the *Boston Globe,* writing about traffic accidents and garden parties and high school football and knifings in the black neighborhoods and drunken brawls in the Irish. Then in my second year on the *Globe,* driving back from covering a "naughty choirmaster" case in Chatham, I saw a turnoff to the Kennedy compound at Hyannisport and pulled in. I was a nothing reporter on a nothing story but as I rolled up the historic gravel drive and stopped, not knowing just what to do or say, a small, shrunken, and very old lady opened the front door. I'm from the *Globe,* I said.

We take the *Globe* already, sonny, Rose Kennedy said, thank you very much.

I explained I was a reporter and not selling subs but was pleased she took the *Globe* as it was the best newspaper around. Rose Kennedy liked that, confirming her judgment as sound, and she asked me in for an iced tea. Which was how I got what's believed to be the last rational interview the old girl ever gave. The *Globe,* delighted to have the story but uneasy with a cub, played it big. If cautiously—good newspapers are always cautious—in the second, metro section, instead of out front, where it belonged.

It was that Rose Kennedy story that inspired Garfein, the assistant city editor (dayside) and a devout man, to inform the staff, "People talk to Beecher. They tell him things. You don't learn shit like that at Harvard. Nor even here in the city room of the *Boston Globe.* It's a kind of gift from God and Stowe has it."

Now, a dozen years later, as Labor Day neared, I was fully recovered from my injuries and with my book's first draft nearly wrapped. I'd already resigned from *Newsweek* and in September was scheduled to join *Parade* magazine to write six pieces a year at a handsome figure. The *Parade* editor, Walter Anderson, had read my dispatches, knew I'd tangled with Algerian zealots, had seen my file out of Baku and some of my stuff on Bosnia.

But it was the pieces on Princess Di that I did for *Newsweek* from their London bureau that drew Walter Anderson's eye. Not that they were all that difficult to do. After all, my girlfriend at the time was a member of the young royals' set, like Diana Spencer herself except younger, a Sloane Ranger, one of those chic young people who lived in or about London's Belgravia and Sloane Square, forever popping up in Nigel Dempster's column in the *Daily Mail*—Dempster who styled himself "scourge of the upper classes," yet lived off their droppings. I'd been born in Paris when my father was stationed there as American naval attaché (my late mother was French, a mannequin for Chanel, and maybe one of the first bulimics) and for the past five years I'd been back there in Europe, working as a correspondent. So I had news sources and hung out in the right places, with a membership at the Hurlingham Club, where I played tennis on grass and rated elbow space in the Connaught bar. Nights I hung at Vingt Quatre and Kartouche's Basement and other trendy joints along the Fulham Road but could still get into Annabel's and Tramp and book a table at Langan's. I'd interviewed the elegant Armani in Milano, the new Prix Goncourt novelist in his atelier on the Left Bank (he enjoyed a Turkish waterpipe; I stuck to Gitanes), and General Lebed in the Kremlin before he was sacked ("A de Gaulle in the making or a future dictator" ran the headline), and spoke pretty fair French. Anderson liked writers who knew stuff like that, had been there and done that, and knew their way around.

You know how Clint Eastwood ducks the press and doesn't do Letterman or sit still for a lot of interviews? It was Anderson who came up with the idea of sending Norman Mailer out there to Carmel to do the interview. Eastwood was so delighted he drove down himself to welcome Mailer at the airport, drive him out to the house. The most macho writer in America meets Dirty Harry! That's how they played it; that's how it was. It was stuff like that that was special about *Parade,* the Sunday magazine that's the biggest in the world with a circulation every week of something like forty million, and now its editor had dangled a big money offer. Plus the whole summer off to finish the terrorism book I was doing for Tom Dunne at St. Martin's Press.

You couldn't ask for a better deal. And most appealing of all, it would get me out of London, overnight no longer a town I enjoyed, not since an admirably kinky (though very well brought-up) young woman, whom I was convinced was mad about me, ran off with a chinless, but titled, wonder.

So I took Walter up on his offer, and sailed back to the States aboard *QE2* to spend July and August out on Further Lane doing the book, before starting work at his magazine. Two months to wrap up a hardcover book wasn't all that much time and I plugged away pretty diligently, starting each day with a brisk swim in the surf off our own patch of beach, getting fit again after Algiers. But I tried to duck the East Hampton dinner and cocktail party circuit. Not that even if you wanted, you could go totally into hiding.

One morning on Newtown Lane a small black convertible, very nifty indeed, honked at me. Peggy Siegal, the PR woman. I waved instinctively before realizing it was Peggy. Coming back from Dreesen's with my newspapers, I saw her again, parked at the curb this time and talking animatedly into her cell phone, all the while very carefully detailing the dashboard of her convertible with a long sort of quill, a very precise feather duster indeed, getting into, and meticulously so, every nook and cranny. Quite industrious she was.

Hello, Peggy, I said, who's on the phone?

I don't know why I did that. Causing mischief, I suppose.

But Peggy took me literally. Claudia, she said, say hello.

So I said hello to Claudia Cohen, who was a gossip columnist and very rich and for about an hour and a half had been Senator Al D'Amato's girlfriend. Which no one who knew either of them understood.

"Where are you?" I asked.

"Manhattan," she said.

So we had a brief chat. She didn't know me very well nor did I know her. We were impeccably courteous. It was all somewhat surreal and when I handed the cell phone back to Peggy I hoped no one in East Hampton who knew me had witnessed this odd scene.

What with such encounters among others, my life out here last summer wasn't entirely monkish. I took a drink several places. The young schoolteachers and boutique clerks hung out at Santa Fe Junction on Fresno Place and The Grill on Newtown Lane and those were fine places and I went there, enjoying the occasional encounter. But I had two serious hangouts, one The Blue Parrot in the village down a brief alley next to Ralph Lauren's shop, a vaguely Southern California–Mexican joint run by surfers and named for Signore Ferrari's saloon, the Sydney Greenstreet establishment that competed with Rick's place in *Casablanca*. I wasn't a surfer but I enjoyed eavesdropping on their shop talk, learning that the best lubricant to use on your board was something called Dr. Zog's Sex Wax. The East Hampton Blue Parrot advertised its cuisine as "killer Mexican" and had a battered upright in the corner where not Dooley Wilson, but Billy Joel might drop by and play a few tunes. He and Christie Brinkley had made the place their own. And now that she had moved on, Billy played solo. Movie people and Joe Heller and covergirls and photographers and Jerry Della Femina and

Dave Lucas "the lawn-care king" and, for a time, Bobby
De Niro hung at the Parrot. And having recently lost a
girlfriend, I could empathize with Billy Joel.

My other hangout was out at a marina on the Three
Mile Harbor Road, fronting on the water, and was called
Boaters. Boaters was rednecked and tough, though it mellowed some in summer when the big cabin cruisers and
yachts came in with Wilmington, Del. or Palm Beach or
the BVI painted beneath their names on the stern, most of
them fiberglass Donald Trump wanna-be boats but a few,
the vintage sort. These grand old boats were all highly
polished wood and brightwork and shellac and skippered
by rich old men, whose faces looked varnished as well but
whose ripe younger wives were strictly brightwork. It was
these trophy wives who occasionally struck up friendships
among the young roughnecks who worked summers
around marinas and boatyards and drank at Boaters. In
season Boaters wasn't quite the bucket of blood it could be
in midwinter. Though even now at Boaters you drank Bud
from the bottle and had bumper stickers on your pickup
that said things like, "My kid can beat up your honor stu-
dent." Or "Forget 911. Dial .357."

The gossip columns seem unaware of the phenomenon,
but, yes, we do have good ol' boys in East Hampton. In
ways, the town is as rigidly stratified by caste and socio-
economic class distinctions as anything in Faulkner's Yok-
napatawpha County. We have our patrician Sartoris clans,
our redneck strivers like Flem Snopes and his idiot cousin
Isaac. It said something for the egalitarianism of cash that
among our best families were Ben and Bonnie Krupinski.
Bonnie was one of the locally famous sand and gravel Bis-
trians; Ben had been beatified in an inexplicable puff piece
by the *New York Times* as "contractor to the stars." And
might still be cringing over it as, for one, Village Hardware
on Newtown Lane installed a small, needling sign in its

window: "Bernard—hardware purveyor to the stars." No matter, Ben and Bonnie might be the very richest of East Hampton's humble. Or the humblest of our very rich.

One of the local volunteer firehouses had in addition to a Coke dispenser, another that parceled out cans of Schaefer beer. When too many minor accidents occurred, some that involved simply getting the trucks out the front door, the Fire Department cracked down hard on drinking on the job. They didn't banish the dispensers but raised the price of beer. By fifty cents.

Like the South, we have our rich, have our poor, and in places like Boaters, often they collided.

There were on Further Lane French people from Houston named de Menil. French people from Houston? Never mind. Over the years they went to Harvard and UCLA and collected Picasso, Jasper Johns, Rothko, Twombley, and Rauschenberg. One even converted to Muslim Sufism. And the family built a vast place designed by Charles Gwathmey, which, being droll folks, they christened Toad Hall. My family clashed with them once (they were generally congenial) when they purchased an antique farm somewhere up-island and moved the barns and outbuildings, the whole damned thing, to Further Lane on oversized flatbed trucks that reached out and in rushing past, tore at and damaged our trees, snapping off great limbs.

So we had the de Menils. And we had a gin mill that locals dubbed Club le Bub, "bub" being what natives called themselves and each other.

My father's people, as you know, were old East Hampton. I am a Beecher Stowe IV. They sort of repeated names over and over in our family. Not much imagination. My father's place on Further Lane was hardly the most impressive house in East Hampton. Our house had four acres while most of the neighbors boasted eight or ten or more. But it had been in the family for generations and was a handsome old shingled, chimneyed, and gabled "cottage" with access across the dunes to the beach and ocean, its own badly weathered red clay tennis court my grandfather had put in and where Tilden and von Cramm once played a "friendly," an efficient little apartment above the garage where my dad's housekeeper, a handsome, sturdy Scandinavian woman, lived, and at the head of the graveled drive a shingled old two-bedroom gatehouse, which he'd long ago decided should be mine. After five years away I'd spent most of the summer pounding on the book and reacquainting myself with a part of the world I thought I knew pretty much all about. And which, it was going to turn out, I no longer knew all that well.

FOUR

The potato farmer's daughter who became "America's Homemaker" . . .

Meanwhile, there was Labor Day weekend to get through, and one last, big party, a season-ender along Further Lane at Hannah Cutting's spread. Hannah would shortly be closing down her house to return to Manhattan. Before flying to Katmandu with a small reconnaissance party of wealthy female hardbodies, climbers planning their latest assault the following spring on Mount Everest, the first by a largely female team since that tragic, frenzied, and well-publicized fiasco a few years back when eight climbers died. So Hannah was giving a little cocktail on the lawn for a couple of hundred people to bring down the curtain on yet another summer and, incidentally, to take the salute she obviously considered due her own fame and daring.

Hannah was not one to hide lights under bushels.

But having failed to crack East Hampton's WASP Establishment as she desperately hungered to do (she invited the local gentry to dinners and lawn parties and no one came; chums put Hannah up for membership at the Maidstone Club only to be quietly advised to withdraw her name rather than suffer the embarrassment of a blackball), Hannah reached out largely beyond the Old Money set in casting her parties, inviting the new people with their New Money. And snarling her defiance: "I tried to be one of them, tried to be a WASP, played at being 'that nice Mrs.

Cutting, Andy's wife.' But it didn't take and I didn't take.
They knew I made the money and Andy didn't and that I
hadn't come out of the Seven Sisters but was from Polish
Town in Riverhead. And to hell with them!"

Didn't matter to Hannah if some of her New Money
guests offended local sensibilities and sent shudders
through the Establishment. Hannah was "Tess of the
D'Urbervilles" with attitude. And, like the Serbs, she was
forever at war with somebody. It didn't seem to matter if
Hannah won; it was the hostilities she enjoyed.

As I say, Hollywood and other famous people had long
ago discovered East Hampton, so by now it was nothing
unusual at a lawn party such as Hannah's to see movie
folk, often someone as big as Spielberg. He'd had a place
for years. Geffen, too, now was here. Only Katzenberg
was missing. Or else you could have convened a board
meeting of Dreamworks right there on Hannah's lawn.
Ralph Lauren and Betty Bacall had sold up and moved,
Ralph a few miles down the road to Montauk. But cur-
rency maven George Soros and Mort Zuckerman, who
owned the *Daily News*, and Peter Jennings were here, and
Don Hewitt of *60 Minutes* and the just-separated-but-
dating Kelly and Calvin Klein (how do married people
"date"?) and Jann Wenner and his friend and William
Simon and Ms. Basinger (she and Alec Baldwin had a
house nearby), and Sting, who'd rented the de Menil place
on Further Lane for a hundred and fifty grand for the
month. Bruce Wasserstein, the merger king, lived on Further Lane. William Simon, former Secretary of the Trea-
sury, just off it on Windmill Lane. Nora Ephron and Nick
Pileggi. And lots of beautiful women, some I admired on
Further Lane, plus others.

Such as Hannah Cutting herself.

To some she was an American heroine, self-made and
courageous. To others, an anything-but-sacred monster,

grasping, hard, and appalling. Depended on whom you asked. Sometimes you wondered if they measured the richer of the self-made men as strictly as they did the self-made women. Like Hannah. But never mind. The public adored Hannah, bought her books, followed her on television, wanted to *be* her; people who really knew Hannah, some of those who'd climbed with her on Everest, well, they held contrary views. Jealousy, maybe? Old Money resentment of the New? Pure snobbery? Bitchery? Hannah thought it was all of the above.

I'd go to Hannah's party. Why not?

Hannah Cutting's great green East Hampton estate was called Middlefield.

It was Middlefield long before there was a Hannah Cutting, reference to the fact all of Further Lane had long ago been a pasture called, in geological terms, the Eastern Plain. Farmers for several centuries had worked and fertilized these pastures (no irrigation was ever needed in a place ringed by damp bays and ponds and ocean) and even today, eighty years after the first mansions, like Hannah's, went up, the topsoil is rich and dark and three to five feet deep before you encounter just plain dirt and the local clay. Middlefield sprawled leisurely south for a quarter mile or so toward the ocean, over twelve verdant acres from lovely rural Further Lane to high grassy dunes and then a rickety old wooden catwalk and stairs down to a manicured beach and the Atlantic Ocean beyond. The whole centered on a wonderful old shingled "cottage" with more rooms than are easily counted, twelve-foot-high brick chimneys, broad, shaded verandahs, impressive terraces, tall hedges screening a red clay tennis court and a splendidly boulder-bordered amoeba-shaped pool.

On this pleasant Saturday afternoon in and out of the house and around and across a parklike setting that might have graced Balmoral, beneath lodgepole pines and towering maples and through an array of formal gardens and manicured grounds and across closely cropped lawns in the dappled shade of great elms, strolled invited guests and waiters, wandering minstrels, and, imported from Manhattan for the occasion, a troupe of mimes togged out as tarot cards that cavorted aimiably about, a house of cards in human form. It was left to each of us, even Hannah, to read in their caperings our own future.

Ms. Cutting's guests were a mix of young and old, of East Hampton people and imports from Manhattan, Eurotrash and a few, very few, of the more iconoclastic among the landed gentry. There were the usual pretty girls and journalists; how did you give a party without them? There were the merely rich and the decidedly famous. Well, what else did you expect? Hannah was New Money, you might sniff; East Hampton is like that, WASP and anti-WASP, New Money versus Old. A recent *New Yorker* cartoon captioned "The changing face of East Hampton" pictured an amiable fellow in a business suit, trotting along Main Street under the elms, strewing dollar bills, and cheerily calling out, "New Money for Old, New Money for Old!" This might well be the West Egg of 1925 at Gatsby's place but for the hairdos, the cut of the clothes, the unhummability of the music, the cars without running boards or rumble seats.

Hannah's lawns were of such a perfection, it was said locally in jest, that while most people have theirs mown every Friday, Ms. Cutting had the entire lawn replaced weekly with new sod. The "watchdogs" of The Ladies' Village Improvement Society didn't actually buy the "weekly sod" nonsense, but there had been harsh words over whether Hannah "shoots up" her grass with frowned-upon hormones (she was not much for environmental activism, forever feuding with Brass and his Baymen, and, during chill months, sported sable and mink as if to spite, defiantly, PETA and the animal lovers). There had also been wrangles with neighbors on either flank over when the privet hedges ought to be trimmed and to what height. For all her "good causes," her admirable energy, and follow-through, Hannah was second only to Mrs. Lawrence (who built that "TWA terminal" building of a house down on the beach, which cut off poor Lee Radziwill's view of the sunset) as the most despised woman in town. Several years back Hershberg the real estate man finally sold out and moved to Boca when she won a lawsuit to have a dozen of his trees removed as obscuring her pond vistas and then promptly planted a dozen mature trees of her own to obscure his.

She was as litigious as the Jarndyce family in *Bleak House* and Sullivan & Cromwell at 125 Broad had a small but expert team of white-shoe attorneys assigned permanently to the Hannah Cutting lawsuit account.

Which was one reason those privet hedges were significant. As the tulip is to Holland and the palm to Beverly Hills, the privet hedge is to East Hampton. There were those who believed in having their privet trimmed with geometric precision by gardeners using plumb lines and surveying instruments; others who preferred their hedge wild and thick and bushy. Whatever its shape, the privet is everywhere, tall and green, dividing up enormous properties. And a good thing: neighbors (like Hannah) can be difficult and a tall privet, like a stout fence, settles more arguments than it causes. What is it they say, good fences make good neighbors?

I don't mean to sound patronizing or smug about Hannah's crowd. I knew some of them. Liked a few. I even had a sneaking, contrarian admiration for my hostess. Hannah Cutting was a grand story. The Czechoslovakian potato farmer's daughter from Riverhead who'd become "Amer-

ica's Homemaker." Hard work, guts, taste, an instinct for
what Americans wanted, an enormous vitality, a physical
toughness that had driven her in her thirties to become
something of an alpinist. Meanwhile, left behind in her
luminous wake, a weak and malleable husband bearing
an old East Hampton family name. To some, she was a
self-made success story of heroic proportions; to others,
Lucrezia Borgia. As a reporter, I delighted in colorful orig-
inals like Hannah Cutting.

Which didn't mean we were pals.

Unless they were strictly Maidstone Club, High Episcopalian, Ladies' Village Improvement Society, and all
that, Hamptons parties in high season, even along Further
Lane, occasionally had their freak-show aspects, not quite
up to Fire Island or Key West standards, but still.

Hannah Cutting's season-closing party was campier,
more outrageous than most. The man who was then editing *New York* magazine (and would shortly be sacked on
account of falling subscription renewal rates, down from
71 to 67 percent) was something of a genius who had sent
out a virtual SWAT team of reporters and photographers to
capture on paper that final weekend of summer at Hannah's. As industrious were their efforts, what the occasion
really called for was William Hogarth. Only a Hogarth of
Gin Lane and *The Harlot's Progress* could do justice to
this bunch. Maybe the Hogarth who painted *A Represen-
tation of the March of the Guards Toward Scotland,* with
its magnificent chaos of weeping and roistering, drunken
kisses and brawling, a portrait of his countrymen and
women that was chaotic and ludicrous, ghastly and inso-
lent.

Hannah's invited gallery of grotesques, her real-life
imagining just who were truly the rich and famous, was
everything Old Money found wrong about East Hampton
last summer:

Ross Bleckner, the artist, showed up with his latest Boy Toy who went about assuring people, "but I have a real job! Really I do. I know you despise me. But I work! I work!" Demi Moore came in with her head shaved for a role, compulsively spanking Donna Karan on the ass. And what was that all about? Bianca Jagger lectured people about poverty in Central America and denied she was a fag hag. Yoko Ono ran back and forth to a car, opening and slamming its doors as a pretty boy sprinted after her, calling out, "Mother!" Susan Sontag, of the skunk-streaked hair, sat silent and staring at walls. A man who poured drinks on people until they threw him out. Another fellow who said he kept a tiger shark named Smiley in his swimming pool. But didn't swim, himself. A third who pugnaciously challenged people to hit him. "Hit me! Go ahead! Take a swing at me. Maybe I'm HIV-positive. How can you know until you hit me?"

One husky blonde with a crew cut who'd driven up on a Harley introduced herself, possibly mistaking me for someone important.

"My name is Ralph," she explained. "I'm meeting my girlfriend here. Have you seen her?"

A woman named Precious Mommy told anyone who'd listen just how she loved animals but admitting that very morning, "I ran over a squirrel!" And the trippy Jesus in pirate earrings who kept telling other guests how he began life wearing a gorilla costume delivering invitations to parties such as this one, "but now I *know* these people. And *they* know me!" A famous covergirl, slightly out of it, sat in the backseat of her own Mercedes parked halfway up the gravel drive, upright but fast asleep at five in the afternoon. Murphy, the book promoter with an uncanny knack for getting authors on the morning shows and even *Oprah*, and had a place somewhere out here, came at me wrapped in his accustomed wreath of cigarette smoke,

muttering, "fabulous. Just fabulous." I had no hint of what
he was talking about but to Murphy, understatement was
a sin. Anything even marginally "good" deserved "fabulous" or better adjectives.

All of these folk and more would have made the *New
York* magazine cover story if it hadn't been scrubbed in
favor of the murder.

I worked the lawn, glass in hand, the grotesquerie made
tolerable by the champagne, mingling with fashion designers and actors and TV news anchors and other stars,
feeling like a blend of Robin Leach and Nick Carraway. I
was marginally enjoying the show when Hannah's corporate keeper came along, Hideo Hegel, U.S. rep for what
was nicknamed the Seven Samurai, the huge Japanese
conglomerate that bought Hannah and Hannah's company
for millions and paid her other millions each year to front
for them; Hegel actually ran the thing. He was big, ugly,
and competent. Oh, but he was competent, an interesting
mix, half-Japanese, half-German, his late father a Nazi
general who spent World War II in Tokyo as German
military attaché. People played on his name, snidely re-
ferring to him as "Hideous." Not Hannah. "The Axis Powers," that's what she called him, and to his face, rude and
dismissive. Hegel took it; I don't think he liked it. Having
to account for Hannah to his masters in Tokyo, the Seven
Samurai, he seemed to me to be leading a humiliating life
of quiet exasperation. Except for those hours he whiled
away with his girlfriend.

"Hallo, Stowe. You know the Countess, of course."

"Of course."

I'd met them before, had seen them in Manhattan and
around the boroughs in Europe, and he knew my father by
reputation. The Countess, a blonde invariably described by
Liz Smith as White Russian, was nearly as tall as Hideo
Hegel but much better looking. She belonged to him and

provided services at which one could only, and pruriently, guess. The Samurai paid Hegel to keep an eye on Hannah Cutting. The cynical suggested they also paid the Countess to keep an eye on him.

"Hello, Beecher," said Howard Stringer, the television supremo. That was a shock, seeing him at Hannah's, and I said so. Stringer grinned, a big, amiable Welshman. "I know, I know. She's a piece of work. Three networks in five years and she screwed every one of us. I should know; we stole her show from Ted Turner and Barry Diller stole it from us. One of these days Murdoch'll steal her from Barry. You live by the sword, you die by the sword. If she pulled that stuff on CBS in the old days, Bill Paley would have sent someone to bump her off. Someone classy, Frank Stanton or Murrow, so that it would be done properly, even elegantly so."

Stringer was at her party, he admitted, "for the food and drink, since that's the only profit I'm ever going to get out of the woman."

Beyond Stringer, a knot of men crowded around a slender young woman with dark brown hair down to the small of her bare and very lovely back. You couldn't get close without being pushy. "She's some sort of publishing hotshot from London. Works for Random House," I was authoritatively informed by a man I knew from the Maidstone Club. "Out here for the care and feeding of one of their best-selling authors, I suppose. Got some sort of title." I assumed he meant this in the corporate sense. In the crush of admirers I couldn't tell if the girl was with anyone in particular. She was awfully pretty, with a wonderfully husky Belgravia voice, slurring her speech in a London manner I knew by now pretty well and found irresistible (could I still be carrying a small torch?) and I was considering whether just to barge into the scrum, when someone else came along and said "Hi."

This was Hannah's grown daughter, Claire. Her "plain daughter" was how the unkind put it.

Claire had her mother's coloring and good bones and a vigorous twenty-something body bordering on the spectacular, but the wire-rim glasses and a sulky, resentful look spoiled the effect. I don't know if Claire squinted because she had the wrong lenses but it scrunched up a face that could have been a lot more attractive. Hunched up her shoulders as well, forcing her to peer straight ahead by bending forward. The peerless Hannah clearly had a set of East Hampton values to which her only child was not even attempting to live up. And when someone told the girl, "Your mother's looking for you," Claire's shoulders slumped and she cringed slightly, as if anticipating a blow.

Hannah, it was said, demanded of her daughter a certain standard.

As a journalist, I was interested in relationships, curious about this one; as a polite guest I said to hell with it and took a fresh glass off a waiter's tray, enjoying the spectacle of rich people queued up for the free lunch at buffet tables, nudging each other for advantage at the smoked salmon and toast; the small, chilled local lobster with stiff homemade mayonnaise; the caviar being spooned up. As we waited our turn at the Beluga, one sleekly tailored gent introduced himself as "Donna Karan's orthodontist." Now what the devil do you respond to that, "I've long admired her molars"? I nodded and half-grinned instead and he took his caviar and went on across the lawn, quite pleased and introducing himself to other fortunate folk.

"Oh, champers. Do let's have some, Teddy; there's a good fellow."

It was the English girl, the one with the Belgravia voice who worked for Random House. I was about to say something when I recognized the man with her, the one on whom she was urging the champagne.

"And D.P. at that," she was going on. "I say, this Hannah does have style."

I looked over her shoulder at the bottle from which they were filling the young woman's flute and, she was right. The champagne was Dom Perignon. The flute wasn't shabby either, Waterford at a glance.

Her escort was Crossman, the Wall Street man. Odd, according to the columns he was attached at the hip to that pretty Foley girl. Well, when you've got that much money . . .

The young Englishwoman was right about the champagne. And about Hannah's having style. Further Lane wasn't chardonnay-in-plastic-cups and never had been. Even the New Money people seemed to understand and be happy about it; having earned their way up to Waterford and Dom from chardonnay and plastic. I wished I knew Crossman better; then I could have said hello and been easy about it, and he would have had to introduce me and . . . but by now they'd wandered off and I watched her go; even in departing, she was lovely.

I took mental notes on the more notable guests; you never know when you might have to write a piece and it's better to have taken notes and not use them than to need notes and not have them.

There were plenty of names from the columns; you know who they were.

Then there came a rather ugly moment over the buffet. Hannah had made her appearance, daughter Claire obediently tagging along, while around Hannah was a half circle of flatterers and the curious, asking her about Nepal and climbing and this upcoming Mount Everest recon. Will you be going along with your mother? someone asked Claire, but it was Hannah who answered crisply for her daughter in a voice that carried. "Not my Claire, she's afraid of heights." It was a cruel thing to say publicly and you could see the girl recoil and redden.

I felt badly for Claire but then exactly at that moment Hannah saw me and gave me the benefit of that wonderful broad-mouthed smile and an extended hand. For a microsecond I thought of not taking it, because of what she'd just done to her own kid. But that would have been rude, stupid as well. So I grabbed her hand and shook it vigorously and we exchanged a pleasant word or two as I thanked Hannah for including me in her invitation.

By eight the sun was falling into Hook Pond across the fairways of the Maidstone Club course and the young beauty who worked for Random House had vanished (I assumed with the very fortunate Mr. Crossman), so I got out of there. I hadn't brought my car. I lived pretty close and why bother with the parking ritual. Even though there were neatly dressed young men in identical khakis and white polo shirts parking the cars and, now, unparking them. The sleeping covergirl's vehicle was still there but she wasn't. Perhaps some caring person had taken her away to . . . rest. That was where I saw Claire Cutting again, down by the parked cars, hanging out, I guess, more comfortable with the boys parking cars than with her mother and her mother's friends, no longer cringing like a beaten cur. I wondered if Hannah always treated her daughter that way, wondered why her former husband, Cutting, punished himself by attending her parties as he had this one, hanging about on the fringe and quietly getting soused. Did Hannah enjoy having him there, pinned in his misery like a specimen butterfly to the corkboard? Did she derive pleasure from humiliating Claire? As I walked up the gravel, turning once to be sure a following car wasn't about to nudge me into the hedge, I could see Claire necking with one of the car-parkers, bent backwards and splayed halfway across the hood of a pickup I recognized as Claire's, her arms around the boy's neck, his hands moving. A bumper sticker on her pickup said, "I'm not driving fast; I'm flying low." Claire and the boy seemed to be on the verge of doing both.

Hey, end of summer romance, not unknown out here.

I walked home along Further Lane, passed by limos headed for Manhattan, or to the miniature East Hampton airport that could, just, take the smaller private jets; and by the Range Rovers and custom Hum Vees and less pricey Chevy Blazers and Jeeps, by BMWs and ragtops and other local cars leaving Hannah's, their red taillights burning holes in the summer night. I watched a little tube, tossed a salad and burned a steak, drank most of a bottle of a nice Lynch Bages Pauillac 1990, and went to bed early. Tomorrow was a Sunday but I'd be putting in another long day at the laptop, rewriting and editing the damned book.

I confess to having had absolutely no sense of dread or foreboding about tragedy to come nor did I dream that night of bodies on the beach. So much for my being such a hotshot reporter. But as I fell asleep I told myself I'd been right to thank Hannah for asking me and to take her hand.

And now we had a killing in the village. On a beach where I swam as a boy. Not more than a few hundred yards from where I now lived.

FIVE

The night swimmer
among the sharks . . .

Two o'clock in the morning is a dangerous time to swim alone in the sea. Anyone around here can tell you that.

Some hours after that season-ending Labor Day weekend party at one of the great East Hampton oceanfront "cottages" that adorn Further Lane, the beach is empty and stilled.

The noisy shore birds sleep, terns and plovers, cormorants and gulls, as the usual sea fog of these hours drifts onshore, masking rather than concealing a disciplined, rhythmic line of low waves. There is little breeze; no surf to speak of. The early September moon is already down and scattered stars peek through the thin fog. Dawn is hours off, even false dawn. Fitzgerald once, and famously, called Long Island Sound a great wet barnyard, the most domesticated body of salt water in the hemisphere. That's all very well. But the Sound is up there brushing Connecticut twenty miles north of here. For us on the south shore of Long Island, it's no docile, domesticated sound, but a real ocean out there, the Atlantic itself. Beyond the modest surf line there is in the darkness the occasional swift swirl of disturbed water as a big fish, a striped bass, maybe a big blue or a school of feeding blues breaks the surface in hungry pursuit of baitfish. Further out, even in these latitudes, much larger, more dangerous fish hunt.

During the warm weather months it is not a good idea to swim by night among the baitfish.

Vaguely, through sea fog and at a distance, something else now breaks the surface, scattering small fish. But this is no hunter. Just a swimmer. And a good one, stroking slowly and powerfully in an easy crawl, broad shoulders working efficiently to cover yards with every stroke, long legs scissoring in rhythm. Once through the courtesy surf the swimmer, a naked woman, rises from the water to wade the last few paces, splendid body glistening, seawater streaming from her, emerging from the night ocean and striding strongly up the steeply sloping beach toward the high dunes that for centuries have held back the Atlantic.

Everything about the bather conveys strength and purpose. No longer a girl but magnificently mature, tautly muscled yet lithe, a closely cropped cap of ash-blond hair sleekly framing large eyes, high cheekbones, faintly Slavic, a generous mouth and strong jaw. As she nears the dunes the woman pauses, stoops to retrieve from the sand a big white terry robe of the sort deluxe hotels provide and then beg you not to steal. Even in the act of reaching and stooping, her magnificent body does little to suggest this is a woman of forty.

Now, the robe tossed casually over one square shoulder, and as she nears the base of a tall, rickety, steep but familiar stair leading up to a wooden walkway spanning the fragile dunes, the woman tenses, hesitates, sensing rather than seeing someone there at the top of the laddered stair in the starlit shadows.

"Hello?" the swimmer calls, not yet knowing who it is, only that it must be someone who knows her habits, knows her ways . . .

Then, as the other person moves for the first time, and despite the dark is recognized, the swimmer says, icily:

"Oh, it's you . . ."

These are the only words spoken. The last the swimmer will ever speak, as, still naked with the robe slung, she climbs briskly, efficiently up the old stair to the top, strong hands gripping the wooden railings. Then, from above and without warning, she is hammered savagely on the top of the head by some sort of crude club and slumps loosely, knees caving in, hands desperately gripping the rails as she teeters, trying to keep from falling to the beach below, her brain just marginally functioning, calling up not what is happening to her now but images from the past:

A small girl, blond and plump, running through Polish Town in Riverhead toward the school bus . . . a handsome young man in a Yale letter sweater . . . a television studio's camera, red light on, focused on her . . . a cover of *Time* magazine bearing her face . . . the crisp feel of a newly issued stock certificate with her own name in all that lovely scrolling and engraving . . . a great house on Further Lane that, after so many years of striving, belongs to her . . .

So it all ends, just like this?

She lunges upward in an instinctive final spasm of self-survival, striking out at her attacker. But as she does, there is a savage second thrust, this time to her chest, not a clubbing blow this time but a shocking, spearing, stabbing pain. She falls, fatally wounded, backward from the stair, thudding heavily into the sand, her life's blood ebbing, and yet with a powerful instinct to live, half-crawls, half-squirms as if doing a crude, clumsy backstroke, even as she is dying, back toward the womb of the nurturing ocean.

Then, nothing. And atop the beach stairs where the killer waited in the fog, there is no one, only an empty catwalk across the dunes leading to the faded wooden steps now stained with crimson, already turning dull brown as it dries.

* * *

Early next morning with the sun barely up, a lone vehicle, a rusted red pickup festooned with fishing poles cradled into racks on the front bumper, churns its way slowly along the damp sand of a quiet East Hampton beach, closely skirting the surf, past the big, old, weathered, shingled mansions of the rich, set high on the grassy dunes overlooking the ocean.

The fisherman, a local Bayman named Leo Brass, drives with one practiced eye on the empty beach ahead, the other on the water, seeking out the swooping and plunging and diving seabirds that will tell him precisely where the big blues and striped bass are feeding. Brass earns his money by physical labor, as a commercial fisherman, but he is an educated man, by avocation a naturalist; and often in these complicated times even he is confused by conflicting loyalties. He has been out here since three A.M. and is driving slowly, wondering whether to get out and take a leak. Three hundred yards from the Maidstone Club he sees something and hits the brakes, skidding to a stop and nimbly leaping to the sand before the pickup has stopped rolling.

It is the nude body of a woman, lying face up, dead eyes staring, at the edge of the tide, cropped hair strewn with seaweed, glistening in the low sunlight. And, oddest thing of all, from the woman's left breast protrudes what seems to be a heavy, primitive wooden stake perhaps two feet long. In the final years of the second millennium in one of the more sophisticated enclaves of America, a woman of whom much of the country has heard and whom Leo knows, and well, has been skewered by a homemade spear. Brass kneels there at her side for an instant, looking down. He not only knows the dead woman, but knows her pierced breast as well, knows her entire body. And intimately so.

Staring down at her dead eyes, Brass licks dry lips and

wonders briefly if his mouth is dry but it isn't. Confronted
by violent death, Leo Brass is shaken, but still able to spit.
And does so now, into the sand in the lee of her body. He
continues briefly to kneel there looking down at the dead
woman. Mourning? Remembering? Or marveling how
erotic her naked body looks, despite the butchery. Then,
his meditations accomplished, he rises to grab his cellular
phone from the truck and dial East Hampton 911.

Small fishes drawn by blood wriggle in the shallows
but there are no footprints or other tracks in the sand, the
ebbing predawn tide having neatly, if inconveniently,
scoured the Maidstone beach. Now Leo Brass, distracted
despite himself and his noted machismo, remembers that
his bladder is full and he'd better urinate before the cops
or anyone else comes along. There'll be questions and
people and red tape and cameras, considering the identity
of the stiff. Better take a leak now. He steps to the edge of
the water and unzips his jeans. As he relieves himself into
the ocean, little fishes scattering in alarm, Leo looks again
at the corpse. Christ, even dead she looks good. She always was a woman that took care of herself.

Some body, she had; some woman, she was. Despite
himself he grins in memory.

Much of this, and more, East Hampton will learn over
the next few hours and days from police reports, the eye-
witness testimony of Leo Brass, a coroner's jury, through
local rumor-mongers, and from the feverish accounts of
ambitious reporters on the daily tabloids and the evening
news.

Not within memory had there been a capital crime on Further Lane.

Oh, a wife-beating, perhaps. Driving under the influence. The usual adulteries. Drunkenness. The enjoyment
behind private and privileged walls and privet hedges of il-

licit drugs. A gay-bashing at Two Mile Hollow Beach, where smooth and wealthy older men cruised youngsters in Speedos. Petty theft. Unconfirmed whispers a prominent restauratéur kept a torture chamber, cells, manacles and all, in the cellar of his house. For homicide, you had to go back to 1919 when Captain Chelm came home from France after the Great War to find his lonely young wife in bed with her second cousin Ruggles, whom the Captain promptly shot.

Since then, nothing of this sort.

Which was one of many reasons why wealthy people live on Further Lane and why a distasteful real estate ad (it was soon pulled) referred to a per-acre price for land in the area as "south of the highway and north of a million," and why what happened last September on the sand east of the Maidstone Club shattered so many innocent (more or less) illusions.

SIX

A stake of sharpened privet
driven through her cold heart . . .

The dead woman was Hannah Cutting.

For the first day or so, on Sunday and Labor Day, I took only neighborly, personal interest in what happened. Not professional. There was local shock at having a violent death at our doorsteps; more general shock that the victim was such a celebrated person. TV and newspaper reporters swarmed over the little resort town, complicating the already congested Labor Day weekend traffic and aggravating townspeople. Good thing my old man and his Nordic "housekeeper" were going off to Europe and wouldn't be back until next month; traffic jams in East Hampton were to him an especial irritant. He'd barely tolerated the annual Hampton Classic horse show, which ended September first. And that was miles away in Bridgehampton! And soon the damned film festival would begin. Although I did no digging into the case and had only a normal curiosity, having been at Hannah's home mere hours before her death, I was instinctively and by reflex starting to gather information. Reporters are like that.

Fleshing out fevered accounts in the press, my primary source was a detective named Tom Knowles, a boyhood chum (we split when I went off to Harvard and Tom joined the Marines) who was now a plainclothesman on the small East Hampton P.D. and was professionally irritated that one of the town's rare homicides had been taken over (force majeure!) by Suffolk County with its sizable and quite competent homicide squad. Knowles realized this made sense but he was nonetheless, as he admitted to old pals like me, slightly pissed. You get someone murdered in a small town, the town cops want a piece of it. Especially a man like Tom who single-handedly had taken on and knocked down Leo Brass in the company of numerous and pugnacious Baymen and brought him in to be booked for mischief against Simon Krantz and his contentious dock. Knowles liked Brass more than he liked the wine baron but the law was the damned *law*. Tom was the sort of fellow you might cast to play Inspector Harry Callahan if you couldn't get Eastwood, only half Eastwood's age but every bit as much "Dirty Harry," tall, rawboned, hard, handsome, and with a deep voice that came out of his scrotum. Someone once said of Tom's look, "even his cheekbones have cheekbones."

A good cop besides, and, as I say, pissed. Which made him, for me, an even better source.

To start with, according to Knowles and others who knew the situation, there was nothing suspicious about Hannah's taking a midnight swim. When the water was warm, as it is in late summer, she often swam way out, at night and alone. A good swimmer. Whatever happened to her occurred after she was back on land. Second thing? She must have known her attacker and well since she was apparently naked, carrying her robe, when confronted, and yet had made no evident attempt to cover up or flee. There were two blows. Hannah was walloped over the head, said the cop, which stunned and may have knocked her out. That was all. Didn't finish her. The lethal blow came shortly after, a deep stab wound to her right breast penetrating to the heart. That's what killed Hannah Cutting.

The odd thing? The weapon was heavy and blunt but it

was also sharp, a sturdy length of privet hedge honed and fashioned at one end into a crude but quite deadly spear. The blow to the head, which apparently came first, stunning Hannah, must have been made by the thick handle end of the stake. Which, following swiftly on, had been turned around for that killing spear wound to her breast. Any prints? Anything offering DNA labels? No, said Knowles, the attacker had worn gloves, but the police thought the attacker, from the angle of penetration, might have been left-handed.

Maybe not, I remarked, he might have worn a left-handed glove to avoid leaving prints, and therefore had to use his left hand.

When Tom looked dubious, I said:

"All kinds of folk wear two gloves in summer, people who garden, genteel old Episcopalian ladies, that sort of person. But then there are right-handed ballplayers and right-handed golfers, both of them wearing a single left-hand glove. Unless it's one of Mort Zuckerman's softball team, I'd look for a golfer."

"Harvard," muttered Knowles in disgust, hating to have civilians offering theories. I enjoyed needling him and suspected I'd scored.

What else? He shook his head in posthumous admiration:

"Beech, that Hannah was something. First the knockout shot to the head, then the puncture wound right through her, and she was still alive."

Being a Marine, and a cop, Tom Knowles admired toughness.

The victim, not accepting the undeniable clinical fact she was already dead, had refused to die, but had squirmed away on her back, that ghastly spear protruding from her body, only to make it all the way to the water's edge and then to die, but not easily. An extraordinary feat, Tom admitted, considering that second blow, the stab wound, might have killed anyone almost instantly. But she'd not died, not just yet. Or had she been dragged dying, maybe by the hair, down to the water by the killer? Tom suggested that possibility as well. No footprints, unfortunately. An ebbing flood tide had seen to that.

"Hannah Cutting's hair is cropped short," I protested.

"Enough there to get a hold on it," Knowles persisted, then, "You covering this story, Beech?"

No. And I wasn't. That was the truth. A day or so later it wouldn't be true but I never lied to Tom. Not then, not ever.

The newspapers and the tabloid TV shows were, understandably, out of their minds. A glamorous and famous woman of enormous wealth, style, and power, widely admired and recognized, fiercely controversial in some quarters, had been found stark naked and murdered on the sands of America's most elegant beach resort, a wooden stake (as one overstimulated headline writer put it) "driven through her cold heart!"

The press reported the facts amid wild tales of vengeance, feuds, sexual license, plots and rumors of black magic, and (nothing was too far a reach for headline writers at the *New York Post*) "orgies among the de-beached and rich."

The briefly most fevered theory featured allegations of devil worship, voodoo rituals, and, yes, that favorite of sexually heated gothics, the Black Mass. Here was a female victim, stripped naked and spread-eagled (not so, said the cops!), pierced by a clearly phallic device, the sharpened wooden stake; and wasn't Hannah, after all, a lapsed Roman Catholic? And weren't the Hamptons officially (and famously so) part of the Roman Catholic Diocese of Rockville Center? What could be more obvious?

There was talk the bishop was in confidential contact with the Jesuits and might summon an exorcist.

An illegal Haitian immigrant, meanwhile, employed in nearby Wainscott by a sod-laying firm, was arrested and closely questioned as to his whereabouts the night of the crime, and his belongings thoroughly ransacked for beheaded chickens and other possible clues to voodoo practices and unspeakable acts. Once the poor man proved to have an alibi, he was swiftly re-arrested by immigration authorities and hustled off. The immigration people hate to let a live one get away.

Almost as exotically, according to detective Tom Knowles, the local Indian Jesse Maine headed the list of suspects, having recently and quite loudly been fired as a handyman by the dead woman on her complaint that he'd used her own personal bathroom while working around the house. Hannah, a housekeeping fanatic, had flown into a powerful rage. Jesse, with quite a rap sheet for drunkenness and violent behavior, was overheard by several reliable witnesses threatening to "get back at" Ms. Cutting. But Jesse hadn't yet been charged. He was a popular figure on the nearby Shinnecock Indian Reservation in Southampton and the authorities didn't want an "incident" especially this weekend, the annual Labor Day Reservation Pow Wow that drew thousands of spectators and hundreds of Indians from other Eastern tribes.

"Bringing in Jesse during Pow Wow would be like busting the Pope Easter Sunday at Solemn High Mass in Vatican City," Knowles had said.

Another thing about Jesse, he and detective Knowles and I all played ball together (against the angry and trouble-making Leo Brass) in one of the Hampton summer leagues when we were kids. Tom was the fastest of us, Jesse maybe the strongest, Brass the loudest, and I also played.

Jesse the Shinnecock, like most of his tribe, was of decidedly mixed blood. "I'm seventy-five percent black, one hundred percent mean, and I'm all Shinnecock," he was fond of boasting when in drink.

But he was hardly the only possible killer.

Hannah had her enemies. Half the people in town had reasons to dislike her; with the other half, she "got along." Since for five years I'd been away, returning only briefly on home leave or summer holidays for family reasons, Knowles's narrative became for me a sort of personal "Greek chorus," not only in regard to Hannah's death, but on recent changes here in the little town where both of us spent some or all of our youth. The Knowleses were old East Hampton and of modest means; the Stowes old East Hampton and well-off.

"No one resents the old families, Beech, for having a few bucks. It's the new bunch, the carpetbaggers, the actors and rock stars and Wall Street arbs, the fashion designers and hairdressers, this latest swami with his patter about Rosicrucians, about Merlin and mystic numbers. They arrive here and start to throw their weight around and treat blue-collar types like me as picturesque local color, as if we were part of the scenery, sent here by central casting for their amusement. Billy Joel, now, he's swell. But that Sting, he'll look right through you. I encountered him one day on Main Street and said hello."

"And?"

"He nodded, smiled, and called me 'My man.' "

Hannah Cutting was New Money but was also old East End, from Riverhead, and that confused people; they didn't know quite how to react to Hannah. As for motive, there were plenty who hated her guts. Tom Knowles tugged out of a seersucker jacket pocket a narrow spiral notebook such as good cops, and good reporters, carry, and checking his notes, he read them for me, ticking off the usual suspects:

Max Victor, Hannah's former partner, sloughed off when she sold herself and the company to the Japanese. Victor was paid millions but not the fortune he believed he was owed; he drank and had an unhealthy letch for unsuitably young women; was still resentful and rarely referred to his ex-partner except as "that bitch;"

Hannah's former husband, Andy Cutting, the product of aristocratic if tired loins, wearer of the old school tie but these days a nonentity celebrated largely for having once shared Hannah's bed. He'd long ago been dumped by Hannah and had been sliding downhill ever since;

Her East Hampton nemesis and neighbor, the very WASP (authentically so; she didn't marry into it as Hannah did!) Pam Phythian, a doe-eyed, Aztec-profiled, lean, athletic woman about Hannah's age who was particularly offended by Hannah's alpine grandstanding: "Everest, Everest, Everest," wailed Pam, "you'd think she was Tenzing Norkay!," naming the Sherpa who accompanied Edmund Hillary on that first ascent. Pam and Hannah had been fellow members of an Everest expedition that ended tragically with eight alpinists dead. The traumatized Pam hadn't climbed since while an apparently insensitive Hannah was planning another Everest assault. Once climbers on the same rope, relations between these two savvy, powerful women had soured into viciousness. Hannah moved onto Further Lane five years ago, Pam's family had been there for five generations (one set of cousins spelled the name "Fithian"), and the two strong, attractive women were now at the point of scheduling competing dinner parties, backing rival charities, arguing over whether their commonly bordering privet should be trimmed back and by how much. If Pam played for the Artists in the annual softball game behind the A & P, Hannah volunteered for the Writers' team. But would a perfectly respectable woman kill over such trivial things?

You jest! Of course she might. Or so I told myself.

Pam was hardly the only one out here who hated Hannah. A famous, flamboyant interior designer, Roger Dafoe, whose stock in trade plummeted when Hannah on her TV show critiqued his finest work as "boasting all the elegance of an OTB parlor"; Hideo (Hideous) Hegel, who lost face with his superiors in Tokyo, the Seven Samurai, because of Hannah's never-ending, and to them, insulting and arrogant demands;

A brawling bayman Hannah once accused of molesting her in a local restaurant. "Hell, her jeans were painted on and I gave her a little pat on the ass. How'd I know she was Hannah friggin' Cutting?";

Boobie Vander, a covergirl recently dropped by Hannah from her TV commercial and endorsement contract, a costly and unpleasant blow made even more painful with Hannah's widely repeated reference to Boobie as "having a few miles on her odometer";

Stringer, the big television CEO, who only Saturday evening suggested Bill Paley would have had the woman "bumped off" for dealing traitorously;

Hannah's grown daughter, Claire, whom she patronized and bullied (and who might have good reason to welcome her mother's death);

And even the Bayman who discovered her body, Leo Brass. He and Hannah were at opposite ends of the environmental debate clashing only last spring over composting rules (he lived off but cared about nature; she enjoyed and exploited it). And Leo had an arrogance to match her own.

Plus former lovers and people Hannah Cutting used, abused, and climbed over on her way to the top of the ladder. Even the summer's pet swami, having been snubbed, carried a grudge.

There may have been other suspects at this stage unknown to the police or to anyone else, including me. And a few in Tom's notebook, like Boobie Vander, turned out to have been on entirely different continents when Hannah climbed that old wooden stair to meet her killer. But had we cast nets sufficiently wide? Where was PR woman Peggy Siegal that night, Peggy, the "flack from Hell"? Where, too, Claudia Cohen? Had she an alibi? What of Senator D'Amato himself, a Long Islander by birth and breeding? Where were Mikey and Mickey the night Hannah bought it? As far as I was concerned, and considering all the people who fought with or disliked or envied Hannah, just about every single one of us was a suspect but Brooke Astor, who already had everything Hannah ever wanted, and who rarely if ever came to the Hamptons.

This was what caught at the sleeve of imagination and piqued the curiosity of so many of us: Who killed Hannah Cutting and why?

SEVEN

People who live here think themselves special, touched
by the hand of God . . .

By Tuesday morning the long holiday weekend had ended
and East Hampton was emptying out, frustrating the homicide detectives. Streisand was back in L.A., Martha Stewart in Connecticut, Donna Karan on her way to Lyon and
Zurich to buy fabric for the new collection. Demi was on
location somewhere. Others scattered this way and that.
My own father would be off that very day for Norway and
the salmon beat he'd taken on the Merdal, and his annual
tour of the parishes, Copenhagen, Paris, London. How do
you force rich and famous people to stay around to be
questioned simply because they knew her or she attended
the victim's last cocktail party?

The answer, you don't.

Also, by Tuesday morning, I was no longer merely one
of the loitering curious; my summer-long idyll ended. By
Tuesday, I was on assignment, covering the Hannah Cutting story.

Anderson phoned early that morning from his office at
Parade on Third Avenue in Manhattan. The editor, aimi-
able but firm, told me to shelve the several assignments we
discussed. "Right now, Hannah Cutting's our story. You're
out there, you knew the woman, you attended her last
party, you know the setting and the cast of characters. You
probably know most of the suspects. Her death is pure

melodrama; it's her whole life that fascinates people. Who
was Hannah? How did a poor girl become a millionaire?
Where did she come up with the idea for that first best-
seller, *The Taste Machine*?"

And, the editor wanted most to know, "How did Hannah
Cutting get to Further Lane?"

Anderson cut his teeth as a general assignment reporter
for the Gannett newspapers and he knew cops solve murders; reporters don't. He didn't want me chasing clues and
grilling suspects but finding out the truth—not about her
death—but about the living Hannah Cutting. . . .

"You *own* this story, Beecher," Walter Anderson
growled cheerfully as he hung up, a softspoken man, but
you could sense the iron beneath, which left me feeling
rather like that anonymous little reporter in *Citizen Kane*
dispatched by his boss to find out about Rosebud.

By now, the television crews had gone back to town
and the print reporters were reduced to haunting the Suffolk County DA's regional office in Southampton, waiting
for news and trying to goad someone, anyone, into making an arrest. Why couldn't the cops just go in there and
grab that goddamned drunken Indian Jesse Maine right
out of his wigwam? Touch off a riot? Well, yeah, maybe.
But, hell! A famous woman's dead and no one's been
charged! Riot's a small price to pay. Besides, when did
Indians last riot? This is Long Island, not the Little
Bighorn. And if it came down to that, an Indian uprising
might turn out to be an even better story, Wounded Knee
and all that. . . .

There was a brief flurry of excitement when Hannah's
ex-partner Max Victor was arrested for allegedly groping
a young woman sitting next to him on the Hampton Jitney.
Ever since Hannah, damn her!, sold the company out from
under Max, he hadn't had much luck. She was his curse,
it seemed. And now this . . . when he'd barely touched the

girl's leg reaching for his book, a biography of Jane Austen, for God's sake.

Preliminary autopsy results were released. The knock on the head caused concussion; the stab would killed Hannah. And, Tom Knowles told me, they were learning more about that primitive spear. Not only was it privet wood, carved to a dangerous point, but it was carefully hardened by flame, having been turned over a charcoal fire. Privet hedge? Charcoal? Not much of a clue there; in an East Hampton summer you could hardly turn around without encountering both. The place was a-crawl with barbecue fires and lush green hedge.

But why kill with a spear in the East Hampton of the nineties? Silly, and stereotypical, but it nudged me toward starting the *Parade* magazine assignment with Jesse Maine. Not that my father thought it a very good idea.

"Why not have a talk with Leo Brass? I don't have to tell you he's a violent, difficult man, and he did find the body. Used to throw the javelin, didn't he? Jesse's okay, Beecher. Watch yourself when he's been drinking and watch yourself around Leo period. Just because they both know boats and water and hunting and fishing better than you, don't get carried away with a romantic notion you're dealing with noble savages. Noble they can be but savage they are. Be sure you know whether it's Jekyll or Hyde up to bat that morning." Those were the only warnings my father included in a brief farewell address before being driven to JFK for his flight to Oslo.

I'd walked down to my old man's house to see him one more time and say good-bye. "He's on the beach, puttering about in the kayak." This was Inga who kept house for Admiral Stowe and quite possibly was a lot more than that to the old man, a strong, strapping blond woman in her forties, Nordic, placid, crisply attractive. She treated me and just about everyone else with a cool courtesy and no more, reserving more powerful emotions for my father. She might have given the late Dag Hammarskjold the time of day. Or His Majesty, King Olav, but beyond that, very little. There was no one on the beach though out past the surf I could see a lone paddler working hard, coming in. Didn't take long. "Hi, Beecher," my dad called out as, timing the waves, he brought the sturdy ocean-going kayak smartly and smoothly up out of the shallows and onto the damp sand.

"You look ready for the Olympic trials," I told him.

"Next time, maybe."

He rolled nimbly out of the boat and we both lifted it to let the water run out before walking up to the house together, the two of us easily lugging his kayak fore and aft. My father was in his sixties and didn't look it, didn't feel it. He was even taller than I was, lean and suntanned, no varicose veins in the long, sinewy, boater's legs. Inga laid out a marvelous mixed salad and cold salmon with green sauce and a young inexpensive Sancerre and then vanished into the house to finish packing. Or so she said; she kept her place, never eating with us if I was there or he had guests. Inga observed appearances. Over lunch I told my father about Anderson's assignment, to take back tracings on Hannah Cutting and write the story of where she'd come from and how she got to Further Lane. I was a bit uneasy about it, I admitted. "I've never before written about Further Lane. After all, we live here. This is home."

"You've been a reporter everywhere from Boston to Bosnia and there are people living in every place you've written about, Beecher. Why should Further Lane be sacrosanct? Sometimes I think that's just about the only thing wrong with this place, that people who live here believe themselves to be special, touched by the hand of God. When they're just people who happened to have a little money and the sense and taste to want to own a piece of this part of the good green world."

"I know, I'm being oversensitive."

"You're a journalist and a good one, if I'm any judge, based on those pieces you wrote from North Africa and Yugo. Writing about your own town—well, maybe a touch of delicacy and tact might be called for. Beyond that, write the truth, be fair, be yourself."

He was the moral spine of my ethical core, always had been, and I listened to what he said. Their car was coming at three to take them in to JFK so after lunch I thanked him and said good-bye, wishing him good luck with the salmon, and then mentioning as a postscript I was going by the Reservation to see Jesse, and getting a cautionary bit of paternal advice.

Despite fatherly counsel, I drove the twelve miles to Southampton and then the few miles more to the Shinne-cock Reservation. There were still two Indian tribes on Long Island; the other was the Poospatucks at Mastic, both sets liberally intermarried, mostly with blacks but also some whites. Jesse, typically, was more black than Indian. On the reservation side of the highway an Indian in a shanty bright with garish signs promising savings was selling cigarettes by the carton without the excise tax, so I bought a carton of Luckies. Not to smoke. To get him talking. He looked more Sicilian than Shinnecock and took me for a cop and wasn't very talky until I showed him the press card.

Jesse lived in a pretty nice little house with a healthy garden down by the shore on Shinnecock Bay. He had a green thumb and was handy with tools, and it showed. A nubile young woman came out barefoot and said he didn't want to see nobody. Not cops, not reporters, not nobody. I didn't know if she was his girlfriend or one of his kids. Jesse was capable of coming up with either. So I shouted in at him that I was Beecher Stowe from Further Lane that used to play ball with him and how more recently he'd done work for my old man. Jesse chewed that bit of vital information for a little and then shouted back.

"They find out yet who killed the bitch?"

This wasn't very diplomatic of Jesse, speaking ill of the dead, especially when he was among the leading suspects; but when he came out to shake hands I said no, and did he have any ideas?

Yes, he said, he did. "If I killed her, Beech, and I thought about it a few times, there would have been lots more wear and tear on the body, I can tell you."

What kind of person would use a spear as a weapon, did he think?

That seemed to puzzle Jesse for a time.

"Some of them Guatemalans and Aztecs and such they got mowing lawns along Further Lane, them fellas got strange ideas. Voodoo even. You might inquire of them if you speak the lingo."

No, he never heard of local Indians using a spear as a weapon, not since the old days. Not since they got guns. And when the long-ago Shinnecocks did use spears it was mostly for fish or as harpoons for whaling, and back then they used hardwood for the shaft and topped the spear with flint, and later with metal when they could get it. Who ever heard of a soft wood like privet hedge, hardened in flame, for a weapon? Didn't make sense; it was just stupid.

It occurred to me *Town & Country* wouldn't have believed this conversation. They had their own image of the Hamptons; a man like Jesse Maine had no part in it. Nor maybe did a leg man like me.

Then Jesse had an idea: "That Swami fellow down there near you on Further Lane. You might look into him for sheer nonsense. He's got them rich bitches out on the lawn in their skivvies, barefoot and dancing all but naked to the tom tom, eating bees' honey and pondering the Ouija board. They've all given up martinis and espresso, traded them in for scalding water. Swami went to Hannah for contributions and sponsorship but she was too smart, or too mean, to fall for that shit and chased him off. Maybe Swami had a grudge. . . ."

That would be a swell story. I could see the *New York Post* headlines now, could imagine what *Hard Copy* would do with it. We talked some more, not getting very far, and when I left Jesse waved me off and shouted out hallo to my old man.

Hannah Cutting had her faults but Mr. and Mrs. Kroepke stayed loyal. They were the husband and wife team who lived on her property, the missus cooking and keeping after the cleaning woman and the other day servants and people recruited to wait and bartend parties, and the husband driving and butlering and supervising the gardener and lawnmower man and such. Been with her a long time; still there now. They had a yellow plastic crime-scene tape stretched across the head of the gravel drive, but after I showed my press card and indulged in a little palaver, the cop let me in as far as the gatehouse, where I phoned through. Kroepke said okay, I could come up to the house. The couple sat there in the kitchen on straight-backed wooden chairs; that was their turf, the kitchen and below stairs. Mrs. K. made coffee and we talked. I didn't get a lot from them but what I got was first-rate, blue chip, 24 carat. About how Ms. Cutting was working so hard these days. Not on business, the way she always did, but on the book. Her book. She was at it hour after hour. It had sort of taken on a life of its own, Kroepke said, and Mrs. K. said so too. And it was a blessed shame she'd never finish it now. Her story, her life, and never to be finished when it had become such a passion and a holy cause for their mistress . . .

Hannah Cutting's book.

EIGHT

Harry Evans said something about sending someone out to look for the manuscript . . .

I didn't know the whole story about her book but I'd heard some of it.

It all derived from Hannah's being such a control freak. There were already a couple of books out about her, one of them dull and worthy and officially authorized. The one people were buying was the trashy version, decidedly unauthorized and a best-seller. She was furious about it and began talking about setting the record straight and settling scores. So Harry Evans at Random House put on a full-court press and lured Hannah away from the house that had published her earlier self-help books. He got Hannah signed up to write her own story, which Liz Smith informed us would have Ms. Cutting "naming names, taking numbers, and kicking butt." That was months ago. How close was she to completing the job when she died? Maybe Liz Smith got it wrong and this was just another in a series of the decorate-the-place-yourself volumes she pumped out that sold so well? Or simply ego massage and self-indulgence, preening and posturing? Or would this be a really big one, with Hannah telling the raw and maybe bitter truth and avenging herself on enemies by getting it all down on paper? Did this book-in-progress have anything to do with her death?

I phoned Mr. Evans in Manhattan. He tap-danced for a

while even though both Random House and *Parade* were owned by the same gentlemen, the brothers Newhouse. I thought it impolitic for a brand-new hire like me to bring that up; let it occur to Harry Evans on his own. I'm not sure whether it did but in the end Harry told me he was himself in the dark. And he sounded frustrated, even sore about it.

"She told me she was working hard and piling up the pages, but beyond a treatment she was required to give us before we went to contract, I haven't seen a word."

She was doing the book herself, he confirmed. No ghostwriter. Was Hannah talking into a tape recorder or writing on a computer or longhand on legal pads or what? Harry said he'd recommended a word processor but really didn't know. She told him she'd dictated her earlier books to a crack stenographer. This time, she'd do it herself, concerned about confidentiality. With a book this big they'd take it any way it came in and hire transcribers. He said something about sending someone out, a young editor, to look into the manuscript's whereabouts.

"Appreciate your pointing my editor in the right direction, Stowe. Place like East Hampton can be confusing to a stranger."

"Sure, Harry," I said, not really meaning it. Evans and his wife had a place on the East End but not East Hampton. I knew the town and they didn't. I also had a competitive journalism assignment and why should I give anyone else a leg up? In this business, you don't "blacksheet" anyone, you don't hand around copies of what you have or what you've written.

Stupid of me but I hadn't asked the Kroepkes if Hannah was using a computer or writing it out longhand or what. When I phoned the Cutting house again to ask, I got the answering machine so I left a message and spent the afternoon working on my own book, clearing my head of

Hannah Cutting, enjoying the warm, cuddly memories of downtown Sarajevo during a mortar attack, and those jolly days and nights in Algiers when the mullahs stripped and stoned decent women for wearing Western clothes instead of the veil and I got shot in the . . . well, I got shot by sticking my nose in.

At about six I got in the Blazer and drove up to Boaters for a beer. You weren't supposed to dance but when the old jukebox was being fed, people danced. No one tried to stop them. Everyone smoked, everyone drank, everyone danced. That was Boaters. They had everything but gypsy violins and the Don Cossack Chorus. I had a beer and then another and looked around. Among the dancers, Claire Cutting.

Bereft of a loving mother, but clearly not in mourning or rending her garments, the newly orphaned and devoted daughter Claire danced. The girl who freely admitted in comparison to her mother that she was herself inept and artless, danced. And well. Or, at least sexily. Healthy young body. If she traded in those granny glasses for contacts with decent lenses . . .

And she was dancing with Leo Brass, the Bayman who found her mother's body on the beach. When they got back to the bar during a break, she went to the ladies' room and I moved in, squeezing between a couple of locals. Knowing how bristly Brass was, I kept a distance from him, watching him as I drank, waiting for Claire to come back. Tom Knowles told me while I was away Leo hadn't mellowed much. "Remember Crazy Frank, Beecher? He must go about two-sixty these days but one night during a full moon he and Leo got into it. Leo threw Crazy Frank off a highway overpass and damn near killed him. Crazy was laid up for days . . . two or three of them."

Brass was one of your black Irishmen, maybe six-four with huge hands, rawboned and fit, with the crow-black hair hanging lank, through which from time to time he ran a cheap plastic pocket comb. From the size of him, good tight end material. I'd known Leo for years, played ball against him, didn't like him very much. Wherever he went, acolytes followed. Pugnacious little men who drank too much and got into fights they inevitably lost, they stuck by Brass, testifying to his significance. Unlike Leo, the acolytes were unattractive to women or to anyone else, although to him they were faithful as the Twelve Apostles. He had his other adherents, a motley fringe of neo-Fascists and Green Peacers who saw him as a Populist hero, stuck to Leo like napkin lint on a navy suit, and argued passionately he ought to be in politics. And in truth, with all his ranting and that brief mustache, when a lock of black hair dipped over one eye, he resembled a tall Hitler.

Some people felt Leo belonged in Washington; he'd do well down there with Gingrich and that crowd.

Leo himself? Women liked his athletic, cocky, to-hell-with-you look. Some liked it a lot. Men had varying opinions. Was he a blowhard peddling blather though undeniably entertaining? Or a true menace? He was big and tough enough to be dangerous, sufficiently intelligent to be more than that. Lethal? It was possible.

Unlike me, who can't carry a tune, Leo played piano by ear, had a voice, and was a gifted mimic, doing a more than passable James Cagney as "Yankee Doodle Dandy." Years before in the Wild Rose bar drinking with Leo and others, I'd gone home early. At some point the phone rang. It was LaRuffa, a mutual friend: "You gotta come back. He's never been this bad. Everyone's going crazy, buying rounds . . . and women flailing about and rooting him on . . ."

Leo, doing his "Yankee Doodle Dandy" act, was prancing and singing the entire length of the bar and then out the saloon door and onto the Sag Harbor pike, where cars swerved to avoid accidents and honked in alarm.

"I'm asleep, LaRuffa. Tell me tomorrow."

But lying abed I could see Leo in my drunken, drowsy mind's eye. And in ways wished I were there. Leo had talents and commanded loyalties few men have. Or deserve. For all his university education, he was pushy and obnoxious, grabbing a CPA by the lapels and lecturing him about accountancy. Or an engineer just back from building a railroad in Lapland, with Leo informing him why the ties these days were cast concrete rather than wood. Or telling a veteran police detective he knew nothing of law enforcement. One night a visitor from South Africa was at The Grill, an actual white hunter, and before the evening was over Leo Brass was instructing the man in the correct method of stalking wildebeest.

Much powerful grabbing and yanking of shirtfronts and lapels accompanied all of this, even when Leo was congratulating a man for the birth of a child or a killing in the market.

"By God, I'm proud of you, you son of a bitch, showing the damned bastards."

And with the fortunate, or unfortunate, fellow, smiling his gratitude as his head was jerked back and forth, this way and that, very nearly shaken from his shoulders.

That was Leo Brass, whose specialty at bars was telling people they were full of shit. And occasionally throwing people across the room.

Claire Cutting came back now and I took my drink and went to her, pushing past people.

"Claire, it's me, Beecher Stowe. I was at your mother's last party and I wonder if we might . . ."

I didn't get very far. Nor did the "fight," such as it was, last very long. Claire's friends were young, tough, and muscular. Also very protective. Especially the Bayman who didn't like Hannah very much and, coincidentally, had found her body. Now here was Leo Brass "protecting" her daughter. Two or three other locals broke it up before Brass and I got very far. "Beecher's no snooper. He grew up here. Hell, he's as Bonac as any of us . . ."

"Bonac" meant you belonged. Short for Accabonac, an old East Hampton Indian word. True "Bonackers" were born here. "Bonac against the world, bub!" That was the popular local slogan and some of these boys took it seriously. And belligerently. But then, Leo didn't have to be told who I was. He knew very well. We'd played ball as boys, fought as teens, feinted and maneuvered, had drinks together on occasion, yet didn't even pretend to be friends.

With Leo Brass you got a mixed message: intelligence and good looks melded to behavior you might have expected from a redneck in *Deliverance*. And it was Leo whom my father suggested I question first about Hannah's death, my father, who'd spent a lifetime gathering intelligence, assessing and analyzing, and then imparted his knowledge to men who commanded task forces and air fleets, who oversaw our national security.

Tom Knowles said Brass and Hannah had fought, and recently. The clash was over an issue that could only have occurred in East Hampton. She'd accused Leo of clandestinely introducing half-grown and voracious snapping turtles into hers and other ponds in the village to eat the ducklings that were fouling the bottoms with their excrement (more delicate folk preferred the term *guano*), thus encouraging the growth of stifling algae.

On the other hand, Tom said, Hannah was hardly a local heroine, and who gave a damn what she thought? Brass was to some a charismatic figure, a persuasive, even spellbinding speaker, and there was wild talk of running him for Congress from the East End. After all, there were Long

Island people who go to Jones Beach on the Fourth of July
and ever after think of themselves as outdoorsmen. Others
if they've crossed from Orient Point to New London, Connecticut, on the car ferry, consider themselves mariners. A
politically incorrect rebel like Brass might appeal to such
easily convinced voters.

But these were incidental concerns; my questions dealt
with the late Hannah Cutting. Questions I couldn't conveniently ask right now, not with Leo & Co. sufficiently
lubricated to interrupt. And brutally. Well, I told Claire
Cutting, being as pragmatic as Leo Brass, "I'll catch up to
you some other time."

Back at the gatehouse there was a voice-mail message.

"Ms. Cutting was using a laptop computer to write her
book. An IBM laptop." It was Mrs. Kroepke's voice.

Tom Knowles and I met at The Blue Parrot. With the summer people mostly gone, Billy Joel surfaced. He didn't
like their gawking. Billy was a big hero to the East Hampton Baymen who made their living as commercial fishermen. He'd been arrested a couple of times at the Baymen's
protests over striped bass and haulseining restrictions, and
local folks admired a man who'd stand up and get arrested
for you. Tom and I got a table in back where we could
talk and still hear Billy's piano over by the bar.

The detective said of the people who might be considered hostile to Hannah, Suffolk Homicide had cleared
about half as having alibis, solid witnesses to their whereabouts Saturday midnight. The covergirl Boobie Vander,
for example, was in Paris on a shoot. Peggy Siegal was in
Manhattan at a screening. Senator D'Amato was addressing an Italo-American dinner in Baltimore. Jesse Maine
was still under suspicion. "But until we have a lot more, no
one's going to ignite a race riot out here, Beech." I was
tempted to enter Leo Brass's name in nomination as a

leading suspect, the bastard, just to get back at him. But my father wouldn't have approved. He and Harvard were ethically opposed to bearing false witness so I didn't. Princeton or Notre Dame might shilly-shally; Harvard didn't! Instead, I said I was going up to Riverhead, to the East End's Polish Town, where Hannah came from, where she grew up, searching for roots. Knowles was skeptical but gave me the name of the parish priest and a couple of other people I might see. "If what you're really after is her story and not solving murders, that's where you start, Beecher."

I guess Tom was still suspicious as to my motives. Funeral arrangements hadn't yet been announced and the body hadn't been released. There were questions and her next of kin, Claire Cutting, wasn't being particularly helpful. Was her mother Catholic as she had been as a child? Episcopalian, as she seemed defensively to have suggested in interviews? Jewish? She was too damned smart and successful not to be, or so it was said by the usual local anti-Semites. The coroner was still doing tests. No drugs found, only the alcohol that might have been explained by a drink or two. No more. She was dead before breaking waves washed over her; no water in the lungs. What did all this mean?

We talked a bit about the death weapon. "Jesse Maine says privet's a dumb wood to use, that it's too soft."

"Maybe that's the reason it was sharpened, hardened up over flame," the cop said. What sort of person would use a stake or a spear to kill? It was noted that Leo Brass was once a champion javelin thrower. Yes, but . . .

God, this was crazy, arguing about wooden spears and javelin-throwing in the final years of the millennium. As we spoke, I kept seeing Hannah's trim, strong, handsome body and imagined how it looked now, cold and dead and carved upon, on the morgue's cutting tables, slid in and out of the refrigerated lockers for yet another chill session under the scalpels.

"That's the trouble," Tom said loudly, and a waitress turned.

"What?" I asked.

It wasn't just that Jesse was a hothead and Brass a troublemaker and Hannah Cutting a pain in the ass, the detective said.

"East Hampton wasn't like this when we were kids." There were all these local frictions and stresses that had become potentially dangerous, according to which side of the argument you were on. What to do about the thousands of Canada geese who spent all autumn and winter shitting on the Maidstone fairways? What about hungry turtles munching and gnawing on downy little ducklings? A petition to ban those noisy leaf blowers, for another example? Which led, inevitably, to the famous snobbery, not by one of our more prominent Bourbons but by Hannah Cutting, now endlessly repeated over cocktails, that leaves and cut grass shouldn't be blown away by raucous machine but raked by hand:

"That's why we have Guatemalans," Hannah declared wickedly, "to rake lawns."

People took offense, Tom said, and who knew what Hannah, notoriously acid-tongued, had additionally said or who else she had angered? Was it Hannah, or six other people, who remarked there were really any number of Hamptons: East, South, Bridgehampton, Westhampton, Beach Hampton? And then there was that lovely, verdant stretch between Bridgehampton and Sag Harbor where a number of black families lived:

"Lionel Hampton."

In her defense, that's what their neighborhood was

being called by the blacks themselves who lived there. Okay for local blacks to make jokes; not for the rest of us. WASPs are allowed to twit WASPs; Catholics, Catholics; Jews, Jews. In a time of correctness, if you weren't black you didn't do Amos and Andy routines or spoof a black this side of Rev. Farrakhan.

Racism? Snobbery? Elitism? Probably all of the above. East Hampton was still a town where you weren't considered to belong until there was a village lane bearing your family name.

There was one odd sidebar item. In Manhattan, at an East Village gay club, Knowles reported, a man named Roger Dafoe had been arrested for getting into a minor scuffle with another guest. Nothing would have come of it had Dafoe not made something of an ass of himself, claiming he was on a party to celebrate the death on Long Island of a woman named . . . Hannah Cutting. The first cop on the scene, accustomed to drunken hair-pulling in Greenwich Village joints like this one, ignored the man's boozy babble. A second cop, more alert, recognized Hannah's name. A famous woman, recently done to death. And of whose death by stake of privet hedge he called out with evident glee, was "so *very* East Hampton!" They pulled him in and held Dafoe overnight on vague but plausible charges and in the morning, when he was sober, he was questioned.

"And?"

"Dafoe admitted he hated the woman, that she'd damaged his reputation and hurt his business, and came up with some sleazy stuff about her early career that he claimed included an exotic stint as 'Madame Hannah, all fetishes explored.' Beyond that, he claimed not to know what the police were talking about. Must have been drunk, he said. And seemed able to produce on demand responsible witnesses who would swear to an alibi. Most of them attractive young men."

Billy Joel was still playing the piano when I got out of there.

NINE

Of course you think I'm beautiful.
Everyone does . . .

September in the Hamptons is grand, the best time.

Hot, sunny days, warm ocean, cooling evenings, the big fish running and the traffic gone, the season's first football on the tube, and it was terrific being back here in September after five years. Even if Anderson had put me right to work. Living in Europe was wonderful, beyond all telling. And then September came along and you remembered a place like East Hampton existed.

I was sprawled the next morning on a battered old chaise out on the lawn of the gatehouse in a faded denim workshirt and knee-length khaki shorts that had once been respectable, reading the *Times* and having a second cup when the phone rang in the kitchen. The voice, even with the lousy connection, was like bells.

"I'm at Exit Sixty-one on the Long Island Expressway on my cell phone, Mr. Stowe. How do I get there from here? My name's Alix Dunraven and I work for Harry Evans. Who sent me out here on a vital mission and who, incidentally, practically sends love . . ."

The connection faded in and out, and above it, the roar of speeding traffic didn't help nor did a persistent static that sounded like a dog's yipping but I was too stunned for rational objections and by reflex went ahead and gave this unknown woman the directions. About an hour later a very

cool old E-type Jaguar convertible, British racing green
with its tan top down, crunched onto my gravel and skidded to an elegantly competent stop. It was piloted by a
young woman with her long dark hair up in a silk scarf to
keep from blowing and with what I already knew to be
brilliant blue eyes hidden behind the latest in shades:

Crossman the billionaire's girl from Hannah's party!

I chose to ignore the silver gray miniature poodle sitting
next to her on the front seat, regarding me as if I'd been
whistled up for its amusement and curious to know when
I'd begin the performance, rolling over and begging for
dog biscuits.

She (the young woman, not the dog) got out of the car,
wearing a sensibly full-skirted midcalf silk dress of some
summery floral design or other and gave me a brisk handshake. I'd not quite gotten her name over the static and she
gave it again.

"Dunraven, Alix Dunraven. Mr. Evans provided me
your name and number. I've been dog-sitting for an absent
chum and had to fetch Mignonne along. I don't even like
dogs all that much; un-English, I know. But she's been
awfully decent about it so far, one must admit, hasn't bitten me or tossed up in the car or anything. She seems quite
smitten with me. Are you a dog man yourself?"

I scowled, or tried to. It was hard with someone who
looked like Alix Dunraven.

Defensively, she shrugged, as if slightly ashamed to
have admitted she didn't like dogs all that well, being a
Brit.

Mr. Evans, she said, had urged her to call upon me as
sort of a repository of all useful information East Hampton might have to offer, as if I were not only Harry's best
and closest friend but a one-man Michelin guide to the
place and its delights. I barely knew Evans but didn't argue
the toss, just standing there, listening to her rattle on in that

husky Belgravia drawl, enjoying how the easy morning breeze blew the silk dress, rustling it gently against her long, slender body. As she suggested, even the dog seemed infatuated by her and made no fuss at all. As to how I felt about Alix Dunraven, I guess it showed in my face. She gave an impatiently tolerant half smile, her attitude toward me, toward the world, being pretty much:

"Of course you think I'm beautiful, everyone does, but let's speak of important things. . . ."

Instead, she was really saying, "I've called ahead to this bed and breakfast thingie for a room, the Mauve House I believe, d'you know it? I do hope they won't be difficult about dogs and how do I get there from here? But may I freshen up first? That's a bloody long drive and not many petrol stations where one might hazard a pit stop. . . ."

She let the poodle out to romp on my father's lawn for a bit while I showed Ms. Dunraven into the gatehouse to the downstairs john. The one upstairs was nicer but I hadn't yet made my bed and you know . . .

When she came out, looking splendidly "freshened up," I gave her coffee and told her where the B & B was, some number Buell Lane, and how to get there, and we sat there on my old Adirondack chairs in the sun while the poodle sported about and then I said:

"Just why again did Harry send you to me? I don't understand exactly what I'm to . . ."

"Oh," Alix Dunraven said airily, "it's about Hannah Cutting's book. I'm this year's Tony Godwin laureate."

"Tony Godwin?"

"Yes?"

"Who's he?"

She was generously patient with me.

"Each year in London book circles there's a ferocious competition among young editors. The winner gets to spend a season in New York, working for Doubleday or

Simon & Schuster or Putnam's, much as you Americans
send Rhodes scholars to Oxford or a promising under-
graduate to spend a junior year abroad at the Sorbonne . . ."

"And you won this year's Godwin competition?" Before she could respond, I corrected myself: "*Ferocious*
competition?"

"Well, yes, not to be pompous about it, but yes. I work
for Rupert Murdoch's publishing house in London,
HarperCollins, but now I've been dispatched by Random
House to pick up the Cutting manuscript and fetch it to
Mr. Evans. Very simple, actually."

"And my part in all this?"

She frowned. I liked it very much when she frowned,
how it crinkled her nose and made those eyes seem even
bluer. Was she even old enough to be the most brilliant
young book editor in London? What the hell were they
feeding child editors these days? Wheat germ? Straight
gin? Speed?

"Well, I thought it was pretty clear. You called Mr.
Evans about Hannah's book, seemed to know quite a bit
about it, and he gave me your name. . . ."

"You were at Hannah's party."

"Yes," she said, "rotten timing that. I'd never been to
your Hamptons and was desperate to get some sun and,
just coincidentally, have a few encouraging words with
our hot new author Hannah Cutting. Thought I might impress Mr. Evans if I did. So I came out with a man I know
whose mistress was unavailable with root canal and I
begged him to take me along. Then it turned out he was
frantically anxious to dump me and get back to his girlfriend in the city to soothe her pain—God knows how, a
randy business indeed, I suspect. Barely gave me an inde-
cent tumble. That Miss Foley of his must be quite something. He had his plane waiting at your darling little local
airport and we left even before the party ended. So I

missed the murder. Hard cheese on me. When Harry, Mr. Evans, realized I'd actually been there all the time at Hannah's, practically a material witness, and got nothing out of her and left before she was killed, he was quite cross. Sent me right back out before dawn this morning in a regular fit of pique."

I liked that. She'd gone to the party "with a man I know." Who had a "mistress." Didn't sound as if she and Teddy Crossman were, well . . .

"I'd attempted to talk with Ms. Cutting about the book project at her lawn party but she gave me short shrift. I was at a disadvantage, besides, not having read even that first best-seller of hers, *The Taste Machine*. I'd seen the magazine she spun off, *Hannah's Way,* and rather enjoyed it. But that was it; I was no expert on Hannah Cutting. She must have sensed it and cut me dead. Neither the time nor the place, that sort of thing. Still, I kept after her. Even stressed the significance of the Tony Godwin Award and how it meant so much to my career and to United Kingdom prestige, 'Buy British' and all that. At Random House they stress we're to take initiatives, never be discouraged or flag in the quest, that in a great symphony orchestra even the second cello is important."

"I'm sure," I agreed, knowing little of cellos, first *or* second.

"But I got bloody nil out of Hannah about the current manuscript. Very stiff she was. She was 'accustomed to dealing with Mr. Evans himself,' she'd have me know! and no snip of a girl or slip of a girl, I'm not sure which it was she called me . . . And if Harry weren't available, she'd 'be delighted to chat with his boss, Mr. Vitale. Or *his* boss, Mr. Newhouse.' If there was anyone superior to Mr. Newhouse, she'd contact him as well. Told me off, right and proper."

I agreed that Hannah could be stern. But resisted a wisecrack about there being *no one* "superior" to Si Newhouse. Then Alix Dunraven gave me a big smile.

"But I know you! At the party, over where they were ladling out the D.P., and I made Teddy get me some. You were there knocking back the champers yourself."

"Yes," I said, unreasonably pleased that she remembered me, recalling how she'd looked then, enjoying how she looked now.

"Well," she said, suddenly very businesslike and efficient, "I'd best be off to the Mauve House . . . what a curious name . . . and get at it. Can't let the side down. Mr. Evans will be expecting reports every hour on the . . ."

When she and the poodle, who, despite the odd growl, I must admit was awfully well behaved, were back in the car I repeated directions to Buell Lane and told her to phone me if she got lost. We were in the book. Stowe, Beecher, on Further Lane. Phone number 324-something-something. I'd have tattooed the number on her wrist (or other places) if she'd let me. . . .

As she turned around and drove slowly up the gravel toward the Lane, she adjusted her rearview mirror.

To look at me? If I were pondering such possibilities, I must be more hung up on that lost girl in London than I thought, and feeling sorrier for myself.

Or was Alix Dunraven simply checking out her hair?

I returned to my coffee and paper in a pleasant daze. The coffee had gone cold but I found it extraordinarily bracing, even tasty, and reread with enormous interest dull stories I'd long since digested. I was even feeling more tolerant about dogs. Here I'd called Harry Evans to pick his brain about Hannah's book and he'd turned around and sent this honey to pick mine. And I'd been admirably shrewd, not simply caving in while confronted with Alix Dunraven's beauty. I hadn't told her that I knew what her employer Mr. Evans didn't seem to know. That there might not be an actual paper manuscript. Only an IBM laptop on which Hannah was working assiduously when she died. Information I knew and Alix didn't.

What a fine name she had. Alix Dunraven . . . Sounded like something out of Noel Coward. Or Waugh. And what a delicious morning this was turning out to be.

TEN

Higgins educated Liza Doolittle;
Hannah pretty much educated herself . . .

When you want information in a small town you see the clergyman, the cop, the editor of the weekly paper. When the small town is someplace like East Hampton, you also drop in on the current guru.

I called ahead. Sure, he said, come on over. The Swami was living near the Amagansett end of Further Lane in a house that an admirer had provided for the season. It was where he worked his wonders. He spoke fluent, unaccented English. I don't know quite what I'd expected, an ascetic Tibetan, a wild-eyed dervish, a scrofulous towel head, Richard Gere. He didn't sound like any of those.

There were already a dozen or so cars parked on the gravel, Beamers and Benzes and Jags mostly. Ragtops predominated. From around behind the house came noises. Screams, actually. I thought primal screaming went out years ago with Peter Max paintings but I must have been wrong. Swami came to greet me, a smallish, very neat, and well-conditioned-looking gent in a tank top and shorts, both pristinely tennis white, with blond-dyed hair and piercing violet eyes. No caftans currently in sight, no Jesus hair. He was probably thirty-five.

"I am Mr. Kurt," he said. "Some call me 'Swami.' You must be Beecher Stowe."

We shook hands. Nice firm grip. I like a firm grip. Behind Mr. Kurt twelve or fifteen quite attractive women in their thirties or forties danced about the lawn in a loose circle, alternately grunting and letting out screams, keeping time to a big old wooden metronome he had set out there on the grass, its wand going back and forth, back and forth.

"They're testing the fluidity of the doors of perception," Mr. Kurt whispered an aside, so as to let me in on the secret but not break the mood. From what Jesse said, I expected diaphanous gowns, incense, "the beat beat beat of the tom-toms," and sexual excess of every manner and sort. But these women were sensibly dressed in workout clothes, as if this was a Health & Fitness Center like the one Martha Stewart's daughter operates. I wasn't sure whether to call the guru "Swami" or by his name. And would have felt foolish doing either so I took refuge in cop-speak, addressing him as "Sir" and asked about his run-in with Hannah. Angry, was it? Belligerent? Threats exchanged?

"I've been questioned about that earlier. By the authorities. It was very simple. I'd provided her a precis of our devotions, snorting ketamine off each other's bodily parts and, as you've just witnessed, testing fluidity of perception, looking into the fundamental meaning of tie-dye and studying the clouds."

Swami looked skyward and I murmured, soothingly, "Sounds reasonable." He went on.

"But Hannah seemed unable to distinguish the mountain trail from the celestial track. The rest of our little congregation, most of us, were blessed with the gift of being able to find the humor in death and in human excrement oozing between the toes. Not Hannah Cutting. When I quoted the wizened old Hindu baba and asked Hannah to submit to having a lactating woman squirt breast milk into what I reckoned to be her otherwise unseeing eye, Hannah flailed out in anger, turning viciously upon me. It was a stunning rejection, I must admit, nearly violent. I'd asked her to join our little group, suggested an appropriate donation, and she told me to go away, she said she'd been to the carnival before. Not a very respectful or reasoned attitude, but of course I backed away and accepted it without argument. A tranquil soul needs no additional angst."

Sounded like Hannah to me, telling him to fuck off, I thought, but didn't say so. Swami must have sensed his devotees were slacking off so he wheeled angrily to face them, stuck out his tongue, and growled, "Yaaaaaaauuugh!" Or that's how it sounded.

They all stuck out their tongues then and growled back, "Yaaaauugh."

Mr. Kurt was that summer's "consensus guru" and he assured me all these sweaty women swore by him. He said he'd seen Hannah only two or three times after that, around the town or at a cocktail, and they'd not spoken again.

Donna Karan, on the other hand, he told me, was a great supporter, introduced to him by Peter Guber's wife. They all went on retreats together in various shrines and holy places and prayed on cliffs and along the shore and had grand times indeed. What was going on here now on the lawn was sort of summer school, relaxed and outdoorsy. Swami explained he had a small staff, a juice-fasting expert, a psychospiritual counselor, a choreographer, and a chap he described as a veterinarian cum body-piercer cum astral-surfer. Mr. Kurt handled the vital stuff himself, the meditation and primal screaming and other chores. As well as private consultations after hours. He didn't offer anything about enema treatment and I was too shy to ask.

When I thanked him and turned to leave he pressed on me a business card (curled at the edges as if he'd handed it around before or used it to clean his fingernails or floss a stubborn tooth). "If you ever feel in need of a spiritual renewal," he said, "or some excellent hash cookies."

I was on the verge of telling that, as a Protestant, unlike more pliant people, I rarely felt such needs. Instead, I held my tongue, promising insincerely to give him my business, when and if, and then I turned the car 'round and headed west on Route 27 for Riverhead, where I had appointments.

A little juice-fasting and astral-surfing goes a long way with me.

The hottest controversy in Riverhead in recent years was a proposal to sheathe the historic Polish church in vinyl siding. Some parishioners were holding out for aluminum and others insisted a simple traditional paint job would do (the pastor wanted vinyl). Now a poor daughter of the parish, grown enormously rich and celebrated, lay dead.

The priest was a skinny young man, slightly addled, who thought I was there about the vinyl siding. When we got that straightened out (I made a point of *not* telling him I was an Episcopalian), he showed me the register, birth through death. Hannah's family were Czechs but on settling down in pre-war Riverhead's Polish Town were instantly tagged as "Polacks" along with the rest of them. Hanna (no terminal *h* yet) Shuba. Born 1953. Baptized. Confirmed. Married. To a forty-year-old, Pilsudski. Hanna was then sixteen. Five months later, a child born, baptized. The father looked at me.

"It is not unknown for there to be premature births. There are occasionally viable five-month pregnancies," he said, shrugging.

"Of course," I murmured softly, not wanting to appear cynical and slander the dead. Or scandalize a man of God.

Two years later, the priest said, came the funeral for Pilsudski, leaving Hannah (she had the *h* now) a widow at eighteen with a small daughter. She paid for a high mass, even a tenor. God knows where she found the money. That was the extent of his information as he'd been here only a year. I wished Father well in the unfortunate matter of the vinyl siding dispute and got directions to the police station.

Tom Knowles had provided the name of a tame Riverhead cop, an older man who remembered the family. And young Hannah Shuba. Wild, he said, shrewd, too, but wild. Was known to have spent the occasional evening in the backseat of a car. Local boys were all hot for her but when she had options, Hannah went for summer people and rich kids. Long before she ever lived there she had East Hampton tastes. The old cop had no idea who might have wanted her dead. But he sure remembered she had the cutest little bottom in the Hamptons and that she swung it around.

He sent me on to the old man who used to own the shop where she clerked later on, after Mr. Pilsudski died. The man was retired and might no longer be all that cogent, the policeman alerted me. Good thing, too. The old gent, Mr. Ober, lived these days with his sister in a big old frame house on a scruffy, weedy plot near the stone bridge where the Peconic River cut through the old town. The sister hadn't known Hannah when she worked in the store; her brother had, but she gave gave me fair warning. "He's not the man he once was. Keen, he was. You didn't skin Elmer Ober. Not in a deal, not in business. Oh, but he was keen. No more. Just sits there in his hat talking to the dog about television."

"Oh," I said, not knowing what all that meant. I shortly was to find out. Mr. Ober was inside the house in the cool gloom some old houses provide even at midday in summer. And wearing a hat. Otherwise, just his underwear, old-fashioned underwear, what they used to call a union suit. He sat there on a sofa, an old man in his underwear with a Panama hat squarely set on his head while a big dog sat next to him on the couch. Both man and dog were focused on a large television console on which an old black-

and-white movie was showing. I thought I recognized George Raft but couldn't be sure. Mr. Ober was talking. To the dog.

"Don't trust that feller on the right. He's not a reliable sort. Keep an eye on him. The feller that just left, with the raincoat, now, he's okay. You'll see. They hold back clues in the first few reels. Catch you up in the story without revealing all. Too early to reveal all. It comes in later reels. Build the tension, there's the secret. You have to watch for it. Uh oh, look at this one. What's she up to? Nice pins, though . . ."

Mr. Ober might no longer be keen, as the sister warned, but he knew his movies. And appreciated a well-turned leg. The dog listened to the old man, tongue lolling damply, pointed ears reacting to his voice, and seemed to be watching the screen with equivalent concern.

Mr. Ober's sister made the introductions, including the dog.

"That's the neighbor's dog, not ours. He comes over every day to visit my brother and watch television with him. They like to watch together."

"Oh."

Mr. Ober and his dog stared at the TV with enormous interest, and obvious pleasure, as James Cagney got out of a big car with running boards, chauffeured by Frank McHugh, and nipped nimbly across the sidewalk to a nightclub, moving as he always did with that dancer's grace. Mr. Ober was telling the dog, "That's Jimmy Cagney now. You watch, he'll straighten this bunch out. . . ."

After I'd asked a few questions and wasn't getting through, to either the old gentleman or the neighbor's dog, I thanked them all and left. As the living room door closed behind me, the dog's tongue was out, lolling.

The newspaper editor was fuzzy-cheeked, too young to have known the Shuba family, but when I gave him dates he pulled out the dusty bound volumes. Pilsudski died grotesquely, suffocated when a cesspool he was digging caved in. You live in shit, you die in shit. Who was it said that? A year or so later Hannah married again, to Andy Cutting this time.

Driving home from Riverhead didn't take long and I thought I'd better stop to see Andy. He was drunk. Only late afternoon but he was already soused. I can come back some other time, Andy, I said.

"No, Beech, draw up a pew. If I can't talk to old friends . . ." And then, boozily but cogent, he talked to me:

The Cuttings were a fine old East Hampton family. Old Money, as well, except that Andy was apparently the one member of the family who never learned to count. His business acumen was zero and his share of the family fortune was eroding rapidly. Hannah must have seen something in him. To raise her daughter and pay the bills, she'd clerked in Elmer Ober's shop and moonlighted cleaning houses. Her mother baby-sat and Hannah worked hard with energy and lavished attention on good wood and china and silver and glass. She never stole. Or broke things. Or skipped a cleaning day. A Hannah-cleaned house shone, sparkled, shimmered. She appreciated the fine things she came across in the great houses she cleaned, things she didn't have, and cared for them as if they were hers. She seemed to have some primitive notion that marriage to Andy would provide, if not the things themselves, a passport to getting them. I'm afraid I'm a disappointment to you, darling, Andy told her. I don't have the knack; I keep losing money whatever I do. . . .

Don't worry, the girl assured him. Teach me a few things and I'll make the money for both of us.

She was a quick study and hers was a crash course in quality, with Andy the sometimes befuddled, often reluctant tutor, urged on by his young wife: Tell me about sil-

ver. What was the purpose of the hallmark? Who is Billy
Baldwin? Is he as tasteful as Sister Parish? In china, is
Spode as good as Wedgwood? Sheffield steel, is that the
best? Or that German stuff, Solingen? What about glass,
is it the lead that makes Waterford so desirable? Tell
me about furniture. Who was Morris and what do his
chairs look like? Who was Queen Anne? I never heard of
Bauhaus. What is it? How d'you tell fakes from antiques?
Does champagne have vintage years the way Bordeaux
does? Why do the Brits call it claret and we don't? Is ve-
neer good or bad? Was Frank Lloyd Wright a great architect or just a publicity genius? She learned by asking
questions; she learned by osmosis. Other Cuttings, who
still had dough, lived well. When the outsider Hannah was
permitted among them, she took notes. Higgins educated
Liza Doolittle; Hannah Cutting pretty much taught herself.

The cops had been there, Andy said, and the TV crews,
the tabloids, even the *Times*. He was beaten down, still a
handsome, decent man. But tired. Andy lived not grandly,
not well, in a rented apartment over Bucket's Deli up by
the railroad station. He knew it was a comedown; I knew
it. So we mutually ignored the *House & Garden* details
and talked about Hannah. When one of the six or eight
daily trains pulled in, the apartment shuddered and its windows rattled and chipped coffee mugs moved around on
the shelves. Further Lane was two miles and a zillion dollars away.

The problem wasn't getting Andy to talk about her; it
was getting the poor bastard to shut up.

I'm still in love with her, he said. "She dumped me and
I still love her. She sucked the marrow out of my bones
and gave me the drop and here I am sobbing into the cov-
erlet because she's dead. Wish I knew who killed her. I'd
get him."

Him?

"Got to be, Beecher. She turns men into swine or whatever crap it was Hemingway wrote of Brett Ashley. Women hated her; men loved her. You kill the people you love; not the ones you merely hate."

Andy wasn't as drunk as he pretended. But he went on and on, how ambitious, how clever Hannah was, how competently she'd picked his brains, how his family resented her, how she'd ruined him at the same time he'd found in her lush body and nimble head everything he'd ever wanted. . . .

I made him some black coffee on his own hot plate and left. I can take only so much cheap sentimentality. Which was how it came off. I had this sense Andy was role-playing. Maybe there'd been too many interviews by *Entertainment Tonight* and *Hard Copy* or by people from the Geraldo show. Jesse Maine hated Hannah and yet I didn't think he'd killed her; Andy Cutting loved her. And might have.

ELEVEN

*Looking for sea shells, staring up at the big houses on
the dunes . . .*

I got a surprise that evening when Claire Cutting came by
the gatehouse on Further Lane, saying, Look, I'm sorry
about what happened at Boaters.

No problem, I said. I shouldn't have tried to talk to you
so soon after . . .

I don't mind, she said.

There was still light and we sat down outside on the old
lawn chairs and she began to talk. She was like Andy now,
compulsively talking about Hannah. But then people who
knew Hannah well seemed unable not to, people like that
old cop up in Riverhead, who remembered her teenaged
rear end. Hannah had a way of taking hold. I thought there
might be beer on Claire's breath and when I asked if she'd
like a Coors she said sure and I got two from the fridge.
Why this contrast to her previous sullen silence? Don't
tell me it was just having a beer or two. She didn't explain.
But somehow it seemed essential that I should understand
there was nothing weird about Hannah's last swim. It was
okay if I took notes, she said. And then she proceeded to
tell me just how weird such swims were!

"Hannah read somewhere that big sharks, the dangerous
kind, swam in close to the beach at night, hunting baitfish. In Florida, where they knew about such things, most

people won't swim at night. Hannah, being Hannah, determined that night swims were in.

"You swim with the sharks if you have guts."

That, said Claire, was how her mother was, that was her posture. East Hampton wasn't Palm Beach, of course, and no one had been eaten by sharks along here in human memory. But Hannah Cutting was intent on meeting the challenge. You climb Everest or try to, you go swimming with sharks. . . .

I cut across Claire's theorizing. "You and your mother get along?"

Hannah (she called her Hannah, never Mother or Mom) wasn't easy, she admitted. "I admire her." Then, and flatly, "She was involved in too many things to have time for nurturing. I'm a disappointment to her. We are not close."

She had, she said, no idea who might have wanted Hannah dead. Her mother rubbed people the wrong way. People like . . . Pam Phythian. Hannah talked of mountaineering as a way to show up other people, show up snobs like Pam. Survival of the fittest. There was bad blood between Pam and Hannah. When did that start? And why? I probed with questions a devil's advocate might pose:

"Yeah, but you don't murder someone who showed you up, who rubs you the wrong way," I protested. I thought maybe you did; but I was trying to get a rise out of her. Claire seemed uninterested. The Queen is dead; long live the Queen: that seemed her attitude now. She was all over the place. Could she be on something stronger than beer? Why not? Her mother wasn't dead a week and here she was being grilled by some nosy reporter.

I was rude, I guess, but I kept at it, asking more questions. Who knew if I'd get another opportunity, not with Leo hanging close and ready to throw his weight around. And me, if he could. Surprisingly, she answered some of my questions. Truly? Well, I couldn't know that. One answer rang true. I asked just why she thought Hannah was so tough on her only child.

"She made it out of Riverhead and Polish Town and onto Further Lane, trading in poor for rich, swapping old friends for new. I was a sort of throwback. I like the locals. I hang out with a blue-collar crowd. I drive a pickup instead of a Beamer. She'd die to belong to the Maidstone; I couldn't care less. She's into self-improvement and I'm not, she's a powerhouse and I'm, well . . . I'm not her and she seems to consider that an offense."

She spoke like that, in the present tense, as if Hannah weren't dead.

Then, thoughtfully, "I think she really always wanted to be a WASP. She had to work summers and after school as a kid, so except for swimming and being naturally coordinated and pretty strong, she couldn't do sports. But tennis was a big thing out here. So Hannah decided to learn tennis. Got a coach from the Maidstone, bought a SAM."

"What's a SAM?"

"A sports action machine, a kind of robotic tennis pro. Fires shots at you at various speeds from lobs to smashes. A warning light goes on and stand back! Here comes the ball! The SAM Hannah has costs twenty-five grand."

"Oh."

"Same reasoning behind why she married a weakling like Andy Cutting. She was too intelligent to think a wedding could make her a WASP, or even that success and money might do it, but she kept trying, kept butting her head against the wall, and was frustrated by the Establishment. So she takes it out on everybody, WASP or not, and especially on me because I don't share her WASP ambitions."

"Is all that in her book?"

"How would I know?"

"Haven't you read any of it?"

Claire laughed, the sound brief and caustic, as if to say, "Are you kidding?"

"Do you know if she was nearly finished writing it?"

"No. Only that it'll settle a few scores."

"Which scores? Pam? Hideo? Leo Brass? Andy? Jesse Maine . . . ?"

"I dunno. Just that she said that once when she looked up from the laptop and I asked how it was going."

I chewed that one over. Then, "Are you the heiress?" I asked, realizing it was none of my damned business but asking regardless.

She stared into my face. Quite coolly she said, "I haven't the foggiest, Beecher. I've never seen Hannah's will; if she left one, and if there is, I'm quite certain I'm not the executrix. Attorneys are handling everything. Hannah doesn't have much faith in my judgment." The last time I'd seen her, I thought of Claire as a whipped hound, cringing at her mother's name.

She didn't cringe now, and her shoulders didn't sag. No longer did she squint nearsightedly into the middle distance, neck bent. In so many ways, she conveyed the impression she was no longer cowed. Confused and maybe sedated or a little stoned, but not scared or bullied. Hannah's death had liberated her child. Unless by some legal fluke she was disowned, Claire was going to be a very rich young woman. That could help, too, in taking the slump out of your shoulders. . . .

One more thing, Claire said, "She isn't always the automaton some people think. Hannah has her softie side, her vulnerable moments. Sea shells. She has a collection of sea shells from when she was a kid. They didn't have much money and shells were free for the picking up."

"At Riverhead?" There were no sea shells there.

"No, down here at the ocean. Once a year the family

would pile into the pickup truck for a day at the public beach in East Hampton. She looked forward to those outings all spring. Used to tell me about them when I was small, about walking the beach looking for shells and staring up at the big houses on the dunes. A little kid searching for shells and looking up to where the rich people lived. In houses like the one she bought and I live in now."

I nodded. Let her talk. Maybe there'd be something else I could use in my story, like this about the sea shells and staring up at the big houses where the rich lived. Good stuff, that, the dead woman as more than just another rich bitch who'd scored big. And still swam in the night ocean.

"And for all of her famous, even ruthless, efficiency, Hannah can be a bit of a pack rat. With a roomful of junk. Not throwing away things that hold meaning, no matter how silly to anyone else, no matter how worthless otherwise. An old shoebox of sea shells. A beat-up old climbing rope from that Everest expedition when those people died and she didn't. Her first tennis racquet. Never had a racquet until she married Andy Cutting and he bought her one and she practiced at the cement courts behind the high school. Or against the handball wall behind the A & P. Rich people played tennis; it was important to Hannah that she learn how. At least be able to get the ball over the net. Stuff like that . . ."

I walked up to the Further Lane gate with her.

"That freak-show crowd she had to her last party. If she was so intent on impressing the WASPs, they were hardly . . ."

"Oh, that was defiance. She'd sucked up and been rejected so now she was being naughty."

"But for a woman who became famous for teaching American women how their homes and their gardens and even they themselves ought to look and behave, to think of that bunch as her set, it doesn't make sense."

Claire didn't look at me but at the gravel drive in front of her as she said, very softly:

"Hannah's got good taste in everything but people."

At the head of the drive a pickup was parked, waiting. Not Claire's. In the dusk I could just see the driver's profile. Surly, he looked. Maybe he was pissed off that Claire'd come to my house to apologize. Or maybe this was just one of his surly days, when he wasn't doing Jimmy Cagney impersonations.

"Cheer up, Leo," I called out brightly, "maybe you can run over a raccoon on your way out."

Leo Brass didn't say anything; just looked at me, measuring an enemy.

TWELVE

*I wasn't out to earn the Good Housekeeping
Seal of Approval . . .*

Alix Dunraven was back in the morning.

I'd hoped she'd call eventually but I hadn't expected it to be this soon or that she'd show up in person.

"I got hopelessly lost," she confessed. "Finally purchased a map at the stationer's. Couldn't make head nor tails of that, either. Might as well have been celestial navigation. I called Harry for divine guidance and he told me to throw myself on your mercy. So here I am, groveling, really, 'umble as Uriah Heep."

She didn't seem to be groveling nor did she appear especially humble or in any way did she resemble the Uriah Heep either Dickens or I would recognize. But she was too good to look at to quibble. So I just grinned.

"Besides," she said, "I didn't like the Mauve House awfully."

"Too mauve?"

"Oh, decidedly too-too. A rum place, strictly poofter, of course, but being British, I'm more than accustomed to that. Many of my dearest friends, all great chums, are poofs. But this East Hampton bunch, oddly, are very stern about dogs. Those chaps usually dote on having poodles about."

What I couldn't know and wouldn't until much later was that Evans ordered her back to me, convinced for some reason that I knew more than I was saying, about where the manuscript might be. Alix was to get close to me and find out. Even if it meant throwing herself at me and moving in. Nor did she or Mr. Evans seem to care about the bad name they were giving the poor Mauve House, which had always enjoyed an excellent reputation.

There was apparently great excitement back there in Manhattan at Random House. Hannah Cutting's book was going to be big when she was alive. But dead? With a sharpened stake of privet hedge through her breast? Huge! So went a wildfire of gossip through the hallways of the publishing company. The marketing people salivated. Even the salesmen were excited. And you know salesmen.

Trouble was, neither Evans nor anyone else knew where Hannah's manuscript was.

And in the book biz, if you can't find the book, you may have a little problem. Especially if the author is dead. Because trouble calls for a trouble-shooter, Harry Evans had whistled up Alix Dunraven, who filled me in in colorful detail about all these goings-on at Random where, amid considerable drama, a sales meeting had been informed:

"A bloody spear, hardened in flame, thrust through her black heart? My God! It's a cover of the *Times Book Review.* It's a network miniseries. It's bigger than a miniseries! A movie. No, 'a major motion picture.' One that 'reeks of Oscar!' With Streisand playing Hannah! Glenn Close! Sarandon! And Hanks in there somewhere . . ."

Except that, there was no book. No miniseries. No movie. No Oscar. No Streisand and Hanks. *Forrest Gump* sounded like a more promising idea when it was still moldering on Winston Groom's back burner.

Another major difficulty: Evans and his people were dealing with an author new to them. Hannah's first book, the national best-seller, *The Taste Machine,* and each subsequent effort, starting with *Hannah's House* and going on through *Hannah's Garden, Hannah's Kitchen,* and the like, had been published by bitter rival Simon & Schuster. And over there at S & S, where Michael Korda and the others who'd shepherded Hannah from best-seller to best-seller, knew Hannah Cutting and her writing methods intimately and in ways Harry's people couldn't, they were hardly likely to put themselves out to assist Random House in recovering a manuscript S & S probably believed ethically and morally should have been theirs.

The phone rang.

"Harry Evans here, Beecher. Has Lady Alix driven over yet this morning? I told her . . ."

That's how I learned about that title of hers. That it wasn't a corporate label but something regal and inherited, bigger than Lady Di's. Besides being gainfully employed by a prestigious London house, HarperCollins, and now temporarily by one of the biggest Manhattan book publishers, Alix had a curriculum vitae that resembled *Burke's Peerage.* Maybe the *Almanach de Gotha* as well. And looking as she did as a bonus.

Alix Dunraven's daddy was the fourth senior Earl in Britain. The family title dated back to Henry IV, whom the first Dunraven had served both gallantly and fiercely, slaying and eventually being slain, in the jolly tradition of the time and in the service of his liege master, the King. Lady Alix's square name was Alixandre (named for the unfortunate last Czarina of Russia, a third cousin several generations removed); she was twenty-six; she'd taken a double first at Oxford (in Greats and History, having written dissertations on "The Confessions of Saint Augustine" and "Clive of India"); worked briefly for British *Vogue;* had recently only just gotten out of a quasi-arranged marriage; and had been taken up by Harry when assigned to Random by the Tony Godwin Award folks. Evans, married to Tina Brown, was one of the few important men in Manhattan who really knew women. And in Alix he early saw not just a luncheon companion or a charmer, but someone he could dispatch to a little mess of one sort or another and be reasonably confident she would straighten things out and within an acceptable time frame. Would have made a good sleuth, a great crook. Scotland Yard and the Mafia both loved people like Alix: competent, swift, efficient. Ruthless?

No, a woman who looked like this couldn't be . . . ruthless. Well, perhaps.

Harry kept her around because she was beautiful, she was London, she was . . . good. Recently on a new tell-all yarn about the royals, a book she didn't write or edit, she'd been able to nail a few potentially embarrassing errors and to flesh out one or two anecdotes with firsthand information. You sent Alix out to do something; she usually did it. She wasn't all that professionally trained; with her, it was instinct. Sort of in the way I got Rose Kennedy to talk about the family, Alix had a knack for finding things. How big a job was it finding a lousy book manuscript that had gone missing? Which probably still resided quietly inside an IBM computer somewhere in the house. And, as he had once said of his own wife, Evans paid Alix a sincere compliment: "She has the cunning of a rat."

Now the "cunning" Alix was attempting to co-opt me.

"Harry said you and he talk often. That you've been most helpful in this matter. He suggested I spend lots of time with you."

I hadn't been very helpful at all, I wanted to say. Instead, "If you've checked out of the Mauve House, where are you staying?" I asked.

"Oh, I'm not staying. Just a day or so, until I find the manuscript."

That's when I realized this gloriously beautiful but almost total stranger was actually moving in. Which immediately raised in me several powerful but conflicting emotions. She was confident about being allowed to move in, about eventually finding the book—confident about most things. She was also tall and slender, had that long, dark hair and those disarmingly innocent blue eyes, and was dressed by Ungaro. And now that the Mauve House had turned out to be too . . . mauve, she was descending on me. She and a dog I didn't like much and that she barely knew. When she saw hesitation in my face, she leapt right in:

"You're an author yourself and apparently very good at it. I'm a book editor, and we both understand that between writers and editors there's a kind of tacit but quite genuine entente cordiale. And here I am . . ."

When I didn't actually snarl, she smiled, and nodded toward the Jag's boot.

"There are three pieces of luggage there, if quite convenient."

It wasn't quite convenient, but okay. Hardly the moment to play churl. Louis Vuitton, the three of them, matching and chic. Even her laptop had a Louis Vuitton carrying case. That was a first. Think of it. Louis Vuitton laptops!

As I reached into the boot to lift out the luggage, the poodle yipped and went at me, as if she suspected I was stealing them.

"Oh, gosh, I guess she thought— Are you hurt?"

"Hardly broke the skin," I said through clenched teeth, intent on behaving gamely, but giving the poodle a dirty look.

So much for the entente cordiale.

Screw Harry for sending this bird, *and* her dog, to my father's house, giving her my name, my number. But I was after the Hannah Cutting story. And if that required offering bed and breakfast to Lady Alix Dunraven, so be it. What better source material could there be in getting Hannah's story than sneaking a first peek at Hannah's own book?

And maybe this kid could find it. For Random House. And for me.

And I felt the old pull, fiercely remembered from London in the spring when my girl ran off. Alix meant to use me to help her get Hannah's manuscript. And I was intent on using her for just about the same purpose. One of us was going to get screwed. And I didn't necessarily mean in bed though that was hardly an outcome to be dreaded if indeed it happened.

There were two bedrooms in the gatehouse and I lugged her Vuitton luggage upstairs to the smaller and put out some fresh bed linen and towels. I wasn't going to start making beds for the people at Random House, even ones whose daddies were earls and who looked like this. This wasn't a Holiday Inn and I wasn't out to earn the Good Housekeeping Seal of Approval. When Harry brought someone home to stay overnight, did Tina Brown change the sheets and put out fresh towels? While we were making our little domestic arrangements my phone rang downstairs.

It was Evans. Again. Checking up on the towels and fresh linen, I supposed. "Yes?" I said, being chilly about it.

"Hello, Stowe, good of you to take in a waif. She'll be no trouble, I assure you."

She and Evans talked some more. Some nonsense I didn't quite get about E-mail in cipher. I enjoyed myself looking at her, this girl who was going to compete with me in tracking down Hannah Cutting's manuscript. What a joke. She wasn't in my league on a sleuthing job like this. Had she ever fled from Sarajevo or been chased by mullahs? Which of the two of us was it got Rose Kennedy to talk, and on the record, about Teddy and the family?

But Her Ladyship might turn out awfully pleasant to have around, you had to admit.

THIRTEEN

Next thing there'll be graffiti on the
Presbyterian church . . .

Hideo Hegel and the Countess were still in town. His mansion's rental ran until October first. But they were packing, getting out. Orders from Tokyo. Did the Seven Samurai blame Hannah's death on Hideous? Or the sum total of all the grief she'd given them, alive and dead? Strange people, the Japanese. Eat their fish not only raw but still alive. I must ask Hideous about that sometime. But not now. He seemed reasonably happy to see me. The Countess, well, let's not get into that. Maybe she sensed I was a threat to her lover, her checkbook. Hegel gave me another facet of Hannah. I already sensed the contradictions, depending on the source: control freak, the swimmer with sharks, the gutsy loner, the instinctive genius, the sex symbol, the social-climbing alpinist, the pain in the ass, the admirable striver, the backstabbing bitch, the passionate lover, the anal-retentive mother, the uncanonized saint, the child of impoverished Polish Town collecting sea shells and staring up at the palaces of the wealthy. How true or accurate any of this was I didn't yet know. I was getting a wildly chaotic though more rounded view. Not yet a portrait, but more than a sketch.

Hideo's take was that of a monster.

"Stowe, a real ball-breaker she was. And I do not say this lightly.

"A true ball-breaker. With no appreciation of Samurai tradition and the legend of the Forty-seven Ronin who were prepared to disembowel themselves out of loyalty to their master. Or of Prussian probity. Or even the Old School Tie."

He went on in graphic detail about Hannah's tantrums and wheedling. I cut him off. "You can't be serious."

"Be a good fellow, Stowe, and hear me out. There's worse." When I shrugged agreement to hear more he smiled thinly, a sort of smile halfway between the pleasure of trashing his late business colleague and disgust at what she'd done.

"Three years ago she visited Tokyo for the first time since we acquired her business. You've read the figures, the Samurai paid nearly a billion for her controlling stock, a lot less to her partner, Max Victor, and on top of that we named her chairman of the U.S. affiliate at five million a year. I was installed as president to watch over things. And then she was invited to visit the home office so to speak, get to meet the Samurai, see aspects of Japan the average tourist couldn't possibly get to. And to preside over the launch of the Japanese edition of *Hannah's Way* magazine and the opening of a chain of Hannah for the Home boutiques. For a week Hannah got the deluxe guided tour of Japan, everything but an audience with the Emperor (he inclined his head slightly in deference). We trotted her around to palaces and temples and tea pavilions and sumo matches, visited the company's manufacturing plants and our finest retail shops. At the end of which, at corporate headquarters in Tokyo, a reception was laid on, a sort of farewell tribute before she flew back to the States, the affair to be carried live on Japanese television. All terribly *comme il faut*. The Seven Samurai, I assure you, do these things well. No expense spared. Influential members of the press, prominent political figures both from the government and the loyal opposition, leaders of society, the top publishers and fashion designers, a cousin, on his mother's side, of our Emperor." Hideous again made a little bow and I tried to look respectful. He resumed. "Let me set the stage. Late afternoon and even Tokyo's notoriously changeable weather cooperated. Through the windows of our office tower you could see clearly the snow-capped peak of sacred Mount Fuji off there fifty miles in the distance. Everything was perfect."

"So?"

"Several brief welcoming speeches were made, people were presented, and then Hannah was handed an arrangement of the most lovely flowers by a troupe of young girls in traditional costume. Everyone stood back, waiting expectantly for what surely would be a gracious little thank you from our distinguished visitor and then, on with the festivities! But no, not Hannah Cutting. She remarked on the loveliness of our young girls and said how pleased she was that they, at least, seemed admirably chaste, pure, and virginal. And she hoped that despite sexually perverse and wicked forces all about, that they would remain that way. Innocent young women owed it themselves to resist commercial pressures seeking to cash in on their vulnerability. On and on . . .

"What was this all about? The Seven Samurai began to look at each other. Members of the government cleared their throats. The Royal cousin looked apprehensive. What was coming next?"

Hegel knew how to tell a story. I found myself waiting for the punch line.

"It was then Hannah said during her week in Japan she'd been reliably informed that on the Tokyo subway system the most popular vending machines were those frequented by perverts and dirty old men, which purveyed, for a hefty price, the soiled underwear of teenaged Japanese schoolgirls. . . ."

I looked at Hideo Hegel.

"You're shitting me."

He shook his head.

"I swear to you, Stowe, those were virtually her exact words to a roomful of distinguished Japanese on the final day of her first visit to Tokyo." He paused. "It was unknown for an honored guest to throw up such an insult into your face. My superiors, the Samurai, fell over themselves getting out of the room and that evening and the next day her remarks were all over television news and in the papers. Not since Commodore Perry had the Japanese people been so insensitively treated by a Western visitor."

"What did she have to say for herself? Anything?"

"I got her aside and asked her later why she'd gone out of her way to insult her business partners, causing the Samurai to lose face before so many important people.

"She said, 'They're a smug, self-important bunch and I just wanted to puncture their pomposity. I thought they'd get a laugh out of how ridiculous it all was. Until you people learn to laugh at yourselves, Japan will never be a great nation.' "

Hideo looked at me. I was beyond comment and waited for him to go on.

"Of course I submitted a resignation of honor for having visited such troubles upon my company and my country. The Samurai, generously, declined to accept it. Needless to say, while she continued to work for us, Hannah was never invited back."

"What she said about vending machines selling girls' panties, did she just make that up out of sheer mischief?"

"Oh, no. The underwear machines are very popular. Everyone knows that."

Now I was silent, shaking my head in disbelief.

"Well, then, why get so upset . . . ?"

Hegel looked at me sternly. "My dear Stowe, it's extremely rude to tell people unpleasant things they already know."

I gathered myself.

"But who killed her?"

"Don't ask me," Hegel said, "I got there too late."

I'd not taken Alix along. She didn't seem put out. Had her own fish to fry, she said, a list of people to see starting with Hannah's servants. Fine. I was determined to play the cards close myself and did nothing beyond showing her places on the map. That afternoon at The Blue Parrot I had a couple of Pacificos. Michael the barman was shaking his head, mourning lost innocence. What? "Damned woman's dead less than a week and someone broke into her place. Next thing we'll have graffiti on the Presbyterian church . . ."

According to Michael a sneak thief or someone had gotten into Hannah's pool house by breaking a window pane in a back door. No one could say when it might have happened and very little if anything was missing. The Kroepkes gave the cops a brief inventory of stuff they couldn't find, cautioning that Ms. Cutting often discarded things carelessly, and items thought stolen might simply have been thrown out. Apparently not among the missing was that nifty new laptop computer, on which Hannah was supposed to have been writing her book. The burglar must not have been a computer nerd, overlooking an easy-to-lug and very pricey laptop and not taking much else of value. Good news for me, the PC still being there. Now how did I get my hands on it?

What was still unclear, had the small window just been broken or had the window been broken earlier and simply not noticed? Maybe the break-in happened earlier. Maybe even the night Hannah died. An estate that size with a number of outbuildings, one small broken window could go unnoticed for weeks. . . .

I called Tom Knowles and we met for coffee at John Papas's café. Tom had no theories but he was looking into it. "See if you can get me a look at that laptop, plus the floppy disks, if any. . . ."

"We've already looked," Tom said. "Thought there might be a clue on her computer as to who might be menacing her, if anyone. She was supposed to be writing a book or something."

"Yeah, that's why I want to see that laptop."

"Waste of time," Tom said. Very definite about it, as well, but not very forthcoming, not the way he usually enjoyed humoring me. Instead, he dropped the subject of the computer and focused instead on the broken window. What puzzled him was why anyone had to break a window to get into Hannah's house. Almost everyone in East Hampton had a key. The plumber, the cleaning woman, a pool boy, the electrician, the snowplow guy, the carpenter, the winter housewatcher, the . . . Well, you get the idea. That's how it was out here. Rich people installed expensive burglar alarm systems or retained security patrol companies and then handed out keys to the front door to people they ran into at the hardware store.

Tom wouldn't be surprised if Jesse Maine had a key. How else would he have gotten in to use Hannah's personal toilet?

I didn't really care about where Jesse took a leak or if he left the toilet seat up.

"The PC, Tom. Can I very quietly and confidentially sort of scroll through the directory? Check out a few disks?"

"No."

This wasn't the Tom Knowles I knew. He might not go along with my idiocies. But he didn't usually just cut me dead like this.

"What?"

"There are no disks. She didn't know how to do them."

"Well, the PC itself. She was writing a book on it. Worked on it every day. Had been doing for months. Random House bought the book already, paid a lot of money. That hard drive could have some interesting stuff on it for this piece I'm writing, plus other stuff that maybe, just maybe, could tell you and me both, something about who might . . ."

"Beech, you Harvard guys make great reporters. But lousy cops."

"Oh?" I was kind of miffed by that. I never wanted to be a cop but suspected I might be reasonably good at it.

"Yes. We had the same idea you had. A few days earlier. And we pulled the PC in for a day, had our house nerds check it out."

"And?"

"Nothing. Not a frigging word. A clean hard drive. No disks, no A copy. No C copy. Nothing. That's what the nerds say."

"But . . ."

"You're right, Beech. She'd been working on a book. The Kroepkes said so. Claire said so. Mr. Evans at Random House had been told by Hannah that she was writing a book and had negotiated a contract and paid her an advance. Hannah herself confirmed to people she was working on it and she had no overwhelming reason to lie unless she was up against . . . what is it when you can't get the next sentence out . . . ?"

". . . writer's block."

"Yeah. Only there was nothing on the computer. Not a

goddamned word. Everything had been downloaded, all deleted. Every trace gone, wiped out."

I just looked at him.

"Doesn't make sense."

"It does if you shut up and listen," Tom said.

"Oh?"

"Yeah, the department's own local Bill Gates tells us there were maybe one hundred eighty thousand characters on the hard drive. Say, thirty to thirty-five thousand words. A good chunk of a book, especially one an amateur was writing."

"But . . ."

"They'd been erased. Every damn one of those characters, every one of those thirty thousand words. We don't know what they were. Can't retrieve them. We only know that many characters, that many words, were typed into the laptop by the late Hannah Cutting."

I didn't say anything. Tom finished the thought.

"Someone erased what Hannah wrote. Maybe Hannah herself for reasons unknown. Maybe whoever killed her. Maybe third parties unknown. Maybe Martha Stewart, for God's sake, envious that anyone else out here might write a book. Or her daughter or the Kroepkes or Peggy Siegal or someone else."

"Any ideas?" I said.

"Yeah, someone who knows how computers work. A newspaper reporter like you, even . . ."

FOURTEEN

Young Hannah once worked in the Further Lane house she now owned.

My father's place was situated on a narrow plot between Further Lane and the ocean, hemmed in on two sides by the houses of the rich. To the east, Toby Montana, the singer and bride of the music mogul who was CEO of her record company. He was fortyish and thrice-married; she was half his age and frighteningly talented. They'd had their house for two summers now and no complaints. Except that choppers delivered them and took them off again, with attendant noise. Beyond that there was nothing exotic except Toby herself. She was fond of sunbathing nude. My father, who spent a career gathering and analyzing information, complained about the choppers but forgave Toby, saying he'd seen her himself sunbathing several times, through his 7 × 50 field glasses. "Splendid young animal," was his judgment. That was his intelligence training manifesting itself even in retirement; he got to the heart of the matter and drew conclusions.

Had Toby and her husband understood the privacy quotient, the value of a good privet hedge, her nude swims would have gone unnoticed by the whole damned CIA.

On the other, western flank, we had Miz Phoebe. Miz Phoebe was a wealthy man's widow, feisty, bigoted, ancient, dotty. My father and I both enjoyed the old girl and joined her for the occasional cocktail. Miz Phoebe would go on and on about the Decline of the West, blaming crime and disaster and most everything else on "gangsta rap," "Gay marriage," and "the Geraldo Rivera show." At her age, she lived mainly in a nostalgic past, recalling Lee and Jackie Bouvier growing up just across Further Lane in that great gray and white stucco mansion which once belonged to the Bouviers and was now the Meehan House. "Such nice girls. Such good posture . . ." Miz Phoebe recalled the Bouvier sisters, reminding lesser people that "posture always tells."

Then Miz Phoebe dropped her little bombshell over a Manhattan she'd invited me to have with her in my father's absence.

"That girl who died on the beach down by the Maidstone, Hannah Cutting? You know she lived on Further Lane years ago."

I protested that she hadn't. "No, Miz Phoebe, she grew up poor, an immigrant Czech family scratching out a hardscrabble livelihood in Polish Town in Riverhead. I've gone up there to look into it and it's true." Quite so, said Miz Phoebe; little Hannah wasn't actually *living* on Further Lane but working here as a teenaged au pair girl, what they called back then "a mother's helper," to one of the great families, the Warrenders. Working the summer in one of the several great Warrender "cottages," for one branch or another of the wealthy Warrender Clan.

In fact, Miz Phoebe said, if memory serves, the young Hannah worked a summer in the very house she now owns! Or had, she added decorously, until her unfortunate death.

Speaking of house keys, I'd given Alix Dunraven a set. Not necessary, really, since no one I knew ever locked the doors on Further Lane unless you were going away. I don't know; maybe I was attempting to distance myself from her, provide her an easy independence.

I'd never enjoyed being a houseguest, didn't especially like having houseguests. Better for strangers to stay in hotels. But this guest had the potential for being different, or I was starting to think so. Our brief contact so far had been a bit awkward, edgy. Then why were we so relaxed next morning?

Credit Alix for that.

I was up early, hoping she'd sleep in late and we wouldn't have to be artificially polite. I'm not great before coffee. And I was inordinately self-conscious about being alone with her, sure I'd do or say something stupid and she'd go off. Harry had dumped her on me and yet I didn't want to lose her. Not yet, certainly. Instead, whether she heard me at the coffee or the morning birds had called her, she came into the nice country kitchen the gatehouse boasted, maybe the best room in the small house.

"I've been admirably behaved thus far," she told me, "even walked the dog." She paused. "Hope you don't mind her doing the necessary on your nice lawn."

"No," I said, thinking my old man would kill me for it, not being a dog fancier himself. But he was in Norway, stalking the noble salmon. The poodle, however, must have read my mind and growled.

"She's remarkably well trained," Alix assured me in comforting tones, aware I'd been bitten once already. "For a dog, I mean."

Well, I said, hope you slept well, being hearty, though not feeling it truly. But she did look fine.

I should have been up earlier, made the coffee myself, she said. Are you good at it? I inquired, not knowing precisely where the conversation was going nor what to say, but only admiring, furtively, her body under the tie silk robe she was wearing, though only just. "No, I'm awful at it. Perhaps it's best you press on and I'll watch." So I made the coffee and we sat together there at the kitchen table and drank it and before it was over, we were laughing at how badly I did coffee, almost as badly as she confessed doing. And I was telling her what good doughnuts Dreesen's made, the grocery store, and how one of these mornings I'd . . .

But still, we fenced. She had appointments and chores; so did I, and I kept them to myself. Didn't, for one, tell her about the cleanly scrubbed computer from which quite possibly the precious manuscript she was looking for had recently been removed. As for her chores?

"You know, before getting into publishing, I thought about trying your line. Worked on a newspaper for a time myself, one of the Fleet Street dailies, during the Long Vac at Oxford. Making tea and running errands and shepherding the Page Three Girls . . ."

"Oh?" Was she now going to tell me how to do my job on the basis of a summer as a copygirl?

"It was on *The Sun,* one of Mr. Murdoch's tabloids. Everyone reads it and denies they do so."

"I know. Anyone who's lived in London knows about the Page Three Girls."

The Page Three Girls were in there and featured every day. Winsomely topless every day as well.

"Pa was apoplectic when I announced I was working there for the summer. Cursed out Rupert and me both." She paused. "Though I suspect he thought the Page Three Girls rather jolly. I used to catch him giving them a careful look."

I thought about my own father watching Toby Montana through binoculars.

But Her Ladyship was off on another tack.

"I found myself brooding about Hannah last night in bed. A woman with all that she had going for her and then, at the pinnacle, to be summarily butchered like that on her own doorstep. Can that ever again be a happy house?" She paused for an instant, and then asked, "Do you believe in ghosts, Beecher? I mean, here we are, the two of us, picking over poor Hannah's bones. If I were so dreadfully slaughtered as she was, I'd strive vigorously to come back and haunt everyone. Weep in the night, rap on tables, set pet dogs to howling, cast funereal chills over things, give all of East Hampton nightmares."

I chewed the question over for a bit. Ghosts? Wasn't the sort of thing I thought much about.

"I dunno. Do you?"

That was clever, I told myself, turning the question back on the questioner.

"Oh, yes, of course. And I'm surprised you haven't taken a philosophical position on it. All these big old houses out here on the sea. Places like this in Cornwall and Devon simply pullulate with ghosts. There was a lovely little film years ago called *The Uninvited,* with Ray Milland, I believe, an old house on the Cornish cliffs. Super, I promise you, sheer but quite elegant horror. Surely along Further Lane someone's encountered a shade or two. . . ."

"Well, I . . ."

"Take my Pa's place at Kingston Mere. We have a white nun who appears on the stair and sobs, wringing her hands and all that. Terrified me as a child. The stair was just outside my nursery and I spent the first decade of my life half-stifled, sleeping with my head under the pillow so she couldn't get at me. A wonder I didn't perish of emphysema."

"But surely your parents took steps to . . ."

"Oh, they nattered about it. Said a proper house ought to have a ghost or two. Insisted a good haunting did wonders for the rental or resale value of an old house, that everyone knew that. Beastly of them, come to think of it, permitting me to grow up perpetually terrified. Finally, I turned the whole business into an asset, inviting girls from

my school to come stay overnight, especially girls I envied
or didn't particularly like. The weeping nun paralyzed
them with fear. Sent them back to school thoroughly chas-
tened with their pants wet. It was smashing! By the time
we graduated, everyone at my school wanted a ghost."

I promised to check with my father when he got back to
determine whether *we'd* ever had a ghost. I felt I owed
Alix that.

Now she shifted focus yet again.

"Good," she said. "Now in my brief forays through the
village, it appeared to me there were any number of super-
looking boutiques. If I'm to be here for a few days I'm
running somewhat short of clothes. Don't want to let the
side down by looking frumpy, y'know."

No, of course not, I quickly agreed. As if she could ever
look "frumpy." But it would keep her occupied for the day
if I knew anything about the East Hampton shops, and
give me time on my own. I'd barely begun digging into the
story of who Hannah Cutting was and how she got from
Polish Town to Further Lane, the story Walter Anderson
wanted. I wasn't getting very far with the assignment but
instead found myself inevitably being drawn into another
story entirely, the one not of her life but of her death.

I kept trying to steer clear of that story, leaving it to
cops like Knowles, and to stay with the assignment. Trouble was, maybe, just maybe, they were the same story.

I was talking to all these people, asking all these questions, when all the answers might be in a book Hannah
Cutting was writing when she died and which nobody, not
Random House who'd advanced a million for it, or this
beautiful troubleshooter of theirs, or even the police
seemed to be able to find. But who downloaded the text
and why? Where had those 180,000 characters gone? Did
they no longer exist or did the thief have plans for them?
Did someone erase them out of sheer mischief or igno-

rance and not recognize the value of what he had? The way the bandidos who killed Humphrey Bogart in the last reel of *The Treasure of the Sierra Madre* threw away the gold dust from his saddlebags thinking it was useless dirt, when they were scavenging for coins and pelts? Fred C. Dobbs, that was Bogie's name. The stuff I remembered.

No point pursuing that. There were still leads unexplored. But I wasn't sharing my information with Alix Dunraven. Not yet. Not quite yet.

I really ought to go see the Warrenders. Follow up on what Miz Phoebe Allenby said, that Hannah worked for them long ago, maybe in the house she later bought and where she died. Finding a Warrender was no great task, not in East Hampton. There were a dozen of them in the phone book. But I didn't make any calls. I knew where at least one Warrender was likely to be. And I began with him, began with a drunk at the bar of the Maidstone Club. A club sufficiently exclusive to have quietly warned Donald Trump, while he enjoyed a temporary summer membership, not to apply for full credentials lest he be turned down. And had treated Hannah Cutting every bit as chillingly.

But a club which tolerated eccentric, even dubious behavior, on the part of old members, the Old Money set who founded the Club, men like Jasper Warrender.

Jasper was one of the Warrender cousins and a midday regular at the bar. His golf game had developed an incurable hook and not even the new oversized putter seemed to help his shakiness on the greens, and out of desperation he had turned, in all seriousness, to consulting the bottom of a glass. A Jack Daniel's man. I felt slightly guilty about pumping a middle-aged souse in my father's club but still . . .

"Sure," Jasper said, he remembered Hannah Shuba. A quarter century later and over the Jack Daniel's, Jasper recalled, "She was only a kid, a teenager, fourteen or fifteen, but a hot little number. She was like honey and we were all buzzing. All of us, me included. Even Cousin Royal home from Yale after his junior year. And you know how goddamned particular and stuffy Royal is, how hard to please, even then." I stood Jasper a couple of drinks and got a little more. Miz Phoebe was right; young Hannah worked that long ago summer in the very house on the grounds of which, a week ago, she was murdered.

When I phoned the Kroepkes that afternoon they were still upset about the break-in. Nothing seemed to be missing. But you didn't sleep easy if you knew strangers had been on the property, had broken in, even if it was just the pool house. I pumped them tactfully, I hoped, double-checking about the computer. Did they know if Hannah left any disks behind? I asked. No, said the Missus, Hannah was hardly a computer literate. Used the PC pretty much like a fancy typewriter, writing right onto the hard drive. Disks would have been beyond her, Mrs. Kroepke said. She had a secretary for that.

"How about her secretary . . . ?"

No, said the housekeeper firmly, Ms. Cutting gave precise instructions to the secretary that she'd be writing the book herself and didn't want anyone messing with it. The secretary handled her correspondence, typed her magazine articles, but didn't touch the book. "At this stage, it was much too personal. I heard Ms. Cutting say that. She even took to typing on it out there in the pool house where she wouldn't be disturbed and no one could look over her shoulder while she worked. Very close she was about it. There was a steno helped her on the other books, going back to the very first one, *The Taste Machine*. No steno this time, no private secretary, just Ms. Cutting and her laptop. Top secret and all that. Which wasn't usual for Ms.

Cutting. Hannah, I mean Ms. Cutting, she loved the publicity. Only when it was good, of course."

"But how can you be sure there were no disks left behind?"

"Mr. Stowe, I never saw a disk. I don't think she'd have known how to insert one. Just about the only thing Hannah, I mean Ms. Cutting, couldn't do. And do well."

"But she was so damned competent. Sure a floppy disk wouldn't be beyond her."

"I don't think she trusted anything with such a silly name. 'Floppy disks'? They couldn't possibly be good enough for her own life story."

"Could I take a look at the laptop?"

Mrs. Kroepke shook her head. "Nossir, she wouldn't want it. And the cops told us to keep it locked away in case they needed it for evidence."

I nodded, ready to hang up.

"Oh, one other thing," she said. "They finally released Ms. Cutting's body. The executor claimed it, a lawyer from Sullivan and Cromwell at One twenty-five Broad Street in Manhattan. Claire didn't want to, didn't think she should."

And the funeral? I asked.

There would be none. Cremation. Later on, somewhat vaguely, a memorial service might be held and . . .

Even in death, Hannah was not to be accepted or paid tribute to. A rich and successful and important woman was dead and nobody hung crepe or lighted candles or tossed a trowel full of earth on the pine box. Ozymandias had it better than Hannah. At least he'd once had a statue.

I slept badly that night. I'd learned something but wasn't sure quite what. Besides, Alix Dunraven came home late. After I was asleep. What the hell was she doing out so late? Where did she go? And with whom? I told myself I was being silly, feeling avuncular about a woman only six or seven years younger. I could hear her moving around, talking to the dog, imagined that by now she ought to be undressing. I was being protective, concerned, and could see her barefoot and sleepy-eyed in that silk robe in my own kitchen. Was starting to imagine how she looked without that silk robe in my own kitchen. Or my bedroom. And not feeling one bit like kindly old Uncle Beecher. . . .

FIFTEEN

The Hound of the Baskervilles
in poodle's clothing . . .

For year-round residents of the Hamptons, people like Admiral Stowe and his son, me, those days immediately after Labor Day were the finest of the year. The crowds gone, the water warm, the sun still high, the beaches near empty, the cranes and cormorants fishing, riders and their horses trotting along the beach, maybe a couple of college boys spiraling a football on the sand, a deer here and there shyly blinking in the sunlight and dashing nervously away. A red fox at dusk hunting pheasant. A hawk circling. An osprey fishing. Schools of big blues working along the beach, scattering the baitfish into panicked flight. Big stripers, too. The last college girls daringly topless within view of the pursed-lipped ladies of the Maidstone. Reduced prices on Ralph Lauren merchandise at the Polo shop on Main Street. Parking spaces on Main Street and even in the A & P lot. Seats for the first show at the movie house. Vehicular traffic along Montauk Highway had slowed to such an extent that those silly-looking guinea hens Billy Joel raises at his place, odd birds with big fat bodies, long necks and tiny heads, felt sufficiently confident to scurry across the road between cars, leaving motorists more startled than the birds.

Honest people had ended their vacations and were back in the counting house, the Hollywood studios, or behind their Manhattan desks. East Hampton was left to the natives, the Bonackers who make their lives and their work here, and to the rich, for whom all of life is a vacation.

I loved this place in September. Even if there was talk of a hurricane out there and possibly coming. And when I couldn't work something out in my head, the lead to a story, the answer to a puzzle, I tossed my Old Maine canoe atop the Blazer and drove up to Three Mile Harbor to launch the boat and paddle about for an hour or two, thinking, pondering, wondering . . .

The storm, if it matured into one, would be called Hurricane Martha. Nice irony there, a big storm named for yet another famous local woman who'd surely had her differences with the late Hannah Cutting.

At this juncture when I couldn't seem to break through to the next stage of Hannah's story, someone with whom I was being awfully canny, not letting on much to her, came to my assistance. Alix Dunraven. She didn't intend to help me out; it was an inadvertent break. And it all came about because I'd given Alix the names of a couple of local places for lunch or a cool drink or the bathroom facilities when she was out shopping. And, despite its bathroom, I'd included The Blue Parrot on my short list of pit stops. Trouble was, Alix went there with her borrowed dog. I'd been halfway down Main Street, talking with Wendy Engel who used to own the pottery shop when I heard the ruckus.

"What the hell was she thinking about, Beecher?" demanded Roland the manager, whose small white dog, Little Bit, had just been rather roughly treated by Alix's Mignonne.

"I'm quite astonished myself by her ferocity," Alix was assuring Roland. "I am so terribly sorry. She's not really my dog, just on loan, and I don't even like dogs all that much. And certainly never suspected Mignonne to be the Hound of the Baskervilles in poodle's clothing."

Roland was barely listening, intent instead on murmuring solace and binding up Little Bit's wounds, which, in all candor, seemed more damaged pride than actual hurt. Lee the owner, a tall, handsome Navy brat raised in Hawaii, came out to tend the bar while Roland, and his dog, recovered. Lee rarely mixed a drink himself and this was something of an event. On the basis of which, I bought a round of drinks for the bar, to ease trauma, and included Roland. Not that it mollified him completely, but it was a start.

"What the hell do you feed that dog? Or do you intentionally keep her mean and hungry?" he asked Alix, who instinctively bathed him in the diffident flirtatiousness she might several years before have utilized on an Oxford don about to ask her to defend her thesis on Saint Augustine or old Clive.

"She's actually the property of a chum of mine, a French woman who works at the UN as a translator. We've Manhattan apartments in the same building and she had a stroke of luck when her married boyfriend was dispatched to Bermuda for a week on business and used his frequent flyer miles to take her along instead of his wife. And please, Beecher (this to me rather than to Roland, who hadn't the foggiest what she was talking about), don't ask me to justify the morality of all that. At Oxford, ethics was not my strong suit (then, once again addressing and bestowing enormous charm on Roland), but there I was caught up in this gripping situation, though ethically dubious I quite agree with Roland, and this dog was at hazard. So I was stuck minding a poodle. And then my employer dispatched me to East Hampton and along she came. Barely know the animal, actually, and I'm stunned at this untoward aggression on her part."

Alix again bestowed her most winning of smiles on Roland. "Mignonne and Mr. Stowe, for example, get along smashingly. Perhaps because they're both unusually articulate in French, as you know."

This was not precisely the truth since the dog had already bitten me once, and growled occasionally, but I bought another round and when it seemed evident Little Bit wasn't mortally injured and about to expire, Roland was soon back to his usual cordial self. Then Lee bought a round, as owner, which also didn't hurt. And Kelly Klein came in (without Calvin) and she and another very attractive blond woman took stools at the bar and ordered daiquiris and that lent a little chic to the place. Alix helped, as well, putting herself out a bit to make up for Mignonne's savagery, leaning forward on her forearms at the bar, providing Roland with both her dazzling smile and a suggestion of cleavage.

Talk about a double first.

Then, in an unconsciously inspired moment as Roland went off to tend to other clients, she said, "Since I can't get anyone in East Hampton to point me even vaguely in the direction of the missing manuscript, I thought I might just go see the richest people in town, one after another, door to door like a salesman, starting at the top and working my way down to mere millionaires. Hannah Cutting's people, the Kroepkes, are very decent folk but they're servants. Don't dare give too much to a snooper like myself. Won't even tell me if she were typing the story or scribbling it longhand on foolscap. Nor should they, out of sheer loyalty to their patronne. Not at all. Can't blame them a whit, but rich people, with no sworn allegiance to Hannah, why should they care? They're the ones who might just possibly put me on to the whereabouts of Hannah's manuscript. It's the rich who always know where the body is buried, don't they?"

"You're the rich one; you ought to know."

"Oh, rubbish, we've all those titles and honours and a little land (Daddy's place in Berkshire, Kingston Mere, was on forty-five hundred acres, I'd read somewhere), but no real money. It's why I'm a working girl."

Her idea sounded dumb. Or so I told Alix. But why not?

"Tony Godwin laureates are not 'dumb.' We may be drunk or perverse or debauched or other things but rarely dumb."

I was enjoying needling so I ordered another round and asked, "Have you ever actually edited a full-blown book?"

"Scads of them."

"Name one recent book I might have heard of."

"A brilliant account of the East India Company by an historian named Fellowes. It's all about . . ."

"I know, I know, Clive of India and 'The Mutiny' and all that. We're not totally uneducated here, y'know."

"Well, indeed you are. There's much more to it than that. Did you know, for example, that Elihu Yale, the man who financed Yale University, made his bundle trading in spices as a representative of the East India Company?"

Well, now that was interesting intelligence for a Harvard man to have, with the new football season coming on.

"No, I always suspected there was some sort of shady business about it, being Yale and all, but no, I didn't know that."

"Well, it's a thrilling story and I commend it highly to you. Lots of gore, as well, skirmishes and full-rigged battles and the most gruesome of tortures, the Dutch, surprisingly, being especially fiendish! Native cruelties as well. One poor ship's captain was nailed to a log by the locals and sent floating downriver to be eaten by crocs. That sort of thing."

Alix looked inordinately pleased at the prospect, perhaps imagining me stapled to that dreadful log.

But I didn't say so; instead, I paid for the drinks. Fobbing her off with some sort of plausible excuse, I shamelessly co-opted her "dumb" idea of dropping in on the rich and asking questions and headed for Further Lane. After all, I wasn't getting very far, either, and who knew how long Mr. Anderson's patience with me might run? Nor did I bother to reveal what I knew and she and Random House didn't, that Hannah's computer had been scoured, that there was nothing there. Nor would I have to go door to door looking for the rich or start with the As and go through to the Zs. There were plenty of rich people out here and I knew most of them.

I was concealing what little I knew from her and she was surely concealing from me whatever Evans had given her. Did either of us know much yet? Were we even being especially clever? Probably not.

My real edge was that I knew, and she didn't, which of those rich people were here twenty-five years ago when young Hannah Shuba first appeared on Further Lane; and that she worked for but one of their families. I could start with them, with the people she actually worked for: start with the Warrenders, start with the head of their clan . . .

But first, a little legal advice.

SIXTEEN

*A possible chairman of the Fed
if Greenspan ever left . . .*

Plenty of lawyers live in East Hampton, weekends and summers. But they hang their profitable shingles on buildings in Manhattan. There are only a dozen or so lawyers listed in the yellow pages as practicing in East Hampton. Two of them, deliciously, located on Muchmore Lane. I was after Judge Henty.

"I'm not practicing anymore, Mr. Stowe," he told me courteously. "Retired three years ago."

The Judge (he'd been a town magistrate and the title was accepted as honorific but he liked to be addressed that way and was a genial old soul, so why not?) had been the lawyer for the people who sold Hannah Cutting her Further Lane estate in 1990. As we sat in big wicker chairs on the broad shaded verandah of his frame house on Lily Pond Lane, he told me what he recalled of the closing.

"The Warrenders didn't want the house anymore, not since the old lady, Royal's mother, passed away. Royal had his own place nearby. Jasper had a place. Horace lived in California and the girls were off married. And the market was good so the agents found a buyer easily and the estate asked me to handle the closing. Hannah Cutting had a team of lawyers come out from Sullivan and Cromwell. We met in my offices upstairs over O'Mally's Saloon. The price had been agreed (nine million and change as he recalled) and the whole affair should have been routine. No liens on the property. Hardly, since these were Warrenders who were selling, and Ms. Cutting clearly had money. So the thing ought to have been settled in an hour or two."

"Except that . . . ?"

"Except that Hannah showed up. None of the Warrenders did; they left it to me to represent their interests. Hannah had plenty of white-shoe firepower but she was hands-on, I can tell you, and just about drove everyone batty. If you've seen my old offices, they're pretty small, spartan, too, and there was Hannah Cutting flying around that little room like a Valkyrie, picking up on and challenging every phrase, every stipulation as if she were Mr. Justice Holmes handing down precedent-setting opinions from the high bench. She found fault with the survey of the property and intimated the surveyors had been bribed to falsify property lines. Hannah dotted *i*'s and crossed *t*'s that weren't even in there. Demanded to know why no member of the Warrender family showed up. Were they trying to pull a fast one here, staying away so later on they could assert they never agreed to this or that? If she could take the time out to be present, busy as she was, why couldn't they? Oh, she was a caution, she was, and I tried my best to respond but she kept cutting me off. Rudely, too. Even the Sullivan and Cromwell boys were embarrassed and she was their client. Did everything but delve into my rolltop desk in search of secret compartments and listening devices. Hannah was doing a regular Leona Helmsley bat-outa-hell imitation and a pretty good one at that. At one point threatening that unless they did a better job, she'd move disbarment proceedings against her own attorneys."

Why did the Judge think she was so uptight? Wasn't this a kind of culmination for her, a splendidly triumphant moment she should have thoroughly been enjoying, sufficiently wealthy and successful to be able to pay millions to purchase a house where she once worked as a kind of servant?

"That was the odd part of it. I don't believe any of us knew that. She was just another New Money millionaire buying into Old Money East Hampton. Happened all the time. And customarily, the New Money folks are just delighted when they get their mitts on one of these old cottages here along Lily Pond or over there on Further. Not Hannah. Not as bitter as she was. I never did quite figure it. And I didn't know until you just told me that she'd worked in the house years back. Must have been that. Why else would she carry on like a spoiled brat when the birthday cake was there just waiting for her to blow out the candles?"

The Judge didn't know; neither did I. Maybe Royal Warrender could shed some light.

His vast house perched on the dunes, a twenty-bedroom place on eight acres, the house designed by Rodolphe Daus, a Mexican architect who'd studied in Berlin and at the Beaux-Arts in Paris and had put the place up in 1910, a cheerfully eclectic mix of Tudor and other mostly English architecture, 175 feet long and three stories high, with lots of stone arches and a huge stone conservatory. The thatched roof alone, when it had to be replaced several years back, cost two million dollars. The house was built by one of the robber barons of the era, Warrender's great-grandfather, and was of a similar size and epoch as Hannah Cutting's, built by yet another Warrender (and an architect who'd gone a decidedly different and less ornate direction than Rodolphe Daus when it came to style).

I'd met Royal Warrender before and was able to talk my way in. His man led me through the ground floor past doors and turnings and down corridors to a bookish study. Evening, with the sun dipping from view, the final rays slanting in through mullioned windows. Curiously, for late summer, a fire burned in a hearth that must have been twelve feet across and seven or eight tall.

"You've been asking questions around town," Warrender said after gesturing me to an easy chair in the sort of soft old leather cracking slightly that you saw in good men's clubs where members dozed with the *Wall Street Journal* opened but unread on their ample laps. "My cousin Jasper said you were pumping him at the Club."

"That's what reporters do, Mr. Warrender."

"It's no secret Jasper occasionally takes one too many."

"We chatted over a glass." I was damned if I were going to let him bully me. Besides that, I was Harvard and he was only Yale. Though you don't rub that in with your elders.

"You're Admiral Stowe's boy."

"Yes, sir," I said. Being deferential was okay; letting yourself be bullied was not.

"I'd have expected manners from Beecher Stowe's son. That sort of thing just isn't done, even by journalists, one member of the Maidstone grilling another, especially one in his cups."

That drew from me a grin. Evidently Mr. Warrender knew nothing of my father's well-earned reputation for dirty tricks on behalf of his country. "Burning and turning" was what they called it in those jolly Cold War days. My father had stories, I can tell you. The grin may have puzzled Warrender. Anyway, it stopped him from hectoring me and even got him answering a few questions.

"So you do remember Hannah Shuba as a kid working around your parents' place?"

"Sure, cute kid, if it's the same one I recall. A lot of the old families brought in local girls every summer to help out. Any number of them over the years. My mother took in one or two every summer. A help to her and a few dollars for the child. Can't say I saw anything in Hannah that would suggest one day she'd be rich and famous. Just another pretty young girl. It says something about America that a kid who once cleaned house comes back to own it. Damned shame what happened to her . . ."

Warrender, now about fifty, tall, handsome, courtly, was as powerful and admired as anyone on Further Lane, a brilliant merchant banker being considered by the Clinton White House as a possible chairman of the Federal Reserve if Greenspan ever left. He was a philanthropist, a sportsman, recently widowed, a pillar of the community, a future governor of New York, perhaps, maybe one day a President. The one flaw: Royal Warrender had just undergone a tricky heart-valve operation. His doctors insisted the heart was sound; the problem was technical. Others whispered of a potentially fatal cardiac condition. I suspected his circulation, which might explain a summer fire to ward off chill. And the blanket across his lap. Or maybe it was just this huge stone pile was damp and chilly. Warrender himself declined to discuss the matter during this period of recuperation and was maintaining a low profile far from Wall Street in East Hampton at his vacation home. There'd been some theorizing in the political columns that the White House, and not his doctors, wanted Warrender under wraps.

Whatever the motivation, he didn't give me very much beyond a few memories of a long ago summer and a cute young girl who worked for his mother. When I asked him about Judge Henty's recollection of the closing on the house and Hannah's odd behavior, he sloughed it off. "Wasn't there," he said, "and Henty never made a point of it. Not to me. We sold, she bought, and they closed. Her check didn't bounce." I pressed the question of Hannah's book, and he waved a dismissive hand. "Too many celebrity autobiographies now. All that kiss and tell stuff. Cheap thrills for the crowd."

How did Royal Warrender know it would be "cheap thrills" and "kiss and tell"? Did he have reasons of his own for not wanting to see Hannah Cutting's book published? When I pressed him he went along for a time and then there came a point . . .

"That's enough, Stowe."

"I just want to know . . ."

He shook his large, handsome head. "I won't be harassed in my own house by reporters."

I looked around. "I'm alone, Mr. Warrender."

He got to his feet now. My "wit" had not gone over.

"This conversation is ended."

"I still have questions."

He looked hard at me.

"Who owns *Parade* magazine? It's a Newhouse property, isn't it?"

"Yes, Advance Publications is the parent company. The Newhouse family owns Advance."

He nodded.

"I know Si Newhouse. If I must, I'll give him a call."

"Lots of people call reporters' bosses to complain, Mr. Warrender. Usually, it doesn't work."

"I'm not 'lots of people,' Stowe."

We shook hands and I left, the implicit threat hanging behind me on the genteel air.

Fine, my first assignment for Anderson at *Parade* and I'd ticked off one of the most admired and influential men in the country. His threats were quietly, politely put, of course, but given Warrender's power, no less real. I fell back on the old reporter's consolation that, well, this is the work we do, getting the news, raising hell, discomfiting the comfortable.

But for the next few times the phone rang, I thought, "Uh, oh, here it comes."

SEVENTEEN

She's not our sort,
not our sort at all . . .

Next stop, Pam Phythian, the quintessential East Hampton
clubwoman who didn't even bother to be polite about her
locally famous feuding with Hannah.

When I pulled up in the driveway of her place and
parked alongside the tennis court, she was just finishing a
game. Pam and another tall fit woman in proper whites
were hitting the ball hard, running hard, the September
sun glistening off them as they worked up an honest sweat.
After a particularly well-played point (the other woman
won it with a backhand), I applauded.

"Who's that . . . ? Beecher Stowe?"

"Yeah, sorry. I can come back later."

"No, we're finished. Martha's beat up on me sufficiently for one morning."

That was the first time I'd met Martha Stewart, taller
than I expected. More relaxed, as well. I'd heard of her as
something of a control freak. Instead, I got a crisp handshake and a good smile. After she and Pam had exchanged air kisses, Martha drove off and Pam slung a
towel around her neck. We sat on old unpainted Adirondack chairs on the lawn next to the court and talked about
Hannah.

"What can I tell you, Beecher? I disliked her intensely.
Not our sort at all. Symptomatic of developments here in

the village I don't like. Every year there are fewer people like us, more people like . . . them."

"You mean, like Hannah."

"Yes. And don't tell me I'm being a snob; I know I am. It's snobbery and tradition and playing by the rules that distinguish people who belong here from those who don't. Because I was brought up playing the game, I'm a pretty fair tennis player. Hannah couldn't play worth a damn. But she was so intent on getting good she hired the Maidstone's pro to tutor her privately and paid out thousands for one of those ball-throwing machines they have at the Club called—"

"I know, a SAM. Twenty-five thousand bucks. Claire told me."

"Well, then, you know what I'm talking about. If I got up a committee to raise money for new elm plantings on Main Street she'd counter by announcing an AIDS benefit. Or a hospice of some sort. Or a petition advocating mixed-race adoption. Didn't matter what the cause. Or even if she believed in it. When some of us signed petitions against that new A & P, Hannah decided a superstore was just what the village needed. It was as if having scaled East Hampton, she had to kick everyone else off the summit. She's like that on an actual mountain; I've seen her. I talked the organizers into letting her join that Everest climb and I've regretted it ever since. Hannah drew up her own set of rules, never seemed to have heard of team play."

"Well, she'd made it on her own pretty much."

"She had a Cutting for a husband. That's hardly . . ."

"You know Andy as well as I do, Pam. He's not all that much—"

"At least he's a gentleman. She's no lady. Or, wasn't."

I was about to respond, "He's a drunk." But why? Then Pam said, still furious:

"I suppose we're all in that book of hers. Getting back at everyone she ever envied and resented. Shocking to think a fine old publisher like Random House would stoop to . . ."

I wanted to hear more about that, about Hannah's book, but Pam was focused on another irritant, obsessively so, returning again and again to the matter of competing cocktail parties.

"Hannah began harassing me socially about two years ago. If I asked people to come by for Saturday drinks, casual wear, she'd schedule a cocktail the very same day and hour, but specify cocktail dress. If I threw a more formal affair, she asked people to party al fresco in Bermuda shorts. Since we were inviting some of the same people, it forced guests to change uniform in mid-cocktail so to speak, to make choices, to side with me or with her. Caused difficulties, friction among friends, between husbands and wives. She did it just to be difficult and didn't seem to care whether anyone enjoyed the parties or not."

I mentioned I'd been to her last party and she picked up on it.

"No one minds that her parties were noisier or boozier or even if they involved sex, if that's what went on. Our Maidstone Club crowd does very well on that sort of thing itself. It was the class of people she attracted. And that the wrong people were always taking off their clothes. You don't mind sin; you do care about manners."

That was about all I got out of her, that apparently everyone knew about Hannah's book. Other than that, Pam Phythian hadn't been much help. Oh, but she was bitter. It surprised me that Hannah had gotten under her skin to that extent. A Phythian ought to be above it all, not getting down into the gutter with an arriviste like Hannah. There must have been more to it than competing benefits and scaling Himalayas. Pam and Hannah were about the same age and both were physical, attractive women.

A man?

Or had something happened on Everest when those people died that Pam blamed Hannah for, even now? Or had it been Hannah who blamed Pam and might have been about to do it publicly in a best-selling book?

On the strength of her thoroughbred bloodlines I took Her Ladyship to dinner at Jerry Della Femina's restaurant on the water, the one with the five-meter Olympic racing sailboat moored right there inside the bar, fully rigged, sheets and mainmast and all. We took her car, the Jag, after she sort of sniffed at my Chevy Blazer. Hell, it couldn't hurt my reputation around East Hampton to be seen in a Jaguar and especially with someone who looked like this. When I said something about liking the car she was pleased.

"British-built. I buy British if I can. Poor old mother England. If those of us who live there don't buy British, you can't expect the Yanks to. One can usually rely on British-built goods. Not clothes, of course, unless it's underwear from Marks & Sparks or waterproofs from Aquascutum. But cars and whisky and Purdey guns and flyrods and things."

She was a Sloane Ranger, all right; I knew the type. Except that I was starting to suspect Alix wasn't a type but an original.

It was the first weekend since Labor Day, and Hannah's death, and if the story wasn't leading the evening news anymore and had vanished from the front page of the tabloids, out here in East Hampton there was still plenty of gossip. The latest involved a suspect in the pool house break-in that followed. One of the local Baymen, an unsavory character named Schmid, who'd earlier been scrutinized and questioned (he was the fellow Hannah once

accused of fondling her), had been pulled in again for
DWI, and discovered to have an unexplained two thousand dollars in his jeans. Cash. None of your damned business where I got it, he told the cops, who kept him
overnight and gave him an appearance ticket in the morning when they released him, sober. But they'd assigned
Tom Knowles to the case. Where would a layabout like
Schmid have gotten two grand unless he'd stolen something from Hannah's place and handed it off to a fence?
Who knew? But I was careful not to tell Alix Dunraven
that the detective on the case was a pal.

Nor was Lady Alix being terribly forthcoming with me
as to what she knew or even suspected about Hannah's
manuscript. We were both being oh-so-clever, keeping the
other in the dark lest we lose advantage. So we compromised by smoking my cigarettes and talking about London
and our mutually disastrous recent love affairs. Della Femina's wine card had some pretty decent vintages on it and
we put a couple of bottles to good use as the sun fell toward the distant shore of Three Mile Harbor and the light
through the restaurant's opened windows softened into
dusk. Alix actually knew my former girlfriend and even
the Old Etonian she'd gone off with. Great chum of Prince
Charles, Alix said, and that was about the best she could
say for the cad. "Chinless wonder," I muttered.

"Oh, that's a bit stiff," Alix replied, "talking that way
about our future king/emperor."

Not Charles, I protested quickly, "the chap my girl ran
off with."

"Oh," Alix said, relieved of the duty of having to defend
her sovereign. Or even "Fruity Metcalfe," her recent but
former fiancé.

"Fruity Metcalfe? You were going to marry a guy
named Fruity Metcalfe?"

"Well, it's not that astounding. The family name's Met-

calfe. He's the Viscount Albemarle. But everyone calls him
Fruity. Have done since Harrow."

"Oh, then that's all right then," I remarked.

"Don't be shirty about it. He's sweet. Quite dotty about
me. And we practically grew up together. Awfully good
family. Boys like Fruity, they were what I knew when I
was young. Not at all hard cases like you. . . ."

Talk about being shirty! Though secretly I rather liked
being thought a "hard case" and when she expressed interest in one, I bought her a good cigar.

On the basis of the cigar and a few glasses of wine I told
yarns about East Hampton.

"You've got to understand, in an old place like this,
there are always strange people."

"Just like England."

"Ever since sometime in the last century it's been a considerable artist's colony, something about the light. Later,
people like Motherwell and Ernst and Jackson Pollack
lived here. Pollack died in a car crash on Montauk Highway. Marcel Duchamp the Dadaist had friends here and
visited weekends. Traveled light. Wore two shirts and removed one when it became soiled. About the turn of the
century rich men's sons, bitten by the art bug, took off to
Europe to learn to paint. One young fellow spent three or
four years studying and painting in Venice and was so
taken by the place that when he returned to East Hampton,
he brought back with him a full-rigged Venetian gondola
and regalia. Used to launch it Sunday afternoons on Hook
Pond, right in the middle of the Maidstone Club's golf
course, and be poled about by a local Indian he dressed up
in gondolier's straw hat and sailor suit. The Indian stood
in the stern poling him about with the artist waving to the
golfers, calling out 'Ciao!' and drinking chilled Frascati as
he floated past. Members of the Maidstone nearly brought

it to a vote to have him expelled, disturbing their concentration on the links."

Alix liked that story. She said she liked any story that had people in boats distracting golfers. Also stories with Indians dressed up and Bohemians wearing two shirts.

After dinner, at her request, we drove to Hannah Cutting's place so she could check it out from the Further Lane side. The Kroepkes had refused to see her when she went by earlier. Apparently the lawyers for the estate thought they'd done too much talking already. "Can't we drive in and see it up close?" I didn't think so, I told her. The cops were being a bit brisk about trespassing since the killing and more so after the break-in. But I showed her how to get to Old Beach, between the Maidstone Club and Hannah's property, where we parked the car and left our shoes and went down onto the sand so Alix could see where Hannah'd been speared and her body found. It being a clear, windless night with a half moon and lots of stars it was very pleasant walking there barefoot on the smooth sand with a gentle surf sliding up on the beach to our right. Hurricane Martha, which it now was, hadn't yet reached the Windward Islands, still nearly two thousand miles off.

"Golly, this is lovely," Alix said, "no wonder all you wealthy chaps go on and on so about the Hamptons."

"I'm a journalist. My neighbors are the rich ones."

"Oh, tosh," she said, "I'll wager you've a bundle."

When we got to the rickety ladder where Hannah's murder most foul had been committed, Alix insisted on clambering up. She was wearing a dress and the ladder did nice things for her legs. She'd read the various reports and was able to visualize where Hannah had been on the steps and where the killer must have stood on the old boardwalk just above. She was disappointed all the dried blood seemed to have been taken in evidence or washed away naturally by rain and wind and spray. Then, her face set and serious:

"Spearing somebody on the very eve of the twenty-first century. What do you make of that?"

Somebody with an exaggerated sense of nostalgia, perhaps. Or maybe to throw off the cops.

"There was a Red Indian they suspected, wasn't there?" Yes, I said, Jesse Maine. Still a suspect but as yet no hard evidence.

"That may have been why a spear was used. To suggest Mr. Maine, to implicate him?"

Possible. It had occurred to me after a day or two; it had occurred to Alix Dunraven rather more swiftly. When we'd finished with the scene of the crime she said, "Can we put our feet in the ocean? I've been all summer in Manhattan. . . ."

Of course we could. And did. And strolled along at the edge of the ocean chatting and smoking cigarettes.

"You think the same person killed Hannah and broke into the house? And what were they looking for? Could it have been our precious manuscript?" she asked.

I didn't know. And I said so. Hannah's death was a police matter. I was writing a story about her life. Alix raised a skeptical eyebrow. Smug, she was, weren't death and life the same thing? Oh, yes, smug.

I wasn't getting all that far keeping things from her so I told Alix about Hannah's having worked here on Further Lane as a kid and about her coming back to buy the house in which she once had been a servant. Alix liked that:

"It's all too *Wuthering Heights* to be believed," she said, shaking her head. I thought it more Dickensian than Bronte-ish but who was I to challenge an Oxonian with a double first? Instead, I decided against telling her yet about Royal Warrender. Let her offer me a little something, first.

About Hannah's manuscript, I meant.

EIGHTEEN

*The demon amanuensis
of Hampton Bays . . .*

And now Alix did offer something. "Beecher, where are Hampton Bays from here?"

"Where *is*. Hampton Bays is singular, part of Southampton Town."

"My, you are the grammarian, aren't you?"

Why did Alix want to know about Hampton Bays?

"Someone at Random House told me there's this old stenographer living there who actually typed up Hannah's first couple of books for Simon & Schuster. You know, the self-help things." She looked at a small notebook (she shared that with detectives and me, carrying a notebook despite the Louis Vuitton laptop. And I admired her for it, being a traditionalist and all). "Rose Thrall is her name. I thought I'd talk to her on the off-chance she's been doing some typing and such for Hannah on our book."

I liked that "our," as well, granting me a kind of partnership with Alix on the missing manuscript. Then she promptly disabused me of that idea with, "Random House and I are terribly anxious about all this. Since it's our property that seems to have vanished. Rose Thrall may not know a thing but I think it's worth the toss."

I knew how to get to Hampton Bays but didn't know the local streets and roads that intimately so I said I'd go along and help her find the stenographer's place. Alix thought for

a moment, weighing convenience against confidentiality,
I suppose, and then said, "Right. Then let's get to it."

We took the Jag. And the poodle.

"I'd be mortified if she did the nasty on your nice carpets, Beecher."

My "nice" carpets were decidedly tired old Rya rugs
but it was considerate of Alix to fret, tired as they were.

She'd fetched along a copy of the book review from
last Sunday's *New York Times*. "Hannah's got still another
book on the best-seller list, in the Advice, How-to, and
Miscellaneous category. *Good Taste, Better Taste.*"

"She won't be able to do the talk shows."

"There is that," Alix conceded.

We stopped once for gas.

"What sort of place is it, Hampton Bays?" Alix asked.

"Ham Bays is what the locals call it and it's pretty much
blue collar, with a lot of New York city firemen and cops
owning places here, summer cottages and houses to retire
to, about a half-hour drive from Further Lane, just across
the Shinnecock Canal. At a dinner party one night in East
Hampton a guy named Bill Flanagan, a senior editor for
Forbes, who's written a handful of books, said he lived in
Hampton Bays and some woman asked, 'And how far is
that from East Hampton, Mr. Flanagan?'

"And Bill said: 'About two and a half books.' "

I liked that story and told it whenever I could. Alix hu-
mored me. "My, that was clever of him, wasn't it."

I had to ask directions only once. Hampton Bays had
some fine houses with water views or actually on the bays.
There were plenty of cardboardy-looking bungalows of
plywood or siding with small, above-ground pools in the
backyard and a rowboat or a dory on cinder blocks in
front. Rose Thrall lived at the Peconic Bay end of a rutted
dirt road in a sagging, weathered old frame house that had
seen better days. As had she, on first glimpse. Except for

her hands. As she came out on the porch and then down steps toward where we'd gotten out of the Jag, she was carefully pulling on a fresh pair of white cotton gloves. I guess she saw me looking at what she was doing. Or maybe Alix was staring, too.

"I have rather pretty hands," Ms. Thrall said, "so whenever I'm outdoors, even briefly, I cover them. Don't like old ladies' hands if I can keep them at bay."

"I quite agree," Alix said, "and I say, you do have lovely hands." She did, you know.

Alix extended her own to shake both of Ms. Thrall's and to tell her she was from Random House, leaving me sort of vaguely there, offering my name but little else. Rose was a talker:

"If my life had developed differently and I'd been assiduous about it, I might have had a considerable career as a hand model. You know, doing commercials and print ads for dishwashing liquids and lotions and the like. Instead, I won another sort of fame as Stenographer of the Year in 1960. Kennedy was elected that year and I took three hundred sixty words per minute in a national competition. Gregg. I was always partial to Gregg when it came to the various shorthand styles."

"That's jolly good, three hundred sixty words per minute," Alix said, "isn't it, Beecher?"

"Oh, yes," I said. Alix was doing all the running and desperately wanted me to pitch in. Rose Thrall came to the rescue.

"Come in out of the sun," she said. "Have a refreshment."

We both thanked her. This was going to be cake. The poodle was leashed to the steering wheel and for once was docile, curling up and preparing to nap. She liked the Jag's leather seats. But Ms. Thrall beckoned.

"Bring in the dog. I like a dog around. Had one but it died. Buried it out back there."

Mignonne hesitated and then trotted in after us.

"I suppose it's about Hannah," the old woman said.

She was tall and gaunt and had a breath on her I thought was probably rye. And cheap rye at that. Once we were inside the old house you could smell the booze permeating the wood, the furniture, the rugs. There was a sitting room with a fireplace and some dark, heavy wood furniture, all of it dated. Except against one wall, where the only good lighting was, where Ms. Thrall did her work. A desktop IBM computer, a fax machine, a Xerox copier, a printer, and two impressive-looking electronic typewriters.

"Name your poison," she said in a loud voice, pouring herself a refill of the rye. She was no dilettante when it came to that, straight rye right into a water glass with no intervening ice or mixer.

"Ah, tea?" Alix said, for once confounded. The old woman drank off a third of her fresh glass.

"Lipton's okay? Afraid I don't have milk. Got some lemons somewhere. I like a twist of lemon in a glass."

"Coffee for me," I said.

"Instant?" Without waiting for my answer, and with Mignonne trotting amiably in her wake, she went deeper into the gloom of the house to what I guess was the kitchen. She walked steadily, you had to say that for her, carrying her glass—as if concerned we might empty it once her back was turned—and not spilling a drop.

Alix and I looked at each other.

When we were all three again seated, refreshment in hand, and the poodle curled up contentedly on the worn carpet at our hostess's feet, Rose Thrall started right in, sipping from her glass with the bottle handy next to her.

"I'm surprised someone didn't come before. The police

should certainly have checked me out. Considering all the sturm und drang."

"What sturm und drang was that?" Alix asked. Let the old girl tell the damned story, I thought fiercely, willing Alix to hear the unspoken caution. People talk more freely if you don't press them. I shouldn't have worried; there was no scaring off Ms. Rose Thrall.

"When she got that contract from Simon & Schuster for her first book, I sent a letter offering my services. I read *PW* each week, y'know. That's the trade magazine *Publishers Weekly,*" she explained to me, assuming Alix would already know. I nodded my thanks and she went on:

"Hannah called and asked for samples and references and to make a long story short, she hired me to take dictation and then cleantype the manuscript. She could type herself, she said, but wasn't that fast and found the process boring. It was how I made my living. I enjoy typing.

"I learned a lot about her that first book. I'd go over there to her apartment, I still had a place in Manhattan then, too, and we'd work together a couple of hours. Hannah would pace up and down, gripping a sheaf of papers, notes, torn-out newspaper clips, articles from magazines, pages ripped from books, and she'd rustle through them and dictate to me nonstop, and fast. Barked it out at me and I got it down. I never knew if what I was taking down were Hannah's own words and ideas or pure plagiarism. I couldn't tell until later. After she finished dictating she'd stuff the papers into my hand.

" 'Here,' she'd say, 'if you can't spell something I said or didn't quite get it all down, everything's in here. My source material. You work it out. Bring me the cleantyped pages when you come back.' And that's just what I'd do.

"But when I'd get back to my place and sort out my shorthand and her bits and pieces, it was clear she was stealing right and left. There were articles from *House*

Beautiful and *Better Homes* and *Architectural Digest* and the autobiography of Billy Baldwin and a *Time* cover story about Sister Parish or tearsheets from *Vogue* and the *Times* and articles on Jackie Kennedy's influence on White House décor or how Giverny was furnished and the gardens at I Tatti . . .

"A grab bag of stolen goods. But when I went back that first time and handed over the cleantyped pages, I said, trying to be subtle, 'I assume you'll be crediting your sources in footnotes. Or will you do it in the body copy as you go along?' Well, she just exploded.

" 'There's very little new under the sun, Ms. Thrall, and contemporary women are already too pressed for time, balancing family and career, to be slowed down with a lot of academic posturing. I'm not writing a Ph.D. dissertation here; I'm helping busy American women improve their quality of life and I refuse to harass them further. It is callous and wicked of you even to suggest adding *footnotes* to their other burdens!' "

Rose Thrall put the water glass on her head and swallowed off whatever was left in it and reached for the bottle on the table at her elbow and gave herself another refill. Again, no ice, no water. It was astonishing to see. I wondered how long she could do this. As if she'd seen the puzzlement in my face she said, quite reasonably, "I have every vice but one, Mr. Stowe. A fifth of rye a day being among them. I don't smoke, can't abide the noxious weed. As to having a glass, my physician lectures me about it, goes on and on, but I say to him, 'Doctor, how many of your patients my age sleep a full night through night after night as I do? And have a full set of teeth as well?' "

"My," Alix said, "that is impressive."

"Exactly what my doctor said. You put the screws to those fellows, they eventually tell you the truth and stop trying to cram a lot of pricey prescriptions down your throat. Socialized medicine, it's coming eventually. Despite Hillary Clinton's bungling."

That first book was *The Taste Machine* and it was an overnight phenomenon.

When it came out, Rose Thrall remembered, there were plenty of hostile reviews alleging plagiarism, but Hannah had no patience with them. "The book was selling like hotcakes and Hannah was doing the talk shows and signing two hundred fifty copies an hour in Barnes and Noble's window—and to hell! Women right across the country were lining up to buy it, paying twenty bucks for their cram course in good taste, and glad to pay the freight. Couple of months later Hannah called me:

" 'Rose, I'm going to do another book. Do you want the job?' Well, of course I did. I'd give her a little trouble once in a while about the stealing, doing it for her own good. 'Hannah,' I'd say, 'just change the adjectives around a bit so it won't be verbatim.' Sometimes she would, more often she wouldn't. Depended on her mood. She'd tell me to mind my own business, or that she'd think about it. Whichever, I got it all down in Gregg shorthand and had it back a day or so later cleantyped.

" 'Rose,' she'd say, 'you're a wonder. There never has been a stenographer like you.' I agreed on that, you can be sure, I was in the *Guinness Book* by now, wasn't I? But after a time I felt sufficiently at ease with her that I said, 'You know, Hannah, there's a word I much prefer to 'stenographer.' Amanuensis. Means the same thing; just sounds classier.'

"Hannah laughed. Said she'd heard the word a couple times but frankly didn't know what it meant. Started calling me 'Rose Thrall, The Demon Amanuensis.' And we'd both laugh. . . ."

Didn't sound much like "sturm und drang" to me. More

like a couple of women who worked together and got along. Then Rose got to where it was heading:

"I did every single one of those books with her. Got paid fairly, treated pretty well, and it was the work I did. Her books hit the best-seller lists, each of them, and each time, just as regularly, people would bitch and moan about how she'd lifted their stuff from this article or that book. And of course they were right. Hannah didn't write; she cribbed. And from the best sources. Smart, she was, never stole anything second-rate or marginal.

"By now I'd sold my apartment in Manhattan and was living out here. Hannah was twenty miles away and I had other authors I worked for that had places in the Hamptons, and I was computer literate and so really could live about anywhere and make a living. So when I saw in *PW* that Random House signed up Hannah for a million or more to do an autobiography, a serious one, not just some puff job, I sent her a note. No response. So I called.

" 'No,' she told me, 'this time I'm doing the book myself. I won't need your help. This book is too personal to work through with hired hands. It's a book I'm going to do personally. I don't want any second opinions, don't want any leaks.' That was all, cold as that. Well, I don't have to tell you I drink a little. And I kind of blew up, especially that line about 'leaks,' that crack about 'hired hands.' I said, 'For chrissakes, Hannah, when did I leak any time during all those books I typed up where you stole everything but the title from someone else?'

"Guess I shouldn't have said that. She hung up and a week or so later a lawyer came 'round. Sullivan and Cromwell sent him all the way out from Manhattan. Handed me a legal paper and a check. If I signed the paper, I got the check."

By now the poodle was plopped on her lap, asleep. She refreshed her glass and Alix asked, "What was the paper?"

"A confidentiality agreement. No interviews about Hannah, no statements to the press, written or verbal, nothing about her past books or our professional relationship, no this and no that. She was buying my silence.

"I told the Sullivan and Cromwell gentleman I was sorry but I wouldn't sign. He then suggested I might be letting myself in for trouble and I blew up, told him to go to hell, tossed the check back at him—and it was a good-sized check, money I could have used—and he got out.

"That was the last contact I ever had with Hannah. A bribe and a muzzle. We did every book together but this one, she didn't need me. . . ." She took a sip and said, "Ah, to hell. I had a good run with her. Sorry she's dead. No one deserves to die like that. Not even Hannah."

She looked at me. "They find out yet who did it?"

I shook my head.

"And you never did any work on the new book or know anything about it?"

"Not a thing. Hannah didn't trust me. She as much as said that. Discarded me like an old pencil stub you toss away when it's done its job. A casual sort of cruelty, not as much calculated as off-handed, but cruel nonetheless.

"Damn her!"

As we drove back east, Alix said, "Think she might have done it?"

"Possible."

"I don't think so. I liked her. So did Mignonne."

"I said it's possible, that's all. Just because you and a dog like someone doesn't mean they can't commit murder. And don't forget one other thing."

"What's that?" Alix asked.

"She wears gloves."

NINETEEN

A few skeletons lying about, frozen inside their orange climbing suits . . .

Early in June when I was just starting work on the book, I'd subscribed to just about every on-line service they had on the Internet on grounds I'd be out here all summer without easy access to anything but the local library and the little Book Hampton store next to the movie theater. So whatever faults my terrorism book may have, don't blame research.

No longer now was it Bosnian Serbs or the frenzies of Algerian zealots that tugged at curiosity but whatever it was that happened on Mount Everest. It nagged at me that Hannah's and Pam's hatred (too strong a word?) stemmed from their attempt at scaling the world's tallest mountain. Until then, if not friends, they'd been neighbors and fellow members on various East Hampton committees for the usual good causes. Then came Everest. People had died up there, caught by a blizzard above the eight-thousand-meter elevation. Both Pam and Hannah had limped away on frozen feet and suffered other damage. None of it enduring. Why then had they not forged an even closer bond, having survived such a harrowing adventure? For both these powerful, successful women, Everest must have been a defining moment, one of their rare defeats, yet from which they had both walked away, survivors, tough and resilient. Pam, the only one I could ask, was curt, dismissive, as if merely to talk about an Everest she'd painfully shared with Hannah was demeaning. It was to the computer and the on-line services that I now turned for answers, trolling the Net.

It was some story.

There were two expeditions on the mountain at the same time in early May that year. Not really competing; Everest supplies sufficient competition all by itself. Pam Phythian and Hannah were in the same group headed by a celebrated Seattle guide named Wales. The other team was headed up by a New Zealander, Vorstman, another Himalayan "star." Except for one frightening flash snowstorm between camps two and three and the usual small accidents and bouts of altitude sickness, things went reasonably well as far up as camp four at 26,000 feet, from which the final sprint to the summit, 2,900 vertical feet higher, would be made up and back in a single day.

In a riveting passage I found on the Net, writer Peter Wilkinson described camp four. "A depressing, rock-strewn lunar wasteland even in the best weather. The spot is also an eerie garbage dump: besides strips of shredded tents, discarded bright yellow, green, and red oxygen tanks, spent batteries, empty raisin boxes, and Powerbar wrappers, there is a skeleton or two lying about on the loose shale, still zipped into down suits—grim reminders of the price a moody Everest can exact: 143 lives in 43 years, most of them in this vicinity."

The Vorstman group had the lead and reached the summit about noon, took the traditional photos, exchanged high fives, and started back down. But between the glorious summit, at this hour still brilliantly sunny, and camp four with its seedy, town-dump appearance, the victorious group split up. One of the successful summiteers had fallen ill, down with cramp and unable to walk, and he and Vorstman's right-hand man stayed behind until the sick man could resume the descent. No point in the others coming to a halt as well; they were low on oxygen already with very little margin for error.

It was at this juncture that Wales's people, including Hannah and Pam, a party of ten in all, on their way up, passed some of Vorstman's group coming down. The two teams met on the Southeast Ridge, a narrow and treacherous rib of rock generously glazed with ice and drifting snow. By now the wind was coming up and a thin cloud began to mask the afternoon's sunlight. What with the narrowness of the route, the handshakes and congratulations and good wishes exchanged and photos taken, maybe a half hour was lost. Wales, an amiable fellow, wasn't a driver, as Vorstman was known to be. His clients had paid on average $65,000 for their month's adventure and Wales believed in letting them enjoy themselves. Usually, Everest summiteers observed a two P.M. cutoff; if they haven't reached the top by that hour, they give up and start back down. It was after three when the first pair of Wales's climbers got to the top. The others were still on their way up, the weather was deteriorating, the oxygen was running out, and neither Pam nor Hannah Cutting had gotten past the Hillary Step, so-called, at 28,800 feet, with hundreds of feet yet to be climbed. It was at this point that even the casual Wales concluded that enough was enough.

"We're going down," he shouted to the six climbers who hadn't yet made the top, Hannah and Pam among them. Considering the headstrong egos involved, it was a wonder Wales didn't get an argument. But he didn't. Not then. That came later.

There was another logjam at the Hillary Step. One of Wales's group had begun vomiting and had to stop while Vorstman's right-hand man and his sick client were still there huddling pathetically out of the wind while trying to recover sufficiently to resume the descent. And now it began to snow. Not just a fall of snow but a fierce, wind-driven blizzard. And nothing went right after that. Although the accounts vary, depending on the source (and some of those sources were clearly ill or disoriented or panicked or oxygen-starved), what you got through the Internet was that the parties, both the Wales group and what was left up there of the Vorstman bunch, began to break up. Out of fatigue or illness or panic they just fell apart. Several climbers flatly refused to resume the descent along the knife-edged Southeast Ridge in a gale and heavy snow. At least one became hysterical and cried out, "Just leave me alone. I want to die." Guides cursed out clients as "gutless" and shouted, "If you can't walk, then fucking crawl!"

A few hundred feet above them two men, one sick and unable to move, the other a guide who refused to leave him, sheltering in a makeshift snow cave, made final calls by cell phone to their families and fell into a sleep from which they would never wake. They were the first to die; they were not the last.

Two more were lost on the knife edge of the Southeast Ridge, roped together as they had to be in these conditions. Whether both fell or only one, who then pulled the other, no one knew. Neither body was ever found. On one side of the ridge there was a dropoff of 4,800 vertical feet; on the other, 10,000. By five-thirty, even at these heights, darkness began to fall. The storm kept up. Wind chill was estimated at sixty degrees below zero Fahrenheit. The lead guide could not find the rope earlier fixed by the Sherpas. That was a visibility problem. Or maybe the Sherpas hadn't put in the ropes as they'd been told to do. Maybe the Sherpas had shirked their duty. Now the cursing of both guides and clients focused on the native Sherpas, much of it undeserved. By full night the survivors had reached the South Col where there was deep snow into which they could burrow and within which they might last through the night. Almost everyone was now suffering frostbite and out of oxygen, gasping and bent near-double to ease cramp. Camp four was only a few hundred feet lower down but in what direction? If they continued to stumble downhill in the dark they might pass the tents by a few yards and die of exposure and exhaustion. So they bivouacked in the South Col, all except those still missing above and two more who insisted in going on toward what they thought was camp four. Where was Wales? He'd gone off scouting for missing members of the party.

As for Pam Phythian and Hannah Cutting, they were teamed on a three-man rope with the best of the Sherpas, Ang Thwat. Ang had taken the lead as they set off down the knife edge of the Northeast Ridge with Pam, more experienced than Hannah second and Hannah third at rope's end. Moving slowly down, Ang measuring every step, and in almost zero visibility, so strong the wind, so heavy the fall of snow, they were a tenth of the way down, a fifth, half the way down to the Col and its primitive shelter.

And then, for reasons the Internet did not explain and probably didn't know, Ang slipped and disappeared with a single cry off to the side of the knife-edge. Pam, closest to him, found herself being pulled along by his weight. Behind her, Hannah instinctively and correctly threw herself prone on the other side of the narrow ridge as counterbalance to the weight of the fallen Ang and the sliding Pam. And it was there they hung, in deadly equilibrium, until the rope, having frayed or been flawed, suddenly and dramatically snapped! parting between Ang and Pam. Fatal for him, fortunate for her. And for Hannah, too. Both women now scrambled back atop the ridgeline. Ang was gone; they would survive.

A rescue party had started out when the weather began to break, climbing from camp three through four and on up to the Col. Only one member of the group was able to get that far without bivouacking for the night. He found Wales's party. But not Wales. He passed around his oxygen and headed down again, promising to be back in the morning. By which time the storm would be over.

He was as good as his word. So too the others. By noon a colonel of the Nepalese army successfully landed a chopper on the Col and began to take people off, one at a time. Harsh words were exchanged, people pushed and shoved for advantage at the head of the line, an actual fist fight took place. The chopper came back again and again until all the survivors were at base camp far down at the foot of the mountain.

Eight were dead.

The tantalizing thing about all this? In the accounts carried by various on-line services, no one ascribed blame. They'd climbed the mountain, the weather had gone sour, people died, others survived. No one's fault, just rotten luck. But what of that fist fight in the Col when the chopper began its heroic shuttling of people to safety? No one mentioned that again. No one even noted that to have a fight of any sort, at least two persons are required. No one was to blame for that, either, even when it required at least two people to take up hostilities. Who was it who fought? I wondered. No word on that, either.

Just rotten luck.

Three guides, a couple of Sherpas, three clients were dead. Among the survivors, Hannah Cutting and Pam Phythian. A fund was gotten up. Ang Thwat, the hero martyr, was mythologized as having given his life for the two memsahibs. Pam was the driving force behind the fund, which was to help educate Ang's children. If any; no one seemed quite sure. She put up ten thousand dollars.

Hannah Cutting, always prudent when it came to giving her money away, sent a check for fifteen hundred.

And, as a reminder of what they'd been through, and been spared, it was Hannah who kept their climbing rope, souvenir of that terrible moment when it parted and Ang fell. While Pam and Hannah were saved. How it was that Hannah ended up with the rope when it was Pam who was closest to the hero Sherpa, the on-line services had no explanation.

And ever since the Everest tragedy, two women who'd been if not close friends, neighbors and colleagues back in East Hampton, had mutually and cordially despised each other.

TWENTY

Claire, in a white Speedo tank suit,
was on the ski . . .

Alix and I, on the other hand, were getting along well. In the morning I tried to improve still further the tenor and pace of our relationship. Was I rushing it? She looked adorable over coffee, hair shining and face bright and the silk robe skimming lightly over that long, lovely body. Take her out in a canoe, I thought (such was the manner in which my mind worked!); show her East Hampton from a different vantage point. A Sloane Ranger from London, let Alix see how other folks lived. Even how deftly I handled the canoe. Might impress her, loosen her up, get her telling me things about Hannah Cutting's book I wanted to know. Or things about herself.

I'd conveniently overlooked the fact of her double first at Oxford and being the Earl's daughter and that she tended to make up her own mind about what she'd be doing. On September mornings like this or any time.

"That's all very well, Beecher, but I've got errands first. Mr. Evans requires answers and I've supplied bloody few. He's expecting daily E-mails and getting none. I really ought to go by and try again to talk my way in to meet Hannah's staff—the Kroepkes are they?—and ask a few questions myself." What else she did I don't know but she was back before noon. She hadn't gotten much out of the Kroepkes, she admitted. But at least this time they'd talked with her, having been charmed, I was sure. Alix charmed everyone. And she'd bought several new outfits in local boutiques that looked even better on her than on the window mannequins. She was also proving to be the sort of dogged young person who persevered and wasn't permanently out of sorts when someone chased her off. She just went back again. And she was back in time for us still to go out on the water. Wearing a bikini bottom and an Oxford crew T-shirt and salty-looking sneakers. I'd not seen so much of her legs before. Even in ratty old sneakers they were nice legs. I know it's demeaning of me to make such shallow judgments or to think things like that. But I do.

Alix helped me (really did; she was handy and pretty strong) get the canoe on the roof of the Blazer and stow the paddles and line and other gear inside. But when I attempted to explain to her about her PFD, the personal flotation device the Coast Guard required out here, Alix Dunraven said, and very politely, "Well, you see, I've been in small boats before. I cox-ed the varsity against Cambridge on the Thames my second year at Oxford." She paused. "We won by a boatlength and a half."

Here I was telling her about life preservers and she'd been coxswain of the winning crew in a historic boat race more celebrated than the America's Cup.

"Oh," I said, not very cleverly. Not for the first time I thought I was too easily put down. Especially by beautiful women.

We drove up Three Mile Harbor Road past the little farm where a handwritten sign advertised "Priscilla & Elvis," the 600-pound sow and the huge old goat that lived in a corral outside the faded red barn where the curious pulled their cars over and kids got off their bikes to gawk. "What's that?" Alix asked. "Local joke," I told her. She knit her brow over that, not quite sure about our American sense of humor. There was almost no wind (a good thing;

wind is the enemy of the canoeist), and when we got the
boat launched, she said:

"It's been my experience the butler very rarely does it.
Usually it's the wife. Or the husband. Or one of the children. Don't you agree?"

"I haven't had that much experience solving murders."

Which was my way of asking, without actually doing
so, just how much experience *she* had.

"I mean, theoretical rather than empirical, through reading mostly. Hercule Poirot, Holmes, Miss Marple, Le
Carré, Raymond Chandler. All those chaps, especially
John Buchan. Devilishly clever, don't you think? It was
Buchan taught me the use of simple code, six-number
groupings in cipher, signed with the name of a winner of
the Derby, just as Sandy Arbuthnot, Master of Clanroyden,
used to do whilst foiling The Hun as he communicated
with Dick Hannay, the South African mining engineer
turned general who . . ."

Of course, I said, not knowing where this was going
nor just what the devil she was talking about. Six-number
groupings? Cipher? And who was General Hannay?

"You know . . ." she began a bit vaguely, "how I keep
in touch with Mr. Evans." And then, not vaguely at all,
"Do you suspect the same person that killed Hannah also
broke into the pool house? Or had a confederate who may
have done so? Is there a link at all? Or do we have two
malefactors entirely, one murderer and one burglar? Perhaps more than two, an entire ring?"

I issued the usual protestation that I was writing about
Hannah's life and not her murder. Alix smirked. "Oh,
that's a given, Beecher. Go right on." She tolerated my
line while clearly dismissing it. There was no shortage of
suspects, I had to admit. I told Her Ladyship about various
celebrated local feuds involving Hannah that erupted over
beach-driving permits and whether to set aside a protected

beach for nesting plovers and terns and if striped bass limits were sufficient. She nodded distractedly, not much of a
dedicated naturalist herself. The wind was so calm and the
water so flat, I didn't stay inside of Three Mile Harbor as
I usually did, but steered the boat out through the channel
into Peconic Bay, paddling smoothly, Alix in the bow and
I in the stern, working up a nice rhythm, setting up the
boat well, which lulled me as the canoe usually did on a
calm day. Hell, why not just enjoy ourselves and think of
the missing manuscript as a game. Paddling about with a
pretty girl on a nice day, I might well have been punting on
the Thames (or the Isis or whatever that river is that flows
through Oxford, where undergraduates picnic on cucum-
ber sandwiches and chilled wine out of wicker hampers).
Hannah Cutting's dead and gone and no one seems for-
lorn. If Random House can find the manuscript they've got
a big best-seller and hooray for Her Ladyship. If I find it
first, I've got a good piece for Anderson at *Parade*. Alix
wins or I win or neither of us wins and the damned thing's
gone forever. But no one really gets hurt. Or so I thought.

It was precisely then, in the midst of my facile, com-
placently shallow philosophizing, that a sleek, electric blue
cigarette boat, coming up apparently out of nowhere, raced
past the canoe not fifty yards away and pulling a water-
skier. There were rules in the harbor. No jet skis, no water
skis, five miles per hour maximum speed. But out here on
broad Peconic Bay, only the usual maritime rules of the
road, and the cigarette must have been doing forty! Jesus!
Alix, without being told, joined me in paddling so that the
canoe spun to face the speedboat's wake, bow on, letting
the wake slide under us rather than hit us broadside and
maybe dump us into the water.

"Are people supposed to do that?"

"No, dammit, not that close to a canoe they're not."

She was surprised and I was sore. We were safely

through the wake now but before I could say more, or really do anything, I could see, half a mile off, the cigarette boat turning and starting to head back toward us. This wasn't skylarking now; this was menacing.

"Paddle, Alix, make for that beach to the left."

"Right-oh," she said. Good girl. Didn't waste breath debating.

The big speedboat buzzed us twice more. Leo Brass was at the helm; Claire Cutting, in a white Speedo tank suit, was on the ski. She curved this way and that, in and out so that the towline actually crossed over the canoe, forcing us to duck. Taut line like that could tip a small boat; line like that might break your damn neck if it caught you. I shook my fist and cursed. I could see Leo's face, split in a grin. Or was it a scowl? At speed, you couldn't tell. He seemed to be shouting at Claire, urging her on or cursing her out. The bastard. The roar of the big engine drowned his words. Big Green Peacer and he's trying to run us down. Or have his girlfriend cut us in two. After the third pass they sped off out into open water toward Gardiner's Island and the ocean.

We paddled back inside of the sheltered Three Mile Harbor, where we beached the canoe and took a breather before getting it back atop the Blazer. Alix said, "Now what was that all about?"

"That's Hannah's daughter and her boyfriend. I've been asking questions and apparently they resent it."

Alix looked thoughtful. "I wonder, was he steering the boat that close or was she skiing that close? Which of them did the actual menacing?"

I started to say she was splitting hairs and what difference did it make but stopped. It did make a difference. It was Claire's cigarette boat, one of her "toys." Hannah might have treated her child badly but she gave good allowance. Leo's boat was a big old Hatteras fishing job, a useful boat but not the swift powerhouse a cigarette boat was. Were Claire and Brass a team, and if so, which of them called the plays? Or were they at odds and that was why Leo seemed to have been shouting at her? Why would a guy as fierce as Leo was about wetlands and pristine waters be speeding around in cigarette boats just outside Three Mile Harbor when he had an entire ocean at hand?

I dunno, I said. Then, "You okay?"

"Oh, quite. Nothing quite like a canoe ride to calm the nerves."

TWENTY-ONE

You must have grand times there,
the Queen and all . . .

While we were paddling around and Leo and Hannah's daughter amused themselves at our expense (or may have had more malign intentions), Jesse Maine broke out again. He'd hurt a gas station proprietor in a brutal fight over whether the man was cheating Shinnecocks by watering gas bought by Reservation Indians. Local cops knew the gas station owner was a shifty sort and probably the gas was watered. But you couldn't have Jesse beating people up and sending them to the Southampton Hospital E.R. So he's the Red Indian, Alix said. Yeah. And can be risky to be around.

When I called Tom Knowles he was already at the reservation and I thought I ought to be, too, and when Alix flatly refused to be left behind, we drove down there.

"You gonna arrest him again, Tom?"

"I dunno, Beech," Knowles said. "I hate to keep arresting Jesse. We get along pretty well until it comes to a matter of laws I'm sworn to uphold and he's determined to break. I wish to hell he'd get married again or go fishing or something and stop raising hell. I know he's got grievances but so has the gas station guy. Who's also got a broken jaw." Jesse was a pretty good guy but when he got sore, or drunk, he was dangerous. Tom knew that, so did my father, so did I. But Tom was a policeman, my father was fishing in Norway; I was just a reporter.

Even more dangerous than Jesse, hot bloods on the Reservation, who'd gathered at Jesse's house on the shores of Shinnecock Bay, ready to fight to defend their turf and convinced the cops were picking on Jesse, who, again not wisely, was blurting out that he wished he'd never laid eyes on that damned Hannah Cutting. That she was bad medicine. Everything that happened could be put down to her fault. Ever since she croaked there'd been a hex on him. The whole business had the potential to erupt into a Siege-at-Waco or a Montana Freemen's standoff when a Bill Kunstler–type radical lawyer arrived by limo, issuing high-flown and flowery statements and snarling contempt for a local police force that didn't have a single Native American among its number.

"Oh, shit," Knowles groaned, "we've only got thirty-six officers and no Shinnecock ever even applied." But when the attorney, the Manhattan outsider, offered his smarmy services to the easily angered Jesse, assuring him he was being railroaded, the Indian picked him up and threw him bodily into the water.

"Can't say I didn't warn you," Jesse reminded the drenched interloper. "I dislike pretty much everyone. And that especially includes lawyers."

Then, "Howdy, Beecher. Your Daddy catch any fish over there yet? Tell him I said hello."

"Surely will, Jesse," I assured him. "Say hello as well to Alix Dunraven. She's here from London."

"Well, isn't that fine, Miss. Think of that, all the way from London. One of many places I've never been. You must have grand times there, with the Queen and all, and the way they carry on in that family."

"Oh, England's quite often jolly. I think you'd like it,

Mr. Maine. Except perhaps for the weather. It's usually raining."

Jesse nodded, very thoughtful. Rain meant certain crops might thrive better than others. He wondered if there were muskrats to be trapped and inquired about the fishing. I explained about Alix's daddy, the title and all, his being an Earl, all of which fascinated Jesse. "We got some sachems and chiefs and the like in our eastern tribes. But no earls. Do they have gainful employment or just laze about?"

Alix felt she ought to defend the aristocracy, at least in the abstract, before moving on to more parochial concerns. "They are useful, or so Pa insists, voting in the House of Lords and keeping tabs on those chaps in Commons. But what about your tribe, Mr. Maine, is there a casino?" Alex asked, wanting to be polite. "I've been to the one at Deauville and to Monte, of course."

"No," Jesse said. He was opposed to casinos. On principle.

"And I thought all the Indians had them."

"No, ma'am. You never hear of a Sioux casino. Or a Commanche. Or Cheyenne. It's all these half-assed local eastern tribes got them. Fellas with rusty pickups up on cinder blocks in the front yard but they're too good to pump gas or work in the 7-Eleven."

"Mmmm," Alix said tactfully, unsure of the polite response and not wishing to denigrate one Indian in front of another. I tried to help out. "Jesse works hard himself, Alix, hunting muskrat for their pelts and catching fish for market and growing a little corn and working on house repairs and such. Done fine work for my father who swears by him."

"Correct," the Indian said, pleased at my father's compliments, even secondhand, "I freelance, I consult, and I am available on proper notice for assignments of varying sorts. For a fee, of course. But some of these fellas 'round here, they'll have you convinced they're Shinnecock aristocrats and such just like you Brits, bragging on about ancestors with portraits in gilt frames all over the walls, that their great-granddad on one side was Sitting Bull and on the other, Crispus Attucks . . ."

Alix shook her head, said she knew of Sitting Bull and his enormous exploits, but not of the other man he mentioned.

"Who was he?" she asked. Jesse looked startled.

"Why, you of all people, Your Ladyship, you ought to know. He was a black gentleman who was shot by your Redcoats hundreds of years back at the massacre."

"What massacre was that?" she asked. "We've had any number, regrettably."

"Boston. The Boston Massacre. Attucks was the fellow who practically got the American Revolution started all by hisself. Just by getting shot and killed. A great hero and role model for the rest of us people of color, ever since."

"I should say so, Mr. Maine," Alix said. "And our chaps shot him? You mean that literally?"

"I do."

"Then on behalf of Great Britain, I *am* sorry."

We all paused for a brief silence in memory of the late Crispus Attucks of Boston.

Driving back to East Hampton Alix said, "Will they arrest him?"

"Don't think so. Hope not. But Jesse doesn't make it easy."

In the end, Knowles told Jesse to come in the following day and make a statement. But to come in on his own; the cops wouldn't bring him. That seemed to mollify the Indian, his precious dignity intact and immeasurably pleased by having thrown a lawyer into the water. If Jesse hated anyone worse than the late Hannah Cutting (and most cops), it was lawyers.

We stopped at Sam's, on Newtown Lane. You like pizza? Alix shook her head. No?

"No, I like pizza fine. It's just all too much, you and the Red Indians and African-Americans in Boston being massacred by Englishmen and whether there ought to be casinos, and then that detective fellow, and Claire Cutting and her boyfriend trying to drown us in the speedboat. Mr. Evans will be terribly out of sorts. And my failures reflect badly on HarperCollins as well, back in London. And even on the Tony Godwin Award jury. By this time I'm supposed to have found Hannah's manuscript buried under the floorboards or somewhere and fetched it back so we can get on with producing yet another best-seller that quite conceivably might be optioned by Hollywood as a potential major motion picture. At the very least I ought to be E-mailing daily or even hourly messages in cipher to describe what progress if any I was making in cracking the case. Instead, I feel absurdly guilty, buying new clothes and sporting about with you in canoes and meeting these fascinating people and driving along these lovely lanes, dining in restaurants with sailboats in the bar and now eating pizza and . . ."

"East Hampton ought to retain you to do Chamber of Commerce promos. You make it sound pretty nice." Her being here made it pretty nice as well, though I caught myself and didn't say so.

She liked all our windmills as well.

"I feel a proper Sancho Panza trailing about after you on all these noble quests seeking manuscripts and jousting with chaps."

I liked that, as well, being Don Quixote. But instead of my squire, shouldn't she be the Don's lovely Dulcinea? But I didn't say that, either. Episcopalian reticence.

Alix might be growing impatient but I was getting used to having her around and less uneasy with the dissonance of "houseguest." I was even beginning to hope we wouldn't find Hannah's manuscript all that quickly so that Alix wouldn't be hurrying back to Manhattan. Back at the gatehouse I opened a chilled Julienas from Georges Duboeuf that was only two years old but went down fine with sausage and pepper pizza from Sam's, while listening to some John Coltrane and Ella Fitzgerald on the old stereo.

"Y'know, Beecher," Alix said, "I haven't been here two full days and don't know a bloody thing. But it seems to me that what counts most here in East Hampton isn't really money or celebrity. What counts is roots, how long you've all lived here. The old families, the old land, the traditions and customs. In ways, Beecher, it's rather like Britain, all those stately homes and people who can't pay their bills but they keep up those justifiably storied lawns."

". . . rolling them every day for a thousand years. Yeah."

She nodded, as if trying to figure out what she'd say next and wondering if it made even the slimmest sense.

"Seems to me that if you want to find out something in a place like this, in the Hamptons and along Further Lane, you get hold of someone who's lived here a very long time, centuries, millennia, and you enlist his assistance. . . ."

"No one lives centuries. They . . ."

"Oh, don't be dense, Beecher. I mean a family that's been here that long. Or longer."

"Well, there are the Warrenders. And Tom Knowles's folks. And Pam Phythian. Even my people. And the Spaeths and Gardiners and Cuttings and . . ."

"Longer than that."

I was starting to see how Alix's mind worked.

"Jesse Maine and the Shinnecocks, right?"

"May I have a little more of that wine?" she asked, not quite coy but offering me a half smile. Jesse might not know it yet but Her Ladyship's net was about to be cast wide on the local waters.

The eleven o'clock news said Hurricane Martha had come ashore and violently so in the British Virgin Islands and was zeroing in on Puerto Rico. No threat yet to the East Coast but the Hurricane Center in Miami was watching it to see if it gave sign of making that classic right turn to come north. . . .

TWENTY-TWO

$2,400 for a collie to chase
the sonuvabitching geese . . .

Even though the official season ended with Labor Day,
once Her Ladyship took up residence in my quarters, the
invitations came flooding in. Suddenly, I was enormously
popular. You'd think Princess Di and Fergie, both!, were
bunking in my spare bedroom and entertaining the gentry
with their carnal favors. Enormous wealth or being a partner at Skadden Arps or helming the America's Cup winner
was one thing; having a British title was something far
more likely to impress the local rustics. Most invitations
were shrugged off. Not all.

"Do you want to see Leo Brass up close?" I asked.

"I've seen him, too bloody close in fact." Alix wasn't a
romantic about the realities.

"He was in a cigarette boat; we had a canoe. This time
we're on land. Both of us. Much better odds."

Every year it seemed the Green Peacers had a new
cause. Locally, this time, it was Georgica Pond. And . . .
The Gut.

"What's 'The Gut' if it's not pushy to inquire?" Alix
wanted to know.

Good question. Even in East Hampton people were
vague, confused, about The Gut. I was anything but expert.
But I was game.

"Georgica is a gorgeous pond, with wonderful homes

and a number of great estates bordering its shoreline, one of the bigger ponds in East Hampton, couple of miles long and a mile or so wide. At its southern end it comes up against the ocean beach so that a narrow sand barrier no more than one hundred yards across separates the pond from the ocean. Every year, usually twice a year depending on a ruling from the town trustees, bulldozers cut a breach through that sand barrier at a narrow place called The Gut. Leo Brass usually does the bulldozing, being something of an artist with a tractor. He gouges out a channel so that the brackish water of the pond with all the sediment and fertilizer and rain runoff and such that gets in there can be flushed out into the ocean and the pond can refresh itself with an influx of clean seawater. It's something to see, the pond water rushing out and then, at the next high tide, the ocean rushing in, with all sorts of big and little fish and crabs and shellfish flailing about, with Leo up there atop the 'dozer, waving and taking bows, and people shaking hands with the trustees and snapping photos and lifting a glass to toast The Gut and otherwise carrying on. Like when they have the grunion run in Southern California."

"The what?"

I was getting in deeply enough with Georgica Pond and The Gut to start explaining about grunion. Especially since I knew nothing of grunion beyond what I'd read in *The Last Tycoon* and had never even seen one.

"Never mind." Alix didn't say anything, but did award me the highest raised eyebrow of the week.

There was a problem about the timing of the flushing of The Gut. Some of the big shorefront landowners were pushing for an earlier opening since Georgica Pond was high this summer and lapping at their lawns if not precisely at their front doors. And they were clearly aware a hurricane could be coming this way. Even a modest hurri-

cane meant drenching rains that disastrously might force
the Pond out of its banks and into their homes. The Baymen, led by Leo Brass, hadn't yet said anything but were
expected to hold out for a later, more traditional date, and
to hell with the rich people who had property fronting on
the Pond. Those were the wealthiest people, theirs the
most valuable land. So you understood their position. But
there was something ecologically to be said on behalf of
the Baymen's as well. I had a sneaking feeling that Brass
so loved a fight that if the rich were demanding The Gut
be left alone until winter, he'd be leading the battle to have
it flushed yesterday afternoon. Ornery, he was.

The Baymen's rally was scheduled for eight at Ashawag
Hall on Old Stone Highway. That must have sounded impressive to Alix because she asked, "Must we book?" I
said we'd get in, don't worry, and would in fact have time
to drop by first for a glass at Pam Phythian's. Since both
Pam and Leo Brass were sworn enemies of Hannah's (as
well as having clashed themselves with considerable ferocity over some ecological point of dispute or other!),
we'd be touching several bases in the one evening.

"And who's she?" Alix wondered.

Pam was easier to explain than grunion and The Gut.

"She's a Phythian, which out here is pretty important
stuff. Real old family, lots of Old Money as well. There's
even a Fithian Lane in the village that runs behind the Post
Office down to Egypt Lane. That's how some of the family spells the name, with an *F*. Pam's forty or so; I always
thought resembled Anouk Aimee without the accent.
Damned attractive, tall, lean, and athletic. She was the one
who got Hannah Cutting started climbing mountains."

Pam had never married, I explained. Oh, there'd been
opportunities, suitors, affairs. It was just, people said, that
no one man measured up to Pam's needs and expectations.

"I like her already," Alix said, delighted at having such

a vigorously independent female role model as our hostess.

I was about to say, "and she'll like you, too," but didn't. There were vague stories about Pam and other women, including even Hannah. But they were only stories and you know how people gossip.

As one might have expected, given her lineage, Pam handled things superbly. While other of her guests were practically curtseying to Alix on being introduced, Pam stuck out her hand and shook Alix's firmly.

"Any friend of Beecher's," she murmured, "and especially one so lovely and having come so far."

They were about the same height, both of them lean, but Alix less rangy, not as broad in the shoulder. Both were wearing ankle-length wrap skirts not showing much leg (last summer's trendy look but a shame, I thought). Pam was much tanner except for her hands. A gardener, of course, who habitually wore gardening gloves; and who in East Hampton wasn't a gardener? As we stood there chatting, Jerry Della Femina joined us. He was the big noise on Madison Avenue who owned a smashing home on the dunes and several businesses including restaurants and a small but chic shopping center. Busy man. In his spare time he was suing the town over a freedom of speech issue and had also run for East Hampton town elective office earlier in the year and lost badly. But then, in every election, there are losers. What left a bad taste behind was Jerry's loud complaint that traditional old members of the Maidstone Club ganged up and defeated him and his blue-collar supporters. He was especially irate over one super-annuated old gent who'd been rolled into the polling place in a wheelchair while hooked up to a breathing device. How dare these people?

Jerry's annoyed protest at allowing an invalid to cast a ballot ignited a furious backlash on behalf of the elderly man's guts and public spirit. Jerry was holding forth now

on another matter, brilliant and persuasive in his trademark style.

"These Baymen have the right idea. Get a tough like
Leo Brass up there to put a scare into the Establishment . . ."

"Brass?" Pam said. "What's he up to now?" She'd
hardly been listening to Jerry, almost rudely ignoring his
rant, or that was my impression, but now she seized on
Leo's name.

"Oh, I dunno," Jerry Della Femina said, "something
about emptying ponds and changing the water. Turtles eating ducks or vice versa. And the red tide and the green
algae, or have I got that confused?" Jerry knew very well
what it was all about but enjoyed playing the simpleton
and then, having lulled an opponent, pouncing!

Alix picked up on it:

"It's all a matter of duck feces," she said, "imperiling
fish and crabs and oysters and the like, causing the ag-
gressive growth of algae and raising coliform counts.
That's what chokes out the shellfish," Alix offered, "or at
least so I'm given to understand by Native American and
other expert ecological sources."

Della Femina had not yet met Her Ladyship so I made
the introductions.

"Duck feces? Native Americans? Coliform counts?
What would an English duchess know about all that?"

"Well, firstly, I'm hardly a duchess but I happen to be a
personal friend of Mr. Jesse Maine who . . ."

Pam's face was still intent on something else. On Jerry's
mention of Leo Brass? What was this all about? She'd
battled and publicly with Leo even more fiercely than
Hannah.

Over a glass Pam asked Alix if she played tennis. Having earlier underestimated the English myself when it
came to personal floation devices, I was half-hoping Alix
would tell her, "Why, yes, I reached the round of sixteen

at Wimbledon before twisting my knee against Sanchez-Vicario."

Instead, Alix demurred. "Oh, you know . . . I'm really not match-fit, much more caught up these days in Native American efforts to gain recognition for Crispus Attucks. And about flushing Georgica Lake into the sea."

"Pond," I hissed, "Georgica Pond."

"Well, we're all aware it's hardly Loch Ness." She shot a hostile look at me.

Ashawag Hall was just about filled and we squeezed into seats upfront, which I didn't like because they made it harder to slip out if you were bored. The crowd was Baymen, mostly, plus some serious New Money landowners who didn't trust rabble-rousers like Brass and feared their wine cellars might be flooded or their taxes would go up. There were also the usual wealthy layabouts and retailers and accountants and mergers & acquisitions specialists and Manhattan dentists who'd done well in the market and thought they owed it to America to espouse causes. Even ones they didn't precisely understand.

George Plimpton had been called in to moderate the rally. He did that sort of thing very well and was also available, it was said somewhat mockingly, to tape TV commercials for a local pizza parlor or swimming pool contractor. I admired George immensely. But as a fellow Harvard man I secretly wished he were more discriminating in the enterprises he took up. *The Paris Review* was one thing; pizza parlors quite another. But there were lots of people here who liked George and, because he was quasi-official pyrotechnic adviser to East Hampton, they hoped he might set off a few. People enjoy a good fireworks show.

Billy Joel, as well, showed up. If the Baymen had an event, you could count on Billy. And there were just lots of people who liked Billy and hoped maybe he'd play a lit-

tle piano during the evening. East Hampton was a village
that enjoyed piano music and a good fireworks show. But
this was September and we had to be satisfied with Leo
Brass and The Gut. If that's what he genuinely had on his
mind; you couldn't always tell with Leo. Charisma he had;
consistency? Well, now that was something else. Maybe
there was a hurricane coming but right now, we had dry
brush, dry scrub pine, and most folks were more nervous
about that than a tropical storm and heavy rain. If the
brushfires ever got started again as they did Labor Day
weekend a year ago, it didn't really matter which side of
the snail darter debate or flushing The Gut you favored.

Leo was good. Like all effective demagogues, he conveyed an absolute sense of believing everything he said,
especially the rubbish. Brushing Plimpton aside (you'd
think Leo, too, had a Harvard degree), he addressed, not a
few fishermen in an echoing little hall, but a larger con-
stituency. Channel 12, the local community TV station,
had its camera there; there was a reporter from *Newsday,*
a woman from the *Times,* and Larry Penny, the naturalist
who wrote for the *East Hampton Star,* busily taking notes.
And Alix and me upfront. He saw us, all right, and nodded,
giving us a tight smile. Not saying hello but just marking
that we were there.

Before he started to speak, Alix hissed at me.

"You're right, you know."

"About what?"

"Hitler. He does look like 'a tall Hitler.' "

I hoped her voice didn't carry.

Leo's agenda? Just listen:

"Disaster is good.

"Nature's way of kicking us in the ass and balancing the
scales. You summer people don't understand that. Last
year's Labor Day pine barrens fire in Westhampton Beach
cleared the land. There are seeds that need heat to burst

open and germinate. Five years from now we'll have a better forest there. Let the whole damned place burn next time. This hurricane they're talking about? Good. We ought to have a Great Hurricane like '38 every generation. Scour the beaches, rinse the air, renew the ponds, knock down the dead trees.

"This isn't the Sierra Club. The Hamptons Baymen aren't tree-huggers, we're not amateurs. We're serious, professional, hardworking people, who live every day with nature, work every day with nature. If we don't collaborate with nature, sometimes nature gets up on its hind legs and kills us. We understand that, as well. Every few years a Bayman's boat goes down, a man drowns. We know, as dilettantes can't and tree-huggers won't, that when you rape the sea, when you rape the land, when you rape the sky, there's nothing left to reap or harvest or bring to net. Nature doesn't have to kill you to get even; it can starve you. Practical working people understand this. Farmers, ranchers, commercial fishermen. Spending a few weeks here in summer or dropping by weekends doesn't qualify you. You can't know. We *know.*"

The audience, which he'd just insulted as dilettantes who couldn't possibly *know,* loved it, breaking into applause.

"Here is our agenda for the year two thousand," Brass continued.

"He thinks long term," Alix said quietly, "got to give him that."

"The Unabomber thought long term as well."

"Hush," someone behind us said, hearing Alix and reading meaning into my verbalized thoughts. Alix smiled, sensing support for her point of view. But Leo was already talking, listing his priorities:

"The wetlands are at risk. Swimming pools seem to come first. We cannot permit the East Hampton wetlands to be crucified on a cross of chlorine. The following steps are essential and the very first of them involves foreign affairs and a need for the State Department to become vigorously involved."

He paused, and I must confess, we all leaned forward anticipating his next words. What was this all about, "foreign relations"? This was East Hampton, not Bosnia. What the hell did other countries have to do with chlorine in our swimming pools and whether they were overflowing into the local wetlands? Leo waited until the buzz fell. Then,

"Canada geese! There they are, in their thousands, shitting all over the fairways of the Maidstone Club, befouling the saline inlets and bays of the town, our precious freshwater ponds. Shitting on your lawn. And mine. Foreign birds, crossing our national borders to foul the playgrounds and ballfields of our small children." Leo threw a small bone to moneyed, older folks in the audience, people who had no small children and resented the level of school tax.

"Shitting on your Cadillacs and Mercedes. I studied this problem at MIT, how the acid content in their droppings is eating through nine coats of the finest factory paint on the best automobiles the industry can build."

He paused. We again leaned forward. I could hear Alix's breathing. It did nice, pneumatic things to her blouse and those young breasts within. Leo resumed:

"Washington does nothing about these lousy fowls. A totally supine reaction. No severe representations made to Ottawa. And why not? We didn't take this crap from Noriega? Why let the Canucks dump on us? Has someone been bought off? Or is it racism? Quite possibly." He rolled his eyes a bit, suggesting more than his words. Then, changing pace deftly, he came down a degree or two in fury and went on. "And when Americans, decent people, our countrymen, stand up to the threat? What hap-

pens then, when they resist the invading birds? Upstate in
Rockland County, Supervisor Charles Holbrook of Clarks-
town, rather than shoo away the damned birds, had them
shot, and the fresh meat, tasty at that, donated to the poor.
What happened? Two hundred pounds of goose meat was
seized by the state on grounds it was contaminated by
feathers, dirt, and traces of lead pellets. Starving Americans forbidden to eat a free meal of roast goose.

"In the name of God! Bob Cratchit and his goddamned
family were permitted a lousy goose. We're talking 'Geese
police' here. And think of what happened twelve years ago
when they did something about Canada geese up-island at
the Seawanee Golf and Country Club in Hewlett. Five
hundred geese died, mysteriously. The club had to pay
five thousand dollars in an out-of-court settlement following charges they'd salted golfing fairways with illicit
pesticides. The Lawrence Village Country Club purchased
a border collie to chase off the intruders. Did Washington
strike medals in honor of this splendid dog? Hell, no. The
good people of Lawrence Village ponied up the two thousand four hundred dollars themselves to pay for a
sonuvabitching collie to chase geese.

"Other places they floated helium-filled balloons to
scare off the geese or filled up soda cans full of marbles
and hired day laborers to rattle them loudly. The Fish and
Wildlife one time penned up thousands of geese and
shipped them south to the Carolinas by tractor trailer. And
the geese were back shitting on Long Island before the
trucks . . ."

"Pa and his chums," Alix whispered conspiratorially in
my ear so as not to distract Leo, "would have put paid to
this goose business in a month."

"How?" I asked, also whispering.

"Shotguns. A dozen or so middle-aged old chaps with
Purdey over-and-unders firing away, *bang! bang! bang!*"

Leo moved on in his agenda.

"Bring back the snapping turtle and control the duck population. Ban pesticides that run off following heavy rain into the ponds and bays. Give local stoop labor a break. Eliminate mechanical leaf blowers and let the Guatemalans make a dollar, illegal or not. No new swimming pools anywhere south of the Highway. Bring back ticket clerks to the railroad stations on the East End and do away with ticket-dispensing machines. Reduce the roundtrip cost of a Jitney ride into Manhattan and back."

And then, reaching his climax, he made his announcement about The Gut!

"There's maybe a hurricane coming. And contrary to how the Baymen traditionally vote on this question, this year we're having a small change of heart. We think maybe this year and this year only, we ought to flush early. Like this week."

Not even the Baymen were expecting this and a shocked murmur ran through the room.

"What's that all about?" Alix whispered.

"I dunno."

"But he's terrific. Super! His command of the language. He's got them on their feet even if I don't understand a word of it."

Nor did anyone else.

"He's been reading Bryan, the 'Cross of Gold' speech."

"Who's Bryan? What Cross of Gold?" Alix demanded.

"I'd rather explain about grunion."

From the row behind, people shushed us urgently.

Leo's local popularity among the roughnecks, and with women, as well as his backing by the Baymen might have carried the day. But it wasn't to be; The Walter jumped to his feet. And with reason; this was Mr. Walter Pincus who may have been East Hampton's wealthiest man with 120 acres bordering Georgica Pond, a figure so preposterously

self-important he was invariably (and to his delight) referred to as "The Walter." As was his custom, The Walter
was accompanied by a bodyguard and an attorney, and he
stood now, waving order papers and shouting:

"Brass, you can't just . . ."

The Walter and Leo were old enemies (both men derived a perverse pleasure from their enmity) and they
shouted back and forth, arguing whether and when The
Gut was to be flushed.

"Gosh!" Alix said, "this is wonderful stuff, all the shouting, like a Kings Road pub at closing time. When do they
begin throwing chairs?"

The Walter's voice boomed out one more time.

"The Gut, Brass! What about THE GUT?"

Momentarily, the room fell silent, waiting for an answer. What they got was a low growl:

"You leave The Gut to me. A John Deere backhoe or a
couple pounds of plastic explosive'll take care of The
Gut," Leo Brass said darkly. That lock of hair fell over
one eye and his mustache bristled. All you needed was an
armband and rousing rendition of "The Horst Wessel
Song."

Someone else tried then to get recognized to ask a question about the sacred Indian burial grounds of Montauk
and about some paleo-Indian artifacts recently unearthed.
But Leo and the acolytes and his phalanx of burly Baymen
were already gone, leaving The Walter, flanked by eminent
counsel and Pincus flunkies, cursing as he went.

"Can he do that?" Alix asked, her splendid Oxford education being broadened by the minute. "Can he blow up
The Gut?"

"Not legally. But he can. And may."

As we and everyone else maneuvered among the Ferraris and the pickups to find and get into our cars in the

dark and avoid being run over in the doing, Alix grabbed my arm.

"Isn't that Pam what's-her-name, Phythian?"

I looked around.

"Too late, she must have gotten into her car. I can't see her anymore."

"Maybe it was someone else."

"Probably was," Alix agreed. "Didn't you say she and Leo Brass were feuding?" We found the Chevy Blazer and got out of there safely. Which was something, considering that Leo had, after all, braced me that time at Boaters and then nearly whipsawed Alix and me both with Claire's towline. Odd, that Claire wasn't at the rally. And that Pam Phythian was, or at least was hanging around outside.

TWENTY-THREE

Part of the entourage, the bodacious O'Leary sisters,
nineteen and red-haired . . .

None of these little diversions, the pleasant or the painful,
must be permitted to get in the way of the piece I was
writing for Anderson about Hannah Cutting's life and
times. My first assignment, and I wasn't even close to getting anything new or exclusive or especially gripping on
her quite extraordinary life. The editor had called twice.
Patient, he was, admirably so. But you sensed there in his
voice a distinct edge, as if he was wondering to himself
just what he'd gotten in me. You know, the way a major
league baseball owner feels who signs a starting pitcher for
fifteen million for three years and is then informed the
guy has a sore arm or can't get his curve ball over the
plate. When Walter Anderson hired a contributor, he expected contributions.

I tried to shrug off Leo Brass and The Gut and Mr. Pincus and his armed guards and even being scared by speed-
boats as mere distractions. I'd catch up to Brass one of
these days and have it out. Let the rest of it lay.

Please do not think that after Labor Day East Hampton
simply empties out like a draining bathtub. Martha Stewart and Streisand and the Swami might be leaving or already have left but there remained a small yet resilient
permanent population plus a few new celebrities dropping
by, some drawn by the horse show, others by the upcom-

ing Film Festival, some here simply to enjoy September. We even had people like Meisel the fashion photographer, the one who'd created such a fuss for Calvin Klein with those commercials of juicy little boys in their underpants. Once that stir and outrage cooled and Calvin canceled the last few of his ads (the underwear line was already just about sold out, an enormous success!) to mollify the bluenoses, he and Meisel were thicker than ever. And with the autumn horse show season approaching, Calvin's on-and-off sort of wife, Kelly Klein, would be easing into her jodhpurs, very sleek indeed, going off to garner the old ribbons, leaving Calvin at liberty to enjoy himself.

And now, back came Felton, for several years considered, after Michael Ovitz, the most powerful man in Hollywood.

For someone who lived in Malibu, Sid Felton knew East Hampton intimately, having for a couple of summers rented the Regan (now the Johnson) place just off the Maidstone fairways. That was in his third wife's time; she had sinus problems and whined nasally (and endlessly) about the L.A. smog. That wife was long gone but Sid returned each year for the film festival, much as he did to Cannes and Sundance and Venice. This year, he would come early, drawn by Hannah's death. It was Labor Day when Sid first heard the news. By Tuesday he suspected there was a movie in it, not one of those crappy TV movies with Kathleen Turner but a class movie, a theatrical release, with Glenn Close or Susan Sarandon, and directed by de Palma, someone like that. With Nicholas Cage to play the cop.

There had to be a cop, didn't there? If there's a murder, you've got cops. By Wednesday Felton *knew* there was a movie in it and that night he and the usual entourage flew out to New York on the red-eye and were met at JFK by a convoy of limos that whisked them out to East Hampton and the 1770 House on Main Street, where four suites and several smaller rooms had been booked in Felton's name.

Sid was usually composed. But in moments of stress, he ate Kleenex. I mean that literally. He chewed and swallowed Kleenex. And in recent seasons, due to having had the occasional flop, he's eaten his share of tissues. Despite the flops and the Kleenex eating, *Entertainment Weekly,* in its annual compilation of the hundred most powerful people in Hollywood, still put Sid Felton at nine. His own self-assessment would have put him at effing-well five or six. Eight at the outside, but no higher!

And if you were one of the ten most important people in the industry, limos met you at airports and whisked you places and a 1770 House would set aside suites. Set aside a goddamned floor, if need be.

"Ginny, try keeping your sister from getting too stoned tonight, will you?"

"I'm Margie, Mr. Felton."

"Oh, sure. Well, both of you, try, okay? They're pretty stuffy here. A classy place like this, I get edgy."

"Yes, Mr. Felton."

These were the bodacious O'Leary sisters, nineteen-year-old identical, redheaded twins, an integral part of the Felton entourage, providing personal rather than professional services, and cited recently, both of them, as corespondents in the bill of divorcement of Mr. Felton's fourth wife.

Most of the press drawn by Hannah's death had gone back to Manhattan but Sid Felton's arrival gave the story a fresh spin. The *New York Post* sent Cindy Adams out to interview the mogul; a camera crew was dispatched by Regis and Kathie Lee, another by CNN. The flurry of renewed media coverage was such that one local wag re-

marked East Hampton really didn't need a film festival to
hype post–Labor Day business.

"Just bump off a celebrity every September!"

But Felton and his executive flunky were already out
walking the ground with a cinematographer and a second
unit director Sid trusted, looking up from the beach at the
"death stairs," as the tabloids called them, and considering
camera angles and lap dissolves, while the O'Leary twins
tripped along in Felton's wake, looking for all the world
like the *Baywatch* extras they had, in several episodes, actually been.

Felton was in many ways an appalling man but when it
came to movies, he was nobody's fool, having cut his professional teeth here in New York as one of Don Hewitt's
producers at *60 Minutes,* winning a handful of Emmys before the money (and the starlets) drew him west. There
followed the Oscars. And the wives. And a growing cyni-
cism that matched his talent, his success at making what
Hollywood called "high concept" films, those you could
describe in one or two sentences.

Bittersweet, which he was already using as a working
title for "the life and death of Hannah Cutting," was defi-
nitely a "high concept" movie.

"Think of it, the most glamorous and successful self-
made woman in America, and a looker as well, is found
stark naked, and also dead, on the beach of a spectacular
resort with a sharpened stake through her heart, and a
dozen of the most famous people in the country, plus a
drunken goddamned Indian and her own daughter, among
the suspects!"

It was so gripping a high concept, and so simple, that
Ginny and Margie, the O'Leary twins, thrilled even to
think of it. And wondered if there might be small roles
for them. *Variety* reported Felton was already talking by
cell phone to Joe Eszterhas about a script and quoted him

as saying, "Sure, Joe's written some flops. But memorable flops! No one forgets a Joe Eszterhas flop, never! I assure you."

There was talk, which made both Alix and me nervous, that Felton had information about Hannah's missing manuscript and was quietly talking to cops and others about its whereabouts, letting people know he had deep pockets and wouldn't be reluctant to pay a handsome gratuity to anyone who could locate Hannah's story. I asked Tom Knowles if it were so. The detective shook his head in resignation.

"He came around to the station asking questions yesterday. Beech, wearing an aloha shirt with a very obvious leather checkbook sticking out of his breast pocket and patting it affectionately from time to time. Got to say this for Sid Felton: subtle he ain't."

Each evening at cocktail hour Sid and his entourage, featuring the O'Leary girls in their microminis du jour, planted themselves decorously around several tables on the sidewalk in front of Frank Duffy's place, The Grill, on Newtown Lane. There they perched, enjoying a refreshment, signing the odd autograph, graciously waving at passersby, the curious drawn by Felton's fame, or the lascivious, eager to ogle the bodacious twins. For a day or two Felton's table tolerated Sudsy, gossip columnist for the local weekly paper (the job was unpaid but it got Sudsy invited to parties), permitting him to sit there among his betters and take notes. Until, writing too slowly for Sid's taste and missing too many Felton mots, and having to ask the great man to repeat them, Sudsy was banished.

Only Steven Spielberg, who had long owned an East Hampton house, seemed to find Felton truly offensive and crossed to the opposite side of the street when passing, so as to avoid having to say hello to a man he despised.

* * *

We got hold of Jesse the next morning. The weather was holding, whatever was happening down there in the Caribbean, with sun and low humidity and a few billowy, pillowy clouds only helping define the blue sky. I told Tom Knowles what I was going to do.

"Oh, shit, Beech. You and Her Highness and Jesse? Why, compared to the trouble you'll get into, Wounded Knee was a promising start." Tom never was a great one for having faith.

Jesse, however, liked the idea. Though, typical of him, he was carping from the first. "Don't expect me to betray my own people, Beech. I won't turn in Shinnecocks. Nor other Native Americans regardless of tribal affiliation. I won't play stooge for the Bureau of Indian Affairs, those conniving, graft-ridden bastards. I tell you upfront that I'll . . ."

"Jesse, shuddup. This is a murder you didn't do . . ."

". . . though I might have, Beecher. Never forget that. I am capable of enormous violence when provoked. There have been occasions when . . ."

His pickup followed us back to Further Lane and turned in on the gravel. Alix made tea for herself and Jesse and I drank instant coffee. We sat on the patio and talked.

Since I was leveling with Jesse, at least to an extent, there was no longer any valid reason for keeping Her Ladyship in the dark. So I told her about my talk with Royal Warrender, about what I'd learned up in Polish Town in Riverhead, what Miz Phoebe remembered, all of it.

She listened. But then, "That still doesn't tell us anything about where the manuscript is. And that's why I'm here, y'know."

She was right. But now with Jesse, there'd be three of us looking for it. That was progress, wasn't it? I didn't yet let her in on the fact the laptop had been thoroughly scoured by parties unknown and there might not even be a manuscript anymore. If she were convinced of that, and more importantly if she sent coded E-mails to Harry Evans and if he accepted this unhappy reality, Alix would very shortly be back in her Jag, heading for the LIE and Manhattan. And I was getting more than accustomed to having her around.

She sort of looked at me as if to say none of the above was getting us anywhere. I forgave her. Oxford University was a grand place, I was sure. It didn't necessarily prepare you for actual life.

Then I told Jesse I wanted to know whom he'd seen around while he was working at Hannah's place. Not the Kroepkes or the regulars, but others.

"You mean like Leo Brass?"

"No, no. He's Claire's boyfriend. Of course he'd be around."

Jesse shook his head.

"Him and Hannah, they had something going on with them that Claire didn't know about. Should I go on . . . ?"

Yes, I said, he should go on.

Hannah and a local Bayman? Even one as celebrated as Brass. And one whom she'd publicly cursed out in a nasty squabble over wetlands. That was something I hadn't figured, not with all her social-climbing, New Money ways, and her impatience with Claire who was wasting her time with local rednecks and . . .

. . . who was also sleeping with young and very active Mr. Brass?

I thought I'd better tell Jesse Maine about Leo's speedboat intimidation. "He just being nasty, Jesse, or is there something more to it?" The Shinnecock didn't waste breath on speculation but nodded and took in the information to be looked into at the appropriate moment.

"Who else, Jesse?"

"Andy Cutting," he said. "Andy's around a lot. Looking

like a sick cow and feeling sorry for himself." Then, after a slight hesitation, considerate of Alix, "He's a peeper as well. D'you know that, Beech? Likes to look through windows. I don't know if he checks out what all the local beauties wear to bed, but he sure does keep tabs on what his ex-wife's up to after hours and in private and intimate moments."

That puzzled me. I knew Andy was still carrying a torch for Hannah and looking pitiful. I didn't peg him for a peeping tom stalking his own ex-wife. Then Jesse tossed in a surprise candidate.

"Well, Royal's been there, too. Now why would you think after all those years that Royal might come around? His drunken cousin Jasper, sure. But Royal, maybe our next President? Or at least CEO of a major conglomerate."

We talked about the permutations of that and then I leveled with Jesse about the missing manuscript, without mentioning it might or might not have been on personal computer. Hell, if Jesse'd stolen it from the laptop, he knew already. If not, maybe he could help find it. "You want to ask around, Jesse? No questions asked if it gets turned over. Might even be a modest reward."

Before Jesse got back into his pickup and set off on errands I didn't even want to know about, he squinted at the sky south of us, out over the ocean.

"Hurricane coming, Beech. Oughta keep an eye out."

"When?"

"Oh, four days, maybe five. If it comes and I think it just might."

"Oh, hell," I said, "they usually blow out to sea."

"Hope you're right," Jesse said, "but I don't think so. Sometimes they make the turn and come up the coast at us."

That was when Her Ladyship spoke up:

"I'd listen to Mr. Maine, Beecher. Red Indians or, as one ought to call them, Native Americans, are closer to na-

ture than we are and they know such things. They have
their ways, don't they, Mr. Maine, the Great Manitou and
all that?"

"Well, Lady Alix, I guess some do. Me, every morning
I watch *The Weather Channel.*"

"Oh," she said, considerably deflated.

As if he too, like Jesse, could predict nature and knew
a hurricane might be headed for the Hamptons, with time
becoming of the essence, Evans was calling more fre-
quently to hector his personal emissary into greater speed
of action.

"Of course, Harry," I could hear her soothingly assure
him. "And Mr. Stowe's been awfully helpful. I'd say we'll
be hot on the trail of the manuscript within a matter of
hours. You should be receiving messages in cipher on a
regular basis from here on."

Evans apparently interrupted her and she actually listened for a time.

"Yes, Harry, we've heard those reports out here about
Mr. Felton offering rewards for Hannah's story. But local
authorities consider him something of a windbag and I'm
confident we'll get there first on behalf of Random House.
Mr. Stowe has allies among the authorities and even has a
Red Indian assisting us. Marvelous chap. Squints at the
sky and tells one if there are hurricanes about."

Evans must have said something along the lines of
"What the hell are you talking about?" Didn't faze Alix a
bit, nor did she draw breath:

"Absolutely, he's a sachem or chief of enormous standing. And one of the best informed authorities on the life
and achievements of the late Crispus Attucks of Boston, a
pivotal figure in Colonial history, as well. His name is
Jesse Maine and he's a wizard at predicting things. Mr.
Stowe says he's unerring." She paused, thoughtful. "Perhaps it isn't a sachem that he is, Harry, but a shaman. I'll

check and get back to you on the E-mail with details as to the correct term. But he is cracking good and you can count on us to recover Hannah's story."

We had cocktails and smoked cigarettes and then, as if she were trying to plumb my depths, or perhaps she was just bored, Alix said:

"What really happened there in Algiers, Beecher? When you were shot."

I liked her a lot but I wasn't quite sure I really want to talk about Algiers. My father heard the story. So had Walter Anderson and a few others. Not many people. No matter how noble you'd been or what heroics you'd performed, you weren't eager to go into detail about having been shot in the ass.

"I'll tell you about it sometime," I said, vague and not very enthusiastic, and poured us both a fresh martini.

When she didn't say anything more and I suspected was sulking, I retreated into the usual psychobabble, saying people oughtn't dwell on the unpleasant without first filtering the experience through the seine of time. . . .

"Oh, poof!" Alix said. "If you don't choose to tell me, fine. But don't talk rubbish."

You had to like her, with her built-in shit detector. I was getting to like her more with every day. But then, I was vulnerable.

I don't know how long I'd been asleep when Alix woke me.

"Beecher, there's something going on out there," she whispered, bending over my bed so I could hear. Her hair hung long and loose, she looked sleepy in the half light of a moon through my window, she smelled warm and wonderful in an oversized cotton T-shirt. I sat up.

"What, what?" I asked, still only partially awake.

"Listen," she said.

There was something. A raccoon at the garbage? Wind

in the chimneys? A red fox hunting in the hedges? A prowler? Andy Cutting looking through windows? Old houses make their own sounds in the night.

I swung out of bed, naked, and grabbed khaki shorts from the chair and yanked them on. Then, barefoot, and clutching an old sand wedge from the battered golf bag leaning against the wall, I went downstairs, Alix following so close behind I could feel her breath on my neck.

"Stay upstairs," I said.

"No."

She was always open to reason, Alix was.

At the kitchen door I paused to listen. Nothing. I opened the door slowly and stepped out onto the flagstone. It felt cool, pleasantly so, damp. I walked out onto the lawn. The grass was wet. Dew. Above, stars and a sliver of moon. Behind me, still close, Alix. I hefted the sand wedge in my right hand, ready. What a fool I'd feel like if it was just a raccoon or a garbage hound rooting amid the trash bins. Yet I hoped it was a dog or a 'coon and not . . .

There I heard the noise and almost simultaneously was blinded by a brilliant light and felt the blow and began to fall. After that, nothing . . .

"There now, Beecher, just lie still and try to count back from ten. Take your time, speed is hardly essential, slowly is fine. But I do need to know if you've got concussion."

Alix was kneeling over me where I lay on the grass and my head was wet. But it wasn't blood. Or not all blood. Just a kitchen towel she'd wet under the faucet and wrapped turbanlike around my head.

"Ouch." It was still tender and Alix was probing.

"You're not counting," she chided me. "Ten, nine, eight . . ."

"I can count very nicely on my own, thank you."

"Seven, six, five . . ."

God, but she was pushy.

"Who slugged me? You see?"

"Large chap. Don't know him. Barely caught a glimpse. He swung something at you, I could hear the crack when it hit your head, you went down, and I was more concerned about you than identifying him. He blinded me with a flashlight of sorts and was off in an instant so by the time I looked up again, we were here alone, you and I. Sorry, Beecher, I should have been more alert."

Probably that was the same light that blinded me and possibly it was the flashlight he'd used to knock me out.

"How long have I . . ."

"Oh, gosh, not more than a few moments. The instant I applied cold compresses you began to stir. I say, you do have adventures, Beecher. Nothing dull about you."

From inside the house I could hear an unearthly howl. Now what the hell . . . ?

"Poor Mignonne, I sprang from bed so suddenly to wake you about prowlers, the poor dog must be petrified."

"Have it bark backwards for a bit. That should do it."

Alix gave me a look.

"Don't just lie there, Beecher, the grass is sopping. You'll have rheumatism or something."

"Yes, ma'am."

"*Ooooww,*" the poodle howled.

"I'm coming, I'm coming," she called out as she headed back to the house. I got myself up. Well, could be worse. Alix got into a robe and I toweled off and made coffee and we talked about it for a while—who it might have been and should we call the police—and then deciding the constructive course might be to get some sleep, we headed for our respective bedrooms.

"Beecher?"

"Yes?"

"I was quite right about you, right from the start."

"What?"

"You ARE a hard case. And I am pleased you don't have concussion."

"Yeah, well . . ."

She moved in close enough to me that her T-shirted nipples brushed lightly against my bare chest and reached up on her toes to kiss me very chastely but awfully pleasantly on the lips.

"G'night, Beecher."

I stood there watching her back and her legs as she headed for her bedroom.

"Eight, four, seven, three . . ."

She turned her head, briefly, to look back.

"And witty, as well," she said tartly. But smiling, too.

Except that in the morning neither of us was smiling. Not after Alix found a sharpened, fire-hardened stake of privet hedge driven and viciously so through the soft tan glove leather upholstery of her Jag's driver's seat. Had I been hit with the thick end, as happened to Hannah? And if so, how fortunate was I not to have gotten the spear end of the damned thing as well?

Was the whole business a warning or something more?

TWENTY-FOUR

*Who pays your salary, Rupert Murdoch
or Harry Evans . . . ?*

For no reason except that he was large (Alix's description) and hostile and had knocked me about on earlier occasions, I fixed on Leo Brass as our late-night prowler. Though what the devil he had to gain from snooping and pooping around my place was hard to figure. Sheer intimidation? Might be. Leo's weird sense of humor? Neither Alix nor I knew anything that could damage Brass except that he'd nearly run us down with a speedboat. But it was clear I'd been challenged three times now, twice inarguably by Leo at Boaters and on the water, and a third time, maybe by him again. Since Alix had seen him on his Ashawag Hall soapbox, I questioned her pretty closely. No, she still couldn't say. She'd been blinded by the flash; it had been too dark. He could have been Brass, he was that large, but beyond that, no.

I flirted briefly with the idea of not reporting the incident on grounds it might cause more talk and trouble than it was worth. But with a stake of privet driven through Alix's car seat, that might constitute withholding evidence not in a mere trespass and assault, but in a previous murder. So I called Tom.

"This might be copycat stuff, Beech," he said after having handed the privet over to the lab boys. "The weapon that killed Hannah was whittled by knife and then hard-

ened in flame. This one was milled and then burned. Could
be the same wacko both times but probably not. I'll check
into who owns milling gear around here. Pin down Leo
Brass's whereabouts if I can. How's your head? The lab
found a little blood we assume is yours on the meat end of
the stake."

I was fine, I said. And was. Except that I was building
one hell of a grudge against Leo Brass and thought the
time had come when we'd better have a little talk.

While with Royal Warrender you might be best off
using subtlety and sneaking up on him after getting cousin
Jasper stewed, with Leo Brass you were every bit as truculent as he was. You walked right up to Leo and punched
him in the face to get his attention. Maybe if I got him sore
enough, he'd lose his cool and tell me something. But
when I tried the theory on Alix Dunraven, she pointed out
its one inarguable flaw.

"Isn't he just slightly larger than you, Beecher?"

There was that.

"Perhaps you could send Mr. Maine. He's rather intim-
idating."

I know she was just trying to be helpful but I hated to
have my masculinity questioned.

"No, this is something I've got to do." You don't go
prowling around a man's house late at night, scaring the
poodle, then slug someone with a stake of privet and put
holes in the car upholstery for no reason and get away
with it. Not when it's someone else's dog and my head
and Alix's car and a Jag at that.

But Alix was right about Brass. Not only was he larger
than I, he was a local hero, leader of the Baymen and their
one intellectual, a "green" who knew more than most people about the environment but too rugged to be a "tree-
hugger." His most recent feud with Hannah (hardly their
first) dealt with her purchase of a forty-acre potato field,

one of the last of that size on Further Lane, which she intended to subdivide and sell off for pricey homes at a substantial profit. Brass accused Hannah of ecological rape; she called him a Trotskyite advocating the redistribution of wealth.

I felt possessive myself about that same field. My father liked to tell the story of the time two little girls, about ten, who came to his kitchen door in sheer terror because a local cop cruising past had caught them in that very field, picking up potatoes the harvesting machine missed, and threw such a scare into them my dad had to let them hide out until the police dragnet was suspended. "One of the kids was Heather Robertson, Cliff's daughter with Dina Merrill."

He liked recalling the imagery, that of the daughter of one of the richest women in America and a Hollywood movie star, scavenging for potatoes in a field on Further Lane.

I drove the Blazer but Alix came with me. Just in case I might not feel up to driving home . . . afterwards. I knew how athletic Leo was and with a considerable rep as a fighter. I did have, though Her Ladyship didn't know it, a sort of secret weapon. Which I now told her about, keeping it brief but reassuring.

"Don't be too sure I'm entirely at Leo's mercy. I do have my 'Nixons.' "

"Oh, and just what are they, Beecher? Some variety of crossbow or broadsword?"

I ignored the sarcasm.

"My father was in naval intelligence in a lot of dodgy places during the Cold War and they assigned him a driver-bodyguard who was a career Marine. He sort of adopted me. His name was Guns and he was pretty clever with his fists. And his elbows. And his feet. I was a skinny thirteen-year-old and Guns taught me what he called

'Nixons,' for 'dirty tricks.' I'm a little out of practice but they usually come back."

"Were you prevented from using them recently in Algiers? And damaged as a result?" she asked.

"Well, yeah, a little. My 'Nixons' don't work so well on a mob. But I'm fine now."

Astonishing what this young woman knew. An impressive store of useless knowledge. And she now surprised me again. "It was Leo Brass, wasn't it, who competed at university in the decathlon?"

"Yes, hell of an all-around athlete. Why?" I assumed she was trying to warn me off a confrontation with such a formidable foe.

"Because one of the ten disciplines in the decathlon is javelin-throwing. Mightn't that suggest a link between a spear of sharpened privet and the ferocious Mr. Brass?"

Could be, I admitted. Could also be a red herring offered up to incriminate the innocent and toss a little obscuring dust.

Leo lived out by Louse Point which, despite its name, is a nice neck of land at the east side of Accobonac Harbor. Wonderful boating, nice beach, good fishing when they were running. "Louse Point?" Alix said, turning it over on her tongue to enjoy the dreadful sound of it. "Louse Point."

"Now you stay in the car. Just in case . . ."

"But you have your 'Nixons,' Beecher. We're relying heavily on those, y'know."

"Sure."

I wish I felt as confident as she did. All the Winston Churchill bravado, that magnificent wartime defiance toward a more powerful Nazi foe, seemed to have come down to Alix through the genes. Or did they issue stuff like that at Oxford?

Fortunately, Leo wasn't home.

Claire came out, looking sulky but nothing like the whipped girl Hannah bullied. More pugnacious. Each time I'd seen her since Hannah's death, she'd matured, grown stronger. "He's out in the boat," she said.

I couldn't resist.

"Running down canoes?"

"Go to hell. That was just teasing. If Leo wanted to he could have cut your canoe in half. And you with it!"

"I suppose he could." No point arguing. And I was pretty relieved not to have to fight Leo Brass, at least not yet.

Claire's mood swings were something. Last time she'd come to apologize. I wondered what she'd say if she heard what Jesse said about her boyfriend. And her mother. I must say, Claire was looking pretty good despite everything. If she ever traded in those glasses, well . . .

But she was again hostile. "Reporters," she snarled, "bloodsuckers! Feeding off death, snooping for scandal. Even the cops finally had the decency to take down the yellow ribbons and go away. Page Six and the *Enquirer* went home. But you keep sniffing around."

I told her I only wanted to know what Leo was up to, why she and Leo tried to scare us off. I didn't mention our midnight prowler; I was keeping that one for Leo himself.

"Just stay away. And that includes Hannah's place—*my* place on Further Lane. I told the Kroepkes. You come messing around there and I'll . . ."

I thought I could again smell beer on her breath but this wasn't the time or place to discuss the Volstead Act. There was a bit more of her shouting and then I got back in the Blazer and Alix drove us off.

"Well . . ." I said.

"Yes, well, Beecher. I do admire the way you stood up to Mr. Brass. Even if he wasn't there."

"Thanks."

"But I think it's time we delve somewhat more deeply into the case. How can we determine just who was most fearful of what Hannah's book might tell? Who could be most damaged by her revelations? Had the most to lose? Claire and Leo or someone else? I know they're unpleasant, but are we wasting time on them when it's someone else entirely? Isn't it logical to explore things like that?"

She was very brisk. I think Alix felt cheated, disappointed Brass and I hadn't had a fight.

Couldn't blame her. You come all this way, you want to see the show.

"Might Leo have killed Hannah?" she asked, thoughtful.

"He could have. But don't forget, he found the body. Wouldn't that be calling down suspicion on himself?"

"But they always return to the scene of the crime. Or so I've read."

"That's an old wives' tale."

"Not in my experience," she said. "Don't you recall McCray the Hammersmith Strangler?"

We ended up at the Parrot, drinking Mexican beer and munching tortilla chips. Royal Warrender. He was the one that intrigued her. "Is it possible I might meet him? I mean, without being obvious about it?"

I didn't think so, I said. But I'd give it some thought.

When we got back to the gatehouse there was a message from Random House. Not the boss this time. Evans was apparently too annoyed to get on the phone himself. An aide informed Lady Alix that Page Six of the *New York Post* had a report Random House had panicked over the possibility its million-dollar manuscript was missing from Hannah Cutting's house, that perhaps such a manuscript had never even existed, and since Hannah was dead, no one could say. Random House had a dozen editors and private eyes on the case, pestering wealthy people and tracking down clues all over East Hampton. The newspaper gave as one of its sources on the story "local community activist Leo Brass, the man who found Hannah's body on Labor Day Sunday."

The message to Alix from Random House: "Bring back Hannah's book or don't come back yourself." Put more tactfully, of course. Book publishers are polite folk.

"Oh, dear, they do sound cross." Usually, she shrugged things off. Now she actually looked concerned and sat down at the Louis Vuitton laptop to rattle off some more E-mail to Harry Evans, telling him God knows what in, I assume, six-figure code signed with the names of horses.

I was sore myself and not for the first time at Leo. "Community activist," indeed. I'd activate him! But I was also aggravated at Page Six and realized how dumb that was. I was a newsman letting my feelings for Alix get me in a mood to kill stories and suppress rumors.

Then next morning, by what seemed extraordinary coincidence (until I thought about it), a car pulled up and Warrender's manservant came to the door. Our invitation to dinner was on creamy cardboard, handwritten, as these old WASPs do. Very last minute, Royal's note admitted apologetically, but they were juggling dates with the hurricane coming.

"Want to have dinner with Royal Warrender?" I asked Lady Alix, being very cool.

"Oh, you are the clever one." Had to say this about Alix, she didn't brood, and was already quite cheery.

"Yes, aren't I?"

The truth was that Royal hadn't suddenly dived headlong into the Hamptons' social scene but was simply carrying out an annual ritual of the Maidstone Club, which one of its governors would as likely have flaunted as a member of the College of Cardinals would have snubbed the Pope.

Whatever she'd E-mailed Random House seemed to have resonated with Evans, who now phoned her directly. And instead of reacting to the Page Six business and fobbing the editor off with excuses, she attempted to distract him with tantalizing hints of another book entirely:

". . . I realize all that, Harry, and you're entirely right to be miffed. But not since the Sepoy Rebellion has there been someone like this fellow Crispus Attucks. A Gandhi of his time, a Mandela or a Bishop Tutu, and we shot him down there in the snows of Boston. Shocking, I say, Harry, even at the remove of two centuries. Had he lived, he might have been a Jefferson or Washington even if, as a gentleman of color, he might not have gotten due notice. But Chief Maine has all the data, chapter and verse, and I beg to suggest that, given the proper editing, a book on Mr. Attucks could make him bigger than your chum Salman Rushdie."

There was a substantial pause. After which, Alix said:

"No, no, Harry. Mr. Attucks is dead. Jesse Maine is our chap. Put him together with one of your finest young editors and I'm reasonably sure we'll have a best-seller that may, given the proper promotion, succeed in . . ."

I don't think Evans was buying her act anymore. When she hung up she was chewing her lower lip as if wondering, where do we go from here? But it wasn't only her failures with Random House that were eating at her.

"Beecher, these are desperate moments."

"Oh?"

"Yes; at Princeton, did you study ethics? I'm in something of a dilemma and I could use a little ethical counsel." It occurred to me she was a bit of a nut on ethics but didn't say so.

"Harvard. I went to Harvard, not that other place."

"Oh, I am sorry."

"It's okay. As to ethics, my old man's the one. He always knows right from wrong. But try me, I'll tell you as best I can."

What happened was that London had called. *The Times.* Murdoch owned *The Times* of London as well as the *Sun* with its Page Three Girls and the book publishing house of HarperCollins, where Alix was an editor. Murdoch also owned the *Post* in New York with its busybodies of Page Six. The pieces were falling into place and now someone over there was pressing her for a first peek at Hannah's manuscript, if and when. Why should some Yank reporter get there first? Wasn't as if Alix were an employee of Random House. Her firm was HarperCollins. The Random House business was pro tem and honorary. She had sacred responsibilities and loyalties to London, not to New York.

"As if I were a leftenant in the First Fusiliers and had been seconded to the King's Own Scottish Borderers," she said. "Or at least that was how they put it to me. My primary allegiance was to the old regiment."

"To Rupert and *The Times.*"

She looked gloomy.

"That's what they were telling me. But what would you do, Beecher?"

I'd never been very good at such questions and admitted as much. "Do what you think is right, Alix. To whom do you owe professional loyalty? To HarperCollins or Random House?"

"Oh, God, I dunno." She loved HarperCollins but was proud of her Godwin Award and grateful to people in New York, who'd been welcoming and gracious.

When she froze up and didn't answer, I said:

"Tomorrow, when you wake, and before you think or make cold, rational judgments, are you a Brit or a Yank?

The First Fusiliers or the King's Own? Who pays your salary, Rupert Murdoch or Harry Evans?"

She regarded me in agony. An ethical quandary on top of Page Six and threats from Random House.

"Oh, shit," she said.

TWENTY-FIVE

*It made the turn! The hurricane made
the damned turn!*

Desperation inspires rash acts. So does too frequent the
rereading, at an impressionable age, of books like *The
Thirty-nine Steps.*

Buchan's thrillers are meant to be read and enjoyed but
not acted upon as practical guides to conduct in the wan-
ing years of the twentieth century. I don't mean that Alix
Dunraven followed literally the example of Sir Richard
Hannay and his World War One—era chums as they confounded and battled The Hun, but the accounts of their
adventures and defiantly gorgeous gestures in the face
of adversity and peril surely planted seeds. So that now
at a moment when she should have been keenly focused
on the recovery of Hannah's unfinished manuscript, Her
Ladyship decided admirably, if not prudently, to do a
Madeleine Albright and negotiate peace between the war-
ring factions.

Without letting me in on it, she drove up to meet Claire
Cutting to see if between the two of them, something
might be sorted out to prevent Leo Brass and me from
damaging each other. Though, as she later confessed, Alix
wasn't nearly as concerned about Leo's health as about
mine. Which didn't say much for her confidence in my
"Nixons" but was nonetheless very sweet.

To this moment I don't know precisely what went on

between the two women but when Alix and the poodle got
back to Further Lane and skidded to her usual racing stop
on the gatehouse gravel, she was smiling broadly.

"My watch says nearly four, Beecher. We've not much
time. She insists you and Leo foregather on neutral ground
and we're to be down there on the beach by five."

Alix was wearing olive green corduroy jeans, sneakers,
and a "Smashing Pumpkins" T-shirt so she didn't have
much changing to do.

"What the hell are you talking about?"

It rushed out of her then.

"We're meeting Leo Brass at five down by The Gut.
Claire said that's where he wanted it to be and when. Quite
precise about it, she was, five P.M. at The Gut. I said, I
suppose Beecher will know where that is and she laughed.
Rather rude of her, I must say. You do know where it is,
don't you?"

Yes, I knew where The Gut was. What I didn't know
was whatever possessed Alix to . . .

"Well, I drove up to see Claire and I laid it right out. If
Beecher comes up here again and Leo's at home, there's
certain to be ill-feeling and all sort of difficulty. Even violence. I told her that in plain language. Much as in *The
Three Hostages* Dick Hannay told off that cad Medina
after he'd spit in Sir Richard's face while Hannay was pretending to be hypnotized. I told Claire we knew Leo was
behind that midnight prowl and the stake of privet through
my car seat and the cudgeling of your poor head and we
simply weren't going to stand for it anymore. What with
my Random House connections and yours with *Parade*
magazine and that nice Mr. Anderson of yours, we were
anything but helpless. And you have various police officers as chums, besides.

"I suggested you and Leo meet and talk it all out like
civilized people and not go bashing each other like angry

children. Or rugby players in a pub. Negotiate an armistice
of sorts, the way the Germans and Russia met at Brest-
Litovsk and hammered out a truce. Your only interest was
writing a story about the late Hannah Cutting's remarkable
life and times, and mine was in retrieving a manuscript
she'd sold to Random House and that now was missing.
Neither you nor I was the least bit interested in trashing
Hannah or discomfitting Mr. Brass. We had, in fact, and I
told her this with considerable emphasis, even attended
his recent speech at what was the name of that hall? . . .
and had sat there most attentively and in agreement, to a
great extent, with his defense of the wetlands and so on
from those dreadful geese flying down from Canada that
have him concerned. And rightly so."

Okay, I said. She hadn't left me much choice, had she,
dammit? Refusing to meet Leo now would brand me either
a coward or mulishly stubborn.

We drove down Lily Pond Lane to West End and as
close as we could get by road and then drove along the
beach another half mile and parked the Blazer and shucked
our shoes. I showed her the pond and The Gut and the jetties they have down there. We don't have many East
Hampton jetties and a good thing, too. Jetties cause all
that erosion there along Dune Road in Westhampton. Or so
most people believe. There was a fisherman out on a jetty
surfcasting and west of The Gut you could see people
strolling or a kid throwing pebbles into the surf. We
walked along, the water washing against our feet and an-
kles, still September warm. It felt good. No Leo Brass, no
Claire Cutting. I looked at my watch.

"What time did you say, five?"

"Yes. She was crisp about it, 'five, precisely,' Claire
told me, 'at The Gut.' Though to tell the truth, I had no
idea where it might be but knew that you would."

Good. Maybe they weren't coming. Maybe I wouldn't have to fight Leo after all. I was here and he wasn't. I began to feel pretty good when Alix said:

"Splendid, and right on time. Here they come."

Great. I watched Leo's pickup roll along the beach toward us with only marginal enthusiasm.

"Remember now, Beecher," Alix whispered as they got out and came toward us, "be patient. They didn't sign the Treaty of Versailles the very first day of the conference."

Brest-Litovsk and Versailles; she thought large, in global terms, you had to admit.

It was reasonably polite if not exactly chummy to start with handshakes and hellos. It was a nice day with the sun still up and a fairly good surf but metronomic, no chaotic chop or crosscurrents but nice big waves coming in and breaking, and the four of us stood there at the edge, water lapping at our bare feet where the waves washed up and then fell back down the slope. But once we'd gotten past the pleasantries, as was his style, Leo started in, Mister Bombast.

"Let me tell you, Beecher, I'm not a man to be pushed. Not a bit of it. I saw plenty of your kind up there in Cambridge the year I spent at MIT, all you WASPs secure and smug in your frayed button-down shirts and old tweeds and flannels, your properly worn cordovan shoes. And I was the outsider trying so hard to do the right thing and shined my shoes and wore a proper suit to class just to show respect. What good did that do me? The suit was polyester and my shoes wrong and you snickered at it. At me . . ."

Not me, I said, I never . . .

Brass waved a large, dismissive hand. "Oh, hell, I know that. Don't be so literal. It was guys like you, Harvard men. I'd see you around, people like you and Plimpton in the old school tie, meeting with a wink and a nod and exchanging the secret handshake. 'Penn State? Penn State? Oh, dear, he must be a coal miner, the ruffian . . .' "

Even now, and sore, Leo's gift for mimicry was pretty good. I could hear nasal Boston in his tone, see Harvard Yard in his gestures. And could sense class resentment that went deeper than either words or gestures.

"I know all about the media, too. You fellows looking for dirt, hassling people, stealing the photo of the dead kid right off the grieving goddamned mother's night table. I've seen plenty of it and right here in East Hampton. Bunch of phonies, preening and posturing about their by-lines, while all the time they're . . ."

Claire stood next to him with Alix a few yards off from me, toying with a bare foot in the sand, moving a seashell around aimlessly. For once she was silent. Claire looked sore but she, too, kept her mouth shut. Let Leo and me paw the ground and snort. I guess that's how the women felt. Some summit conference. Leo picked it up again.

"That's another thing about Boston, me slaving over the Bunsen burner in labs, carrying a full academic sked, working nights behind a Cambridge bar, and driving a bulldozer weekends on construction sites for rent money, and you a hotshot on the *Globe*, hanging with the Kennedys."

"The hell I . . ."

"Sure you did. I read all about it. With the pull you had, you should have stayed in the navy. You'd be halfway to admiral by now."

"I wasn't in the navy. That was my old man."

There was an edge to our dialogue now and Alix stepped in brightly, looking to defuse it. "I met an admiral once," she said. "Pa had him to dinner at the house. Randy old chap. I wasn't sixteen and he had a hand on my leg before the savory was served. I told all the girls at school and they were agog. The admiral and I were quite the topic for about a week."

Claire knit her brow and Leo stared for a moment. Then he picked up again:

"Well, your Ladyship, I can tell you and your pal Stowe here there are mighty changes coming. A time when family connections and school ties don't matter. It'll be the new men, not old admirals but the technocrats who know all this shit, that'll take over and run things. We'll . . ."

"Oh, tosh," Alix said. "I've heard all that rubbish before about 'the new men.' The Labour Party trots it out every election and then the Tories win again. I'm sure Tony Blair will be standing there in Commons and droning on about 'the new men' until the very moment the government changes again."

Well played, Alix, I thought. But Claire reacted.

"You're not in England now. This is the United States where . . ."

Leo didn't let his girlfriend stop him either.

"Clear, clean water, protected wetlands, an end to pollution and acid rain, reasonable limits on striped bass, liberalized rules for the haulseiners. More snapping turtles and fewer ducks in the ponds. A genuine crackdown on Canada geese that goes far beyond what . . ."

I let Leo go on for a bit more and then I'd had enough.

"Leo, was it you who came skulking around my place the other night? Who walloped me over the head and vandalized the Jag?"

He just looked at me, furious. Leo wasn't used to being challenged. And certainly not interrupted while in full oratorical flight. I didn't feel great about doing it but at some point you've got to call the guy on this stuff. Instead of answering, he went to his best pitch—the Brass bluster.

"Don't you try pushing me around, Stowe. I know your

old man's a big deal and you're this big foreign correspondent. But I ain't answering questions when how the
hell do I know if you're wearing a wire or your girlfriend
here. I know my rights and won't be bullied."

"I can assure you, Mr. Brass, as I told Claire earlier
today, my sole objective in all this is . . ."

"You talk too much," Claire said.

Alix turned to her:

"Why, Claire," she said sweetly and not meaning it,
"and how *loudly* you talk. I hadn't noticed until just now."

That was when Claire flew at her and both Leo and I
stepped in to break it up. The women were fighting while
Leo and I attempted to make peace and just then, a shout
stopped us all.

"HEY!"

It was Jesse Maine in his pickup, racing toward us
across the sand. We all four swiveled toward him, hostilities temporarily suspended.

"Hurricane's comin'!" Jesse shouted. "Hurricane's
comin'!"

The pickup skidded to a stop and he jumped out.

"It made the turn!" he shouted. "The damned hurricane
made the turn!"

Then, more quietly, "Well, hello there, Your Ladyship,
Claire, Leo, and Beech. You folks better break up this little tea party and start getting ready. We got a couple of
days but Hurricane Martha's headed for East Hampton."

Alix shook her head in admiration.

"You and *The Weather Channel*, Jesse. You're amazing."

I was staring out at the ocean and the sky. Was it my
imagination or had a veil already insinuated itself between
earth and the lowering sun? I glanced over and Leo, too,
was looking out with an eye far more practiced than my
own, looking up, gauging the wind, scrutinizing the sky.

"Come on," he said, to Claire I guess but maybe to all of us, "there's work to be done."

"Here at The Gut, Leo?" Claire said.

"Here and elsewhere. Lots of places, lots to do. But yeah, here at The Gut."

TWENTY-SIX

The Survivors Supper was that night . . .

It was something of a tradition, one which I'd forgotten, ever since '38 (with time out for the War), for the Maidstone to host a "Survivors Supper" after Labor Day. Evening dress, of course.

This year it was Royal Warrender's turn to play host. He was too young to have endured the Great Hurricane of 1938, "a wind to shake the world" as one contemporary witness called it, but he knew the stories. And older members, such as Miz Phoebe Allenby, who'd actually survived the big blow, could weigh in with personal and often thrilling anecdotes. This year, with another huge and potentially dangerous storm working its destructive way through the Bahamas, heading for Florida and then, as Jesse Maine had just reported, making that classic turn up the Atlantic coast toward Hatteras, Long Island, and New England, the survivors supper took on a special piquancy. But the Maidstone did not permit things that hadn't yet happened to dilute the evening's pleasures. Nor had the recent death of a neighbor, Hannah Cutting of Further Lane, done more than layer over the affair with a small irony.

"I have the suspicion this evening was arranged entirely to get us here," Alix whispered over cocktails. She was wrong, I knew, but it was curious that we'd been placed at Warrender's own table, set by the pool amid lighted tapers. He and I were hardly friends and Alix was an outsider, though in an ankle-length floral silk sheath bought off the rack at St. Barth's on Newtown Lane, surely a welcome one. The other guests, all perfectly respectable WASPs, might have been sent over by central casting as representative of the Episcopal Church and Brown Brothers Harriman. At least that's how impeccably well-bred they looked; the impression a stranger might get.

At dinner (our table numbered eight), Alix was placed at Royal's right at the head of the table. The conversation was good, the sort of table talk that makes a party. Hannah's death figured in it, of course, plus hurricanes and the upcoming film festival, which most agreed had been artificially created by local merchants to hype business in slow October. "I don't see why we need a festival at all," Miz Phoebe complained, "if there's one at Cannes and another at Paul Newman's place out west ('Robert Redford's,' someone hissed), why must East Hampton be plagued?" There was considerable debate on this. "They're not the A-List, I admit. But hardly riff-raff . . . except maybe for that Felton man, with his twin doxies." Pam Phythian thought the O'Leary sisters good for East Hampton. "Some of us, and I include myself, are at risk of becoming terminally stuffy. A roué like Felton and a couple of tarts make for a nice change of pace." Miz Phoebe and several others harumphed at this astonishing notion.

Also hotly debated, if a really major hurricane, a category five, say, hit our coast today, what would go; what would survive?

Warrender was pretty good on this. "Take my place. Built 1910 or so. Fairly well constructed but awfully close to the dune. I suppose if the ocean came full across the dune and not just spray and wind, but actual big waves, nothing would stand up to it. Not my place or Phoebe's or the (he may have hesitated imperceptibly) . . . the Cutting house. But if it's just wind and not solid green water, well, we might lose shingles or a brick chimney or two, maybe lose the whole damned roof. But I think the houses would stand." He paused. "They did in '38."

There were many theories about what happened to Hannah, none of them terribly convincing. I noticed Royal offered very little.

An odd thing. Claire Cutting was there at another table. But then, why not? She wasn't a Maidstone member but owned property along Further Lane and such folks were asked as well. With her, looking surprisingly smooth in a rental shop tuxedo, Leo Brass. He avoided my eyes but Claire was gracious. She, at least, hadn't been trespassing on my lawn the other night and perhaps Leo had. Except when doing his James Cagney impersonations, I could take Leo or leave him and preferred the leaving. I liked Royal Warrender the more we all drank, the later the evening wore on. He had manners, bearing, brains. Would make a helluva Fed chairman. Could he have been involved in Hannah's death? Or the theft of her book? What possible reason could there have been that . . .

"Stowe."

"Yes?"

"You and Lady Alix, we've had a good talk over dinner about this part of the world. Would it amuse her to see another of the old Further Lane cottages? She's been asking about my place."

"That's fine, yes."

Warrender was being uncharacteristically expansive. He and I were standing a bit apart from the others waiting for Alix to get back from the ladies' room. Then, getting swiftly to the point, and talking low, almost in a whisper, and not at all that chummy, "You've been asking a lot of questions. You and Jesse Maine. You have him on the case now, too, don't you? You and Lady Alix. I want to know what you're up to . . ."

"We could talk about it right here, do it tonight," I said, not going to be bullied.

"No, not tonight. Not in front of everyone. Let's talk at my place. Where there won't be interruptions or eaves-dropping. Call me in the morning. We'll set something up before the damned hurricane hits. If that's what we're in for."

After Royal dangled that tease about calling tomorrow to set up a tour and a full and frank face-to-face, Alix and I went dancing. By now much more talk of Hurricane Martha. Perhaps it was the hour, perhaps the growing tension, perhaps the drink, or the coming storm, but when we got home she asked if I'd take her swimming.

"Will you take me swimming?"

"Now?"

"Yes."

We changed into swimsuits and walked down over the spindly catwalk to the stairs and the beach and dove into the black ocean and a surf already building before sprint-ing back up the beach to grab big terry towels and wrap ourselves against the chill to hurry to the gatehouse. Then, without bothering to shower, Alix Dunraven and I made love for the first time.

"Golly, Beecher, let's do that again," she said with un-feigned enthusiasm.

"Why, yes, let's."

Except that she tasted of salt and the ocean, the touch and the feel of her was everything I'd imagined.

She liked my bedroom better than hers, she said, and be-fore I was awake had moved her things in from the smaller room she'd been using. Only trouble with that was that Mignonne came along, the poodle, who didn't at all like my being in the same bed with her (temporary) nurturer and growled menacingly. I began to feel like Roland the bartender's dog, Little Bit, and wondered if I were about to be attacked.

"Speak to her in French, Beecher," Alix suggested. "She so enjoys your accent."

So I murmured a few lines of the old Française and wasn't bitten so maybe Alix's theory was correct. And we felt sufficiently secure about it to go right ahead with what we were doing without fretting over Mignonne's frame of mind.

Sunday morning Alix got into her car before I woke and went up to Dreesen's for doughnuts and the Sunday papers. I began seriously considering a declaration of love.

I called Warrender to arrange our visit but there was no answer so I took Alix to the local Episcopal church, not so much for the praying and all that, but to show her the place and because that's what people on Further Lane do Sunday mornings; they go to church and buy the *Times*. You heard about sex orgies and cross-dressing and such in the Hamptons but the reality was the Sunday papers and buying Dreesen doughnuts and going to church. By now even the preacher was asking for a prayer that we be spared the hurricane.

The exodus from East Hampton and much of coastal Long Island began in earnest Sunday afternoon. I watched the NFL on television in the den while Alix curled up next to me on the couch in what proper people call dishabille, smoking my cigarettes and doing delightfully distracting things. Jesse Maine came by and she scampered to put on a robe.

"You ever consider a lasting relationship of some kind with the aristocracy, Beech?"

"I barely know her, Jesse."

"Yeah, well . . ."

He said they were boarding up windows in all the big

houses along Further Lane, the windows fronting on the ocean.

Alix, back and discreetly covered, asked if that meant the hurricane was truly coming. "That's what *The Weather Channel* says, that it made the turn and it's coming," Jesse told her. She grinned, delighted that her theory about Native Americans' predicting the weather was turning out to be accurate. Maine had a few other matters to report. "Leo Brass is out there in his boat, pulling his lobster traps. Claire Cutting's with him. She's got strong arms, that girl, pulls a lobster pot well as a man. And you know it's gonna be bad when lobstermen like Leo pull their traps. Too damn much work putting them out to respond to false alarms." There was another thing. "Royal Warrender's evacuating his people, the servants and such. Says he'll ride it out."

Royal told us that over dinner the night before. Except he didn't say he'd be there alone. Alix looked at me. I guess she was thinking what I was, that here was a man with a damaged heart and he was sending away anyone who might be able to help if and when . . .

I did whatever battening-down chores seemed sensible both at my father's house and my own little gatehouse, storing patio furniture, taking down hanging plants that in a high wind could become projectiles, closing windows, clearing the rain gutters of muck and dead leaves that might clog the drains, that kind of thing. Alix pitched in and afterwards we went to The Blue Parrot, where they were rigging for a hurricane party, with surfers coming in exhausted but exhilarated by the waves and the promise of even bigger and better surf to come. Lee the owner told about surfing at home in Hawaii and bought rounds of drinks while jolly waitresses fetched bowls of tortilla chips and salsa. Roland's dog, that hangs around there waiting for a drunk to feed her a chip or two, did a sort of dance atop a barstool and we all cheered and got tipsy. "Good thing we left Mignonne home," Alix said. Only Billy Joel was missing. "I had so hoped he'd be there," she complained, "you claimed he practically camps out, pounding at that piano virtually every night." So I took her down to the beach as a treat for what might be a last walk before the hurricane. The wind was blowing harder now but it was the ocean that was dramatically up, lapping at the base of the old dunes that guarded the beachfront "cottages." In the dusk a few surfers were still out there on their boards. Way out, nearly half a mile out. Crazy. But try telling them . . .

The eleven o'clock news was all hurricane. See, Alix said, Jesse was right!

We slept together again but by two or three in the morning were both awake, the house shaken by the wind, the first rain showers slashing against the shingles, the hurricane still hundreds of miles away but putting out warnings. About four-thirty I gave up the effort and got out of bed and pulled on khaki pants and topsiders and a faded sweatshirt. Alex got up then too and went into the kitchen to make coffee. She didn't do it very well, there were probably people who did that sort of thing for her at home, but she looked awfully good trying.

"Maybe you ought to put on some clothes, Alix," I suggested.

"Oh, quite."

The electricity was still on and would be for a while, thanks to the East Hampton's fathers' insistence power lines be buried rather than strung. I tapped the old barometer hung on the wall of the kitchen and it read 28.60, which was low. And it was trending lower. I put fresh batteries in a couple of flashlights and left the portable radio on in the kitchen so if the electricity went we'd have the news. WCBS was saying the storm was still tracking up right along the coast with its eye off the Delmarva peninsula. This was not encouraging. By now Alix was in jeans and sneakers and a big old Brooks Brothers shirt of mine worn shirttails out, smoking a cigarette and quite contented.

"I imagine it must have been like this in London during the Blitz. Except here you don't go down into the Underground and the Thames is hardly the ocean." She considered phoning Random House to check in with Mr. Evans but thought better of it. "It's too early and anyway, he'll just natter at me about the missing manuscript and I'm rather running out of lies."

There was room in my dad's garage for her Jag so we rolled it in there, getting pretty wet. The rain wasn't steady but came in bursts. The wind was stronger and some good-sized limbs and plenty of small branches were down all over the lawn. Whatever else Hurricane Martha brought, there was going to be a hell of a cleanup. The poodle didn't seem jittery or anything. So much for vaunted canine intuition and barking just before earthquakes struck and such. Mignonne just curled up with us on the old leather chesterfield while Alix played around licking my ear and I stroked her hair and other pleasant parts.

And then she said, "You know, Beecher, all the men I know, or most, are so smooth and smug and sleek. And you're not. You've been, I dunno, bruised a bit. I don't mean to sound critical, and is 'bruised' an appropriate term?"

She was kissing me in various places, licking them clean before she did, and I was understandably distracted but tried to maintain a cogent conversation.

"Quite appropriate. But last thing you were telling me what a hard case I am. Now I'm damaged goods. You ought to make up your mind."

"Maybe you're both."

"And?"

"I like it that you are. I know a little about the Algiers business. I called it up on the Net. You did something heroic rescuing that woman but you don't go about striking poses or affecting a limp and wearing the old DSO in your buttonhole." She paused, thinking of something. "Do you know your great man William Faulkner was in training for the air corps or something at the end of the First War and never even got to France, never mind the fighting, and ever after walked with a limp and claimed he had a silver plate in his head?"

I didn't know but liked having her tell me things like that (and also being licked) and so now that she'd asked again and for no other good reason whatever except that I tend to dramatize myself a bit during times of impending crisis, I decided to go ahead and tell her about Algiers.

And what happened to me there.

TWENTY-SEVEN

*I could no longer see the bright
pink Chanel suit . . .*

As perhaps you know, the place to take your sweet morning coffee in an Algiers March with a north wind whipping off the Med is on the sunny side of the Place. People think Africa is hot. Try Algiers in a windy March. I was there outside one of the three good, or otherwise so-so, cafés they have there with their comfortable big wicker chairs at a small, matching table with barely enough space for an ashtray and matches. The French newspapers hung on rattan sticks to be read but not stolen, and when the early plane is in, sometimes that morning's London papers are there as well. The café I liked best and on this morning was patronizing was Boulevard's.

"Mr. Beecher, a fresh cup?"

"Yes, Ahmet."

It was shortly after nine on a Tuesday and I sat with my *Figaro* and the *Paris Herald-Trib* and a day-old *Times* of London (there were headwinds and the morning plane from Heathrow was late) sipping sweet and scalding coffee and rooting the sun higher above the bank tower and other buildings on the far side of the place so we would get more of its warmth. The rush hour was ended and but for the usual idlers and beggars and would-be guides, there were mostly local businessmen and very few tourists lounging there in the early sun and having coffee. Tourism was down badly, and why shouldn't it be, with all the craziness?

It was why I was here—the "craziness"—why *Newsweek* sent me.

Algiers—and what was happening here—scared even old hands who knew North Africa and its people and admired its ways and culture and could get along both in French and pattering the local patois. Islamic Fundamentalism was a mighty force channeled for good or bad. Here in Algeria a ferocious struggle was playing itself out between a beleaguered government, only marginally effective but moderate or relatively so, and a rebellious zealotry, whipped into passion by the younger and more militant mullahs. Latest arena in the confrontation was fashion!

Algerian women, and even foreigners, not wearing the traditional veil had been harassed in the city's streets. Several had been stoned. One woman was beaten, raped, and then murdered as, or so it was reported and believed, mullahs looked on approvingly.

"Ahmet."

I mimed signing a check and tugged out the Gitanes from a shirt pocket and lighted up. At the next table four Japanese tourists took turns shooting videotape of themselves and the colorful passing street crowd. Fools! I was here on assignment, paid to be here; what was their excuse? Maybe they were making a TV documentary. The videocam was big enough.

"Allo, allo!"

Ahmet was there with the check on the little tray but was looking past me out into the place through a gap in the parked cars to where a knot of idlers and passersby had gathered about something, the way children are drawn to an injured bird. I asked what it was.

"Not good, Mr. Beecher."

It was then that I saw the mullahs. Then that I saw the woman in the pink Chanel suit.

The knot of idlers exploded into a small mob, as scores of men, perhaps a hundred, came running toward the idlers, the crowd of them growing all the time. At its hub a woman I could see only intermittently as the mob swayed and pressed in, then fell back. I could no longer see the bright pink Chanel suit.

"Ahmet! The police. Call the . . ."

I looked about. Ahmet, the faithful one, the best waiter at Boulevard's, had vanished. So, too, the local businessmen. These days Algerians smelled trouble and got out quick. The smart ones. Over to the side near the tabac, a lone policeman stood watching. Making no move toward the growing fury. Only the Japanese tourists, stunned, remained, witnesses to what was now a brutal scrimmage in which a woman, nearly naked, was being systematically pummeled and kicked.

"Quick! I'll need your camera," I shouted at the paralyzed Japanese, leaping to my feet and without waiting for a response, snatching the videocam and sprinting into the open Place toward the mob, knocking aside two applauding mullahs as I went.

"*Attention! Attention!*" I shouted in French as I ran. "*Say Enn Ennnn! Say Enn Enn!*"

I worked for a magazine but here in the Third World, CNN was more instantly recognized than any magazine or newspaper.

"*Say Enn Enn!*" I cried again, holding high the videocam, and shoving my way through members of the mob closest to and assaulting the now naked and bloody woman.

And, by some miracle, men actually backed off. I shoved the camera out at arm's length as if taping the air, no longer shouting but now grinning my cameraman's joy at finding something to shoot, crooning my pleasure and winningly so, in a melange of French and Arabic. "Yes, yes, a little smile here. Good, that's it. Super! More of you, that chap there! Again. Fine, I love it. *Say Enn Enn* goes prime-time! Great footage. We've got you all on tape now. More smiles, hands above your heads. That's it, wave them about. Lots of broad smiles. Oh, lovely. Wonderful stuff . . ."

I wasn't sure myself what I was saying, suspected it made no sense, so I just kept shouting and fending off the crowd with one hand while, somewhat vaguely and surely out of focus, I operated the Japanese camera with the other, all the while wondering just what the hell to do next.

"Great, guys! You there (this to a grim-looking mullah), say 'cheese!' You know, *'fromage!'* but with a huge smile. That's IT!, *mon vieux,* old chap. Great. Looking good, lads."

Another mullah was actually adjusting his headgear, in effect tidying up and metaphorically shooting his cuffs, ready to be photographed. I could see blood on his hands. The woman's blood.

"Super!" I called out. "Say Enn Enn! Lights! Action! Camera! Mister De Mille!"

I was standing over the naked woman now and except for bruises and scratches and a bloody nose and mouth she looked okay. She was on her hands and knees and that was something. Once a mob got you down and put in the boot, you didn't get up again. I pointed the camera at her, getting her into the lens while I motioned the others back. Incredibly, they gave way, wanting me to be able to get a good shot.

"Death to the infidel!" someone shouted.

"Marvelous!" I called back. "Right on!" I was speaking English now without actually meaning to, but it was the soothing cheer in my voice that moved them, not the words.

"Okay, fellows, I'm just going to move the lady a bit. Better camera angles, you know. Nothing fancy, matter of composition and the lighting. Step back there, you chaps, don't want shadows. Peter Arnett stuff, this. Or the Scud Stud out there on the hotel balcony, remember?"

"Death to the infidels!"

"Right on!" I responded. "Tippicanoe and Tyler, too!"

I had the woman by one hand now, gripping her bloody bicep and steering her out into the open square a few paces removed from the crowd. She was crying a bit but under control, not sobbing or threatening to collapse, and letting herself be steered. Good. She's functioning still. If I was going to get her out of this, I'd need help. Hers. Quite incredibly, considering the scene, traffic continued to roll over the cobbles of the Place, buses, private cars, vans and bicycles, even a police car, which didn't even slow. Everything you might expect of a modern city but Rollerblades.

"Here we go," I said, still crooning comforting nonsense. The one thing I didn't want was to appear threatening. Or we might have two "infidels" being torn to pieces in the Algiers street. The naked woman, curled into my body for protection, seemed alert.

"Thank you for your assistance," she murmured in good but accented English.

"Excellent," I said aloud. She was functioning. I needed that.

People, who out of confusion or impressed by the "CNN" camera had briefly fallen back, now began to crowd in once more.

"Just stand still and smile," I whispered. She nodded.

Then, trying to will authority into my voice, I called out in French, "Back there, everyone, if you please. Left to right, want to get everyone in the shot. Don't want chaps feeling left out, y'know. On the evening news tonight. Everyone. Call the neighbors, let 'em know you'll be on. Prime-time stuff . . ."

The mindless prattle worked once more as the mullahs, now under the spell of the cameras and wanting the shot to be a good one, exercised their authority, shoving and pushing men into a more orderly if straggling semicircle. "Good-oh!" I shouted. "Couldn't do better at St. Cyr, *mes amis.*"

"Game girl," I murmured an aside, no longer sure when I was speaking French, when English, when amiable rubbish. We had a little space now and a pause to reflect. But I was still at a loss. How could we break away? The mob would be on us in a few meters. I might outrun them; a barefoot, battered woman, never. Not on these cobbles. Then I heard the klaxon and the shout:

"Mister Beecher!"

Toward us across the Place rolled an old Citroën, smoking badly and rattling and rasping, lurching this way and that on decrepit springs. At the wheel, Ahmet the waiter, window rolled down, one hand waving, a Gauloise stuck between his yellow teeth, very much à la Jean Gabin.

"Mister Beecher!"

The passenger-side door suddenly swung open, brushing the very skirts of the mullahs who now, affrighted and impressed, pulled back, thinking perhaps this was an Iman arriving to preside over the show. Or even an Ayatollah.

But it was only Ahmet the waiter in an antique Citroën. Into which I literally threw a naked woman I'd never met and followed myself, leaping acrobatically atop her, apologizing as I landed.

"Sorry about that."

"Not at all," she responded in English.

Behind us now came shouts and curses in several languages and prayers and imprecations on our heads, upon all three, the infidel woman, the *Say Enn Enn* correspondent, and the driver of the old car who might be a Muslim but was most assuredly a traitor to God and to decent, pious people, and if he were, a man to be chastised most severely.

"I'm Beecher Stowe," I said. "Here, take my jacket. It'll have to do until we cross over into friendlier jurisdictions."

"It'll do nicely, thank you," she said, cheerful despite her wounds, trying to grin through split and bloodied lips, despite her proximity to death.

"A shame about your suit. Chanel, wasn't it?"

"Yes, from the January collection."

Ahmet drove swiftly, alternately cursing at and murmuring flattery toward the Citroën, through the downtown and out into the city's suburbs where a facsimile of freeways might begin. But the chase was not ended. Behind us, automobiles had picked up the chase, and from one car or another came the single crack of a rifle. And then, swiftly following on, the *pop pop pop* of an automatic weapon. Well, I thought, I've heard gunfire before. Been in firefights. And then, in this complacent mood, and rather shockingly, I was hit.

"Oh," I said, or rather grunted, "that hurt. That hurt like bloody hell."

Ahmet, as he should, ignored me and kept his eyes on the road, continuing to keep us clear ahead of our trackers. "Here," the woman said, "hold tightly to me. Let my body absorb the pain."

I looked up into her black and rather lovely eyes.

"Sure, you do that, Ace," I grunted through the pain and through tightly clenched teeth. Ahmet, fortunately, had friends. And that very afternoon, before there was further damage or international incident, they flew me out of the country in a small plane, my wound crudely bandaged and pillowed, to sit upon cushions flying west toward friendly

Tangier, while a beautiful black-eyed woman, battered and bruised but no longer naked, bathed my brow with damp towels, as if it were fevered, which it was not, lighted cigarettes that we both smoked, and poured Black Label Scotch that I gratefully drank.

Her name was Princess Tati, a member of the Saudi royal family, who'd rashly, she now admitted, ignored rumors of danger. "I'd been told such things happened to women who wore Western clothes instead of the veil. But when one lives mainly in Paris and London, well, such nonsense is hard to credit."

"Women have been beaten. Raped. Even killed, for 'such nonsense.' "

That sobered her. Then, feeling damply uncomfortable, and yet aware of awkwardness, I said, "Your Highness, excuse my impertinence, but could you check to see if I'm bleeding again?"

"Avec plaisir."

She wasn't a nurse but using my linen handkerchief and wads of tissues from the plane's tiny lavatory, she got the wound sufficiently stanched to get us to Tangier without my bleeding to death. A series of limousines, alerted by radio, waited to whisk Tati to the palace (the King of Morocco was both a distant relation and an ally) and me to the hospital.

My father, a pragmatic sort who knew about such things from personal, even painful, experience, phoned me in Tangier and, after the usual paternal expressions of love and concern, remarked that if you had to be shot, some preferred the fleshy part of the calf. Or a non–bone-breaking clean wound in the upper arm.

"But I've always felt, Beecher, if you're to take a bullet anywhere, being shot in the ass is better than most."

I thanked him for that.

"Golly, Beecher," Alix said when this interminable account was finally done, "having saved Tati's life, I'm bowled over that she didn't put herself out to be, y'know, accommodating to you."

"She had both a husband and a lover, Alix. But she did send roomsful of flowers and a most cordial note of thanks."

"Least she could do," she said glumly, rather disappointed that Saudi princesses weren't more impulsive and demonstrative than your ordinary British royal.

"I'm sure," I said, accepting reality and not choosing to argue the toss.

Alix tried to make it up to me for Princess Tati's failures by taking me back to bed and doing a few provocative things we'd not thought of doing before. Or with quite this urgency.

It was awfully pleasant. I almost forgot Hurricane Martha working its way toward us.

TWENTY-EIGHT

My, but you are a great beauty . . .

Because we were young and healthy and excited by the coming storm and needed to do something, anything! rather than just wait for a new "wind to shake the world" (and having just made love), we got in the Blazer and drove around visiting neighbors along Further Lane. Some of the houses were completely closed, the occupants gone, fled to higher ground. Miz Phoebe was in residence and her maid, who answered the door, warned us off. "Oh, don't get her started. She's a terror this morning. Ranting and raving. We didn't have this many hurricanes in the old days before television put on the *Geraldo* show."

I thought Miz Phoebe might have a point but we went on. At Claire Cutting's house (I still thought of it as Hannah's but it was only a week or so, wasn't it?) we'd barely stopped the car when she came out onto the front porch. I'd half-expected Brass to be there, truculent and threatening, but there was no sign of him. Maybe he was securing his boat. Claire asked, cuttingly, I thought, "Still snooping, Beecher?"

"Only looking in, Claire, just looking in as neighbors do," I shrugged and got the car turned around.

"Not terribly matey, is she?" was the extent of Alix's reaction. Being British, she understood about bad manners.

There were lights on at Warrender's and ignoring his suggestion that we phone ahead and make an appointment,

I went right up to the door. What the hell, hurricane's coming. But when we rang no one came. Maybe he'd come to his senses and followed the servants. But no. When I pushed at the door it opened and we found him there in the library, looking through the picture window at the ferocious ocean.

"Sit down, sit down," he said, but not with his usual tone of command. "Forgive me for not rising, Alix. I'm not all that well."

He'd had a bad night, he said. Chest pain. No, he was pretty sure it wasn't cardiac. Probably he'd simply dined too well. No, he hadn't called his doctor. The damned fool was in Manhattan and what good would that do?

When we were seated he said he'd passed the restless night reading *Lear*.

"The older I get and the more alone, the more I understand Lear. Or think I do. Almost three decades since Yale and English Lit." Alix took him up on it, saying *Lear* was a favorite of hers as well, and that she hated the bad sisters and empathized with the good one, the one who truly loved her father the king. "Was that Cordelia or Regan?" she said. "I know it wasn't Goneril."

Not that I was sure which daughter it was, but I did wonder again about that double first at Oxford.

And if Royal Warrender was acting as mad as Lear, still here riding out the storm like a dying king, just what the hell were Alix and I doing a few hundred yards from the ocean with a hurricane coming ashore? Well, I told myself, I was watching over my father's property; Alix was looking for her precious manuscript. Healthier motives those, much healthier than playing Lear on the stormy heath. Thus assured I turned to considering what, if anything, we could do for Warrender.

He apologized for not being a better host and sent Alix somewhere deeper into the house to rustle up coffee or cold Cokes. Under his East Hampton tan I thought he was paler, wasted, looking older by far than his fifty years. Whatever that nocturnal pain had been, cardiac or not, he was drained.

"Look," I said, not knowing quite how to phrase it, considering Further Lane's strictures against being pushy, "my car's outside. Four-wheel drive. And Southampton Hospital's only twelve miles from here. We can give you a lift and have them take a look to be sure everything's okay. Couple of hours from now we may not be able to make it to Southampton the way trees are starting to come down."

He shook his head. "I'm not going anywhere, Beecher. I'll ride it out here. If I have to die it'll come in my own house surrounded by familiar things and not in a strange room in a strange place connected to tubes and machines and people I never saw before telling me what to do. I've had it with hospitals."

Alix came in then with a tray of soft drinks. The water for coffee, she said, was heating. "At least I think it is. I must say your stove is an impressive affair. An awful lot of buttons. I should have read engineering at Oxford. Hope I pushed the right one."

He smiled at her, that winning Warrender smile they always mentioned in magazine articles about him, speculating on his bright future, a future that was somewhat in doubt right now. "I'm sure you did, Alix." He paused. "My, but you are a great beauty . . ."

She went to him then, leaned down and kissed his forehead.

It was after he'd sipped a ginger ale that he seemed to have made up his mind, come to a decision about something. Maybe about whom he could trust. With the hurricane coming and his house emptied except for us, he didn't have many options, did he? Maybe it was simply that Alix was a beautiful girl who'd just kissed him. Whatever the reason, he needed to confide in someone, maybe anyone. So with the wind rising and the hurricane coming, he started to talk, beginning with a sort of valedictory.

"There's a tradition of service in this family. As there is in other clans of great wealth. You could be of different political orientation and yet admire the things both Roosevelts did. Or Nelson and Jay Rockefeller. Or Ave Harriman. Prescott Bush and his son. Some of the Kennedys. I was brought up in that way of thinking and I've pretty much lived my life by certain rules of conduct. Of service to the nation. Of decent behavior. Of honorable intentions. Sounds fuddy-duddy, I guess, but it was how we were trained.

"Yet twice I've broken those rules. Once nearly three decades ago. The other occasion much more recently."

He paused. As if wondering if he were doing the right thing in trusting us with his story. Or just being foolish, playing the garrulous old man blathering on. Or thought he might be dying and wanted someone to hear him out. And then, having made up his mind, Royal Warrender told us about young Hannah Shuba.

I was home from Yale that summer, he began, very full of myself. A Warrender, of course, with all that conveyed both here on Further Lane and in a broader context. With a few dollars. Captain of the swim team. Just tapped for 'Bones. Practically engaged to a swell girl named Rockefeller. And here came along this little Czechoslovak kid from Polish Town in Riverhead, working for my family, right off the potato farm, cutest thing you've every seen, a little blonde swishing her bottom and her ponytail both, and looking wide-eyed at me as if I were something special. I guess I thought I was. But then so did Hannah. She had a big crush on me, she said. "Crush" was an okay term to use then, I guess. I came home early in June and by the

Fourth of July had forgotten all about Miss Rockefeller, even about Skull and Bones. I was twenty-two and Hannah was fifteen and I knew it was wrong but couldn't stop, couldn't keep my hands off her. And she wasn't making it easy, working around the house and the garden in a little cotton dress and no bra. I couldn't let my old man know and especially not my mother. The usual class distinctions, y'know, the old school tie and all that.

I took her swimming nights. She'd sneak out of the house and meet me behind the old cabanas. I'd come down from the Maidstone Club and we'd get undressed and do the usual things, and a few unusual, and then swim way out. She was a strong swimmer and I was very good. We'd hold onto one another out there, bobbing up and down, kissing and wrapping our legs around each other, and then swim back in and make love all over again, using one of the cabanas. Just about every night, neither of us could get enough. She said she was nuts about me and I guess I was crazy, too.

Then, the end of August with Labor Day coming and classes beginning at Yale, she told me. She was pregnant. "Preggers," that's what sophisticated people say. Not Hannah. "I'm going to have your baby, Royal." That's how she told me and she was happy. Not upset or hysterical or making threats or demands or anything. Very very happy. And when I started to mumble something about paying for an abortion, she hushed me. "No, Royal, I'll have your beautiful baby." Sure, I thought in a panic. That means I'll have to marry her and it's bye-bye Yale for me and hello Park Avenue for her. But that wasn't Hannah Shuba. Not then it wasn't . . .

Alex and I were leaning forward now, caught up in Warrender's narrative. All around the growing storm twisted and boiled and churned and pummeled his big old house atop the dune.

I agonized for a day or two, Royal resumed, then I knew what I had to do and went to my father and told him. Told him about the baby and that I was going to marry Hannah. I didn't realize how naive I was. My father went into a cold rage, telling me the bitch was a little gold digger playing me for a sucker. If I had to sleep with her why didn't I use something? "I'll hire private detectives," he said. "That girl probably slept with half the Baymen in East Hampton and every potato farmer in Riverhead and you announce it's *your* baby? Didn't they teach you anything at Yale, Royal? She's a Catholic, isn't she? I'll have her name read out from the pulpits of every Polack church on the East End."

I started to say they were Czechs and not Poles and that she . . .

He shut me up pretty fast. "I'll ruin this girl and her bastard."

It was all very J. P. Marquand. No way was he going to let me marry Hannah. The whole Warrender clan sprang up protectively around me, the way the Shinnecocks gathered 'round your pal, Jesse Maine. It's how primitive tribes behave; it's how the Warrenders behave.

Hannah, on the other hand, he said, still impressed by the Warrenders' place in society rather than repelled by their chill cruelty, and slightly dazed at age fifteen by what had happened to her, reacted very well. No tantrums, no screams of outraged virtue, no demands for my name or even for money. The sexy little teenager with a potato farmer for a father behaved as Warrenders were supposed to do: with class!

She returned to Riverhead, where her mother "arranged" things; she married an older man, the cesspool digger, had "their" baby, a girl she named "Claire" because it sounded "classy," sounded nice and WASP, and she kept her mouth shut. No appeals, no tears, no whispered confidences about just who Claire's father "really" was. The cesspool man died in that accident and Hannah remarried. This time, more "suitably." To Andy Cutting. He had a little money and a good name. He was a WASP and Hannah had begun to understand they were the people who ran the world.

Andy Cutting was mad for her. He was also a weakling. And Hannah by now realized that she was anything but . . .

Royal was winding up his tale.

Hannah learned from Cutting. And since she knew something about food and came from a family with a tradition of service to the Moravian aristocracy in the old country, she started a small, freelance catering service and within a few years had a Manhattan operation as well, a caterer and a good one, to corporate clients and society affairs and, eventually, to the rich and famous. And by then she was rich and famous herself. And no longer so sweet or so simple.

And in all the intervening years Royal and Hannah never spoke. They found themselves on the same street, even in the same room at times, they passed on Main Street and occasionally in Manhattan. Yet they never spoke, never did more than nod. Neither seemed to want to bridge gaps. Nearly three decades passed. And then Random House announced Hannah Cutting was writing a book in which she was going to "tell all."

"But you know the story from there," Royal Warrender said.

TWENTY-NINE

The rest of it was pure venom . . . settling
scores . . .

After his yarn had played out, Royal looked almost chipper, vivacious, as if weights had been lifted. Alix sat there, brow creased, thoughtful. I think she felt as I did; it was a wonderful narrative intelligently told. But did it get us any closer to the mystery of Hannah's death or the whereabouts of the famous manuscript and, perhaps, its unfinished symphony of life along Further Lane? It was up to me to ask:

"Royal, do you have any notion of where Hannah's book is now?"

"Yes, Beecher," he said so quietly that at first I didn't grasp what he was saying, "I have it."

I would not have been as surprised had Royal informed us he didn't own a house on Further Lane and had in fact never been to East Hampton. But he was going on:

"I knew she worked on the book in her Further Lane house and even where she was writing it, in which room, and how for the first time she was using a word processor. So it was the simplest thing in the world to drop by and grab it."

"But how did you know all that?"

"Hannah told me. Bragged about it. Taunted me with nasty little hints. She had the goods on me and on lots of others and once she had it all down in book form between hard covers we'd realize it. She went on and on, saying she wrote for an hour or two every morning without fail in the little changing room she had out in the pool house, that she had a new IBM computer, and wasn't bothering with frivolities such as floppy disks. She was getting back at everyone who'd been hard on her or put her down. She worked right off the hard drive, instead of a disk, though she didn't use the terms."

"But you just said you and she never spoke. Not a word."

"Not until last year. Then, things changed."

"And after all that time, after all her success, she was still sore at you?"

"Hostile's more the word. And it was a hatred that grew through the years as she matured and grew more resentful of my youthful failures. But only intermittently so. That's the puzzling thing. When my wife died last year Hannah wrote me a note. The usual polite condolence and when I got around to sending out those printed acknowledgments I scrawled a line at the bottom about how much I appreciated hearing from her. Well, that broke the ice. We saw each other a few times. She wasn't a hot little teenager anymore but in ways she was just as desirable. I would have been drawn to her if she'd been more stable. But there were these violent mood swings and outbursts. One moment she'd laughingly, rather cleverly be musing on what a good wife she'd make to an ambitious man like me. That it was true that behind every great man there was a great woman. The next she'd be snarling resentment for my having amused myself with a naive kid, toyed with her and then walked away from responsibility because I was in awe of and afraid of my father, obsessed by family and position. Next thing you know, she'd be in what she used to call her 'angora sweater mood,' sexy and open and vulnerable. I suppose it's hard for people who don't really know Hannah to think of her as either naive or vulnerable. But there were times . . ."

Alix and I waited for him to resume the narrative.

"Late Saturday night of Labor Day weekend, early Sunday morning actually, I walked down Further Lane to her place. She was leaving for Nepal any day now on that Mount Everest foolishness and this might be a last chance to find out what she'd written about me and what steps I might take, legally or otherwise, to protect myself and avoid a scandal. I was under strict orders from Washington to keep my nose clean for these next couple of months or the job at the Fed would be out the window. Not only that, anything foolish on my part would redound against the President, hurt his chances for a second term. I knew her house and property and the outbuildings as well as she knew them. But only the East Hampton place; once she was back in Manhattan in her apartment or at the house in Vermont, I'd be helplessly out of my depth. Further Lane was my turf; it was now or never. As I expected, the back door to the pool house was unlocked and I let myself in, wearing cotton gardening gloves to avoid leaving prints, moved quietly, paused now and then to be sure she wasn't there working late over the book, but the place was empty. So I nipped into the changing room, which she'd fixed up like a rec room of sorts, and sat down to work at the computer. With a magnet it didn't take long. There was only a single, quite lengthy entry in the directory . . ."

". . . some hundred and eighty thousand characters, I believe," I put in, unable to resist interrupting his rather smug account.

Warrender looked at me, his brow wrinkled. Then he resumed, not permitting me to draw him into an exchange.

"When I'd done what I came to do, I left, wrapping my knuckles inside the glove in a handkerchief to avoid being cut and breaking a pane of glass to leave behind the suggestion of a break-in and thinking myself a crafty fellow indeed. It was then I heard Hannah's voice."

Alix and I both sat up. Were we about to hear the story of her death?

"It came from down at the beach somewhere and I couldn't make out the words, only a few words, a sentence or so, but it was Hannah. I knew the voice, recognized the tone, rather put out. There was no response, not that I could hear, but I didn't hang about. I got going. If Hannah was up and about no reason why she mightn't head this way. So I took off and fast and walked home along Further Lane, twice dropping back into the hedge when headlights approached."

"But Hannah? You can't recall anything more?"

"No, just that she spoke. Sounded annoyed . . ."

"There's a difference in how a woman speaks to a man and to another woman," Alix put in. "Could you sense if it were one or the other . . . ?"

Royal shook his head. We'd gotten out of him all we were going to get. "That's why I didn't say anything to the police about it. Wouldn't have helped their case and would just have gotten me into a mess trying to explain what the devil I was doing on her property at two in the morning, breaking and entering her pool house."

He still hadn't gotten to the heart of the matter so I said: "So you went home, turned on your computer, and read her book."

"I did. That very night. Starting off, of course, with the early chapters. Those which might, and from her warnings, *would* indict me as the worst breed of sunovabitch for having seduced and abandoned an underage girl employed by my family. And then lacking the guts to stand up to my old man and marry her."

Neither Alix nor I said a word. He went on:

"There was a good deal of stuff about Further Lane and

the house and rich people in general and the Warrenders in particular and her youthful response to it all, her first sustained exposure to wealth and privilege. But as for a love affair, only a few sentences. I have them committed to heart by now."

Alix nodded. He was the sort who would remember. Warrender waited a moment and then, after running a tongue over dry lips, he said:

"She wrote only that, 'In that summer when I was fifteen, I fell very much in love with a handsome young man of wealth and good family. For me, a dream; for him, unsuitable and impossible. I was, as young girls are, heartbroken when September came and he went back to college, leaving me forever.' " He paused. "That's about it. I went on and read the rest but she was dealing with other times and other places, with a first marriage to an older fellow and a child, with people other than my family and me."

"So despite all her threats . . ." Alix began.

"At least in this draft, Hannah wrote nothing to damage me, nothing to get back at or disgrace the Warrenders."

"And as for the rest of it?" Alix said.

"Some of the rest of it was pure venom. When people said Hannah was writing the book to settle scores, they were right. If and when that book ever comes out, it'll be the Crash of '29 all over again, with distinguished people we all know going out high windows."

I had one more question and I asked it now.

"Where's Hannah's manuscript now? I assume you kept the disk you downloaded onto and didn't just toss it away or erase the memory."

"Correct."

"Have you plans for it, something to suit your own purposes?"

Royal was again vibrant, even playful, relieved to have told his story to someone.

"That's for me to know and a reporter like you to find out. Go home now while you still can. We can discuss this after the storm. When the hurricane has passed and if by any chance we're all still alive . . ."

I started to get up but Alix was having none of it.

"But that simply isn't good enough, Mr. Warrender. I've been dispatched here specifically to reclaim a manuscript Random House has paid royally for."

". . . and which I have and for now, at least, am going to hang onto."

"Rubbish!" Alix said firmly. "Even Communist China is at last coming around to recognizing the protection of an individual's rights to intellectual property. North Korea is said to have been considering similar concessions. Can a future chairman of the Federal Reserve Bank do less?"

"Can and will." Warrender seemed to be enjoying this, rallying swiftly back and forth across an argumentative net with a beautiful young woman. Some of the color was back in his face.

"And when I report to Mr. Harry Evans the gist of what you've just told us. Do you believe he'll simply write off a substantial investment in advance royalties to say nothing of the millions a book like this could conceivably earn, and not consult with eminent counsel?"

Warrender looked up at me.

"Beecher, will you please take her home before I suffer another cardiac and expire right here on the spot?"

I had my own need for the disk and my own argument to make. That all I had to do was to phone Tom Knowles and inform him the great Royal Warrender was an admitted burglar. But with the rain slashing against windows and the wind rising to a screech, I thought we'd better put it all off for tonight. After all, he hadn't flatly refused; said he was going to hang onto the damned thing "for now."

Besides, if he hadn't destroyed or erased Hannah's story already, was he likely to do so now? Especially as there was nothing in there damaging to him.

"Okay, Alix. We'll talk again to Mr. Warrender after the storm. When he's slept on it and is feeling better."

"But . . ."

My God, she was stubborn. I was liking her better all the time.

I took her arm and as we started to go, Warrender had one more request. "Lady Alix, would you be so kind as to go back into the kitchen and turn off the stove. We never did have that coffee and I shouldn't like to burn the house down before giving our hurricane its turn at bat."

"Of course, Mr. Warrender," she said as if there'd never been an argument. "What a goose I am."

Alix and I battled our way through the rain and wind to the Blazer and drove home, dodging a falling tree at one point, and driving up on the shoulder to avoid others already down. Other than talking about the storm and the usual conversation, two things were bothering her.

"What two things?"

"How you knew precisely how many characters were on Hannah's laptop when you've been claiming you hadn't the foggiest where the manuscript is?" She sounded pretty sore about it.

"Police sources. They examined the computer and found stuff had been erased. I had no idea what the manuscript said or where it was, just that at one time it comprised 180,000 characters."

"Oh, all right." She was grudging but she seemed to be accepting my story.

"And the other thing?" I asked.

"You know, of course, Beecher, what Mr. Warrender told us."

"Sure, that he stole the manuscript and was relieved to learn that despite everything Hannah hadn't trashed him and that you and I could go to hell."

"No, I mean besides that. He was telling us that Claire Cutting is his child."

It was some night. And it was only starting.

THIRTY

*The pond came out of its banks and there
must be a thousand trees down . . .*

I still don't know how either of us got to sleep at all but we
did. The last thing I remember was the gatehouse shaking
as if whatever held it to the foundations had come loose,
the very timbers creaking and groaning, sheets of water
whipping against and over the windows. Just what kind of
beating would mere glass take before imploding inward on
us, I wondered. Was the surf by now well up in among the
dunes and headed this way, which old shade trees were already down and which would fall next, and did my father's great old house still stand?

It was after four when Alix woke me.

"Look, Beecher, up there. Stars! You can see them as the
clouds race past."

She was right. How bright with promise they were
against the night. The hurricane was dying. Or nearly so.
By five I gave up trying to sleep and got up. Off to the east,
just south of Montauk, a full sun came up at dawn in a
rapidly clearing sky scrubbed clean by the storm. The gray
ocean still boiled in fury but here at the house the wind had
dropped off to mere gale force, what seemed by contrast a
preternatural calm. The house stood though you could not
say that for many of the great trees. There was no power
but the portable radio in the kitchen filled us in. The hurricane had skirted the East End of Long Island before roar-

ing across Martha's Vineyard and the Cape and was north-east of us now, intent on battering Maine and the Canadian Maritimes. All up and down the eastern seacoast there was enormous damage but only two dozen dead. We were fortunate, the experts said. We got lucky this time.

Alix was attempting yet again to brew coffee. And not greatly successful at it.

"The electricity's off, darling."

"Oh. I thought you might have dry cell batteries or something else terribly clever."

For once in the morning, she was dressed. We'd both gone to bed that way, right down to sneakers and topsiders just in case we'd had to get out during the night with broken glass underfoot. I was starting to realize I preferred her naked when, as if she read minds, she began to strip. "What?" I started to ask, when she cut me off. "I hope the shower works. I'm grungy." She was just about naked when there was a honk outside. Jesse Maine in his pickup.

"The roads is hell, Beecher. I drove a good bit of the way along the beach. You oughta see Georgica. The pond came out of its banks and there must be a thousand big trees down. That Mr. Perelman will be raising hell and suing somebody, you can be damned sure."

Alix had dashed away when Jesse came into the kitchen and would shortly return in that tie silk robe of hers.

Jesse looked at her in that way of his, open and frankly lascivious, saying, "My, my," admiringly and with the worldliness of a man who'd had four wives, and I remembered what he'd told me earlier, how I ought to consider tying in with this girl.

He was right, I suspected, but not wanting anyone—even Jesse who'd been well and truly married and understood the drill—living my life for me, I just grunted and went about checking out the gatehouse. One broken window in the bathroom had let in some rainwater but it was already drying on the tiles. My dad's house lost some shingles and one of the chimneys. But except for some fine old trees down and broken limbs everywhere, that was it. We'd been lucky, as the experts said, damned lucky. Unlike Ron Perelman, I wasn't in the mood to sue anyone. Especially not with Alix Dunraven here. I recruited Jesse to the cause and we began calling on houses along Further Lane. Maybe someone was worse off than we and we might help.

Some houses were shuttered, locked, and empty. Those folks had gotten out and I didn't worry about them. If they had damage, it wasn't going to go away. Miz Phoebe was still at her station. The maid came to the door.

"I hope this is important because she ain't in a mood for trivialities. I never heard her curse so."

Principal among Phoebe's plaints, that day the Sally Jessy show was scheduled to have on yet another of the O.J. trial lawyers, latest one out with his own book about those farcical legal follies.

"I never miss one with Dershowitz. Or that Darden fellow. Or Shapiro. I can take Marcia Clark or leave her. But the others, I love to hear 'em lie. And now they say we won't have television until maybe tomorrow. If the cable's buried underground, why can't I have my talk shows?" She was also concerned we might be confronted right here in East Hampton by looters. "Just mind you, what happened in Los Angeles when they acquitted those cops of beating up that poor man. Though why anyone would go into a store and come out carrying a refrigerator, I hardly know. . . ."

Like Mr. Perelman, she was in a mood to sue someone.

We went past Claire's house, stopping at the head of the drive so as not to give her an excuse to chase us off again. The house looked okay and except for all the trees down, so did the property. Hannah sure would have been sore about what the wind had done to her roses along the fence, though. After that, we moved on to Warrender's, Jesse in his pickup and Alix and me in the blazer. We had to leave the cars on Further Lane and walk to his house, there were so many fallen trees, and big ones, lying across Royal's long gravel drive. Once again no one came to the door at my knock and I shoved it open.

We found Warrender lying facedown in the great parlor that looked out through rows of picture windows onto the beach and surf and the endless Atlantic beyond.

Alix, who for obscure reasons seemed to understand such things, moved without an instant's delay to kneel by him with her face close to his and then with her ear upon his chest. Whatever it was she heard or didn't hear, she set to immediately with a vigorous and apparently competent mouth-to-mouth resuscitation. After a few moments, she looked up, face flushed and breathing hard but marginally pleased. "He's alive," she said. But that was about the extent of it. There was no power in the house and the phone, when we tried it, was dead. Jesse went out to the pickup for his cell phone and got through to Southampton Hospital. No, they couldn't send an ambulance, not with the injuries they were handling locally. If we could get him there the E.R. was operating on a generator. No, they couldn't send a chopper. They were all out of choppers on other chores and errands and bringing in casualties. Lingering winds from the tail of the storm, in any event, made flying chancy.

Is there another hospital? Alix asked. When I said no, Jesse contradicted me. "There's Mattituck. On the North Fork. Riverhead's miles west of that but bigger. If we can get up to Three Mile Harbor and borrow a boat, we can get him over there to one of them in a lot less time than driving along the beach to Southampton."

His own boat was at the reservation twelve miles away

and I had nothing but a canoe in the garage, and this was hardly canoeing weather, not with a heart attack victim to be transported, and who knew what we were going to find at the marina. But it seemed worth a try so we carried Royal outside and lay him down on a blanket in the bed of Jesse's pickup and covered him with another. "I'll ride in there with him," Alix said.

"The hell you will—" I began.

"Just shut up, Beecher. I've trained at Saint Godolph's as a nurses' aide. Let's go, Jesse."

"Yes, ma'am, Your Ladyship," Jesse said, laughing out loud despite everything, a lot like he used to laugh at me when we played ball.

Out the Three Mile Harbor Road you got an idea of what the hurricane did to the back country. It was some mess. Trees mostly and telephone poles and power lines. They don't bury them up there the way they do on Further Lane, you know. At the marina boats, some of them big ones, forty-six-foot Bertrams and such, were tossed about and smashed like things in a children's toy box. The first lugubrious sailors were there before us, observing the damage, with a few of them angry and mystified that their boats, apparently so snugly secured only twenty-four hours earlier, had entirely vanished. The small harbor was covered with floating debris that had once been a grand little pleasure boat fleet.

"Hey," Jesse called, "here's one looks okay."

Alix was still up there in the pickup with Warr̀ow "He's breathing," she reported, "and that's all I white I joined Jesse on one of the spindly docks th̀ d securely had ridden out the storm and at the end ọ̉ securely fishing boat, a twenty-foot Shamrock tethered.

"Richard Ryan's," Jesse said̀ Richard, he's a man knows how to secure a boat́ does."

He was on board and already tinkering with the inboard engine, trying to figure out the best way to hot-wire it.

"Maybe you ought to call Richard on your cell phone first," I offered.

"Time is of the goddamned essence, Beech," he replied, and kept right on tinkering until the engine coughed a few times and began to hum. Jesse was awfully good with machinery, handy with almost anything, but he kept getting in trouble. Hot-wiring someone else's boat was not looked upon at Three Mile Harbor as a very neighborly act but, as Jesse said, Royal Warrender didn't have the luxury of time.

There was a stiff chop but nothing worse, and with Jesse up forward warning of wreckage ahead in the water, I helmed Richard's boat while Alix cradled Warrender's head in her lap and sort of cooed to him soothingly where he lay on the blanketed deck. I don't believe Royal heard a bit of it but she had an awfully nice lap and she was really fine at cooing as well. When we got past the breakwater and swung west into Gardiners Bay, a much bigger body of water, it was more open and we got real waves now and some pretty good swells. Too big a sea, Jesse and I agreed, to make our way straight across Peconic Bay, not with this small a boat and with Warrender so bad. So we altered course to swing due west, skirting the shore, and making our way to Southampton by water rather than by road. At least the wind was going down fast and we made good time passing Shelter Island to starboard. There were choppers up now buzzing overhead and the sun beat no strong out of a cloudless sky. When it was still blowgone as if the hurricane was going to last forever;

A guy in a was over, you wondered at how quickly it had in near the North gave us a lift from where we pulled to the hospital. The Mof Southampton and ran us down k Highway was impassable

but a few of these local roads were okay if you picked
your way. The hospital folks at the E.R. were fine. Harassed by the storm but with generators working, somehow they coped. It was a cardiac, all right, a bad one. I
gave them as many particulars as I could about family and
so on and my phone number and address; then it turned out
Royal's billfold was in his pocket so we got the paper-
work done and got out of there. No one was yet saying if
Royal Warrender was going to make it. But we three had
done our job.

Back at the marina Richard Ryan was on station and
we all had what might be called a "spirited" discussion
about the ethics of hot-wiring his boat but in the end
Richard said we'd done the right thing and he offered to
stand us drinks at The Blue Parrot unless I thought ten in
the morning was a bit early for that. Richard had been driving around town and gave us his damage assessment. No
casualties among people we knew. But then, all the
precincts hadn't yet reported in.

"No one's seen Leo Brass yet this morning. Damn fool,
I hope he wasn't out there pulling lobster traps last night."

Brass missing? And might Claire Cutting be with him?

THIRTY-ONE

A series of terrible tidal waves
sweeping over East Hampton . . .

Driving back into the village we passed those yellow East Hampton municipal trucks with gangs of men wielding chainsaws and tugging at downed trees and limbs. It was some mess. At the Parrot, Roland the manager was tidying up. The big awning out front was in tatters and outdoor tables and chairs thrown about, but beyond that and some rainwater around the windows, the place looked pretty good. Lee the owner was down at Montauk checking his boat and Billy Joel had apparently deserted us. But a few girls came in and so did Morgan Rank, who owns the gallery of primitive art. After that Toni Ross, daughter of the late Steve Ross, arrived, giving the bar a certain tone; she owns Nick & Toni's with her husband, Jeff. Then in came Dave Lucas the lawn-care king and most of Sid Felton's entourage, including the O'Leary twins, driven from their accustomed perch at the sidewalk café by the wind. We all introduced ourselves and Alix looked impressed to have met a moviemaker like Felton and wide-eyed at the sheer physical presence of the O'Learys. "Have you done any acting, Your Ladyship?" Felton was asking, slyly, I thought. By now Roland's white dog was begging for tortilla chips so, considering all things, it was pretty normal. Maybe we should have brought the poodle along, as well. Then we all had a beer, even Alix, who wanted a margarita but the blender wasn't working, so she had a Pacifico too. And Sid Felton was recalling tidal waves at Malibu and what famous movie stars had attended *his* parties.

"Golly," Alix said, "Tom Cruise. Fancy that!"

Then Claire Cutting arrived.

Sweet as could be and looking pretty good, the wire-rim glasses finally traded in for some outsized shades that must have been prescription lenses because she wasn't hunched forward squinting the way she once did. And those tight, faded jeans did no harm nor did the pink tanktop she wore without any evidence of a bra. I mean, a skinny young woman like Alix could bounce around without a bra and not frighten onlookers. But when you were solid and curvy as Claire who took after her mother in that department, well . . .

I recalled what Jesse said about her strength, hauling lobster pots with Leo, those strong brown arms ending, dramatically, in white hands. It was the trademark look of the serious East Hampton gardener, forever wearing cotton gardening gloves—we had by the score here in East Hampton—not only Claire but enthusiastic gardeners like Pam Phythian. Whatever, Claire looked good. Felton was looking her over, wondering who she might be, and Richard even moved down one barstool to give her drinking room. "Hi, Beecher," Claire said, "you folks get hurt at all?"

Last time I'd seen her she was telling me to get the hell off her place. Now she was inquiring after the wife and kids.

"No, we're fine, Claire."

Alix, who didn't like her, then said disarmingly, "How did that nice Mr. Brass come through the storm? He's not been seen this morning yet, I take it."

Claire sensed sarcasm in the question and started to anger, then bit it back. "I've no idea," she said coolly, and then turned to Richard to ask empty questions about his boat. Mr. Felton, having been told who Claire was, hunkered down, which was unlike him, maintaining a discreet and uncharacteristic silence. Maybe he was trying to figure out if Claire's dead mother was yet in the public domain or if in making his film *Bittersweet* he might be required to pay royalties to the family. You had to say this about Felton: he was a professional who knew about costs, below and above the line. While he mulled over the possibilities, Sid ate a few Kleenex. We all had the one and then a second. Then Jesse and Felton had their heads together briefly.

"He asked me to be a technical adviser on the movie," Jesse whispered. "Move out to Los Angeles for a time. Become acquainted with female movie stars."

And? "I told him I'd consider it."

Then Jesse went off on various errands and Alix and I returned to the gatehouse where, it being noon and the sun high, we went back to bed, unclothed this time. "D'you want me to keep my sneakers on, Beecher? Might be rather kinky." You had to like the way her mind worked.

She also wanted to know something else.

"Beecher, I'm confused."

"About what?"

"The O'Leary sisters and Mr. Felton."

"Seems plain enough to me."

"No, I mean, do you think Mr. Felton sleeps with them both at the same time or enjoys them seriatim?"

Primly, I said I had no idea. But while we were making love she returned again to the theme, asking if I'd ever slept with two girls at once and was it stimulating or simply complicated? I shut her mouth with mine and retreated into a silent wonderment as to whether her father the Earl knew how his daughter went on and just what Oxford was teaching young people these days.

Afterwards Alix called Random House to inform them she was still alive and, yet again, hot on the trail of the elusive manuscript. And that for the first time, she could guarantee it hadn't been destroyed or anything, and surely it was merely a matter of hours now. I roamed the kitchen where she was using the phone, looking into cupboards and aligning coffee mugs, self-conscious and embarrassed at the growing ingenuity of her lies, which by now were colorfully describing a series of terrible tidal waves that washed clear over East Hampton, sweeping away houses and inundating roads and marooning isolated farmers and lobster fishermen, and which terrified even the redoubtable Indian sachem and war chief Jesse Maine.

We got up about five and showered together, which wasn't such a great idea. Not only with the electricity down was the water ice-cold, we very nearly went back to bed again, and if you weren't at the Parrot by six, you stood a gaudy chance of finding a barstool. Leo Brass was still among the missing. He wasn't the only one but there were plausible explanations for the others; not Leo. East Hampton had its first two fatalities that we knew about. An old lady in Springs had a heart attack trying to pull a big tree limb off her deck. And a body was found down by The Gut where Georgica Pond empties into that channel cut through the beach to the ocean at times of heavy rain and overflows.

Poor devil, someone said, must have drowned in the storm surge. A few of us lifted a Pacifico in solemn tribute.

No, said Roland from behind the bar. That was the odd thing. The body was that of a man with a terrible stab wound of some sort through his chest. Or so went the rumor.

I borrowed The Blue Parrot's cell phone, the one they hang up beneath a copy of Joe Heller's latest book and the scrawled love note to the place from Christie Brinkley, and called Tom Knowles at the police station. He was out checking storm damage with the rest of them but they'd page his car and get him to phone me at the Parrot. So we had another round of Pacificos. When Tom called back, I didn't even have to ask the question.

"Same damn wound, Beecher. Just like Hannah's. Once again, the killer left the weapon behind. Privet hedge. A stake sharpened with a knife and then honed and hardened in flame. Not milled like the one you got slugged with. They're checking for prints as we speak. No I.D. yet. I haven't been over there to see the body because of the roads. I'll get back to you."

I paid up and got Alix out of there, over her objections.

"I say, Beecher, this is the jolliest spot in town, and I dote on that Richard Ryan chap. And without power and no lights, what's the point of going home so early?"

I repeated what Tom told me about the stake of privet hedge through the dead man's heart.

"Golly!"

We drove around the village looking at damage and checking with a few of my friends not seen since before the storm, all the while wrestling with who might be the man dead in Georgica Pond (Ron Perelman, who lived there and had ruffled feathers? Leo Brass who boasted about "taking care of" The Gut himself? "The Walter"? Jerry Della Femina? Parties unknown?) and what was the significance of a second murder in little more than a week by sharpened privet hedge through the heart.

"Cold heart," Alix corrected me. "All the best writers of policiers use a good adjective and do it that way. If this were Miss Marple it would always be 'through his (or her as the case may be) *cold* heart.' "

"I'm sure," I said, not being a Miss Marple expert.

We drove along Lily Pond Lane to see if Mort Zuckerman's place or Jerry Della Femina's dune house had been

swept out to sea. Neither had. Martha Stewart's lovely
garden had been trashed and there was a big maple down
and what looked like a copper beech. We drove past Ken
Auletta's and then Ben and Sally Bradlee's house, the old
"Gray Gardens" that they bought from Jackie's crazy
cousins—and then had to have the exterminators in before the decorators. They, too, seemed to have come
through. We swung back and drove down Highway Behind the Pond to the beach, where old Mrs. Lawrence built
what *Vanity Fair* called "the house from hell," but which
I thought of as resembling the TWA terminal. The mon-
strosity, unfortunately, was still standing as well. Then we
saw Lee Radziwill, who lived next door and never had
forgiven Mrs. Lawrence, or her architect, that rogue!,
striding past, walking a couple of skinny dogs on leashes,
so we knew Lee was okay.

"Whippets," I said, not terribly sure. Alix looked narrowly at me.

"Borzois," she said briskly. "It's amazing the voids Harvard left in your education, darling."

The "darling" made up for unwarranted attacks on Harvard.

And now Alix turned philosophical.

"You know, Beecher, I've been asking myself just
who's the real villain in all this, and when we talk to people who knew her, it seems to come up more often than not
to be Hannah Cutting. As if she's to blame for her own
death. Being such a bitch and all. Over and over we hear
of her appalling ways and lack of manners. And I'll have
to admit she cut me there on her own lawn. But now someone else is dead as well, and was that Hannah's fault too?
I think we're shortchanging her, y'know; to have accomplished all she did, to come out of nothing and become
someone, she couldn't have been all bad.

"There's not that much time, or energy, for people to be completely evil and still do all the things Hannah did."

We were no sooner back at my gatehouse when Knowles called. The dead man was Leo Brass. Only an environmental whack job like Brass would have gone out to check Georgica Gut atop a bulldozer during a hurricane and it killed him. Not the actual storm but someone who knew him well, knew how he thought, who realized The Gut was one of the places Leo would have checked out as the storm rose in its strangled fury and lashed at the pond and the fragile, protective dune.

Claire Cutting? If anyone knew the dead man, she did.

There was still no power so I cooked a couple of steaks on the Weber grill and Alix tossed a salad and we had a simple dinner on the patio, washing it down with a Châteauneuf du Pape. "I say, Beecher, this roughing it isn't all that harsh, y'know." Fortunately, there was running water and the toilets flushed.

We'd had so little sleep the night before we turned in early. Without electricity, why not, and as the candles turned down we made love. Undressed, this time. Why not, again, since we needn't be prepared to evacuate tonight. I was marginally asleep when Alix shook me awake. "That nice copper friend of yours, Beecher, Inspector Knowles. We've got to call him. Get him to purloin Claire's gardening gloves. He'll find them simply reeking of privet and soot, I'll wager."

"Why?"

"I've been literally tossing and turning, meditating on it. Suddenly, it came to me, at least I think it did. Because in both murders, there were no fingerprints. Claire habitually wore gardening gloves, you could see it yourself, strong brown forearms and those pale hands. And she was the daughter of the dead woman, the lover of the dead man. Poirot and so many other adepts always tell you in a murder case, 'Look to the family! Find the husband! Suspect the wife! *Cherchez les amants* . . . seek out the lovers!' By far the majority of homicides are committed by someone who knew the victim well. Strangers very rarely are found guilty of having . . ."

Once she got on a hobby horse . . . So I said, "Alix, go to sleep. There are hundreds of pairs of pale hands in East Hampton. The Ladies' Village Improvement Society practically requires them for membership."

She was stubborn. "I'm not talking about little old ladies with pale hands. I'm talking about someone strong enough to drive a stake through a human chest who also happens to have white hands."

"Well, what about Pam Phythian? She gardens, she has pale hands, and she, for chrissakes, climbed Mount Everest."

"Mmmm," Alix said, "there is that."

Then, after a thoughtful pause, "D'you think it would be ethical for us to go back to Mr. Warrender's house by dark of night and before the servants return and scout about for Hannah's floppy disk? Mr. Evans would be so pleased if I could somehow produce it."

"Go to sleep. Hot-wiring Richard Ryan's boat is sufficient criminal behavior for one week."

In the morning Tom Knowles was moving haltingly toward Alix's point of view. "I'm asking Claire Cutting to come in. Not to charge her. Not yet. But it's not clear just where she was when Leo was killed. And as far as the night Hannah died, Leo Brass was Claire's alibi and she was his. She's the one person we have who was close to both victims."

"Miss Marple says that's always the one," I informed him, "or maybe it's Hercule Poirot who says it."

"What the hell are you talking about, Beecher?"

I left it at that. When I called Southampton they said Royal Warrender was conscious. Not well but alert and aware. Jesse Maine had gone in to see him and called with a firsthand report. "He looks like something washed up by the tide, Beech, but he's alive. And that's something. I talked to him for a while."

"They said 'no visitors' when I called."

"Yeah, well, you know, I sort of pushed my way in."

"What'd he say?"

"Get the hell out of here."

"Oh."

So much for saving a Bourbon's life. Jesse and I chatted a bit more. "I gotta get out of here now. Security's coming. Tell Richard Ryan I said hi."

Jesse and Alix ought to team up. Neither took the sanctity of law very seriously. Both would have been a cross to bear for Sandra Day O'Connor.

Despite this I took her to Boaters for a drink that night, it being the one East Hampton shrine Alix hadn't yet visited. Besides, I wanted to hear what they were saying up there along Three Mile Harbor about the late Leo Brass. This was his turf. And if I dropped in alone, his Baymen buddies might resent it. With Alix, I'd look less like a snooper.

Or so went the theory; the reality was somewhat different.

"Gosh, Beecher," Alix said afterwards, "I didn't know you were that good a fighter. That was really impressive."

"I lost, Alix. The guy knocked me out the door."

"Oh, rubbish. You made him look inept with all those twists and spins and feints of yours, those devilishly clever jabs and things. You fought with enormous panache. He was fortunate to hit you at all."

What happened was that one of the Baymen not only resented my being there a day after Leo's body had been found, but did something about it. But not until I'd gotten what I went after; a link between Brass and someone else who had as yet only vaguely entered the picture. Pam Phythian!

Alix and I had taken a table in back and when the waitress brought the drinks I got her talking about Leo. About what a shock it was and I supposed lots of people had dropped by to lift a glass in memory, a sort of final toast. Yeah, she said, plenty of them had been in. Including Claire Cutting, red-eyed and sort of shocked. "As if she was on something, y'know."

I said I could understand it. They'd been spending a lot of time together.

The waitress nodded, then, "But that's the funny thing. I thought it was over between them. The way him and that Pam dame have been doing all that ecology crap together."

"Pam? What Pam?"

"The rich one, one of the Fithians or the Phythians, they ought to make up their damned minds how to spell it. She plays tennis and climbed Mount Everest or something, from Further Lane. Rich, long-legged bitch. Racy, y'know. Pam Phythian."

"No."

"That's what you think. Leo and a snotty dame like her? Listen, he's been with plenty of that kind, Maidstone Club and all. And dames off yachts. Leo's an equal opportunity letch." She paused, as if in regret. "Or used to be . . ."

She shook her head sadly at the loss and I wondered if she and Leo . . . Just then the Bayman called Charlie Ray showed up and decided to throw me through the wall. He didn't like it I was sitting there drinking beers when a man like Leo Brass lay dead.

Thank God for Guns and his "Nixons." Without my repertory of dirty tricks, Charlie would have done it, and easily. As it was, I settled for being thrown through an

open door, and for my cleverness, was now being enthusiastically lauded by Her Ladyship.

"I'll wager if you practiced a bit and bulked up, you'd
be throwing chaps through doors, too. I dated, if only
briefly, a rugger player at Oxford and he could throw people about."

"Charlie threw *me* through the door, Alix," I said flatly,
taking a stab at reality, "remember?"

"Beecher," she said sensibly, "if not for your subtle
moves he'd have thrown you through the *wall.*"

There was that, I had to admit.

"Come on, I'll buy you dinner."

I wanted to concentrate. What did Pam and Leo have in
common? Well, environmental concerns, for one. What
else? Sex? She was at least ten years older than he was
but she was very attractive. And physical. Love between
the upper and lower classes was hardly unknown. Funny
though, without any evidence whatsoever, I'd put Pam
Phythian down as possibly more interested in other women.
One of the reasons she and Hannah didn't get along. Pam
might be a lesbian and Hannah was quite clearly the other
thing. Maybe she was bisexual. Maybe she . . .

I embarrassed myself whenever I got off on these tan-
gents, speculating about the sex lives of people I knew.
Disgusting.

We got a table at The Grill on Newtown Lane. Paul, the
manager, was full of apologies for the storm damage not
yet having been entirely cleared up and for a limited menu.
"The generator's got only so much capacity."

Dinner, despite all this, was splendid, especially now
that the sidewalk café was back in action so we could ob-
serve people crawling out from their storm cellars to stroll
along Newtown Lane, greeting each other and being
cheerful. It was like a paseo without the duennas. I kept
puzzling over Pam Phythian's relationship with Leo Brass.

No point asking Alix what she thought; she didn't really know either of them. After dinner, back at the house, I called Tom Knowles, wanting his take on the Pam-Leo business. Instead, "Claire refused to come in voluntarily," Tom said. "I'm asking for a subpoena."

It was on the eleven o'clock news. Claire Cutting, whose mother had been murdered Labor Day weekend and whose "boyfriend" had been stabbed to death during the big hurricane, was being subpoenaed by East Hampton police. "No, she is not a suspect in either death," the cops said. "But we'd like to ask her a few questions. . . ."

"Ha!" said Alix, emerging from the bath into my bedroom halfway through the TV news report. She looked wonderful naked, always did.

"What's that?"

"That's what they always say in England, the police, just before they slap on the manacles and lock you away in the cells. 'A man is helping police with their inquiries. . . .' You only hear that about the guilty ones, I can assure you."

THIRTY-TWO

*"The Fed, you've screwed that up,
haven't you . . . ?"*

Early that glorious next morning, heralding one of those
usual stretches of superb weather after a big blow, the
phone rang and things began to happen at a dizzying pace.

"Wake up, Beech. It's me, Jesse. Turn on the radio.
There's hell to pay."

What happened was that from his bed at Southampton
Hospital Royal Warrender had just confessed to a double
murder, that of Hannah Cutting and Leo Brass. A lawyer
for the Warrender family almost immediately issued a
soothing statement that Mr. Warrender, who only days before suffered a cardiac attack, "was not himself." A very
cautious police statement, mindful of Warrender family
power and connections, and understandably wary of law-
suits, said Mr. Warrender had not been and as yet was not
a suspect in either killing but that of course officers were
now en route to the hospital and would be speaking with
Mr. Warrender if his doctors approved. The hospital was
denying everything. Claire Cutting had not yet been heard
from.

"Why, that's ridiculous," Alix said with considerable
asperity. "He was in no condition to have killed that fellow
Brass. Hannah, perhaps. I can't say. But Leo Brass? Not
a bit of it. I doubt even you, Beecher, could have bumped
off Leo."

"He's shielding Claire. He must have heard about the subpoena."

"And she still doesn't know she's his daughter?"

"I don't think so."

I showered and got dressed only to find Alix ahead of me.

"Come on," she said, "it's up to us to find Claire and tell her about her father." She didn't bother explaining just why it was "up to us."

Alix already had the Jaguar out, first time since the storm, with the top down, the motor idling. I wish I was as sure of our ethical position as apparently she was. Royal had taken us into his confidence. Who was I to play God and tell Claire he was her father? This is why they have shrinks, situations like this. When I confessed my doubts Alix was having none of it.

"Rubbish! Beecher. He's a sick man. We can't have the authorities bullying the poor chap on his deathbed."

There was that, I admitted to myself.

Tom Knowles was at Claire's before we were. "She's not here. Bed hasn't been slept in. The pressure's on to issue an APB. Which will really have it hitting the fan if Claire's not guilty of anything but . . ."

"What's an ABP?" Alix said. "No ABPs from Inspector Maigret that I recall."

"APB," Tom said, "all points bulletin."

"Must remember that. APB . . ." she said, tugging out her notebook and jotting it down.

I expected that at any minute she was going to blurt out what we knew, and Tom didn't, about Royal and Claire being father and daughter. Maybe we ought to tell him. When Anderson gave me an assignment to write about the late Hannah Cutting and how she'd gotten to Further Lane, I don't think either of us thought how complicated it would become, how nuanced. This wasn't a case for a newspaperman but for a theologian.

Tom got back into his car. "If you run across Claire, tell her to call me. She's just making things worse for herself if she runs."

"Sure, Tom."

Easy to say. Problem was, I wasn't sure about anything.

"Where next?" I said, half to myself.

"Southampton Hospital," Alix said briskly, "try to get Mr. Warrender to release us from our blood oaths and let us tell Claire just who she is."

"You think he'll . . ."

"Haven't the foggiest, Beecher," she admitted, "but if he agrees, I'm going to ask his blessing on my retrieving that bloody disk as well. Or Mr. Evans, Harry that is, is sure to sack me. Which'll cast all sorts of unwarranted aspersions on the Tony Godwin Award."

We covered the twelve miles to Southampton in good time, considering there were still trees down and road gangs working the power saws. She was a dandy driver. A double first. And a . . .

Wouldn't be natural for Fruity Metcalfe not to have fallen for her and proposed marriage. I was starting to empathize with poor Fruity. And ponder along those lines myself.

We were too late. As we pulled up in the parking lot Claire Cutting was coming out. Handcuffed, and with a policeman in tow and a woman in civilian clothes that shouted "matron," and who had Claire's upper left arm in a firm grip.

"Well, hello, Claire," Alix said, savoring the scene, "we were so hoping to find you."

"None of that," the matron said, "no communications with the prisoner. Unless you're her lawyers." Claire didn't say anything, not right away. But she didn't look angry at us. Or even very upset about being cuffed. Just thoughtful, as if she were mulling over an entirely unexpected situation.

"Hi, Beecher," the policeman said. "How'd you make out in the hurricane?"

"Just fine, Marty. Lost some trees."

The East End is like that, you either know almost everyone else or you know someone who knows them. The matron didn't know which of us to scowl at first and compromised by looking furious at everyone.

"Hi, Your Ladyship," Claire now said brightly. "Hello, Beech. Heard you got into a fight up at Boaters."

"Got whipped, too. Sorry about Leo."

She half-shrugged but the matron tugged at her.

"Sorry, Beech," the policeman said, "but we got to bring her in. She claims Mr. Warrender's out of his head and that she killed her mother and ol' Leo."

"No!"

"Yessir, we're getting confessions regularly, every hour on the hour."

"Did she get in to see him, Royal Warrender?"

"Yeah, that's where we grabbed her. She had a pretty mean-looking fish knife and there was some shouting. Hostile stuff. Reasonable suspicions Claire was up to no good. That's what the floor nurse said. That's when they called nine-one-one. I figure Claire was out to avenge herself on Warrender for the killings he'd admitted to but by the time we got there, she and Royal were billing and cooing and she was swearing she was the one, and not him, that did the dirty on Hannah and Leo Brass, running them through with privet. And all the time Mr. Warrender was continuing to give himself up as East Hampton's leading serial killer."

"Officer, this is most unusual," the matron said, and as

she seemed to be launching into a pretty stern lecture, Marty shrugged.

"She's right, Beech. Got to take Claire in. Be seeing you."

"Cheer up, Claire," Alix called out sweetly as they went off, "you can always call Beecher and me as character witnesses."

When they were gone, I was of a mind to say the hell with all of them and go home. Not Alix. "With all this confusion we'll slip right into Mr. Warrender's room. Order tea, fluff up his pillows, see to a fresh bedpan, engage him in a little chat, inquire after his health."

She was absolutely intent on getting that floppy disk. Single-minded she was.

If you've never seen Southampton Hospital, we're not talking Mass. General or the Mayo Clinic. Nice place, friendly folks, but small. Not high-tech. We strolled in and went up to the third floor. That's where Jesse told us they were keeping Royal. Beyond the third floor there wasn't much. Just a small utilities attic and the top of the elevator shaft. We peeked into rooms (none of the doors was closed) until we got to Royal.

Considering how close to death he was said to be, Royal was reasonably alert.

"Damned girl, has no understanding of the system. No, one was going to convict me on the basis of a deathbed confession. Tried to tell her to shut up and let her daddy play the hand. Feisty, though, you have to like her for that. Wasn't like that while Hannah was still alive. Claire's grown up, I'd say."

"But she had a knife. . . ."

Royal waved a large, if pale, and dismissive hand.

"Oh, she had intentions. Just goes to prove her innocence. If she'd bumped off Hannah and the unfortunate Leo Brass, she would have stayed home watching television and let me confess my wickedness. The minute she came through that door and started telling me how she was going to carve me up, out of respect to a mother she didn't really even like, I knew she was okay.

"That's when I told her who I was, who *she* was. And she put the knife back and came over and stroked my hair, patted my hand, and in the end, leaned down to kiss my aging cheek. An absolutely gorgeous moment, that."

"But the Fed. You've screwed all that up, haven't you?"

He nodded.

"Yes, and it's a shame. I would have been pretty good at it. Hell of a lot better than Greenspan with his fixation on tight money. But you don't swap your own child for a job. Took me a long time to learn that but eventually it sunk in. Ask your daddy, Beecher. He'll tell you."

Now it was Alix's turn.

"Then who did kill them? If you didn't—we·know that—and if Claire didn't, we have only your word and hers."

"What do you Brits say? 'I haven't the foggiest.' "

She chewed that over for all of a second or two and then got to the gravamen, at least to her.

"Mr. Warrender, may I have your authorization yet again to trespass on your property, enter your house, and take with me the floppy disk onto which you downloaded Hannah Cutting's autobiography for which my employer, Mr. Evans of Random House, has paid an awful lot of money?"

Warrender looked into her face, not giving a hint. Then, briefly, at me. Then back to her.

"And if I give you the okay, will you share it with our reporter friend, Beecher Stowe, who also seems to have both a professional and a personal interest?"

Alix looked at him, looked at me, looked back at him. And then with a cool, professional crispness, she said:

"Mr. Stowe is a journalist after a story; my employer has already paid for and owns this literary property. And I am here in my capacity as Random House's agent."

Sick as he was, and as wasted, Royal summoned a grin, enjoying seeing me get screwed. He never had liked reporters very much.

"I hoped you'd say that," he said. "Shows sand."

"Sand?"

"Grit. Guts. Determination. All the good things."

"Oh, I do like that."

"Come closer, Alix, so I can whisper."

She knelt by the bed as he told her where the disk was stowed and which door was unlocked so she could get into the house. If any of the servants had returned, they were to phone him for an okay. I could hear some of it and considered arguing with both of them but didn't. You don't win such arguments. Instead, I said:

"Take care of yourself, Royal." Then, to Alix:

"Come on."

As she hurried along to the car she said, "He hid the disk inside a book in his library. He told me he arranges all his books alphabetically by author."

"Who's the author? Your man Buchan?"

"No." She thought for a moment. "I don't know why he whispered. You can be trusted."

"Sure, I possess all the Boy Scout virtues," I said mockingly.

"Well, you do, you know. Or most of them. No, it's not John Buchan. A writer I never heard of. John P. Marquand. A book called *The Late George Something or other.* . . ."

I laughed.

"*The Late George Apley.* All about a stuffy old Harvard man years ago. Kind of novel nobody reads anymore."

"But that's just what Mr. Warrender whispered. 'A book

nobody reads so no one would ever find something hidden
there.'"

So much for a Yale man's sense of humor.

"Come on," I said, "I want to stop at the *East Hampton
Star*."

"What's that, the *East Hampton Star*?"

"Local newspaper. I just want to look up something.
And then we've got a killer to find."

She sounded uncharacteristically subdued, as if it was
starting to sink in that she was finally going to get what
she'd been dispatched here to find. "Yes, Beecher, I'm
coming."

"Good. That's the spirit."

THIRTY-THREE

*Hitler did his worst
and couldn't defeat them . . .*

I got what I needed from the newspaper office. At least I
thought I did. There was one more stop.

"Hannah's house. Middlefield."

"What's there?"

"Some old junk. A roomful of stuff Hannah collected
through the years. Claire told me about it once. Where she
may have kept the maguffin. Old tennis racquets, seashells, stuff that didn't mean anything to anyone else but
her. And whoever killed her, maybe."

She looked puzzled. "What's the maguffin this time?"

"It's whatever Hitchcock says the bad guys are after
and the hero finds. It could be a map or a kidnaped child
or a . . ."

"Don't lecture me about maguffins. I knew my Hitchcock perfectly well. I want to know precisely what particular maguffin you're after."

"Dunno, exactly. That's why we're going there."

"Can we get in?"

"We'll get in. Claire's in jail. I think I can handle the
Kroepkes if you help out, do a little tank job."

"What tank?"

"The vapors. Instead of the cool, competent, and highly
efficient book editor and certified Tony Godwin Award–
winning genius you really are, I want your best impression

of a Victorian damsel in distress, right out of Jane Austen."

"You mean batting my eyes, calling for smelling salts, and falling into a swoon?"

That Alix, she grasped a concept pretty swiftly. "Yeah," I said, "going into the tank. The way boxers do."

"You are the clever one," she admitted.

"Subterfuge and stratagems, that's me."

"Richard Hannay and Sandy Arbuthnot would both be proud."

There were a lot of limbs down and a couple of trees and the lawn didn't look manicured as it had, but other than that, Hannah's place didn't seem to have been badly hurt by the storm. Mrs. Kroepke came out when she heard my tires on the gravel. Her husband was up at the shopping center in Bridgehampton, she said. He'd be back soon.

"Just wanted to check that you were both okay," I said.

"Well, isn't that nice. No damage to speak of. Though we're upset about Miss Claire, of course."

"She'll be fine," I told the housekeeper. "We saw her at Southampton Hospital before she was . . . well, you know. I'm sure she'll be out soon. All really just a silly mistake . . ."

That got us an invitation to the kitchen and tea.

"Oh, that'll be lovely," Alix enthused. "I've had a touch of something ever since the hurricane."

"I don't wonder, Your Ladyship. Gentlefolks like yourself aren't accustomed to such hard times, I'm sure. Now you just sit down at the table and relax and I'll put the tea on."

Alix mopped her face with a Kleenex.

"Sorry to be such a bother. Do you have any quinine?" She pronounced in the English way, not with a long "i."

"No, I don't believe so. Not something I've ever kept in medicine chests. . . ."

"Naturally not. Years ago as a child in India, a touch of malaria . . . recurs from time to time . . ."

"Oh, dear. Perhaps I can send to White's Pharmacy. I'm sure they'll . . ."

India! Malaria! Talk about stratagems and subterfuge.

"Fever," Alix muttered. I swore her face had reddened and she seemed slick with perspiration. Was she overdoing this thing?

Mrs. Kroepke was on her feet. "We ought to get you to a hospital, dear."

"No, just if I could use the bathroom. Bathe my forehead and wrists with a damp towel . . ."

When she and the housekeeper had vanished down a hallway from the kitchen, poor Alix leaning heavily on Mrs. Kroepke's arm, I raced for the stairs. From what Claire told me that evening at my house when she spoke of the Hannah few of us know, the little girl who collected seashells and dreamt of one day being rich, of the things she saved ("a pack rat," she said, "a roomful of junk"), but which room? Had Claire said downstairs or upstairs? A room upstairs? I ran up a second flight and then down the broad hallway, throwing open room doors as I went. Bedrooms, all bedrooms. How long could Alix keep Mrs. Kroepke occupied? When would her husband be back? Where the hell was Hannah's room?

Then I remembered. She'd been writing the book out in the pool house. The pool house where the laptop was downloaded of its 180,000 characters. A logical place for her little "treasures," her roomful of junk. But would it be open? Could I get in?

I sped down stairs and out the door and across the lawn to the swimming pool and the house. Blessedly, a door swung easily open.

On the far wall, mounted with some care, a small and not very distinguished collection of . . . seashells.

A Slazenger wooden tennis racquet . . .

Some photos that meant nothing to me but clearly had
to Hannah Cutting.

A length of rope . . .

I was back at the kitchen table, waiting patiently for my
tea, when Mrs. Kroepke reappeared.

"That darling girl. What courage, a bout of malaria and
still on her feet, insisting she can soldier on, and the torments of her childhood in the fever jungles of India and
Ceylon. It's a wonder she's alive at all, and when the fever
isn't on her, usually so frisky. The English. Got to take
your hat off, Mr. Stowe. Hitler did his worst and couldn't
defeat them and no wonder, with even their young people
displaying such courage in the face of Lord knows what.
And the stories she has, all about the East India Company.
Did you know, Mr. Stowe, that the man who founded Yale
University made his money selling pepper and spices?"

I said as a Harvard alumnus I wouldn't be a bit surprised.

When Alix came out she looked remarkably composed.
Especially in view of those "torments" of a childhood
spent "in the fever jungles." Mrs. K., who understood the
proprieties, bounced to her feet.

"Now you sit right down, Your Ladyship, and have
your tea."

Alix shot me a look. I signaled with a nod that I'd gotten hold of the maguffin.

"Oh, but I'm feeling so much better, Mrs. Kroepke.
Amazing what a damp towel can do. I recall one time at
Darjeeling when the fever came and Ma, always clever
about such matters, doused me with rose water and sat up
the night at my bedside, fanning me through the mosquito
netting. . . ."

"Mrs. Kroepke, your offer of tea . . ."

"Yes, it's almost ready."

". . . you've done too much already, and Lady Alix and I have other calls to make along the Lane, checking in with others as to damage estimates and possible casualties."

"Of course. You young people are extraordinary. It's the spirit that won the Cold War. I voted for Jimmy Carter but I've got to admit that Reagan did something. And now you two, no matter what the crisis you pitch right in and handle . . ."

Out in the car Alix said, "Well?"

I hugged her.

"I got it. I found it!"

She shook her head.

"That isn't what I meant. What about my performance? Did I go 'into the tank' to your satisfaction?"

"Super! You get the Oscar! A countryman of yours named Frank Bruno couldn't have folded more impressively."

"Frank Bruno, I know him. One of our finest heavyweight boxers. Splendid fellow. Always loses gallantly."

That was the amazing thing about Alix Dunraven, she had it right, even about English heavyweights.

THIRTY-FOUR

*She was forever on the cell phone
or shaving her legs . . .*

Neither of us talked very much on the way to Pam Phythian's place. She wasn't there.

"At the club, sir. She's got a tennis lesson. Our own court suffered damage."

"Thank you."

I lusted after Alix's Jag but right now, the job we were on, I wanted that Chevy Blazer under my legs. At some point, I might have to go off-road. The Jag was wonderful but it didn't have that kind of clearance.

"Let's go by my father's place. For this, we may need two cars."

"Right-o."

When we each had a car and just before we started off for the club, Alix said, "Aren't you forgetting something? I've got to stop off en route at Mr. Warrender's and pick up the disk from that copy of, what was it again?"

"Marquand. *The Late George Apley.*" I could hardly blame her. We both wanted Hannah's manuscript in any form but Warrender had given Her Ladyship his blessing. Hard cheese on me, as Alix enjoyed saying.

"Okay, just take Dunemere Lane to Main Street and then on James Lane, your first left. Says 'Dead End' but it takes you into the Maidstone courts."

"I'll be there," she said.

The Maidstone Club grounds are spacious with the tennis courts off a distant fairway of the golf course and easily a mile from the main clubhouse. When I got to the tennis shop, where you could have a racquet strung or sign up for a game, there were only two cars parked, one a beat-up antique MG that belonged to Archer the pro. The other, Pam Phythian's classic Bentley. From somewhere beyond the privet hedge I could hear the *pock-pock* of tennis balls. Pam and the pro must be having a hit. I walked around and through the canvases, thought I could see Pam in her tennis whites, no longer required by the Maidstone but clearly preferred. I got closer. It was Pam, all right, looking fine, those long racehorse legs slightly slick with sweat and that good, even tan WASPs do so well. Her tennis wasn't bad either. But when I came all the way 'round the canvases and could see the entire court, she was alone. No pro, no opponent. *Pock-pock,* she hit against the Maidstone's ball-tossing machine with a useful two-fisted backhand and a good, flat, powerful forehand that she slammed from the left side. Tom Knowles said that right from the first, that a lefty drove that stake of privet through Hannah. Well, the cops weren't always wrong. A warning light went on and then, *pock!,* a ball came at Pam and she swung. A terrific return she had. Then, setting up for the next ball, she saw me.

"Oh, hi, Beecher. I didn't think you played tennis."

"Not much, Pam. Came over to see you."

"So you've sniffed out my guilty secret?"

"What?"

"I'm as bad as the late but unlamented Hannah, playing against the ball-tossing machine. The Club's SAM, adjusting the speed so I can't just whack it back routinely every time. I like to be tested. So I go for that Steffi Graf hundred-and-five-mile-an-hour first serve. Even at my age, I like a nice hard ball."

"That's a laugh, at 'your age.' Come on."

"Very gallant, Beech. Thanks. But calendars don't lie."

I was fencing, offering a small compliment rather than telling her why I was here. I wished now I'd waited for Alix. It would be easier to start talking. Not about her tennis but whether she'd killed two people. I was a reporter accustomed to asking questions and trying to get answers. But I'd never asked a question anything close to that direct, not even of a stranger. Never mind the rich neighbor who lived down the lane . . .

"Well . . ." she said, mopping her face and forearms with a crisp white towel pulled from her smart-looking nylon tote bag, smiling easily at me as if to say, yes, I know it's indulgent of me, but I do sweat. And now, Beecher Stowe, why are you here to see me?

"Are you up to speed on the contradictory 'confessions' by Royal Warrender and Claire Cutting?"

"Only that I heard about it on the car radio and the police don't seem to be taking them seriously. Why?"

"Because the cops don't believe either is the killer. Because it leaves us still asking, then who is?"

"And?" she said, as always, very cool.

"And that brings us to you."

"Me? *Me?* Are you serious, Beecher? This isn't at all amusing."

"Not meant to be," I said, deciding to plunge right ahead. Too late now to fret about injured feelings or never again being invited to the annual garden party. I told her that everyone knew she despised Hannah. No argument about that she said, not coolly anymore but decidedly icy. And now we know you were involved with Leo Brass. How do you know that? she demanded. It's all the talk of Boaters, I said, figuring that was vague enough to protect the gossipy waitress from retribution. And insulting enough to get under her hide. It did.

"Me, the talk of Boaters? What would they know about people from Further Lane at a place like Boaters?"

"That you and Leo first came together on some environmental issue. And it heated up from there. So much so that Hannah Cutting heard the talk. Started riding you. Sniggering up her sleeve about Pam Phythian the Ice Queen and Brass the Bayman. Hinted, or at least suggested, maybe even told you outright it was going into her precious book. She threatened to turn you into a local laughingstock. Tell everyone all about your love affair with a common redneck like . . ."

Pam erupted now, slinging her tennis racquet at me so accurately that if I hadn't ducked . . .

"You bastard! What do you know of men like Leo? We had things in common you couldn't possibly even imagine. Hannah wasn't our sort at all. Never was. For her to threaten me was so pathetic. A cheap little social climber from Polish Town. Leo saw right through her. They had a fling once, you know. He slept with her, he slept with her daughter. It was delicious, really, the way he played with them. Then I came along. Leo understood the difference. He was a cut above the usual roughneck Bonacker, the kind of man who could go on, win elections, go to Washington. He and I . . ."

Pam was really chewing the scenery now. Real Bette Davis stuff. Just what I wanted. Get her sore, get her talking. Now I needed backup. Moral support. Where the hell was Her Ladyship?

"Then why kill Leo, why bump off a future senator?" I asked. She made a vaguely dismissive gesture with one of those capable pale hands. So I tried to answer for her, hoping again to goad her into an explosion.

"I think it must have been because he went back to Claire. He'd had his fun with you, the great lady falling for the redneck Bayman, and he thought he could do even better. Now that Hannah was dead, not there dominating her daughter and whomever she married, Leo was looking at Claire a lot differently. Claire wasn't only rich; she was suddenly a lot more attractive. Leo was a maverick and the idea of Hannah playing mother-in-law-from-hell didn't appeal one bit. But now Hannah was out of the way. You'd done Leo a big favor, Pam. You'd cleared the way for a much younger woman to take him away from you, twenty years younger, and one about to become even richer than you. You couldn't accept that. There was something else. When Hannah was killed Leo knew he didn't do it and neither did Claire. Because they were in bed making love at the time. Nor was he sure you did it but he had his suspicions. That's motivation enough, even without the jealousy factor. He was starting to consider going to the police. Or you feared he might. He'd dumped you for a rich, sexy young girl and now he might finger you as a murderer. People kill for a lot less. And when the hurricane came it gave you the opportunity. You knew Leo's passion for the wetlands and all that, knew he'd absolutely have to go down to check The Gut. Great ecological minds work in the same way."

She tossed her head in irritation. "If you're all that bright, why bother killing people with bits of privet hedge? Aren't there subtler ways? Aren't I a pretty fair shot?"

"You and Hannah were forever bickering over the privet. Using a privet stake through her black heart may have seemed to you bleak poetic justice."

She was as truly calm as I was only pretending to be. I even got a smile.

"My, we are clever, Beecher. You'd think you were your father. The Admiral would be so proud the way you put two and three together and get six. You don't add, you multiply. There's privet hedge anywhere you look out here. I've no monopoly on the stuff. Privet is to East

Hampton what the pine is to Maine. The redwood to California. Yet you come up with these astonishing conclusions."

Here was where I started tap-dancing:

"I've been up to your place, broke into one of the greenhouses, stole your gardening gloves. They bore the same combination of soot and privet hedge the crime lab found in the wounds that killed them both, Hannah and Leo Brass."

Her face started to fall apart then. But only for an instant. The old WASP grace under pressure came through. Until, as we both heard a car, she wheeled. It sounded like Alix's Jag. I turned toward the parking lot trying to see if it were. A mistake. When I turned back Pam had her tote bag in one hand and a small but impressive-looking handgun in the other. With what seemed a professional silencer over the muzzle. That Pam, she thought of everything, didn't she?

"Just shut up and stand where you are, Beecher."

"Sure, Pam. No problem." It wouldn't be very smart of her to start shooting people in broad daylight on the grounds of the Maidstone Club but you never knew. She'd killed two people already and had nothing to lose. A weekday morning out of season with nobody around. And with a silencer, to boot. She sounded cool and controlled but why take a chance? People got jittery and started shooting. It happened. I'd been shot in the ass once and didn't want any more of it. Then Alix strode onto the court, seeing both of us but not yet seeing the gun. To Alix it was simply a couple of members having a clubby little chat.

"Hi, there, Pamela. Playing a match? Jolly good to see you. Sorry I'm late, Beecher. The door Mr. Warrender told us was supposed to be open was locked and I had to— Is *that* a gun, Ms. Phythian?"

"How observant. Yes, and I'd like you over on this side of the net as well, please. I'll be leaving shortly in my car and I'd prefer you didn't attempt to impede me."

"Not at all," I said, trying to make it sound as if that were the furthest thing from my mind. As it pretty much was.

Not Alix's, however.

"So it was you that bumped everyone off, I take it? Crumbs, that's a stunner. Not even John le Carré could possibly have . . ."

What the hell was Alix up to? Instead of coming around the net to our side as Pam ordered, she drifted across the baseline. She had something in mind. Just what, I hadn't a clue. But I started talking again, trying to get Pam refocused on me rather than on Alix.

"Clever of you to have known precisely where Leo would be once the storm came ashore. Took someone versed in local topography to know about The Gut and how crucial it is to the ecology of Georgica Pond."

Alix was still moving, a fixed smile on her face. What the hell was she . . . ? Then she said, her voice very steady, "Beecher, how did you get the goods on her, so to speak?"

"The gloves. Her gardening gloves."

"My word, just think of it. . . ."

Pam's voice, hard and angry, cut across our silly dialogue like the crack of a whip. "Enough! There isn't a functioning brain between the two of you. How you stumbled across my path is just sheer rotten luck. I . . ."

Did I see a warning light blinking on? Or was I . . .

"Don't you dare . . ." Pam started.

From somewhere behind me there was a loud bang of sorts and there whizzed past my ear a blur of yellow moving very very fast. *Pock!* Then the same succession of sounds. *Pock-pock!* Facing me, Pam started to dodge, raising the gun menacingly, and then, as a yellow tennis ball smashed into her chest, she staggered and fell.

Game, set, and match, Alix Dunraven.

I used the old length of climbing rope from Hannah's "junk" collection to bind her hands. Then I released tension on the net of the teaching court and had Pam Phythian snugly rolled up like a rug long before the cops arrived and even before she was fully recovered from the thud of that ninety-mile-an-hour serve.

"Fortunate thing she didn't have the machine set to toss up a lob," Alix commented thoughtfully.

Pam, considering her situation, was remarkably composed. Most of her venom was reserved for the late Hannah Cutting.

"I told you she wasn't our sort, not our sort at all. The very idea of her attempting to climb Everest. On the way up from Katmandu she was forever on the cell phone to the gossip columns, posing for photos with the grinning Sherpas, and shaving her legs. To think that a woman so common might one day stand atop a summit where Hillary and Tenzing once . . ."

"And where you yourself also stood, Ms. Phythian," Alix threw in.

"Quite so," Pam Phythian said, pleased at the notion.

THIRTY-FIVE

Ang Thwat spun out into space
and fell into eternity . . .

With Pam at our mercy, I decided to explain why I suspected something had happened three years ago on Everest between Hannah and her that would eventually lead Pam Phythian to violence.

"You were a suspect, I suppose most of us were, no matter how marginally. But when I checked back issues of the *East Hampton Star* I realized it was only a month or so after you returned from that tragic business atop Everest that Hannah was put up for membership in the Ladies' Village Improvement Society and you pulled rank and forced a vote you knew would end by rejecting her. But why? A relatively unimportant matter but you risked embarrassment to kill her chances. Obviously, a few weeks after you both came home, the differences between you had become deadly, far beyond trimming the privet hedge and backing rival charities. It was Everest, wasn't it?"

She just stared at me. Furious and stubborn, sure she could dominate, quite certain I was only making wild guesses.

Very quietly, I said, "The rope, Pam. That length of climbing rope Hannah brought back from Everest. That was it, wasn't it?"

She started to talk then, compulsively. The police had been called and were on the way and I suppose I should have tried to stop her, to have warned Pam against self-incrimination, but I wasn't a policeman or the D.A.; I was certainly no lawyer. And despite being wrapped in tennis netting, she was in no mood to be shut up and seemed in a curious way to be at the center of our attention.

"The traditional approach to Everest is an overland trek of seventy miles or so from Katmandu to the Thyangboche monastery," she began. "It can take two or even three weeks; the porters carry such heavy loads and the country is so rough. May seem like a waste of time, but it works out well, permitting the climbers to acclimate gradually to higher and higher altitudes, helps them put a fine edge on fitness. A mountain like Everest demands more than Tuesdays and Thursdays on the Stairmaster. But our expedition was anything but traditional, half of us high-powered women, 'a dirty half-dozen,' so we laughingly termed ourselves, all of us savvy dames accustomed to having our egos massaged, having our way. So the decision was made to save three weeks and airlift by chopper directly from Katmandu to the monastery base camp and start out from there. I objected, so did a few others. Hannah and the majority would have none of it. She was incredibly eager to push on. She'd cut a deal with one of the TV networks and wanted to get on with the videotaping and the climb and get her adventures on the air. It was sure to sell more books, more magazines, more everything, more . . . Hannah. So we began our trek without the usual preconditioning and with predictable results, pulled muscles, hammies, sprains. On the approach march most of us wore sensible khaki shorts; Hannah sported a miniskirt and kept asking someone or other to shoot photos and videotape of her on the march. She shaved her legs every morning before we broke camp and drove everyone nuts, forever on the cell phone, talking to people in New York and dictating to secretaries back there. A porter broke his leg fording a mountain stream and you could see Hannah looking impatiently at her Cartier tank watch, wondering just how long this latest crisis was going to delay things. A man writhing in agony and she's looking at her watch.

"On the mountain itself, her pushiness actually helped. The higher you climb, the more sluggish people get. They have to be chivied out of their sleeping bags in the morning, forced to saddle up heavy loads and get cracking. Despite her lack of high mountain experience, Hannah was so good at that part of it; you might resent the woman and admire her at the same time. She would have made a marvelous drill instructor at boot camp. And she was fit; that was another thing you couldn't fault her for . . ."

But what happened? I asked. You don't kill someone because she made you get up in the morning and shaved her legs; you threw a shoe at her but you didn't drive a stake of privet through her heart.

It was above camp four that it all happened, Pam said, the camp from which the final assault party would make its sprint for the summit, there and back in one day. Reach the summit or admit failure and fall back. They were running short of options, of oxygen bottles and food and everything else, and worst of all, running short of good weather.

"The monsoon was moving in," Pam went on. "Base camp radio relayed us the weather reports from Delhi each morning, each evening. We'd had a splendid run of almost a fortnight, fine, clear weather and no new snow. But the window of opportunity was closing fast. Delhi reported the monsoon was boiling up out of the Bay of Bengal and headed our way fast. Even the greenest of us knew what that meant; you can't climb above eight thousand meters when the wind blows at a hundred miles an hour and six feet of new snow can fall in a single day. When the monsoon reaches the Himalayas you shut down climbing until

October. The guides chose those of us they considered fit enough to make the attempt. There were two distinct teams. I guess because they thought we were pals, Hannah and I were put together with Ang Thwat the Sherpa on one of them, and from here on would rope up as one. Which displeased both of us since we'd been snapping at each other and didn't really want to be on the same rope. By now, I believe we cordially detested each other."

You couldn't stop her now. What was it that drove them to confession and self-incrimination, she and Royal both, spilling their guts to strangers out of some mystic need to purge themselves of sin? Cotton Mather might have understood it. Or his brother, Increase Mather, or the men who burned the women at Salem. Puritanism and WASP guilt and an irresistible urge to tell all?

"Our rope never did reach the summit," Pam resumed. "Didn't miss by more than a few hundred feet, but by then Wales, our leader, ordered retreat. Snow was falling, daylight fading, wind rising, we were desperately short of oxygen, and the damned Sherpas seemed to have shirked their job of setting up fixed ropes at the steeper places. A grand adventure was turning into nightmare, arguably into disaster. Yet Hannah kept griping. Why couldn't we have pressed on? If she could make it this far with her limited experience, what plagued the rest of us? Hot shots! she sneered. '*Ms. Magazine* Goes on an Outing!'

"Her contempt was something you could feel! We set off back down to camp four and the safety of tents and sleeping bags and primus stoves and radio. Some of us never got there. The storm caught us. One of the Sherpas collapsed. My feet were freezing. I guess we were all pretty badly spent. Even Hannah. But she kept on and on about it, we'd been so near the top . . .

"We were all roped in two-person or three-person teams. We were halfway down the Southeast Ridge when

Conrad and the Sherpa just disappeared. Wales said it was ten thousand feet down that side of the ridge. I didn't even feel a sense of loss. We were all going to die, I was sure. Why mourn the dead when we'd shortly be with them? Wales was shouting at us now. He was panicking, too. All that Seattle cool oozing out of him. I think he was afraid we were giving up, that we'd refuse to go on, would just sit down there in the snow and die. We would have, too, I guess we realized that, but there comes a stage of fatigue and oxygen starvation where you couldn't care less. Die? Why not? Nothing could be worse than this. I know I felt that way. Wales was starting to go back to help one of the Sherpas. I remember screaming at him not to leave us, to get us the hell out of here. I lost it a bit, I guess, and found myself shouting at him:

"'It's only a Sherpa!'

"It was then that Hannah Cutting slapped me. Called me a bitch. A coward. A weakling . . .

"And I was none of those things. I was so much better than she was. My breeding so much better . . . It was just that I was exhausted, worn down, out of my head for lack of oxygen. I only wanted to hollow out a little place in the snow and lie down and die."

She paused.

"We were at that stretch of the Southeast Ridge when it narrows to a knife edge with those terrible voids falling away on either side. Hannah and I were roped together, three on the rope. Ang was leading with me second and Hannah trailing. Tired as I was, and frightened, I was the more experienced climber, I had the better technique. Hannah had that astonishing primal energy but even she seemed to accept that I should be ahead of her. The knife edge was by now more like a razor's edge, so narrow along here it was a matter of putting one foot ahead of the other and keeping your balance, like a high wire act. All this in darkness and with a full gale blowing and heavy snow. Then my crampon slipped, my left foot went out from under me, and suddenly I was falling. It was ten thousand feet down and I knew I was going to die. Only I didn't fall, I didn't die. Ang reached back to steady me and then, so fast I don't know what happened, he slipped and went over the edge. I was pulled down, too, and started to slide after him, pulled by the rope. Hannah threw herself down on the other side of the knife edge as a counterweight and with the rope pulled in opposite directions; I was being nearly cut in half. I could see Ang hanging there over the void, hear him wheezing and helpless. To the other side, Hannah lay flat on her stomach holding all three of us from sliding off into space. But she was losing the fight. Ang and I together weighed too much for her to haul us back. Slowly but surely we were all sliding toward infinity. Hannah was cursing. I could hear her panting, between the swear words. And then, miraculously for us, tragically for him, the rope connecting Ang to me and behind me to Hannah parted!

"Ang Thwat spun out into space, not making a sound, and fell into eternity. The rope had parted, leaving Hannah and me secure, balanced on either side of the knife edge. After a minute to get our breath, we were able to scramble back to our feet. And now it was Hannah who would lead, who'd proved the stronger.

"I started to say thanks, for having been so quick and so strong, for having saved my life. She cut me off with a snarl. 'I didn't do it for you, Pam. I did it for myself! If you fell, you'd take me with you.'

"Somehow, we got down to the South Col and bivouacked for the night. Wales never got back. Two others died in the night. Frozen and exhausted. When the chopper came Hannah laughed at me. 'Better go first, Pam, you poor dear,' that sort of thing, her voice full of contempt. My feet were solid blocks of ice and I was still feeling awful but I wasn't going to take that. I swung at her with my rucksack and knocked her right off her feet. But she was quickly up and hitting out at me. I remember the guides pulling us apart and then I was in the Nepalese chopper and flying and for the first time since the evening before, I realized I was going to live, that I wasn't going to die on Mount Everest."

Pam stopped.

"It was later that day I also realized I'd put myself forever at Hannah Cutting's mercy, that all she had to do was to tell what happened, and I'd be drummed out of society. In a small town like East Hampton if people are laughing at you behind your back, you might as well sell the house, pack up, and get out. It's never forgotten, you're never forgiven for not living up to whatever defines your class. I was the blueblood and I'd folded; Hannah the peasant from Polish Town hadn't. That was four years ago. She's been holding it over my head ever since. And now she was coming out with this book of hers that Liz Smith was saying would name names and tell all. And I had to do something about it now before she left for Nepal and the reconnaissance because she might not be back to East Hampton until next summer. By that time she might well have succeeded in climbing Everest and her book would be out. A heroine and a best-selling author all wrapped in the one sexy Hannah package.

"She was stronger than I was and I hated her for it; she'd saved my life and I'd never been able to forgive her for that."

For all her gush, she was still tiptoeing carefully around one thing. There was still one thing about which she wasn't leveling and telling all. It wasn't just that Hannah might humiliate her in society; it was that Hannah knew something even worse that happened up there on the knife edge of the Everest ridge lines. So I asked:

"The rope holding you to Ang, Pam. What happened to it? Why did it mean so much to Hannah to have a lousy length of old mountaineering rope?"

She cursed at me then. Like Hannah had cursed on Everest.

I pressed her nonetheless.

"Because Ang's end of the rope wasn't frayed but had been cut? By the climber nearest to him and just above?"

"You bastard!"

"I've seen the rope, Pam. It was cut by the climber closest to Ang Thwat. By you."

"She cut it! Hannah cut the . . ."

"If Hannah cut the rope, both you and Ang would have slid off into space. No, somehow you contrived to cut it to save yourself, and incidentally, Hannah Cutting. And in the doing, you killed a Sherpa named Ang Thwat. No wonder you started a fund for his family and wrote a fat check."

"Damn you! If I get loose, I'll kill you too. Both of you. I . . ."

"You won't get loose, Pam. Not with your wrists tied with climbing rope . . ."

Her handsome mouth fell open and she stared at her wrists, wrapped tightly in a length of old rope I'd lifted from Hannah's place. And for the first time, she fell silent. The first police car rolled up then, its roof lights flashing but no siren. These were, after all, the grounds of the Maidstone Club.

Tom Knowles read Pam her rights. "I'd better do it properly," he told me out of the corner of his mouth. "She's a whack job, of course, but she'll have the best white-shoe law firm in Manhattan representing her. They'll plead migraine and PMS and everything but Per-

sian Gulf syndrome, and accuse poor Hannah of casting
spells. My bet is Pam gets away with community service
and a stiff fine. Does the Junior League qualify as 'community service,' Beech?"

"Wouldn't be at all surprised."

Alix wanted to know how I knew that, about her gardening gloves, the soot and the privet, and all that. "I lied.
But she's got a greenhouse. Where else would you keep
gardening gloves? Though I've no idea what's on 'em. . . ."

"And the rope that wasn't frayed?"

"That was no lie; that was the real goods. I figured setting up that foundation for Ang the martyr might be inspired by guilt. Because if the rope really broke, it was
Ang's fault as one of their professional guides, and why
should Pam blame herself? I'm just guessing as part of
her equipment, she had a knife. Hannah suspected it as
well and before they got off the mountain, made sure she
had the length of rope so that Pam couldn't somehow doctor or get rid of it in the unlikely situation they might convene a coroner's jury or whatever it is they have in Nepal."

"So that was why I had to go 'into the tank' at Middlefield, and take poor Mrs. Kroepke off to the loo to bathe
my fevered brow, while you sought out the bit of rope to
see if it really had frayed or was cut."

"That's it, the rope was the maguffin."

Alix shook her head. And then kissed me lightly on the
lips.

"My, you are the clever one."

THIRTY-SIX

*But who was the real villain? Maybe
they were both victims . . .*

So Pam Phythian was under arrest (bail would be set;
Tom was confident she would make it), Royal Warrender
was feeling better and might soon be released from the
hospital, he and Claire Cutting were catching up on a
quarter century of neglect, and Alix had Hannah's elusive
disk.

Except that one more strange thing happened: two days
before the hurricane, which explained the delay in its
being publicly made known, Rose Thrall burned to death.

It wasn't even a police case, certainly no mystery. The
papers and, very briefly, local radio reported that a retired
secretary and professional typist, who many years ago had
won a national stenography contest, 350 words a minute in
Gregg shorthand, had died at her home in Hampton Bays.
An antique frame house, open fireplaces, smoking in bed
(alcohol was not mentioned; no reason to besmirch the
memory of a woman who drank a fifth of rye a day), the
cause of the fire and the woman's subsequent death, were
patently evident.

As a minor afterthought the papers noted Ms. Thrall
had once worked for the late Hannah Cutting, who was
killed earlier in the month. No mention that, and why
should there have been, Alix and I had gone there to grill
Rose Thrall about Hannah's book.

I told Tom Knowles about it now, asked what he thought about a possible link.

"You're weaving gossamer, Beech. The old lady was a rummy. Probably fell asleep with a cigarette in her hand. Happens a lot."

"She didn't smoke, Tom."

"Oh?"

You didn't often surprise a good cop like Knowles. I'd just done so. Tom promised to look more closely into the initial verdict of "misadventure." And to check if any cigarette butts found at the Thrall place matched the brand smoked by, say, Pam Phythian.

Meanwhile, right next door to my place, there was a constant coming and going of helicopters at Toby Montana's. An East Hampton Hurricane Relief Gala was being organized. Her music mogul husband was calling in his markers and the stars were rushing to commit. Ms. Montana herself and such other local idols as Paul Simon, Billy Joel and Kim Basinger would also perform (the committee was attempting to find a gracious way of declining Yoko Ono's generous offer to do a lengthy reading of her own poetry). Alec Baldwin as emcee and fireworks by Grucci with narration by George Plimpton. Even Sting had relaxed his standards somewhat and agreed to stay over a few days to appear. Carl Icahn, not previously noted for charitable works, agreed to serve as a committee co-chair, with the whole thing to be catered by local resident Warner LeRoy, who owned Tavern on the Green in Manhattan. Being auctioned off would be such desirable items as a private consultation with New Age guru Deepak Chopra, a wardrobe of Calvin Klein underwear autographed by the designer, a personally guided tour of Gardiners Island conducted by Lord of the Manor Robert Lion Gardiner himself, and an hour's in-line skating along local lanes with JFK Jr. and his bride. "Put me down for two tickets," I reluctantly told a committee lady who called. Then my father phoned from Oslo:

"The house still standing? You all right?" he inquired.

"Yes, the house is okay. I'm here as well."

I thought he might have asked first about his only child.

Relieved to learn there was no damage, not even any family casualties, my old man then launched into a spirited and detailed account of the salmon fishing. When he'd hung up I confessed a slight disenchantment.

"Oh, cheer up," Alix said sensibly. "No one damaged here and he killed some fine salmon. Well played, both Stowes, father and son, I'd say."

"I suppose so."

I guess I was still feeling let down about the disk, now firmly in Her Ladyship's hands, and all for the greater glory and profit of Random House and Harry Evans—Hannah Cutting's story, the story Walter Anderson assigned me to get. Some start to a new job! I'm this highly touted foreign correspondent with *Newsweek* and the *Boston Globe* behind me and a lifelong resident of Further Lane who knew the entire cast of characters. And I get beaten to the story by a slip of an English girl in her twenties who'd never even seen East Hampton before.

Well, I wasn't going to fight her for it. I'd cobble a story somehow about Hannah's humble beginnings. And with Royal and Claire talking so openly, the mystery of what happened on Further Lane long ago was there for the taking. But it would have been sweet, being able to read Hannah's own account of her extraordinary life, even before Random House got hold of it. What the hell! There were winners and there were losers and I had sense enough to recognize the difference.

"Come on," I said.

She didn't always argue the toss, and didn't this time, but climbed into the four-wheel drive with me without question. It was not only the end of the case, the wrap-up of the story, what Alix and I had together was coming down to an end. I drove up the Three Mile Harbor Road in the dusk and turned onto the little old winding beach road to park. "Let's walk a little." She wasn't really wearing walking shoes but she was game and the light was fading but it was nice at sunset to see the old beach pavilion where maybe a dozen people were lighting up grills and opening beers, talking, laughing, listening to music from a boom box, local people, aware there wouldn't be many more soft evenings like this with summer gone. On the beach someone had a keg and a lighted grill and a man was grilling hot dogs. You could smell those hot dogs, the greasy smoke rising, from a hundred yards off. A couple of teenagers tossed an old football and three or four men in shorts stood knee-deep in the water, using spinning reels to cast for stripers in the dusk and not getting much. Little kids ran around and girls laughed and a baby wailed. And a mother hushed it soothingly. The sun was down now with millions of stars up, and the water on the incoming tide rushed by dark and swift from the sea.

"Nice," I said.

Alix reached out and took my hand.

"Yes," she said.

We walked back to where we'd left the Blazer and got a couple of stools at the bar of Michael's and ordered drinks. Behind the bar a small sign said, "Next time, bring your wife."

Tom had filled me in on what Pam was saying now with lawyers present, especially about the death of Leo Brass, and I told Alix.

"Leo was so much bigger and stronger, the cops were curious how she'd killed a man like that with a sharpened stick. Pam said he'd been drinking and was more than ever full of himself, how he'd straightened out the experts and

told them they knew nothing, how he was going down to
The Gut high up there astride the Cat, ready and willing to
bulldoze The Gut to let in the sea. And then he was going
back to Claire. That it had been fun with Pam but it was
over. Claire was half her age and richer. The Cutting name,
the Cutting money, would enable Leo to achieve wonders,
ecological, political, and otherwise, that would have been
out of reach for a Bonacker. Besides, he grinned lascivi-
ously, 'Claire's pretty good in bed. You know these young
ones. . . .'"

Leo knew how to hurt a woman.

So Pam said they ought to have one final fling, that
she'd go with him and his bulldozer down to The Gut,
fetch along a poncho and a blanket, so with the wind up
and the surf pounding and the hurricane coming ashore,
they could make exciting and even extraordinary love one
last time, right there at The Gut, on the narrow windswept,
rain-drenched strand between pond and ocean.

"And they did," Tom Knowles said, "screwing in a hurricane. And when they finished, Leo was lying there on a
blanket, naked, rain-slick, and half drunk, and Pam took
out another of her handy privet stakes thoughtfully
brought along for the occasion, and just ran him through,
cold as January. And when she was sure he was dead,
rolled his body into the pond, tidied up, and drove home
in her own car, leaving behind the Cat and one dead Bayman. And every clue and track washed away by the grandfather of all wind and rainstorms and a tide washing right
across the beach and into the pond. Hell of a woman . . ."

Alix agreed enthusiastically.

"I'll say! Make love to the chap during a hurricane and
then drive a stake through his gizzard. Wow!"

Detective Knowles said her lawyers had already come
up with a unique defense in the matter of the dead Sherpa.
"Triage," he said, "that's what they'll argue to get that

death thrown out of court. That when one alpinist is inad-
vertently about to cause the death of two more, the others
are perfectly entitled to cut his rope and save themselves.
I don't know if it'll wash but it hints just how clever Pam's
defense is going to be. They'll have everything in there on
her behalf but depositions from Mark Fuhrman."

Beyond that, Alix was still chewing over the metaphys-
ical aspects of the case:

"Was Pam the real villain or was it Hannah?"

"Oh, hell, one of them killed two and probably three
people, maybe four if you count Rose Thrall; the other
was just a pain in the ass. There is a difference."

"Of course. But in a larger sense, I think they're both
victims. And perhaps both villains, as well. If you consider the backgrounds of the two women, so different and
yet so . . ."

That was Oxford talking, debating the question from
two sides at once, and I let her rattle on without offering
much. I was more focused on the inescapable fact our glorious adventure was coming to an end, our week and a little was over. That this bright and beautiful and funny
young woman would go home to Random House and not
to my house. That her laughter would soon be tinkling
once again on the city's East Side and not here on Further
Lane. Alix would be vanishing back into the vastness of
Manhattan among the ex-pats and the elegant, and this
picturesque little episode, this brief encounter by the
ocean, would fade and be forgotten, merely a footnote to
September.

It was silly of me, I realize, this small melancholy I was
indulging, since I would shortly be moving into Manhattan myself, taking an apartment, probably on that same
posh East Side, and that all I had to do was to pick up a
phone and call her. It was simply I suspected what we had
here at a small town in the Hamptons would not travel

well nor flourish in great cities. I knew that I would miss Alix in a lot of ways. I confess even to imagining that without her cheerful, frisky carnality, just how vacant my bed was going to be tonight.

We had dinner and drove back to the house. "You'll be driving back to town then," I said gloomily.

"Yes," Alix said, more subdued than I'd have expected her to be, considering her triumphs. No gloating, no smug self-applause.

"Okay."

She paused briefly. "But not until morning if you don't mind. I'm rather bushed. May I sleep here tonight, leave early in the morning?"

"Of course."

Then, not slyly but with a clear conscience and open face, that lovely face, Lady Alix Dunraven said:

"At the hospital, you may recall, when Mr. Warrender asked if I were going to share what was on the computer disk with you, I was rather precise in my response, almost legalistic. I didn't say yes or no, simply that you were a journalist with your own assignments and responsibilities while I was representing the excellent book publishing firm of Random House. I prefer not to lie, y'know."

I couldn't recall her exact words but what did it matter, this splitting of hairs. And, in truth, she lied like a newspaper; I'd heard her lying to Evans, who paid her salary and whose employee pro tem she was. But this was our last night. I wasn't going to hector her.

"So?"

She smiled, a small, slow smile, and said:

"So I'm going to leave the disk here next to your own laptop on this kitchen table where I know it'll be safe. And where hardly anyone will notice it or think to scroll through it hurriedly, taking a few crucial notes to be used in an article or two that couldn't possibly be construed as competitive with Random House and its plans to publish a quality hardcover book that could, in fact, end up on various best-seller lists and even attract Hollywood and the producers of major motion pictures that . . ."

I guess my mouth was somewhat ajar because when she reached up to kiss me, a very light, flirtatious kiss, my mouth was open, though only briefly, to her tongue.

"I'll be off now, Beecher," she said. "You will be coming to bed shortly, won't you?"

"Yes," I said. "Probably do a little reading first. But I'll be in, yes."

"Super," said Her Ladyship firmly, "that's quite what I'd hoped you'd say. We don't have all that much time till morning and there are one or two things we haven't yet tried."

On that provocative note, she turned and left. As Zooey once remarked of his mother, you do give yourself the exit lines. I didn't say it. Instead I growled, but in silence, try to keep me away. You don't say rude and vulgar things to a proper young woman whose daddy was the fourth (or was it the fifth?) senior Earl in the realm and who had a double first at Oxford, and won the Tony Godwin Award, besides.

THIRTY-SEVEN

Impudent people, who tried to become us . . .

They set bail at half a million and, as Detective Knowles predicted, Pam made it. Local people, most of them (not the Baymen, however, still mourning Leo as one of theirs), were supportive, sympathetic, even cordial. Pam Phythian was Old East Hampton and Hannah wasn't; whatever the crime, that still made a difference out here. The old lineup: WASP vs. anti-WASP; you know who wins that one. The Ladies' Village Improvement Society got up a subcommittee to study whether a Pam Phythian Defense Fund ought to be raised. A board meeting of the Maidstone Club will convene shortly to determine if her membership should be suspended pending the trial. Sentiment is apparently leaning toward continuing her in good standing. On assumption-of-innocence grounds, of course. She was routinely getting the usual cocktail and dinner invitations and I wasn't, in that I may have broken the code (by tattling on a fellow member of the Maidstone). I saw Pam a couple more times around East Hampton, once on Further Lane, the other time buying doughnuts at Dreesen's. She cut me dead. Which was not entirely a shock, considering.

In an interview with *Newsday,* an interview Sullivan & Cromwell urged her not to grant, Pam sketched out what her defense would be at the murder trial. It wasn't anything personal, these things she was supposed to have done, but "a matter of class warfare," the legitimate struggle to pro-

tect and preserve the old values. Pam saw it as a Consti-
tutional issue, the right of a society to defend and maintain
itself against external or internal dangers. Hannah's purchase of farmland for development threatened the common weal; Leo's attempt to blow up The Gut put wetlands
at risk. Pam was nuts, of course, but the argument resonated powerfully among some of the East Hampton Establishment; the Old Money people secretly thrilled when
Pam spoke of defending them and their class against
strivers like Hannah and Leo Brass who, she said, "had
gotten above themselves."

As Pam Phythian viewed it, "These were impudent people. Who tried to become us . . ."

September was nearly over and I was glad of it. Jesse
Maine was still around and we did some fishing and took
a haul of late blues off Gardiners Island. Sid Felton actually did offer him some vague situation in Los Angeles
but Jesse turned it down.

"I was tempted, Beech, the O'Leary sisters and all, but
there are people who belong in Hollywood and people who
don't. I have my little problems here with the Bonackers
and the authorities, but they know me and I know them and
in ways, we're like family."

I'd lost Alix to the city, to her responsibilities amid the
stepped-up frenzy of book publishing in autumn's change
of seasons. Having brought in Hannah Cutting's book
made Alix something of a heroine and Harry Evans even
approved an expense account for her time in East Hampton that consisted mainly of gas for the Jag, one night at
the Mauve House, and any number of purchases from the
clothing boutiques. I missed her a lot, even missed the
poodle growling at me in Alix's bed, missed Alix in Alix's
bed. Where did you find women like Alix who drove like
Richard Petty in Jags and traveled with borrowed poodles

and brought you Dreesen's doughnuts in bed and sent E-mail messages in cipher on Louis Vuitton laptops?

Walter Anderson liked the piece I did for *Parade* and especially that it would run months before Harry could get the book out. When both editors worked for the same company, things like that mattered. The weather turned crisp and we had frost on the lawn one morning. You could feel it on the wind, change coming, and no longer did I swim every day. The striped bass were running thin and the party boats came into port empty. A fresh film festival was cranking up and private jets landed hourly at the airport, disgorging men and women wearing black clothes and handsome folk sporting shades at night were seen in the streets. *Le tout* Hollywood had arrived. And I realized with a shudder I actually knew and had interviewed some of these people. It would be a relief to be moving into the City.

Into Manhattan, where nobody knew anyone; there were too many people there for that.

Look for *Gin Lane*—James Brady's new novel of life in the Hamptons—on sale now in hardcover from St. Martin's Press. An excerpt follows . . .

ONE

Men who were always gloriously broke but attached to the top girls . . .

To write about and understand Gin Lane in Southampton, New York, it is helpful to have lived nearby so that you have at least a passing acquaintance with that rich and famous road and the breed of people who live there. And how this past spring they confronted and coped with what they saw as a threat to their place and their quality of life. It's a lively yarn, quite as colorful as anything in a full-blown and fleshed-out history of Gin Lane, and does credit to only a few of us. Since the cast of characters includes powerful folk who believe they pretty much run the country (and perhaps they do!), much of what happened there on Gin Lane in late May and June with the Southampton "Season" barely under way has been hushed up. No one really wanted it out and especially not the government, neither Southampton's nor Washington's. For most people the president's problems began with the running of the White House interns. But along Gin Lane months earlier, we knew how near he'd come to stumbling into an entirely distinct scandal not of his making; we'd seen evidence of a presidential skittishness none of us yet understood. Probably you've heard rumors, the snippets of truth, those partial explanations, the outright gossip: about how the president of the United States failed Tom and Daisy Buchanan and, for all he knew, might have broken their daughter's heart. And why the earl of Bute never got to dance at his son's wedding, depriving the old gent of "having a gallop about the hardwood with a bridesmaid!" And grounds on which a celebrated fashion designer was arrested. And who very nearly got shot at Cowboy Dils's house and how A. J. Foyt was asked to save the Bridge-hampton raceway and where Mandy Buchanan danced on tables and how the forty thousand honeybees died and why "Nipper" Gascoigne chided his boyhood chum "Fruity" Metcalfe and how Señorita de Playa's splendid pecs were deprived of kayaking on the Nile and why Wyseman Clagett was warning against El Niño and at-tempting to eat his own ear and just who it was sent the Marines ashore. As well as the role played by the Shin-necock Indians and those Argentino polo players and what it was got *Women's Wear Daily* on the case and why peo-ple were squashing lemons into their hair and wearing watches on the wrong wrists and how Nurse Cavell res-cued the Dalai Lama's ambassador-without-portfolio and the future of the shellfish hatchery and bad feelings over Magistrate Hobbes's unfortunate seizure and who bor-rowed Captain Bly's industrial-strength sunblock and why an apparently innocent tango ignited fistfights with the RAF and whether the Eel Lady predicted an early spring.

I realize all this sounds pretty complicated. Maybe I better just tell you how my own good intentions foolishly got me pulled into those and related events along Gin Lane and who was involved and what really did go on this past spring in Southampton. As best I can remember . . .

Further Lane, where my father and I live in East Hampton, is fourteen miles east of Southampton's famous Gin Lane.

And along both of these brief and lovely oceanfront lanes people are forever debating just which of the two Hamptons is better, richer, a more desirable place to live and raise families and enjoy the good life. They also argue just which have been the truly *great* Seasons out here, the vintage summers no one who experienced them will ever forget.

From one celebrated Hampton to the other is but a twenty-minute drive, an easy hour's bike ride along the Atlantic Ocean, and if you are fit, a half-day's stroll in the sun. For places that are so close, the two Hamptons are quite different in style. Book publisher John Sargent, a sophisticated and witty man who long ran Doubleday for Nelson and the family, once attempted in a merry moment to explain about the two villages: "If you're going to dinner in Southampton you wear a tie but no socks; and in East Hampton you wear socks and no tie."

There may be something to that or no sense at all, but there are other, less superficial distinctions as well, I'm sure, and not being either a historian or a social scientist but simply a journalist, I will leave it there. Both Hamptons have their traditions, their accepted ways, their look, and the casual local snobberies that flourish with age along certain roads and at the more desirable addresses. That these snobberies are casual does not make them any less cruel and cutting. Gin and Further Lanes, behind their masking hedges and great, gated walls, possess a haunting beauty, each very lovely in its own distinctive way, and they are linked by a single, narrow road, by the ocean, by a strip of gorgeous beach.

And by money.

When you arrive there on Gin Lane, you find yourself on a narrow, somewhat claustrophobic road with one slim lane in each direction onto which hedges and walls and gates press close. And if you are fortunate, through the gates and thin places in the privet hedge and down the graveled drives, some of the drives so long and sinuous they are interrupted for safety by speed bumps, you may even glimpse the ocean. It is always there, just beyond the great houses and tennis courts and marble pools and rich, rolled and sloping, darkly grassy lawns. But in these precincts, an Atlantic view is exclusively purchased, and even the sand looks expensive. The people along Gin Lane are rich as well, always have been, I guess.

Through the years, and even today, it has been a gorgeous place. Though over cocktails or after golf or inhaling a surely unnecessary final midnight brandy, the subject comes up and the proposition debated by the modernists and those who insist on favoring "the old days". Which really were Gin Lane's best years? Which the best times? The top crowds? The prettiest women? The most lavish parties? The quintessential Southampton Season? Certain glorious years are nominated, specific moments are recalled, various men and women mentioned, this great house or that remembered and eulogized, a road race or a polo match or historic carouse described in exquisite if antique detail, a particularly splendid lawn party praised or champagne breakfast cited. And, inevitably, during these genial exchanges there will be someone who nominates Ten bis Gin Lane (the original Number Ten was washed away in the "great" hurricane of '38, thus justifying the label "bis" on its successor), and others will nod and half smile in amiable memory, and Number Ten bis will get its share of votes as a Gin Lane address ever to be remembered.

I'm from an old Hamptons family (Beecher Stowe being a familiar name out here), but having been born in France, and for a time working as a foreign correspondent, I'm hardly the fellow to make such judgments, and prefer listening to those who claim to know. Maybe, connoisseurs say, of all the good times there ever were along Gin Lane, some of the best came right after the war, from '46 on; 1946 I mean, since in the Hamptons the good times

have been going on for three centuries (of course, bad
times occasionally punctuated the good, though these are
rarely mentioned). But in 1946 and 1947 the world was at
last out of uniform, back home, and at play. Then began
the summers when Angier Duke and his brother Tony
came home from the war to Gin Lane. Ever since, there've
been Dukes at various places here and there along the lane,
these days at Wyndcote Farm, but at that time they had
their house at Ten bis Gin Lane that people, including the
Dukes themselves, good-naturedly and with youthful, self-
deprecating wit, labeled "the Duke Box." From Memorial
Day through Labor Day, what Southampton calls the Season, the house was never empty.

As an agreeable chum of Tony and Luly Duke (Luly is
Tony's wife, and you probably know the man I mean) remembers the house even now, half a century later: "It was
always filled with pretty girls, out from Manhattan, and
White Russians, dashing fellows who worked in PR or
sold expensive fragrances to Saks and Bergdorf or were
trying to get jobs with E. F. Hutton or Merrill Lynch, plus
a few clever men like Serge Obolensky (a prince who had
actually served and knew the tsar!) and his comrades
Count Vava and one Sasha, a Guards officer whose last
name none but Sasha could pronounce, and then but marginally, as well as other men who were always gloriously
broke, but attached to the top girls in a time when the
really top girls looked better than women ever had. Remember? There was Audrey the Conover Girl and Faye the
Powers Girl and, in from Hollywood, a couple of Goldwyn
Girls called Mona and Jill. A French lounge pianist named
Jacques Frey, invariably addressed by the Goldwyn Girls
as "Monsieur Pierre," dropped by in June and stayed the
summer, reminiscent of poor Gatsby's "Mr. Klipspringer,"
camping out there in the sunroom playing piano, the show
tunes everyone could sing and to which anyone could

dance, the tall windows opened to lawns and sprawling patios and dunes and the beach beyond and the ocean's surf, so there was music everywhere, indoors and out, and the laughter and voices of the girls as well . . .

Tony and Angie Duke had enjoyed splendid wars, and so had many of their friends, including the Russians (they were OSS mostly and had been parachuted into dicey places where they did deadly things), and now all of them felt obliged thoroughly to enjoy the peace. Which they did from the end of May to early September, when, in the week following Labor Day, the Southampton house was tidied up and shuttered and they all, Russians and girls and Monsieur Pierre, plus Count Vava and Prince Obolensky, and various Duke boys, returned to Manhattan, simply moving the party from Gin Lane to El Morocco and the Stork.

It was that house, that "gentleman's estate" (in the stuffy, pretentious phrasing of real estate advertisements), which Leicester (Cowboy) Dils bought for $12 million a year or two back and in which he briefly, and flamboyantly, lived until what happened this past spring, at the very start of yet another Southampton Season. Until then, Cowboy had been enjoying himself and delighting his friends, less elegantly but every bit as fully as the Dukes did so long ago, even while scoffed at by his "betters," men who clucked at the very idea of their new neighbor. While the Duke boys' parties inspired rhapsodies of memory half a century later, Dils's contemporary gatherings invited privileged, local scorn.

"Cowboy Dils on Gin Lane? Preposterous." And probably it was. Yet who was there to tell a wealthy American such as Dils that he couldn't buy this piece of property or that and live wherever he chose? Even if he did entertain odd friends and loudly. And was forever threatening to "have a fistfight" with someone. How strangely soothing and old-fashioned the phrase "I want to have a fistfight with you!"

It occurred to the few of us who actually liked him that with Dils, even his hostilities were comfortable and homespun.

I mentioned the differences between East Hampton and Southampton, the distinctions between our Further Lane and their Gin Lane; mentioned as well the links they share: the narrow road, the lovely beach, the ocean on which both front, and the money.

Cowboy Dils understood the money part, I guess, but not much else about the Hamptons or the Season. He was a queer duck with all the usual tics and neuroses, but he had remained very much the westerner, and had a westerner's open, easy, joshing ways. Where he came from, traditions began a few decades back and a hundred years was a long time; here in the East we counted by centuries. There are local people who can count back twelve generations of Hamptons residence, to the 1660s, when Connecticut still owned some of the Hamptons. And from the very moment he moved in, much of what Gin Lane was and stood for eluded Dils. Despite this, there were in Cowboy's time glorious days and nights at his mansion at Ten bis. "Good Gawd A-mighty!" he cried in considerable if primitive exasperation, "I was only trying to make people happy."

It was what Cowboy Dils didn't understand about the place and its traditions that in the end drove him from Gin Lane and emptied that wonderful house which used to be filled with music and laughter and the top girls and dashing Russians, the place at Ten bis Gin Lane they once called the Duke Box.

TWO

What it is in spring that turns men and women reckless, no one could say.

In the good years—and despite our latitude, 41 degrees north, this promised to be one of them—spring comes early to the East End of Long Island, to what is known generically, and in the gossip columns, as the Hamptons. And with spring each year begins a new time we call "the Season."

Along the beach paths and rural country roads of East Hampton and Southampton and Water Mill and Bridge-hampton and Amagansett and Montauk, the old Puritan villages that have bordered the Atlantic since the 1640s, the long, chill winter just sort of vanished this year one warmish, sunny day in mid-April. On Gin Lane and Dune Road and Lily Pond Lane and along Bluff Road and the Old Montauk Highway and on Further Lane, you got those first deliciously teasing hints of a better time: the snow gone, the wind-driven sand no longer abrasive as emery and scouring bare limbs, the ice melted off the brackish ponds. The migratory birds were back and the first silly plants had come up, gaudy with optimistic color in a monochrome land, flirtatious and at risk, daring the last frost, imperiling themselves the way careless men and au-dacious women do, in passion, or in drink. Credit the ocean for our early spring, the moderating effect of sea-water and the Gulf Stream and the onshore breeze blowing across it toward the beaches and over the land. Or so I'm told by old-timers like The Eel Lady, a local seer who sells live baits and predicts weather. That's what she claims warms the East End and propagates and excites our early growths, our premature greenery; what it is in spring that turns men and women reckless, no one can say. Not even The Eel Lady. The way we are, I suppose.

I didn't come back to the Hamptons this year until May. And then, unexpectedly.

I'd been in California to interview an important actress. I won't mention her name here. Not fair, since the interview never came off. But she was one of the biggies with the requisite Academy Award and all that. And good; her Oscar was no fluke. She was as big even as Streep and Close; younger, too. A little younger. A wonderful actress and beautiful woman, and I'd arranged, with her people, to do a piece for the magazine about her new film. And after all the arranging, with her people getting back to me and my getting back to her people (in California, people are always "getting back" to you), when I arrived she wouldn't see me. Didn't even hint she might be "getting back" to me. Just plain sent out word to go away. Something happened. Was she ill? I could understand illness. People got sick and they canceled. No, not that. Well, maybe she'd disliked the new movie's final cut and didn't choose to promote it. No, not that, either. In the end no one ever told me exactly what it was and I never got to see her. But the buzz suggested it was a young man, much younger. They'd been together here and in Europe, France, I believe, and then something happened and he went off. And the joy went out of her and she didn't give a shit anymore and didn't care to hype the film or talk to me or go on Letterman or do those other things actors do. Nor did I find out the young man's name.

So I flew back to New York.

"These things happen," Anderson said. He wasn't happy about it but he said he understood. Anderson is the editor of *Parade,* the largest-circulation magazine in the world, and we were sitting in his corner office at 711 Third Avenue talking about what happened out there in L.A. and about what I might think about doing instead. I'm under contract to write eight pieces a year for Anderson and this was the first time I'd failed to deliver. "Not your fault, Beecher," he said, and of course it wasn't. But neither was Anderson much for trotted-out excuses and labored explanations; few serious editors are. While I was also a professional who took pride in getting the job done. It's no great credit to me, just how Episcopalians and Harvard men were supposed to be, how my father is, how we were in my family. Professionals, who knew the work and did it. Anderson, who'd been a Marine, was that way himself, perhaps one of the reasons we get along.

My new book was out, the one I wrote on terrorism in Europe and the Middle East and North Africa (the king of Morocco having graciously provided a brief book jacket blurb), and doing well with both the reviewers and the *Times* best-seller list, sitting there at an encouraging number six for nonfiction, and until this failed assignment with the actress, I was feeling myself a pretty bright fellow indeed. Anderson was sensitive to mood and didn't want his writers sulking, so to clear the air between us over my failure, he said why didn't I get out of the city. Maybe go out to the Hamptons, now that the weather had turned, to do that piece on the Baymen I was forever talking about, about the last hardcore commercial fishermen we have in our overcivilized part of the world. After all, the *Parade* story I wrote about Hannah Cutting, and how Hannah got to Further Lane, finding fame and wealth, until in the end it all kind of ganged up and killed her, had turned into a pretty good yarn. . . .

"This best-seller about the Gloucester fishing boat that goes down, *The Perfect Storm,* is good stuff," Anderson said. "Same kind of men as your Baymen, I imagine. A slice of America people in the great cities, sitting down to a fish dinner in a first-rate restaurant, never pause to consider. I thought of asking Peter Matthiessen to do the story. He's out there, knows the territory."

"You could do worse. He's very good," I said. "Very."

"So are you," Anderson said, "and you're under contract and he isn't. I prefer to use the writers we're paying already."

That made sense. And who ever said editors considered only the words and not the dollars?

And so that was how a pout on the part of a famous actress who'd lost her boyfriend sent me slinking back to New York unfulfilled. And almost as an afterthought, got Anderson to give me an assignment that, without his intending to do so, would entangle me with Cowboy Dils and whatever demons pursued him.

Not something Anderson expected or I sought. But reporting was the work I did and so it was I found myself getting my bags packed for East Hampton. Anderson was probably right; with the good weather, there was nothing to keep me in the city, and the beach and ocean beckoned. The Baymen idea might work, could be a fine story. They were hard, wonderful, colorful men working a difficult, often dangerous trade. I was already getting enthusiastic about it; I'm that way about a good story. I get worked up, get excited; show me a writer who doesn't feel that way and I'll show you a cynic. Or a burnt-out case. Besides, our house out there stood empty and available, my father, the Admiral, having been seconded by the Pentagon (by the defense secretary himself) to a liaison job at NATO headquarters in Brussels.

"But you don't even like Brussels."

"I know, Beecher," he acknowledged, "but I can't just say no to Bill Cohen. He's a decent man and he called personally and I'm going."

The Admiral wasn't enthusiastic about the post, or the place, but for forty years since Annapolis, his had been a career in which you saluted and went, finding along the way small consolations. So he reminded himself, as the French are fond of saying: "One eats well in Brussels." Thus dismissing the neighbors, as the French are wont to do, with faint praise, and, like Caesar, not all that fond of Belgians, the Admiral shut down his (and my) house on Further Lane, and off he went.

I had additional small consolations as well. East Hampton would be relaxed and casual. It was a place where tradition still meant something; you could go to the bank on that. The Hamptons were traditionally pretty tranquil until the Season began and that would be Memorial Day at the earliest and nothing could possibly happen until then.

Or so I believed . . .